I0718355

Gender Alignments

Her mum used to be her Dad—her Boyfriend used to be a Girl

Arsalan

The EC Publishing LLC books may be ordered
through booksellers or by contacting:

EC Publishing LLC
116 South Magnolia Ave.
Suite 3, Unit F
Ocala, FL 34471, USA
Direct Line: +1 (352) 644-6538
Fax: +1 (800) 483-1813
http://www.ecpublishingllc.com/

Ordering Information:
Quantity sales. Special discounts are available on quantity purchases by corporations, associations, and others. For details, contact the publisher at the address above.

Printed in the United States of America

Story Outline: Ann is broken into a life of unbridled sexual desire by Brian, during his brief foray into South Australia, once he rescues her from the unwanted attentions of some misguided Afghani madrasa students. Ann and Jules tutor Hazara Afghan girls on behalf of the local Refugee Association. Ann is attacked by some of the girls' brothers and cousins, misguided by their Mullah, a situation out of which Brian rescues and then seduces her. As a result, Ann urges her close friend Julia Childers to become Jules, a boy, to provide Ann with lifelong physical and emotional satisfaction.

While Ann's mother, Carla Landers, is dying from incurable bowel cancer, her dad, Hector, meets Glen during an IT training course in Mildura, for his work service provider. They decide, in a series of talks, to live together in future; since neither is homo-erotically inclined, Hector agrees to a sex change of which Clara approves beforehand.

Both Julia and Ann have to overcome, their parents' understandable reluctance to agree to the two underage girls to become a couple, involving as it does Julia's change of gender; they also have to convince the South Australian Ethics Commission before undertaking the extensive course of action needed to bring about sex change, as do Glen and Hector.

The Committee, surprisingly, decides to allow Julia's sex change, on reaching the age of sixteen. Ann successfully urges Jules to ravish her repeatedly even before that gender alignment.

Trevor and Glen, being mature adults with no insurmountable obligations, obtain Committee approval much easier but take longer to become truly intimate; eventually, they manage that, as well as establish themselves professionally, along with Jules' mother, Eileen, and with Aline, a once-local girl, by setting up an industrial estate in the Marianas.

At about that time, a once-famous, then notorious Australian doctor finds himself reinstated and established on Saipan in Micronesia and agrees to operate on both Jules and Hector as no doctor can be found in South Australia even after the Ethic Committee's reluctant approval. Both Jules and Ann's father both start 'self-medicating' on hormones from the Internet;

The girls switch to home schooling in the months previous to the operation; for, other than their biology teacher at St Brendan the Voyager's, their school had proved un-supportive. Once they attend Saipan High School, they meet Angh Vuong Minh.

With the unexpected gift of an actual penis transplant from a fatal-accident victim on Saipan as a bonus, fully 'equipped 'Jules and Ann manage their first-ever legal heterosexual encounter, also involving Angh Vuong Minh whose mother is a part-Vietnamese science teacher at Saipan High, in the school's shower cubicle.

Jules' dad, Trevor, finds himself enrolled in a local consultancy and ends up with a woman reporter sent to cover all aspects of the story.

❦

Actorum Excerptus:

Ann Landers, not quite fifteen as the story starts, wants to be a lawyer and Jules lifelong 'root,' in inverse order. Both she and Julia/ Jules are volunteer tutors to Hazara girls, members of a refugee Afghan ethnic and religious minority in Adelaide, South Australia. Jules/ Julius, a budding scientist, declares undying commitment to Ann via an intranet email intercepted by Keith Gleeson, their computer teacher at St Brendan the Voyager's School in Adelaide,

Jules undergoes a searching Ethics Committee hearing and is subsequently operated on at Dr Mac Groom's specialist clinic on Saipan in Micronesia to turn into Ann's fully masculine lover, as well as that of Angh Vuong Minh, the daughter of a teacher at Saipan High.

Jules nearly dies of acute toxemia and is cured by a traditional healer from Agrihan in the Marianas.

Ann's mother, Clara Landers, a onetime editor, is diagnosed for bowel cancer from which she eventually dies. Her father, Hector, is a branch manager and IT specialist for a work service provider in Adelaide, s/he is to become Ann's 'mother' while in Micronesia to set up a work referral programme. S/he meets Glen during a software training workshop in Mildura, Australia, and agrees to become his future- female-spouse. Glen Hiddings, divorced, then widowed, attends that fateful IT training course in Mildura, prior to a promotion and transfer to Adelaide.

Graham Evans, the girls' biology teacher and Julia's science career mentor, puts the girls in touch with his former lecturer in forensic microbiology, Prof Alan Enderby, who then readies them for the Ethics Committee of South Australia of which he is a past convenor.

Dr Brendan Mc Groom, a once famous, then discredited, gynaecologist and former colleague of Alan Enderby's, is eventually reinstated and at work on Saipan in Micronesia. Since no doctor in South Australia wants to perform the two-way gender swaps required, Ann traces him while researching famous cases of plagiarism and, eventually, contacts him

Ramon Santiago, a local businessman, sets up Glen and Hec on Agrihan near Saipan; they join forces with Jules' mum, so as to create investment and employment on that island.

Brian and Brenda Chalmers are siblings and onetime lovers whose short sojourn in Adelaide triggers Ann's sexual awakening. Brian's and Brenda's parents are a typical career couple, she a lecturer in police profiling on short-term sabbatical in Adelaide; he is an international natural resource consultant.

Mullah Ali Bhuyyan is an Egyptian-trained, Salafist-influenced, remote cousin of Mullah Omar's who survives a purge among the Taliban by fleeing to Australia; in Adelaide, he befriends teenage Afghan boys who struggle at school or cannot find work. He prevails on them to prevent Afghan girls from being educated; their assault on Ann in Julia's absence allows Brian to first rescue, then 'deflower 'the girl, setting in motion much of this story.

Mrs Weatherby -Gladys -, motherly staff at the Refugee Association on Henley Beach Road where the girls tutor, puts them in touch with Heinrich Wohlfahrt, the sixth-generation descendant of German vintners in the Riverland, South Australia; he, too, guides the girls to Prof Enderby.

Eleanor Gildemeister is the no-nonsense but very supportive matron at Final Moments, the palliative centre where Clara Landers life is to end.

Dr Samira Tafreshi is an Iranian-born palliative oncologist, Clara's last doctor, who charms both Glen and Hector who subsequently try not to become involved with her. She supplies Clara with the vital clue for her competition-winning answer--"mashed potato"--which gain Hector and Ann their trip to Saipan and involve the magazine hosting the contest in subsequent events.

Jean-Claude and his sister, Denise, are French Canadian teenagers whose father is on sabbatical at the University of Adelaide; he and his sister speak both Dari and Pashtoo from their previous life in Quetta, Pakistan. He is gay which Ann and Julia discover on their way home from tutoring.

Dr Gloria Paz, a plastic surgeon, having worked against female genital mutilation, is now based on Hawaii and Guam; she does the actual operations on Andy, Jules and Hec at Brendan Mc Groom's clinic on Saipan. Professor Fernando Gutierrez, a Chamorro, Hawaii-based nephrologist, is also Gloria's mentor and lover. Gordon Ilario, Brendan's boss, arranges accommodation and powerful potable elixirs for all and sundry and eventually introduces Trevor, Jules' dad, to investors on Agrihan. Rosetta is his administrator-cum manager; her parents run a very busy home-stay opposite the clinic Oratio and Merv, two Saipan businessmen, employ Jules' mum as their bookkeeper. Señores Nestor and Alcides are elders on Agrihan; Nestor, the Alcalde and Aline's ancestor, wants to encourage industries, hence the two teams, each to feature a parent of Jules'.

Hec and Glen first meet Agrihan-descended girl Aline during a workshop in Central Australia. She joins forces with both and with Jules' mum--who leaves her husband for Glen--. both physically and professionally, on Agrihan.

Felipe, Santiago and Andy are three Chamorro youth born and raised on Saipan. Andy's parting gift of his penis fully 'mans 'Jules but also nearly causes the teenager to die of toxaemia; Señor Alcides from Agrihan cures him, courtesy of an ingredient supplied by Gloria Paz.

Natasha Bertram, a smart and attractive young lawyer, and her friend, Nina Barthold, a magazine Editor, descendant of a once-famous linguist, arrange the entire drama to be recorded for posterity, thanks to Clara Landers' winning competition entry, through Elanca Hartwig, late van Hoogefeld, one of Nina's reporters. Having survived the bomb attack that killed her husband and his local fixer in Kirgiztan, she is to cover the sex change operations on Saipan. While she falls for Brendan, she then teams up with Jules' dad Trevor on his way back to Adelaide.

Andy-Randy Andy, well-known on Saipan, had lost control of his car while trying to avoid an ancient petrol-driven lorry; he had been flung clear and impaled on a concealed star-picket post. Doctor Mc Groom's team, unable to remove the rusty steel that had thrust itself almost though the vertical length of Andy's body, had tried to control toxaemia and the pain that Andy was constantly in.

A few days before Jules' final sex change surgery, a nurse had a brainwave. "Brendan," it was first-name basis during pre-op meetings, "I had another look at Andy, and he's got the most marvellous tool, even though I say so myself. . ." "intact?" Brendan Mc Groom understood immediately; "what a loss to girl-kind!" "the girls are aware of their loss, I dare say".

"elementary, Philomena," the doctor urged her: "what's next?"

"I can do a compatibility test, as long as we control toxaemia. . . if there's not too much of an averse reaction,. . . can we do a biopsy on Andy and Jules, Brendan?"

"in principle, yes, but not without their permission, Philly. . ."

"which means, Brendan?"

"we can't have them on any medication," commented another nurse.

"certainly none that drugs the mind," agreed the doctor.

"Andy will eventually die from his body digesting his crushed organs; for we cannot rebuild or transplant them quickly enough in sufficient numbers," he continued. "we have a few days, provided we do the tests right now."

"are we expecting Gloria?" asked yet another nurse. Doctor Gloria Paz was a crisis- tested reconstructive surgeon, a Chamorra based in Hawaii.

"yes, she is coming to help us with our two sex change candidates; with luck, she'll arrive before Andy dies. . ."

"We may have a surprise for you, Jules,"

Dr McGroom addressed the teenager two days later. Jules, with all the hormones 'he' had ingested over the last eighteen months, had changed almost irreversibly from the fourteen-year old who had first inserted herself into Ann's sex life, but not in 'his' no-nonsense, confident approach.

"I can't wait, "Jules assured the team, with even 'his' voice sounding the part.

"two, to be precise. . . your parents have agreed to your operation to be done a bit ahead of your sixteenth birthday if medically feasible,"

"good news; it hastens the inevitable, doesn't it?"

"quite; they'll ring you today or tomorrow. Now, the other surprise is the possibility of a transplant to help masculinise you further. . ."

"am I allowed to guess?" Jules asked.

"preferably not; it's to be a surprise if we can make it work; we do need your permission. . ."

"not for the sex change, though; not again, certainly?"

"no, merely for another biopsy. . ."

"today, Dr Mc Groom?"

"now, if you are ready; your parents' agreement covers medical intervention prior to the operation but I thought to ask. . ."

"did you tell them the specifics of what you need this extra biopsy for, Dr Mc Groom?'"

"not yet" conceded the doctor. "would that transplant make Ann happy? "Jules wondered.

"If it works, definitely", assured the doctor.

"do I sign anything?"

"no, Jules, I already have a signature on a comprehensive medical disclaimer. . ."

The next morning, the team fronted Andy in his bed:

"Andy, we need you to go without painkillers this morning; can you bear with us for a few hours?" Dr Mc Groom asked the dying young patient.

"why; Dr Mc Groom, do you need my consent for anything? You know that my organs are no good; you said so, otherwise they'd be available for transplant; my driver's licence says so, and I am of age, just"

"you may have noticed that one particular bit of yours. . ."

"my dick? "wondered the boy." It does keep erecting; I don't know how. What a waste!"

"no, that is why we are here, Andy; we have a patient here who could do with your tool," the doctor informed him, "which is why we need your consent to another biopsy. . ."

"he is welcome; what else does he need?"

"a bit of extra length of your ureter. . ."

"the tubing that my piss goes through?" enquired the boy.

"succinctly put; your bladder is smashed, as is your kidney which your body, moreover, is busily taking apart; hence your daily dialysis, but the tubing, as you call it, is largely intact, as is the full toolkit, so to say, nerves, vein and tissues, testicles included. . ."

"doesn't he have a dick of his own, complete with balls?" the boy asked, intrigued.

"Not yet. . ."

"ehh," mused Randy Andy. "Oh, I get it, your sex change kid. Happy to oblige. Where do I sign for the biopsy and when can you do it, Dr Mc Groom?"

"here, Andy; in an hour if that's' all right; no intravenous nutrients for a while, nor painkillers, I am sorry," answered the doctor: "and how did you find out about 'my sex change kid'?"

"oh, I saw two Australian-sounding kids walk past, one an absolutely gorgeous chick, the other, a very deep voice, lovely figure, that's probably your transplant. Well, if my dick gets to make his girl friend a happy woman, then he can have the full works with my blessing."

"and, to this, the people say Amen!" concluded the doctor.

❧

Once Clara had died, Glen and Hector had started to spend afternoons together after work, meeting in the Linear Park or at various cafes in the city close to wherever work had taken them during the day.

It was slowly heading into winter, with the horizontal rain that Adelaide can be justly famous for. Yet, they braved the inclemency of the weather howling through Gouger Street like in a wind tunnel. Glen put his hand on Hector's arm.

"We need to spend more quality time together," he began. "How?"

"take time off together. . ."

"such as a trial dirty 'weekend', Glen?"

"yes; a workmate has a place near Swan Reach, right by the river. . ."

"bit rough in winter, is it not?" wondered Hector.

"yes, my friend has a fireplace and he promised to cut lots of firewood; he needs to flatten a windbreak on his property. . ."

"just for us?" queried Hector.

"probably not," admitted Glen. "The place itself is rented out but the tenant has agreed for his guests to use the house because he is visiting family of his own in Queensland. . ."

"where it is warmer. . ."

"not necessarily; it can get freezing there, too. Anyway, we are meant to sleep in our own tents but are allowed to use the house during the day and for storage, as long as we keep it tidy."

"we could borrow some tents from work; I'll have to find out whether any are needed during mid-year holidays. . ."

"likewise here;. . . have you any tents of your own, Hector?"

"how about you, Glen?"

"yes, in storage; it's years since I took the kids for a tenting holiday in the Sunraysia."

"Ann might not join us without Julia," her father opined.

"fine as far as I am concerned," Glen shrugged; "the girls will have to work it out with Jules' parents."

"do you want your son and his girl friend to join us?" asked Hector.

"they might come over for a few days," his father suggested, "but they have things to do on their own. I might get Roger to drive us, though, if he can borrow his girl friend's parents' van."

The men (both, so far) sat silently for a while, then finished their coffee, embraced and left,

Several weeks later, Ann accompanied Julia home after school. They had coped with their homework with one hand each while holding hands. The girls (yet) then set up a computer template for their hearing with the Ethics Committee and settled down for a huge pot of tea, no sugar, thank you, while waiting for Julia's dad and her brother to return home.

"Staying for tea, Ann?" Julia's mother, the eternal diplomat, asked the girl.

"I'll ring Dad to let him know where I am. . ."

"will he mind, Ann," the lady asked.

"no, Mrs Childers, as long as I let him know each time I am not home for tea. He usually lets me know if he needs me home early for some compelling reason, what with his own working hours. . ."

"when do you actually have to be home, Ann?" "by nine p m."

The girls said nothing during tea; it was not till Julia's mother had brewed a pot of extra strong tea and they had sat down in front of the telly to watch the seven o'clock news that Ann spoke up:

"Mr and Mrs Childers," she began, "my Dad's future partner invited us, Dad and me, to a property near Swan Reach, about two hours from here, during or just before the midterm break. . ."

"would you like Julia to join you then?" her father wondered. The girls nodded.

"we had planned an escape into the sunshine of Western Australia, as Julia well knows; a package tour, no less, four or five for the price of three. . ."

"who is your current girl friend?" Julia enquired of Stephen, her brother.

"what's that got to do with the price of eggs?" he wondered.

"whoever she is, she can replace me as I head off with Ann. . ."

Julia's parents looked at each other, then her father spoke.

"let us think a bit more about it."

"we cannot cancel the getaway," her mother added.

"nor should you, Mrs Childers," Ann assured Julia's mother. "It would be good to have Julia with me, though."

"for this to really work, Jules, you'll have to become a boy," Ann commented. They lay entwined, naked, across each other, unable and unwilling to untangle.

"you kiss very well," she continued; "you are very confident, highly dominant and bonk me all right but there is something missing. . ."

Earlier on, it seemed minutes ago, or hours:

"strip me, pin me down, kiss me, fuck me," Ann had told her friend.

"you mean, disrobe and welcome you, hold you tightly while I make love to you?" Julia translated. "just do it", Ann's reply.

It all had started with an email from Julia-eventually to become Julius – to Ann, a few days after a particularly trying session with the Hazara Afghani kids in the Western suburbs of Adelaide whom the girls were tutoring after hours.

"Ann, dearest dearest Ann, my closest one," the message had begun, "why have I fallen in love with you ever since we started teaching? you love the Hazara girls like a sister, you are patient, you know how to talk to their parents about their daughters ; they listen to you; you are very practical and very determined but also very vulnerable. . . I like that, it turns me on. . . I want to share every single day of our future lives, grow up with you a bit more. . . and always be helpless without you, sex-and otherwise, darling; your 'own-est': Julia."

Julia had used their school's project computer, mistakenly assuming that it would be safe, having just learnt about encryption. Even before Ann had had a chance to see her message, everyone else had, or so it felt.

It was the girl's misfortune that their school's computer lab had to call an IT maintenance man, as their intranet had collapsed upon itself. Worse still, Mr Gleeson, the school's IT supervisor, had chosen to decipher this particular message in the very moment when the technician had overridden the girl's clumsy encryption and the text was slowly threading itself before the two men. They shook their heads in unison;

"good grief!"

"whatever's next!" the technician;

"what do they think of next?" the exasperated teacher:

"she's probably gone home now," he told the technician. "I'll have to deal with her tomorrow. Do you need to work on that particular bit of software now?" he asked the technician "no, mate; what do you want to do; delete it. . ."

"yes, from the other girl's account as well, if you can help me. . ."

"do you want to download it first, Mr Gleeson?" "Glenn. . ." "Malcolm. . ."

"of course; do you think the girl downloaded the text herself. . .?"

"let me have a look; yeah, looks like it, on her USB, I'd say. . ."

"I'll have to think of some suitable punishment for her. . ."

"better you than me, Glenn," ventured the technician.

"do you want to tell the principal or her class teacher?"

"not just yet," the teacher downloaded, and then deleted, the message from both accounts.

"Childers," he briefly said the next day, that being Julia's surname, "come here. . ."

"Julia Childers, at your service, Sir!"

Glenn Gleeson, resisting the impulse to tell her not to be cheeky, showed her the intercepted message, instead.

"The encryption that you taught us seems not to have worked, Sir," the girl commented.

"is that all you have to say, Julia?"

"look, Sir, this is a very highly personal and severely intimate message to. . ." "we know that now. . ."

"does anyone else, Sir," asked Julia, "for you were saying We?"

"none so far, Childers. . . you know full well that we are not to use any school equipment or system. . ."

"you are thinking of bullying, and I agree, but I certainly wasn't doing that, the very opposite, I'd say, Sir, if anything. . ."

"don't interrupt me," her IT supervisor retorted, "no, you didn't bully anyone, just about the only thing you did right. . ."

"look, Sir, unless there is anything else you need to say," Julia offered, "just punish me now and finish the subject. Thank you very much for not telling anyone else so far. . ."

The teacher decided that the girl was usually very organized and cooperative, so known at St Brendan the Voyager's.

"Childers", he started. "I'll limit your computer time to seven hours a week. . ." "groan"

"other than helping younger students or classmates, but under my supervision or that of another teacher; nor will you be allowed to use your personal USB."

("my Secret Lover," Julia thought, "nothing ever gets closer than my memory stick ")

"but how am I to do projects at home, Sir," the girl wailed.

"I am giving you a stick which you must use for work only; I'll check every day for what's on it" "how long am I to be restricted, Sir?"

"six weeks, just before the mid-year tests, Childers", was the reply.

"if there is nothing else, Sir, could I have that stick now, for some work; you may watch me if you like; I need to get started on another assignment and it won't write itself, Sir."

As the teacher reached for her USB-

"no, you can't, Sir; it's not on me. I promise I shan't use it at school; thanks, Sir!" "thanks for what, Childers" the teacher almost smiled.

"for being an understanding person," the girl replied quietly.

Marnie guided the van onto the rear driveway so no one would notice her rinse the car down which, under water restriction then in force, she was not meant to do; she would later help Helen with her school project; meanwhile Brian had work to do. The boy helped Ann out of the van and walked her to Helen's parents' home, kissing Helen as she opened the door.

"Use Simon's bedroom, he won't be in from uni until later; fresh sheets on the bed; bathroom door is open," the girl called out.

Her brother Simon, a journalism student at Flinders Uni and a very untidy but helpful contemporary had band practice that night, Brian remembered.

"you are a good girl, Helen"

"don't I know it, Brian!" Helen called out cheerfully.

Brian took Ann upstairs, following thickly carpeted stairs that swallowed all sound.

"where are you taking me, Brian?" the girl asked him, surprised at herself how calmly unperturbed she was.

Much later, when reflecting on the events of that day, she was to realize how much courage her mother needed each time she had to surrender herself to medical science, as if to an all-consuming lover, aware that her pancreatic cancer would eventually kill her.

"the passage," Brian answered; "bathroom first."

He lifted her arms, manipulated a few buttons and zippers, allowing her clothes to drop on the carpet. He stripped in one swift movement and bundled all their clothing, dropping it in front of the bedroom.

"for later, Ann; come!"

She followed him into the bathroom, unresistingly; what was she being treated for, she wondered.

Brian guided her, turned the shower on and tested it for temperature with his free hand, allowing her to marvel at his well-executed movements. He squatted under the water and eased her on top of himself.

"Support your weight on the handrail", he instructed her, indicating a diagonally wall-mounted rail to stop people from slipping. . .

"with one hand and grip my dick with the other, same as in the van."

All this struck Ann as highly clinical but not at all scary.

"now sit on my lap, legs apart and thread me inside you, slowly and very gently; don't scratch my bit with your fingernails, or else you put me out of action. . ." Maybe she should, at that, but perish the thought, Ann decided.

"tiniest bit painful, some blood," she wondered.

"that's why I keep the shower running, "Brian explained;

"now you can let go of the handrail and take me with your full weight. . ."

He arched into her time and time again and she worked out how to ride him, using her shanks and knees against his ribs and stretching his arms, hard and rapidly, kissing him and not letting go.

Then, surprising herself, she forced his legs apart with her own knees, feeling Brian's strength inside her and yelling in surprised delight.

She got up, as did Brian who lifted her off her feet and carried her into Simon's bedroom, stepping over the bundle of clothes and opening the door with his free hand.

Helen had put a fresh sheet on an otherwise unmade bed and moved some of the most potentially lethal objects onto the floor, he noticed gratefully, stepping carefully so as not to stumble.

He laid her down and entered her straightaway, thrusting into her in ever- faster rhythm.

She arched underneath him, to centre him even more accurately, kissing his hands, lower arms and fingers, willing herself to be his.

"How old are you, Brian?" she asked, later, while they were waiting for the girls to finish the school project. The van shone, gleaming in its newfound cleanliness on the lawn, visible through the kitchen window.

"Just turned fifteen but I play under-eighteen badminton in Queensland," he explained,

"and you, Ann?"

"more or less fourteen, definitely not of legal age. . ."

"my father is an international consultant; he says there are many places where girls are either married or getting ready to be married at your age, even have children,"

Brian elaborated:

"but that is getting rare now. Some girls in Bangladesh have declared their villages a child-marriage-free zone. . . Dad said when he first started, that a family whose daughter was not married or at least spoken for by age fifteen were openly accused of harbouring a prostitute, not just in country India or Pakistan but even in cities, not to mention Northeast Africa."

"I am not a Third-World girl, I'll have you know", Ann retorted.

"so what was all this in aid of?" she demanded, "once you got me off these boys. . ." Brian refilled her tea and helped himself to another cup:

"to get you ready?" "for what? Bonk?"

"not only that; that, too, to get you addicted to good sex; you are quite remarkable yourself, you know, for that very special person in your life," "yourself?"

"you could do worse. . ."

"you are a Me First boy, typical," Ann retorted.

"for the moment, certainly," Brian countered, "you are mine, now, for the time being. . ."

"you morally certain, just because you first rescue and then deflower me?" Ann intoned.

"lovely way with words," Brian acknowledged. "You'll see. . . as it is, we need to find an excuse; you live with your parents; where?"

"near St Oswald's"

"that's close to the Mongolian restaurant, so bad that even local dogs won't scrounge from its bins. . ."

"I wouldn't know that but it does smell awful," the girl admitted.

"Mum is dying of cancer so she is not often home; Dad usually goes and spends time with her after work. . ."

"look, anything I can do, Ann. . ." Ann acknowledged him by placing her hand on his arm.

"is your Mum due home today?"

"yes, she should be home by now with Dad; they'd be worried. . ."

"where would you normally be this late of an afternoon, after your tutoring sessions. . ."

"home or with a friend. . ."

"well, give Helen your number and she'll ring your home; you had forgotten to charge your phone, didn't you. . ."

"earlier on, that is why I could not alert anyone with those boys. . ."

"highly avoidable characters," conceded Brian; "I am glad I was of some help. . ." "some help!" laughter.

"Helen's from a different school. . ."

"but she could be one of the girl tutors, especially since your usual off-sider was away. . .?"

"how did you know that?"

"I know that tutors work in twos and Marnie and I had seen you girls a few times on our rounds. So Helen was an extra tutor today; last year, she was, as a matter of fact, I think; she wanted your help with her own homework and then you realized that you had run out of charge, hence her phoning your parents."

"that will have to do", Ann figured. "Am I to come back here?"

"no, Ann, where do you change buses on your way home?"

"King William, near the Post Office. . ."

"Post Office it is, near the postbox passage, quarter to half past three, on Wednesday, or do you have any after-hours on that day?. . ."

"no," Ann took his hand and kissed it. "you are right. . ."

❧

"did your Mum and Dad let you get away with that?" Julia asked her, incredulously. "huge benefit of massive doubt," Ann conceded, "look, Mum is about to die, it's only a question of time; Dad's company is facing a merger and they are secretly glad that I look after myself most of the time. . ."

"with help from Magic Brian, it seems. . ." "it is over. . ."

"fun while it lasted?"

"oh yes, Jules; he was due back for badminton coaching in Brisbane a bit earlier than expected. . ."

"hordes of girls thrown in?"

"no doubt, Marnie, his sister, is due to leave for China, and they are actually quite close"

"a bit too close?" "sure; still, Marnie is good news; I'd have liked her to stay around a bit. . ."

The girls were having an afternoon snack in the school cafeteria while comparing notes, in readiness for their next tutoring session. A teacher had promised to drop them there on her way home which had given the girls a few extra minutes. Looking around and not seeing anyone within earshot, Ann continued: "while Brian was around, we fucked like rabbits. . ."

"how about the pill. . ."

"supplied by Marnie, on a morning-after basis, Jules. Brian gets you addicted to sex, as he predicted, but also to a male presence, someone to be my man."

"so you don't want me in your life at all?" Julia commented, calmly but visibly perturbed.

Ann grabbed her hand and held it close to her cheek.

"no, Jules; I want you forever but of a different gender."

"I won't be the same person, Ann" "let's see." (echoing Brian)

"what do I need to do to achieve that?"

"clear as mill-mud; sex change, Jules. . ."

"sex on your brain, more like. . ."

"keep your voice down; can't say, girl anymore, can I?"

Julia managed a burst of enraged laughter in reply.

"look, Jules, come and meet us while Mum is at home; if you still want us to remain close we will work on it. . ."

"step by step, you mean?"

"I'll get you to bonk me, even in your present body. . ."

"promises promises. . ." Julia muttered. "would tomorrow be a good time to meet your family; I'll have to let my own Mum and Dad know."

"of course; no problems."

What had brought all this about, you may ask. It began with two people, both male but with nothing else in common; nor were they ever destined to meet, at least not in this life.

A Salafist Mullah called Bhuyan had recently arrived from Afghanistan and was looking for a likely congregation in Adelaide.

Brian, a normally Brisbane-based badminton prodigy, well below the age of legal consent, was nonetheless prone to frequent sexual congress.

Their vastly disparate personalities and respective actions were to have a lasting influence on the lives, moods and minds of hundreds of people, each in his own sphere.

The Mullah, being a very recent arrival, and a Tajik, represented by a minor militia at home, had received scant welcome and had been unable to motivate any Afghan grouping in South Australia till he had a brainwave and focused on the Hazara whom almost every other Afghani despised if not persecuted. Their own Mullah's paperwork had proved inadequate to keep him in Australia, hence, they had no one to lead them spiritually in Adelaide.

Ibrahim had a deep if unsavoury impact on the bulk of the Hazara teenage boys by impressing on them that girls did not need to be taught, that, indeed, it was haram to do so; if the 'infidel 'school system insisted, that put them even more beyond any redemption than they already were, a view with which his charges concurred, having massive adjustment problems of their own, much worse than their sisters and girl cousins. The more sensitive or intelligent boys in his congregation were bullied or otherwise eased out of his madrasa; the Hazara girls found other Islamic communities to hang out with.

Brian, as stated, could not have been any more different; he possibly knew more about the workings of Islam, even at his very young age, than Mulllah Bhuyan and most practicing Muslims. not that that may concern us for the moment.

His sister Marnie, an undisputed expert, had 'broken him in 'at an even younger age, demonstrating to him how to make girls surrender instantly and unconditionally and stay that way; he had the personality to encourage girls to do so and the training to make them want to, as his former mixed-double partner in Brisbane had put it:

"No self-respecting girl would ever be able, or allow herself, to resist Brian. You'd have to be a totally deluded and utterly misguided female to even try," Doris had observed. "mercifully for most of us," she had concluded, somewhat wistfully, "there's only one Brian in the known universe."

His sister, Marnie, had proved no exception to the principle she had taught her brother. She later explained How to the lab pathology technologist at the Well Women's Centre in Milton, Brisbane. Heather would be Brian's permanent consort from the very moment he reached the age of sexual legal consent:

"One day, Brian and I were arguing with our parents, just before we left for Adelaide, and, even though Mum and Dad were right, we managed to get the better of them and then, I still don't really understand what happened on that day, we grabbed each other's hands and ran all the way to Toowong Cemetery; there we stripped each other and, bedded down on some pine needles, kept bonking for hours. . ."

"did your parents suspect anything?" Heather had asked, shaking her head at her boyfriend's-to-be past antics. "Did you protect yourself? "she had enquired. The girls were sharing barbecue duties at their workplace party held in honour of Brian's sixteenth birthday.

"ever since I started working here," Marnie had replied. "I have been on the industrial strength version of the Morning-after Pill, even though Greg is on experimental medication for temporary male sterility. Anyway, "Marnie concluded, eager to make her point:

"we realised that we'd become so addicted to each other that we'd never stick with a partner; we knew it without saying, stark naked as we were. So we dressed, kissed and walked slowly home; we have never done it since; so you are safe, Heather, "she assured the other girl.

"I know he's had acres of girls before and since that day but he only does 'one girl at a time', like Alcoholics Anonymous; he's experienced and you are older, so you should be safe with him."

❧

Marnie had featured in the event that had brought Ann within Brian's unexpected orbit ("he's never done a virgin before!"). Friday afternoons were set aside for tutoring Hazara girls, on Henley Beach Road in the western suburbs of Adelaide. On one such Friday, Julia had quite suddenly been 'discovered 'by a stomach bug and had to leave school early. While tutors are supposed to work in pairs, Ann had found nobody at such short notice to partner her and had not wanted to disappoint her girls who had come to rely on her.

Classes over, and many cups of Afghan tea later, Ann's bus being late as usual, she was surrounded and threatened by the worst bullies among Mullah Ibrahim's stable of such; bystanders, such as there were, chose not to get involved and people driving past on busy Henley Beach Road preferred not to notice through their tinted glasses, with this exception:

Marnie and Brian had bought a decrepit van off a backpacker due to return to Korea and had set up a combined bike/van messenger service during the short few but fateful months spent in Adelaide due to their mother's work commitments as a profiler on loan to the South Australian police, thus earning some money if not exactly keeping off the streets, after school hours.

Marnie was due to return to Queensland within a few more days and then head off for China to lead a summer language camp in Wenshan, Yunnan Province.

Brian, having expertly observed the Hazara girls for some time, noticed their brothers and cousins, as well as the girl they were threatening for daring to teach their sisters.

"Back into that loading zone, Marn," he ordered his sister, "over the kerb if you can."

Marnie, an expert with the van and used to the speed with which Brian could unload his bike for a message run, complied; the boy leapt across the seat, opened the sliding door, cast out his bike with one move, the result of much practice, and hurled himself out, sitting astride his cycle and heading straight for the cluster of boys who had not seen him approach.

"yallah!" he crashed into them, hauled Ann off her feet from right among them, inches away from a particularly mean-looking kid waving a broken secateur in front of the girl, propelled her into the van, swinging her and the bike back inside. With one movement of his badminton-practiced service arm, not matched by anyone in his age group in Queensland, he slid the door shut as his sister was easing out the van a nose-length away from the irate Afghan teenagers.

He sat Ann down, held her tight and leant her head against his shoulder as she started crying with delayed shock.

"Marnie, my sister; Brian, at your service", he intoned. "you are?"

"Ann," the girl sobbed in his ear.

"glad to have been of insignificant help to you (this is how Brian talked, especially to distraught girls); you were lucky there is a diversion, to do with the new railway underpass; Marnie will have to drop me, the bike and my message bag in a minute; you'll hop up front, seatbelt, please; did the buggers take anything out of your schoolbag; no? good, check your telephone, no charge? that'll be right. . .",

Brian commented, turned Ann's mobile off and plugged it into the van's charge outlet, originally meant for cigarettes. Ann obediently moved onto one of the front seats, belted herself in and looked at the other girl.

"thank you very much; nobody else could be bothered. . ."

"people are like that," Marnie agreed, "thank Brian, he may have noticed you with the Hazara girls, you tutor them, Ann?" the younger girl nodded, slowly recovering. "Brian and I keep seeing the boys around, fresh from their Madrasa, whenever we have to use this diversion. . . do you think their Imam puts them up to this?"

"that's what the girls tell me; most of them have battles at home. . ."

"how do they manage?"

"the principal of the Islamic College is a woman and their parents have learnt not to argue with her; if she says that their daughters need remedial tutoring, done by girls, then that's what is to happen, no matter what their older brothers say; their Imam has been a pain in the bum, to be kind to him; he preaches pointless blather, knows nothing; even the parents say that and they often don't know much more. . ." "Mum told me their regular Mullah is inches away from being deported. . ."

"how does she know?" Ann enquired, intrigued.

"she teaches cross-cultural profiling to both the police and the migration people at the airport; that Mullah Bhuyan is also on their list," Marnie informed her.

"what's to happen next, Marnie; I live close to. . ."

"three things; we'll have to find an excuse, get you done and get you home, all this as we finish work for today."

"what do you mean?"

"trust Brian; I personally trained him, he is good; it'll be easier to take my word for it but you'll find out, anyway."

She soon did. The boy slid his bike back in, leapt the seat, dropped next to Ann, fastened his seatbelt and took Ann's hand, getting her to explore his lower frontage. He turned her head and kissed her, gently at first then hard, guiding her hand around his rod and exploring her while Marnie kept talking, obviously unfazed with her brother's grooming of Ann.

"There's a supermarket car park ahead; I'll stop and ring Helen if her parents are back. . ."

Helen, it's me, "Marnie spoke into her phone as soon as they were connected." your mum and dad back? Not for a few hours; fine. . . I am bringing in Brian and Ann. . . we picked her up, quite literally, on Henley Beach Road, some mugs were onto her; you are not wrong; yeah, Brian is on the job; we finished deliveries for the day; could I use the hose and wash our van if I park it on your rear drive?

I know, bloody water restrictions but no one can see it there; I'll park it on the grass so the water can run off while Brian and Ann are busy. . . back against your garage door? as you wish; thanks, Helen; us girls 'll have a coffee afterwards; you'll need some help, Helen? Consider it done.

A few minutes later, the van pulled off Pulteney, parked on a small strip of lawn behind a well-kept sandstone house and Brian walked Ann into Helen's parents' home, kissing and embracing Helen.

"Upstairs, use Simon's bedroom; the bathroom door is open, towels and sheets at the ready. . ."

"a girl who knows what's needed," Brian smiled at her, guiding a perplexed and unresisting Ann onto the second flight, while continuing to make her nurse his tool. He undressed her quickly and expertly outside the bathroom, then stepped out of his clothing and turned the shower on.

Having adjusted it for temperature, he squatted on his haunches and guided Ann on his erect rod, allowing her to slide onto it under her own weight.

"it's a bit less painful and messy for me to come inside you like this. . . yes, that is a bit of blood but the shower will wash it off. . ."

Ann had gasped when she first felt Brian inside her, in shock, some pain, but also in anticipation.

Her body seemed to know what to do; she lowered herself onto Brian and pried his legs apart with her shanks and knees;

"that's a new one," marvelled Brian underneath her, clearly enjoying the sensation.

After some short but intense action, he gripped her elbows and turned Ann onto her back, thrusting into her, in hard, swift expert moves; Ann groaned and pleaded with him:

"Harder, quicker, pleeease. . ." a drawn-out sound till he closed her mouth with a demanding kiss, sealing her fate with his tongue.

Her tiny breasts rose to the occasion and were, in turn, investigated; his strong badminton-player hands explored her arms, shoulders, neck and torso in minutest detail. She kissed his arms and fingers, willing him to continue to occupy her.

He suddenly gripped her wrists, raised her arms above her head and forced her legs tight, with him still inside her and about to come, as was she; only he was kissing her so hard that she could not call out in her desire:

"you caught me; I am yours, "she eventually managed, struggling against his lips. "very true; consider yourself entered into the real world . ."

"Marnie decided to show me how to," Brian had explained, "when I was thirteen, herself pushing sixteen; the works, believe me, a full-on tutorial in applied anatomy, use of tongue, nose, her own breasts and innards. . ." yes, including rectum, her preferred mode of entry, my own ever-increasing dick, balls. . . total-body control on both of us; full-on practice, experimental pills-for-blokes for me, industrial-strength morning-after ones for herself.

We both work for the Well Woman Centre in Milton, Brisbane, even while at school. . . myself as a messenger and maintenance bloke; she as their prime mover and girlfriend to the owner . . .

Brian was happily reminiscing:

"now, Mum and Dad are a sort of power couple; she teaches police profilers-which is why we are in Adelaide; and, by the way, your Mullah Ibrahim is due to be deported soon, says Mum; and Dad is an international consultant, along with my uncle."

"One afternoon," Brian reminisced, "with Mum and Dad both at home at the same time, a rarity, believe me, a totally ordinary discussion turned into an argument which Marnie and I won, even though Mum and Dad were right, in hindsight, sorry to say . . . So we finished them off, in a manner of speaking, grabbed each other's hands and ran off. . . you should have seen their faces . . . all the way to Toowong Cemetery, which is uphill, to boot; we jumped into the mausoleum of one of the Gypsy Kings, managed to get inside, stripped like maniacs and got 'stuck' into each other, quite barbaric, squeals and all, biting, kissing, cuffing each other, me on top, her on top, tumbling, arms and legs everywhere; a miracle the place didn't start shaking in its foundations; it must have been well-built. Eventually, we came to our senses, I stood Marnie against one of the walls, let go of her wrists, hugged her against me and tried to start breathing normally, Marnie likewise. 'we mustn't ever do this again to each other,' Marnie said, eventually. 'we'll never be able to have sex, let alone a relationship, with anyone else.' 'too right, 'I said, kissed her one more time, grabbed her hand and clothed her. We dusted some of the worst bits off and went home, neither saying a word."

Brian had given Ann a lot to think about after their last bout of lovemaking, on a sports ground of his choosing.

The day came,' days always do; they tend to follow each other'. Julia, who was to meet Ann's parents, remembered someone saying this all the time, maybe a distant aunt. It did not make her less confused about Ann's parents, knowing that the girl's mother was dying. Ann had asked her parents, was it all right to bring Julia along for tea.

"yes, dear, certainly, such a nice girl, so very good with your Afghani students"

Ann's parents had once attended a tutors' parents' meeting organized by the Refugee Council where they had met several Afghan parents. While few had any English, someone had praised the girls.

"your father may not be home quite that early from work. . ."

"it is important, Mum; we'll wait for Dad, and I shall remind Jules to ring home. . ."

Ann realized, with a start, that she no longer wanted to use the feminine pronoun when talking about Julia, pleased that the English language did not require you to use gender all the time; unlike German, still spoken and taught in South Australia!! "that may be very sensible, Ann," her father said, completing her sentence, as he arrived.

He helped himself to a cup of tea and some toast and indicated that he was ready to leave.

"I can drop you near Light Square, Julia;" he explained.

"see you tomorrow, Jules," Ann sang out.

She remembered not only Colonel Light's mother had been a princess from Penang who had followed Mr Light Senior when her own father had fallen in disgrace, but also a nearby spot where Brian had made intensely illicit love to her on several occasions, in time for her to catch her bus.

Julia had told her parents:

"I invited myself to Ann's place today; her mum was home and they'd like me to have tea with them soon;"

"that won't happen much more often, I guess,"

Julia's father guessed, correctly as it turned out.

"won't they want to share an afternoon just as a family, with no visitors?" her mum wondered.

"they remember me from that session at the refugee council which you missed. . ."

Julia's father had been away on business and her mum had gone to help a neighbour cope with her baby on that afternoon.

"I really want to have tea with them while they are still a family in one piece, if you know what I mean."

❧

Much as Julia wanted to be part of Ann's entire life, she was not yet ready to tell anyone so.

She did manage to concentrate on her work at school, almost as an avoidance strategy. She slipped only once all day:

"an ellipsis, Sir" "true," her English teacher sighed,

"but I all I had wanted to ask you is to close your book, Childers; you know that I hate you to have your readers or exercise books open when I work with you. . ." "unless you say so, Sir; I am sorry. . ."

"it is an ellipsis of sorts, I admit", concluded the teacher.

Meanwhile, Julia had phrased in her mind what to tell Ann's parents. It boiled down to this:

"I really and truly want to be in Ann's life. altogether, not just as a friend, not only. . ."

She had enough sense not to blurt it out straightaway. Ann's mum and dad had settled on their verandah, shaded by poplar trees but overlooking lavender and ornamental sunflowers.

"Since when have you girls been close to each other?"

Ann's mother queried her gently but persistently,

"and what do you see in each other?"

Ann's father, who would have never asked that, decided that a person with not much longer to live might have a need to ask such searching questions of a teenager.

He reminded himself that young people wanted to be taken seriously, even challenged.

"working with the Hazara girls and their parents, I guess," the girls answered almost in unison.

"we get to observe each other outside of school; we don't compete and we have to make up for each other's weaknesses. . ."

"like playing doubles. . ." suggested Ann, with Brian's prowess in badminton very much in mind.

Her mother agreed:

"like in tennis which I used to compete in as a girl until my university days", her mum offered.

"that's how we met," smiling at Ann's father who had made an effort to get home early.

"Ann would like me to be a boy",

Julia made use of a quiet moment, to a somewhat predictable reaction.

Ann's father gave her a long, thoughtful look.

"aren't you happy in your own identity?" he asked, sensibly.

"I'll be whoever and whatever Ann wants me to be. . ." the girl replied, surprising herself; for she had not known what to answer until she opened her lips.

"You girls need to work this out among yourselves," Ann's mother commented; "be it far from me to tell you that you are both too young. . ." her husband added.

"no, dad, please!" Ann implored him.

"you are right, dear", her mother silenced her husband with a look.

"if you were to ask me," she continued," will I be here in another year's time,

I'd have to say: no; Ann must have told you why; if it were six months: maybe; in three months; probably, but no guarantees. If you girls want to be committed to each other, I shan't stop you, and if one of you wants to turn herself into what is needed to make up a pair, I' admire that; not that I understand it; my advice is to grow into each other, as we all must in a relationship." She paused:

"If my daughter wants to experience you as a male, I guess, in any future life together, then you are selfish, Ann, and I'd like to know why; what happened?"

"or, rather, who happened to you in these last few weeks, Ann," her father cut in, unexpectedly.

"Someone very special," Ann admitted, "and that is all you'll hear from me. . ." "an adult, Ann?" "No, Mum" "a teacher?"

"teachers are adults, at least in a legal sense, Dad!" "a boy?"

"obviously, Mum and Dad, but the rest of my lips are sealed. . ."

"you do have a way with words ", commented Julia neutrally, glad of the chance to do so.

An immediate image of Brian who had said the same thing came to Ann's mind.

"Ann is very good at explaining vocabulary to the Hazara girls, even better with their mums,"

Julia explained. "very patient, very clear"

"yeah, we know that our daughter can make herself understood at any decibel level", Ann's father concurred.

Soon, they started talking about other things, such as school, sports, fun events at the hospice, Julia's parents-her dad an entrepreneur, her mum a personal finance teacher at a multicultural centre:

"that is how I got into tutoring, Mrs Landers", Julia explained:

"several Hazara ladies had joined mum's class, her being a woman, one of which I attended," she remembered.

"would you like to tutor their daughters, Julia?" the refugee coordinator had asked me, totally unexpected:

"if you do, bring a friend along. . ." "may I ask why?" mum had asked.

"we like our tutors to work in pairs, girls especially; it's standard practice. . ."

"I'll ask around," Julia had promised;

"we do have an ongoing Community Responsibility Project."

"thank you, Julia!" the lady, Mrs Weatherby, had replied.

"Take some photos with you so you can show them to your friends. . . it will have to be another girl, you realise, Julia? we are having enough problems with some of the Afghan boys; not that I don't feel sorry for them," she concluded.

Ann's father, Hector Landers, was having a few beers with his course participants in Wentworth one evening on one of the last days of the course; as a software analyst and a qualified trainer, he had conducted a familiarization course for his staff and several colleagues from other job provision agencies from Central Australia.

The day's work over, Hector had ended up seated across Glen Hiddings from Mildura. Without either of them noticing, everyone else had gone to bed, leaving the two in conversation.

"so very sorry, Hector" Glen was saying. . .

"sorry about what. . ."

"I don't know if I should talk, or even know, about it. . ."

"what is there to know, Glen?"

"someone told me that you had actually not wanted to teach this course. . ." "did they tell you why, Glen?" "yes. . ."

⚜

Glen was right: Hector's boss had called him in one afternoon; for their senior programming officer was leaving them for the Middle East at very short notice.

"Sit down, Hector, coffee, tea or something a bit stronger"

"tea will do, any colour no sugar. . ."

"are you comfortable, Hector?" "in which way, Ryan?"

"Look, I wouldn't ask you to leave Adelaide for ten days. . ." "er. . ."

"knowing that you want to spend as much time with Clara as you can. . ."

"while she is alive, naturally."

"have you heard that Harry is about to leave us in less than a week."

"whatever for, Ryan?"

"a very well-paying job in the Middle East, Oman to be precise. The people who are about to hire him did not find out that they had won the software training contract for Sultan Quabooz University till a few days ago"

"bureaucratic wheel-spinning, no doubt. . ." His boss nodded, clearly uncomfortable. "is Harry that desperate for a better-paying job, such that he'd risk a penalty on his contract with us. . ."

"a very sizable one, indeed, which I decided not to invoke; he'll lose his bonus, that's all I want to inflict on him; before you ask, I shall not try to enforce his contract."

Hector, drank his tea. . . His boss took a deep breath, seemingly counting to fifteen, continued :

"his wife's family company had to seek creditor protection. . ."

"a step away from bankruptcy but why?"

"a series of ongoing payments due them which they'll be unable to realize within the foreseeable future if at all."

"sorry to hear that, Ryan; I know that we need to conduct the course. . ."

"so that we can change over to the new Jobfind software the government requires all of us to use, as you know."

"can't we outsource it; everyone else does?"

"There is nobody to outsource it to, Hector. . . you are clutching at straws; even if I wanted to, I couldn't; the government commits us to delivering such familiarisation training."

"Can't someone else?"

"You must be really desperate, no, I shan't ask Harry"

"we do have quite a few trainers and assessors here"

"but none with your depth of expertise with that kind of software; I've already had people at Employment and Workplace Education moan. . ."

"can't we do it in Adelaide, then?"

"look, I am so very sorry; we have a bespoke centre in Central Australia. . ."

"for a sizable tax break!"

"why not, but only if we use it on an ongoing basis. . ."

His boss made up his mind:

"You have no choice; you are entitled to two days off before we start. . ."

"for being shifted more than fifty kilometres and one week. . ."

"for work-related purposes, and we can travel to Wentworth together; do you want to take your daughter along?"

"I need to talk to Clara, fortunately, she's at home. . ."

"well enough for me to come over one evening?"

"it'd have to be tonight or tomorrow, Ryan; will Esther come?"

"make it this evening; we'll take the two of you out. . ."

"thanks, I'll ask Ann to spend the night with her friend. . ."

Ryan looked at his close friend: 'he always falls on his feet', he mused, not for the first time.

"then you know, Glen; it shouldn't have happened, every which way. Yet, you are someone I could be very close to. . ." "same here. Hector." "your wife left you, didn't she?"

"yes," his newfound friend admitted, "how did you know?"

"your colleagues," Hector smiled, "Who did she leave you for?"

". . .a very straightforward person, more's the pity. . ."

"have you forgiven them, Glen?"

"yes, seeing how much they agonized. It was not doing our son any good; I ended up urging them to go ahead. . ." "where's the kid?"

"he's due for the university of South Australia but wants to live with some mates, perhaps better that way. . ."

"that's next year. . ."

"and his girl friend gravitates between home and him; she is working part-time" "do you need someone in your life if you don't mind me asking?"

"yes, we may not have another opportunity, Hector. Are you heterosexual, if you don't mind me asking?"

"Clara used to tell me if I were any more heterosexual I'd burst. . ."

Glen laughed, for the first time that evening.

"that describes me; so a gay relationship is out for either one of us. . ."

Hector thought for a while, then decided he would have to tell Glen at some stage:

"my daughter wants her best friend to be a boy. . ." "she; what?"

"the girls are determined to spend their lives together but in a straight and, apparently, very physical, relationship. . ."

"one of them 'll have to give in, then; I shouldn't laugh;" said Glen;

"now I can sort of see what you mean. . ."

"can you, Glen?"

"Yes, she wants the intensity of a relationship and some permanence, as I see it; difficult to achieve," Glen offered

"And if you are notoriously heterosexual, then you need the other to be of the opposite, not the same, sex. . ."

"ain't it a strange discussion at all?"

"'course, it goes to show how acceptably flexible sexuality is these days."

⁂

Ann's father rang his wife that he had been forced to leave her for a few days to conduct that workshop in Wentworth, he explained:

"Ryan is in a position to fire me, if I refuse any further, for breach of employment contract and he may yet do so,"

". . .hire a software consultant at short notice and exorbitant cost and make it very difficult for you to find work," Clara stated.

"He is taking us out for dinner tonight, he and his wife; can you cope, dear?"

"I'll ring Ann to stay with Julia. . ."

"are you up to it, Clara?" "yes, dear,"

"would you, please, not mention what I told you, unless Ryan brings it up"

"which he will, no doubt, which is probably why he invited himself to make it a bit easier for us. Someone jumped ship?"

"yes, Harry, who normally does these training courses. . . look, I'll be home in about half an hour," "depending on traffic, dear,"

"that is why I am leaving early. . . and I am given two days off, to spend at home." "something to look forward to, Hector. . ." his wife agreed.

Several weeks after his return from Mildura, Ann having gone to her own room to do her homework, her dad asked her mum:

"What would you call me, Clara, if you had to name me all over?"

"George comes to mind, dear. . ."

"no, it'll have to be a female name, surprise, surprise. . ."

"what are you trying to tell me, Hector Landers?" great emphasis on his first name.

They were seated in the kitchen, drinking some very low-alcoholic beer, having found that it refreshed and relaxed her sufficiently to be able to sleep at night without medication.

The fridge was humming away, as fridges do, the microwave indicated the time and the ceiling fan whirred away quietly. The kitchen table, built by Carla's grandfather, would, barring the unforeseen, outlive Ann's grandchildren, in the increasingly unlikely-looking case of her ever having any.

"I am beginning to prepare a new identity for myself for the time. . ."

"post death, you mean. I appreciate that; we have always been honest about me dying. . ."

"how was your day, anyway; sorry for not asking any earlier, Clara. . ."

"I did some gardening, you may not have noticed. . ."

"it was almost dark when I got home"

"of course, dear; then I cooked our tea and cleaned up wherever I could; I think I'll sleep quite well tonight. Do you miss making love to me?"

"of course I do, but as long as you are in one piece, I am content."

She took his hand and finished her beer with her free one:

"simple delights; life stripped to its basics is good," she sighed.

"Now, as to your future cross-gender identity; you told me about Glen and developing that profound understanding with him; I am pleased for you, because the next few weeks and months. . ."

"I know, love"

"so I don't have to spell it out for us. . . what I need to wrap my failing brain around is why Glen Hiddings needs you in a female incarnation. . ."

"he didn't say so"

"but it must appear that way to you. . ."

"yes, and I admit that I don't know but it feels like the best fit. . ."

"for the two of you once I am gone?" "yes. . ."

Clara had obviously found a missing connection.

"If it weren't for Ann expecting Julia to undergo that same kind of change. . ." "except in the opposite direction, remember!" "O yes, I do," she smiled,

"I would not know why-and how-a person would insist on such a profound change in another person. The only explanation is about as strange as the entire situation itself, is that. . ."

Ann's father was all ear.

"rather than go and be found by the right person of the right gender, whatever that is these days, our daughter," her mum continued, "wills another human being whom she wants to be in her life for her qualities, to make that final adjustment, rather than risk life with a pre-existing boy."

She took a deep breath:

"I would like for Glen, and his son, to begin to feel at home here, with us", she decided:

"another one who does not seem to want to risk getting involved with a fully-fledged original female, any more than Ann with a traditionally-developed boy, but evolve the person that is you into his preferred gender."

"so you suggest we invite him, preferably with his son and future daughter -in-law?" Ann's father said: "as it happens, Glen is to take over an office here in Adelaide next month, he doesn't know yet which one, though, and he offered either to employ me or. . ."

"or set you up your own," his wife offered. "two changes; sex and career!" he agreed. "I'll be gone by that time, but you'll have both new work and a relationship to grow into Which won't leave you with much time and energy for grieving. . ." "necessary though it is."

"I agree," confirmed his wife, "but don't overdo it. I envy you; go for it. . ."

Julia, increasingly called Jules by her classmates, had begun to stand behind Ann, with a hand on her shoulder. One evening, as she was watching a feature on telly on the national British dance competition for pre-teen adolescents, the dance mistress explained that the male dancer was to display his female to her advantage. That made sense to Julia, even as-still-a girl and not yet the intentional boy, as her lover wanted.

"no more childhood for you," her mother once said, "but enjoy the years before you have to be an adult."

Julia had matured in a very short time, having to prepare herself for her future role with hormones from the internet. Idling through the school library-not much time for that, these days-she read about a prisoner-of-war in Changi who had been urged to accept a female role in an end-of-year play. Reluctant at first, he had grown into, and been accepted in it so much, that 'she 'eventually walked into the ocean. Jules, not expecting such a drastic end, appreciated the strength of her forthcoming transformation, nonetheless.

⁂

Ann needed to be introduced to Jules' parents as lifelong love interest, sexual partner and future wife, all in one. Mr Childers was a highly specialized consultant and his wife-Eileen-worked in financial management. The girls had endured a stormy tutoring session, one of the Hazara girls' father having attempted to disrupt it, frustrated by avoidable bureaucratic mishap and stirred by their new mullah.

The girls were aware that unemployment, language difficulties and having to be taught everything at once, almost like a child, was behind such unhappiness, as their coordinator had once said:

"doesn't make it any easier for anyone!"

It did help break the ice when they arrived at Julia's home.

"Your dad will be home as soon as he can; he rang just now," her mother had assured Julia who nearly did not listen.?" (role-change discussions would have to wait a few more minutes!)

"You wouldn't believe it, Mum; that bloke got into our classroom and started ranting.

Eventually, Samira who is as gutsy as a 'lioness with cubs'. . ."

"'a demented lioness,' that's what our coordinator called her," added Ann, for good measure.

"she's also smart. . . she texted her uncle who she knew was waiting outside and then got another girl to pass a note to Mrs Weatherby"

"that's your coordinator, girls?"

"so that she would let that young man in, normally a no-no"

"what did he do next.?" Mrs Childers asked.

"Stand in front of that father, saying nothing much; eventually the man left; afterwards, some of the girls decided to walk Soraya home and protect her that way; Samira threatened, via her uncle"

"who looks gorgeous, by the way," added Ann, "like some Middle Eastern warrior film star,"–causing Jules to look at her strangely- "to call the truancy officer as a precaution; she indicated that her girls' brigade might become a permanent fixture. . ."

"at the slightest provocation," asked Eileen Childers, smiling.

"more or less, Mum."

"Could we invite some of these Hazara girls, what do you girls think. . ."

"girls, in plural, not much longer," said Julia. "But yes, some, at least, we'll need to ask around and also work out suitable bus runs so that they can travel home together?"

"Can't we drop them home?" 'her' mother wondered.

"only if absolutely necessary, Mrs Childers", Ann answered; "Why, Ann?"

"their parents might feel under an obligation which they cannot reciprocate; if they agree to the visit at all, be prepared to accept presents by the girls. . ." "certainly. . ."

"something which we can work through with the girls in advance. . ."

"Now, daughter mine, change of topic," Eileen Childers opened.

"what do you mean by 'girls no longer, in plural'? Is it your intention to confuse me, Julia?"

Her once but not future daughter counted till fifteen, looked at Ann, then at her parents and answered.

"I am sworn to a life with Ann, as her livelong lover and-here it comes-future husband!"

The next few minutes were, by all accounts, indescribable.

Eventually, Trevor Childers who had chosen that moment to arrive home, managed to lower the volume of his voice and turned to Ann:

"you are her friend and our guest today; you are welcome but whether you'll always be so, Julia's mother and I have yet to make up our minds. May I ask what your parents have to say to all that?"

"yes, you may," replied Ann, glad that attention had turned away from Jules.

"my parents are coming to terms, mainly with the fact that I decided to have Jules in my life, hopefully forever."

"but neither of you is of legal age, not even that of sexual consent. . ."

"that, Mr Childers, won't always be the case if we are allowed to survive the next few years."

"Ii you were two Hazara girls, instead, and were having this discussion with your parents. . ."

"our older brothers would kill us, failing that, the cousins, or the Imam, would arrange a public stoning,"

Ann answered truthfully.

"but I regret to say that I do not have a brother and I trust Jules' brother to resist the impulse," she continued.

"was it your idea, then?" Mrs Childers, too, had managed to lower her emotional temperature. . .

Ann took a deep breath, counted till ten and spoke:

"the kind of relationship that we both have in mind only makes sense on an opposite- sex basis," she asserted.

"I cannot speak for other girls, or boys, obviously."

"why not choose a 'traditionally-equipped boy', instead, and devote yourself to him, for as long as you like?"

"Jules wanted to be mine; got into some trouble saying so. . ."

"I am glad to hear it", Mr Childers' vocal temperature started to rise again. "certainly, Sir; and she realized that would only work if she were to end up as a boy and not remain a girl. . ."

"so you see, I had the choice of deciding to remain a girl," Julia cut in, standing behind Ann,

"and never be part of Ann's life, or agree to a sex-change and be with Ann forever. . ." "forever?" "we live in hope, Mum."

❧

Julia's parents were experiencing great difficulty remaining calm; to his credit, it was Trevor Childers' turn to breathe deeply, count towards an unknown number and direct himself to Ann, in a low voice:

"We can't stop you from being with each other at school, even though we are sorely tempted; "looking at his wife in confirmation,

"to forbid Julia from working with the Hazara girls"

"Dad!" his 'daughter' interjected;

"that would be very unfair, Mr Childers," Ann commented levelly;

"I agree, Ann, but to the Hazara girls more than to the two of you; what I am telling you, Ann, in particular: it will be at least a few years if ever that we, Julia's parents, would want to see you again in this house; we may reconsider if the both of you are of the same mind in two years which I doubt. . ."

"that's fair enough, Mr Childers", concurred Ann. "would you like to talk to my parents at all?"

"Dad, don't you realise that Ann's mother has only a short time to live?" raged Julia.

"you should have shown that consideration earlier, my dear," commented 'her' mother. Ann got to her feet:

"that, Mrs Childers, was below the belt; I thank you and Jules' father for your hospitality; I shall see myself to the bus stop; see you tomorrow, Jules! You are welcome, "turning to Trevor Childers,

"to ring my parents but, please, keep in mind what Jules told you. Goodbye!" and left the house.

"I hate you!" shot out Julia and ran outside.

Ann turned as she heard Jules follow her, waited for her to catch up and took her hand.

"walk me to the corner," she told her lover," kiss me and then go back home. I know now that you love me. . ."

"These are going to be difficult years ahead, Ann," Jules agreed.

❧

Julia-increasingly called Jules by everybody-ended up at Angela's place for some shared homework; she wanted to intercept a message she was not allowed to receive on the school network and did not trust her own computer with.

Having found out that Angela's parents never checked her laptop, she offered the girl a deal.

"I have most of our work on my laptop and, when we have finished, feel free to copy it on yours; we'll change a few bits, to make it less obvious. You can complete it; if you are stuck, ask me,,"

"okay," said the girl, sipping a disgustingly sweet drink:

"what do you need, Jules?" she asked, shrewdly.

"your laptop, to capture text to download onto my Secret Lover" "your USB?" "yes, nothing and nobody gets any closer. . .", Julia commented, laughing.

"you can check my USB for virus; I've already done it but feel free. . ."

"no, it's cool, so is my laptop; just erase everything afterwards. How long will it take you?"

"reading it; ten minutes max; barring interruption"

"okay, let's start. Something to drink?"

"that sludge, girl? Make us a cup of tea when it's all over, I say."

Julia was studying Ann's Instrument of Unilateral and Unconditional Subordination, of which later. . .

❧

Julia, Ann and several other tutors were having cups of tea with refugee council staff when one of the ladies spoke up:

"I have an appointment with Heinrich next Wednesday. . ."

"who is Heinrich?" asked one of the tutors, Klaas, an Afrikaans speaker originally from Kenya, knowledgeable about African refugees and fluent in several East African languages, whose parents had left during some disastrous post –election strife several years ago.

"Heinrich Wohlfahrt's office acts on behalf of some of our clients pro bono publico; in effect, for free, Klaas," the lady answered.

"Heinrich will also set time aside to help anyone in our team on personal legal issues, once or twice a year each; I want his advice on a guarantee I was asked for. . ."

"one of our clients?" another tutor wondered.

"indirectly; it's confidential."

"of course, sorry. . ." "cool," the lady replied.

Jules managed to buttonhole her by herself.

"how do I get hold of Mr Wohlfahrt?"

"Julia, what do you need a lawyer for?"

"that, too, is confidential and very personal. . ."

"at your age, Julia?"

"you are never too young to have legal problems."

"good grief, Julia. Let me get an event timetable for you from the office; don't go away."

The lady returned with the list and with a name and telephone number written underneath.

"Can we get an afternoon off by ourselves, Ann, other than for tutoring?" she wondered.

"whatever for?"

"to see that lawyer"

"without anyone to know about it, Jules?"

"yes, I want to get started on the sex change bit. . ."

"why the hurry?" "you, Ann"

The girl reflected on that, frowning:

"let us get time off to organize an internship; ask the Counsellor."

"that worked the last time," remembered Julia,

"and I did get some work during the holidays," reflected Ann.

"anyone you have in mind, Ann? "the student counsellor, an understanding lady, took confidentiality very seriously.

"Yes, I may want to do a legal apprenticeship, while I am at school; Rebecca started one last year. . ."

"the conveyancing she is doing after hours, you mean?" "yes"

"and you, Julia? Do you want to get some interview practice?"

"Yes; it never hurts. . ."

"no, it don't," the councillor agreed.

"I'll get you an afternoon off next Wednesday; you'll have to make your own arrangements whether they can see you on that day. Do you have any specific solicitor in mind?"

"yes; we'll arrange it ourselves.; thanks, anyway. . ."

"welcome; I like to see some initiative here"

"Is it true that girls have more 'go' in them than boys?"

Ann commented while smiling at her friend.

"I have no doubt," the counsellor concluded, "that that's often the case. Good luck, girls"

They did manage to get an appointment on the strength of them being tutors. Telephone calls had been made and, being known as responsible young people, both their tutor coordinator and their guidance counsellor were happy to vouch for them. "You are in luck, girls," the receptionist told them when they arrived at the office on South Terrace

"Heinrich's had a cancellation and he'll see you now. . ."

Ann offered the lawyer a sheet of paper.

"thank you for seeing us; you must wonder why we are here?"

"marginally so," he admitted.

"would you have a look at Ann's document first?" Julia offered; "by way of background. . ."

Heinrich Wohlfahrt read it, looked at the girls, re-read it, then paused.

"If this were not such a clear and well-written text, I'd think that you are out of your mind, Ann.

As it is, I have never seen an intern of ours write like that; some of our staff can't. . . How old are you?"

"it says under Roman One Arabic One, Sir."

"fourteen years, pushing fifteen. . . I don't believe it;. Have you shown it to Julia?"

"yes, Sir. It did surprise her. . ."

"I reckon; let me read out some of it:

'I, Ann Landers intend to devote my life to Julia/Jules Childers, as a closest friend, physical partner and future spouse, as soon as physically possible and legally permissible, so as to love, honour, obey and uphold Jules under any conceivable circumstances and entirely at Jules' pleasure and discretion, for as long as she will have me. . .'"

"my preamble, Sir; we were studying constitutions from all over the world."

"Okay; I can see that; now listen to this one:

'Aware of Jules' intention to undertake a change of sex, in order to become a boy and grow up as a man, so as to meet our mutual demands and desires for as long as we live and to please each other. . .'"

"is that what you girls want to see me about?" "yes, Sir," in unison.

"we do give legal advice on sex change, on occasion; the closest we had anything like yours was the case of a girl who wanted to be turned into a boy because the one she fancied was gay. Yours is different again; your Instrument has no legal standing, however well drafted; so very clear, I am amazed. . ." he shook his head.

"we know that it cannot be taken to Court to prove anything," conceded Julia, "but it does have the force of law as far as we are concerned," added Ann. "Julia, how about you?"

"ever since we started working with the Hazara girls",

"which I know about", the lawyer confirmed, "and people have nothing but good to say about you both,"

"thanks, Sir," Ann continued. "Jules wants to be in my life. . ."
"forever?"

"for as long as it takes, Sir. We do have girls coupled at school. . ."

"at your age, girls?" the lawyer enquired.

"may I continue, Sir?"

"of course, sorry, please, carry on."

"we are both 'non-gay' if you need to put it that way" "rather clumsily"

"I agree, Sir. Now, I want Jules with me about as much as she does but for it to work in the long term requires that one of us change sex; Jules chose to be it."

"answered like a lawyer," the solicitor wondered.

"are you girls certain that you won't enter law?"

"I shall, one day, Sir, Will you give me a job?"

"an internship during the year; why not; get your guidance counsellor to get in touch with us; but back to what you are here for. . ."

"to what extent, Sir, does sexual consent at age sixteen free a person to change one's sex without parental permission?"

"I'd hoped you wouldn't ask this bombshell of a question, Julia," the lawyer countered.

"short answer, girls, yes, but you'd have a battle. . ."

"with whom, Sir?" Jules wanted to know.

"well may you ask," was the reply. "The Medical and Legal Ethics Commission for one; do you girls know anything about them?"

"yes, Sir," answered Julia. "Our biology teacher gave us a presentation not long ago."

"then I suggest that you revisit your material, girls, and ask him, if he can keep it confidential. Do your parents know, by the way?"

"yes, Sir, and our biology teacher is cool, as long as we ask the right questions."

"I leave you to it then, girls," Heinrich Wohlfahrt concluded. "and I shall have a listen into what might be the thinking of the Ethics Commission; we have a contact through one of the partners; ring me next Wednesday, during working hours. Would you allow me to take a copy of your Instrument, Ann? Yes?" He spoke into an internal phone.

"pick up your original on your way out, Ann; the receptionist will have it ready for you. It's been a real pleasure and an eye-opener, girls"

"thank you, Sir," in unison.

⚘

The girls-till further notice, that was-fronted their biology teacher after class, and asked him about the Ethics Commission. They had agonised on how to phrase their query, till Julia overheard the cleaners discussing an accident and had a brainwave:

"Sir, does cosmetic surgery involve the Ethics Commission? the material you gave us doesn't really deal with it at all."

"not meant to, Childers; why are you asking," their teacher answered comfortably, relaxed in the girls' presence.

"we know about an attempted acid attack," Julia had pre-arranged this line, so as not to risk Ann gasping in surprise.

"on one of your Hazara girls? How very awful but also. . ."

"on the books, Sir", completed Ann. "If it had been successful and disfigured the girl. . .?"

"you girls realise that I am neither a medical or legal professional but the short answer is: the Commission would be involved, but their approval would probably be automatic."

"who would have to approach them, Sir?"

"you are asking because some of your clients' parents might hesitate."

"How do you know. Sir?" in unison, surprised.

"I am in the Army Reserve and was sent to Iraq some ten years ago, as an onsite scientist on biological weaponry. . ."

"which everyone thought Saddam had," suggested Ann. "Yes,. . ."

"That is how you learnt about oriental cultures, Sir?" continued Julia.

"Yes, unlike our US counterparts at the time, we were given cultural training," their teacher confirmed.

"So, to get back to your question; if the acid attack had been carried out in public and succeeded, such an awful word in that context, parental permission may not be needed for the Ethics Commission to go ahead. Given a rather less drastic situation, however, if parental approval could not be sought or was not forthcoming, a court order might be called for. . ."

"which court, Sir?"

"that would depend on the background and probably on the necessity and severity of the surgery required; the more drastic, the more the Ethics Commission would be involved, especially if minors are concerned. Do you want to tell me more, girls?" "If you don't mind, Sir; it is somewhat hypothetical. . ."

"but, knowing what Hazara girls, in particular, are up against, sort of realistic, is that what you are telling me?"

"yes, Sir; one more question; how is the Commission constituted?"

"who is on it, you mean?. . . do you want to follow this up as a project, girls?" "Yes, Sir, sort of"

"with the Refugee Council?"

"it's been discussed," the girls replied, truthfully, for a change.

"I'll ask a mate at Army Headquarters on Regency Road. . ."

He and Heinrich Wohlfahrt had the same contact, James Enderby, molecular biologist and reader in forensic microbiology, now semi-retired, known also for his involvement in the first rush into Iraq in 2003; someone, after all, had to identify and catalogue victims of all kinds of weapons of mass destruction, unknown or otherwise. This was how their biology teacher had come to know him, whereas Heinrich's law firm had hired him, after his retirement, to help a client defend a mass murder on the lack of conclusive forensic circumstantial evidence.

Both the teacher and the lawyer knew:

"If Professor Enderby were still with the Legal and Medical Ethics Commission, you girls could not see him;" The girls were aware of why: "He wouldn't be allowed to advise us if he were a sitting member, would he?"

They buttonholed their biology teacher once again and asked him:

"where can we catch up with Professor Enderby, Sir?"

Their teacher thought and then directed them:

"look up the websites of all universities in Adelaide, girls; find the one. . ."

"that has him on their list of retired or additional staff, make a few telephone calls, "added Ann;" then surf the net for some details," enlarged Julia,

"and then work yourselves towards a time and place, with luck," concluded their teacher. . .

In the end, the girls enlisted the help of the senior coordinator with the Refugee Council:

"Mrs Weatherby, we are schoolgirls and don't have an office like yours at our disposal; would you help us?"

"your next group is due in forty minutes; you can make a few telephone calls, provided that these are not to call centres; Ann, use the spare phone and you, Julia, use my computer; just don't mess up whatever's on my desktop.?. . ." what is all this in aid of, girls?"

"Social Responsibility. Mrs Weatherby."

"whom are you trying to contact, girls?"

"Professor Enderby, recently retired."

"Oh; I know of him; my sister tutors photography at the University of the Third Age-U3A-in Northern Suburbs and she used his material in one of her classes; I'll ask her and get you some contact details. Is it anything to do with us here?"

"hypothetically so far, Mrs Weatherby."

"well, let me ring my sister straight away", she offered helpfully.

"Vivienne? . ." already on the phone:

"Gladys, how are you?"

"I am fine; remember the photography class. . . oh you are teaching another one; good on you. . . bit hard to do, your sessions are during working hours ; if you did a block, I could arrange to attend; we are permitted that. . . what I wanted to ask you," she got to the point;

"are you still in touch with Professor Enderby, the one with those microbial slides?. . .

Yes, you did show me some blow-ups, quite fascinating. . . could you ring me back within, say, half an hour. . . it's for a pair of our tutors and they need to be back at class. . . two girls, they are just about the stars in our team. . . what they need it for. . . Community Responsibility; they tell me that both their biology teacher and one of our lawyers suggested him; they also left it to the girls to find out how to contact him… yeah, a bit rough; educational, you know. . . you'll ring me back; thank you…"

Meanwhile, Jules had been directed to a science website which she investigated for a telephone number; she rang; the receptionist answered:

"We'll have to find out if Professor Enderby let me pass on his contact details or whether he prefers to contact you. . . it's something to do with the Ethics Committee, you said? I'll put you through to someone else. . ."

"who will I be talking to?" Julia asked.

"Dr Sanders; he gives workshops in responsibility training… putting you through"

Dr Sanders, however, wasn't available and a colleague promised to pass on Julia's number.

Ann, having found James Enderby's publisher's website, typed an email, for it to be forwarded to him. Meanwhile, Vivienne, the photography tutor, called her sister: "You know, we are used to dealing with Professor Enderby by mail, would you believe it?. . . Postbox 1122, Modbury 5090; the girls in the office say; he'd ring sometimes but he'd never leave a number. . ."

"thanks, I'll tell the girls, Vivienne. Say Hello to Norman; drop in this weekend if you like, for a barbecue?"

Several days later, Ann had a text message on her phone; could she and her friend see him at his publisher's, would they let them know when; he, James Enderby, was intrigued with the idea of undergoing a medical intervention to benefit another person and would like to know more.

The girls went to see their biology teacher once again.

"We managed to get Professor Enderby to contact me yesterday," Ann started. "amazing; did someone at the Refugee Council help you?"

"yes, Sir."

"someone rang the school, they put the call through to me and I put them in touch with your counsellor," their teacher assured them.

"In confidence?"

"we do discuss students among ourselves, or we tend to consult your class teacher or else your parents. We know you both as responsible girls. What can I do for you now?"

"We need an afternoon off, so that we may consult Professor Enderby at his publisher's. . ."

"James hasn't changed; he can be very elusive. . ."

"his army background, maybe?"

"you could be right, girls, never thought about it like that. . . Look, let me ring his publishers; I know his editor. . . what day would suit you girls?"

"next Wednesday, between ten and twelve, Sir," Julia said.

"we need to admit to something, too; seeing that you are about to help us; we really wanted to ask him about the ethics of surgical intervention to benefit or oblige another person, not an acid attack, as you may have been led to believe. . ."

"are you talking about infibulations, female genital mutilation?" their teacher exclaimed, aghast.

"I didn't know that Afghani were into that."

"Hazaras aren't, some Afghan tribes practice it, but not universally," the girls assured him.

"but the intervention we want to ask him about is every bit as drastic as that," Ann added.

"anything at all to do with your tutoring, girls?"

"indirectly;" answered Jules. "if we promised to tell you in detail once we have talked to your friend?"

"Well, it seems that I must settle for that; let me see whether ten or eleven o'clock next Wednesday suits him; I'll let you know"

"thank you ever so much." The girls meant it, too.

In having to arrange a morning that suited James Enderby, their teacher obtained permission to miss school for three hours on that day so that they could take the kind of buses that would get them directly to the publisher's office ; as a result, they both arrived as the office opened.

"Welcome, girls, tea of coffee?" they were greeted on arrival.

"would you like to have a look? Professor Enderby has been delayed in traffic, as per usual this time of the morning," the receptionist told them.

"which one of you girls is going to be the scientist?"

"that's me," indicated Julia. "Ann here will be a fully-qualified lawyer when all this is over."

"sounds ominous," commented the receptionist, smiling.

"you girls will be in good hands with Professor Enderby. I'll make us a pot of tea. Won't be a minute, girls."

Julia went through some back copies with great interest, being absorbed in an article on algal bloom.

A gentleman entered: "Are you making us a pot of tea, Marj?" he called out to the receptionist in her kitchenette.

"yes, James, we can all have a cup. Girls, come over; Professor Enderby is here."

"good morning, girls," he greeted them courteously. "Let's have a cuppa first; tell me about yourselves and then we'll talk shop, whatever you need to find out from me."

They sat down companionably and started talking about their work with the Hazaras.

"they don't do infibulations, do they?" the professor asked.

"no," assured him Ann, "very rarely so; others in Afghanistan may, Baluchi possibly," she continued.

"that's not why we are here, Sir. Did our teacher say that? If he did, we need to apologize to him and you."

"are you girls going to tell him what you want to know from me?"

"yes, we promised him"

"take your cups over, girls; I may use the editor's office for a while," the ethicist told them.

"as to infibulation, to get that out of the way; it is normally East Africans and, perhaps, Yemeni who we know of in Australia, rarely South Asian Muslims, you are right there, Ann"

"it is an offence, Sir, is it not?"

"yes, it is considered a medically unwarranted physical insult; we do have it contested from time to time, to do with life prospects in their respective culture; it is punishable in Australia wherever the act occurs. . ."

"ours, Sir, is rather different," Ann, the prospective legal eagle, assured him: "Two questions:

Does sexual consent include the right to a sex change; if so at what age?" very deep breath:

"what is the thinking of the Ethics Commission on medical interventions undertaken to benefit or accommodate someone other than the patient?"

"that is a very intelligent, if underhand, description of the cultural ramification of female genital mutilation, coming from a teenage girl," the biologist wondered.

"last one first, Julia; the Commission will consider, not necessarily approve of, it as long as the intervention is not a criminal act of coercion, blandishment or intimidation but sought in free will. We do get the odd girl and adult young woman who want a sex change because the one she fancies happens to be gay. . ." the scholar told them.

"the most attractive boys often are," the girls nodded, in unison.

"yours must be for a different reason, I take it."

"very different, Sir," Ann assured him: "the very opposite, if anything; we are both so heterosexual to be ready to burst. . ." "powerfully put, girls; do explain!"

"show him your mouthful of an Instrument of Unilateral Subordination, Ann; did I get that right?" offered Julia.

"you did," said Ann; "I high-lit the segment that we want your advice on, Sir;" and gave him the neatly-typed document to read.

Professor Enderby shook his head: "Did you write that, Ann?"

"yes, Sir, by myself, on someone else's laptop; it took a hour, then I downloaded it on a dedicated USB and got Jules to delete it on a friend's computer."

"a wise decision; would you allow me to upload it from your memory stick, Ann?" "certainly, Sir, who do you need to show it to," she enquired.

"nobody, at the moment; be assured. . ." He sipped some tea, watched the girls do likewise ("they have learnt not to speak for the sake of saying something," he decided.).

"extraordinary", he said at last. "the very short answer to question one: possibly yes but highly contestable at Court; someone adult might have to take on the case for you unless you, Julia, are prepared to wait another few years; Question two: the Commission tends to take a dim view of such drastic and comprehensive an intervention as a 'gender alteration', except in response to an individual need, but that of another person, even in a relationship, yet may not consider it frivolous, especially if the other person-you, Ann?" the girl nodded, "intends to, and insists upon, being involved in the entire lengthy process, which I take you do?"

"yes, Sir, definitely!"

"leave it with me, girls; as I am not a current member, I am free to advise you. . ."

"yes, we were told that," in unison.

"I'll let Mrs Weatherby at the Refugee Council know how to contact me for a reply; do your parents know?"

"yes, Sir; we told them, and their reaction. . ."

"the Commission will need to hear them, as you can imagine; I don't need to, just yet, how they feel. . ."

"we'll tell you, nonetheless, if you don't mind," offered Ann: "my mother is dying and my father is also considering a 'gender alignment' in the interest of a future relationship. . ."

("good grief!", thought the professor, understandably).

"Jules' parents reacted rather differently, again."

"do your parents control your mobiles, girls?"

"yes, they do," in unison.

"So Mrs Weatherby is your best bet, girls; thank you for a most unusual experience, and I mean it; bye for now. I'll ask the editor if one of their staff can drive you part of your way; buses at this time of the day are sheer potluck. . ."

⁂

Meanwhile, Ann's father and Glen had begun to see each other almost daily; Glen had brought his son, Roger, along, on one of Ann's mum's better days.

"consider yourself family, Glen, you, too, Roger;" Clara had said.

"Ann never had an older brother," she commented, smiling at Glen's son;

"and I am getting myself am extra sister, Clara," the boy had replied, "not always easy."

It was an exquisite autumn day; they were sitting outside, except that Julia was standing behind Ann, one hand on the girl's shoulder, as had become her habit. "Jules, sit down", said Ann's father.

"let her, Dad. . ."

"not much longer, Ann," commented Roger.

"Too true; we may find ourselves competing who can get done faster, Jules or you, er, Dad!" laughter all around.

It was a nice day, not as blistery wet and unpleasant as South Australian afternoons can be mid-year. They listened to the birds and to a light breeze blowing through the canopy of some very old gum-trees; Clara's lovingly-planted shrubs were in their last blossom and native bees used the warmth to gather pollen for winter. They sat in companionable silence, drinking tea, savouring the quiet around them, with only the minutest roar caused by distant traffic.

"We do love you, Mum; we'll miss you.," Ann said finally, quietly.

"even though with your Dad lined up. . ."

"to take over from you? It'll be very different. . ."

"but very fulfilling"; Glen and Ann's-so far, father-looked at each other and nodded.

"When are you about to start hormonal treatment?"

Ann said, wishing almost instantly she could swallow her words.

"we do 'tactless', don't we?" countered Julia.

"never mind, dear," Ann's mum assured her, "once you start living with my daughter, you'll have to tell her' change feet' on occasion, as part of lifelong commitment." Her father answered, smiling:

"Glen and I are about to see a specialist; that in itself will take time, merely to get an appointment; I am also in the process of getting my colleagues to accept me in my future identity and role," he continued.

"that's when you realize what kind of village Adelaide really is", added Glen,

"because we deal with the same people at work. I never realized how accurate one of my Malaysian interns was. . ."

"what did she say, Dad?" asked Roger.

"she called it Kampong Adelaide."

"okay; I sometimes feel that half the Malaysian population is here and the other half in Perth," Roger commented.

"do you get to Malaysia very often, Roger?" his future 'stepmother' asked him. "yes", answered Roger, evidently at a loss how to address Ann's 'present' father.

"my Eurasian girl friend lives there;"

"she was at school here," explained his real father;

"that's how we know each other; She and I are going to teach Burmese refugee children on Penang in my gap year; for they are not allowed to enter regular

Malaysian schools. . ."

Roger explained.

Julia went to see the guidance counsellor.

"You are very close to Ann Landers, aren't you?"

"yes, Mrs Sedgway; we are".

The lady explained: "in that case, she'll need every bit of your friendship. . ."

"what do you mean?" began Jules, then she realized; "Her mum must have taken a turn for the worse. . ."

"Look, Julia, you know about the need for confidentiality; don't you agree, Childers?"

"Yes; sorry; but also, thank you"

Soon afterwards, the girls found themselves in the same class.

"Bitch, why did you not tell me?"

"I would have. . ."

"when?" "when the time was right. . ."

"look, Ann, the time is never right for that kind of thing. . . it's your mum, isn't it?"

"How did you know?"

"well, I didn't, now I do, and I am with you!"

"it may be a bit awkward, Jules. . ."

"did your mum have to go back to the hospice, Ann?"

Julia stretched out her hand to touch Ann who moved away, distressed.

"She is not expected to leave it alive. . ."

The girl was close to tears.

"When are we going to visit her?"

"I am leaving early today; Dad"

("provisionally and not for much longer," she added mentally) will pick me up. "us," intoned Jules.

"don't make it hard for me, Jules, please. . ."

Julia took her, by now usual, deep breaths, counted and said:

"you don't know, bitch, how hard it is going to get. Let's go somewhere else, people don't have to hear us argue all over the corridor."

The girls found an empty storeroom and Julia continued:

"you have only one mother-we won't talk about your dad's long-term options-and you are about to lose her. If we can't face that situation together, we'll never make it. . ."

"meaning?"

"if you stop me from going with you to see your mother, today, not in a few weeks, but now, I won't feature in your life. . ."

"How?"

"I'd change schools, if I have to, Ann; it's not what I want to do but if I'm not allowed to be close when it counts I don't want to be with you at all, ever". "it's not so much I. . ."

"if your dad ("until further notice", Julia added to herself) is against it, you know what to do."

"it might be the hospice: close relatives only," countered Ann.

"then you and your dad know what to do!"

"I guess so, Jules."

Ann rang her father later that day, during a break when students were permitted to make and receive calls.

"Julia is coming along this afternoon; she is organising time off as well."

"do you think that's a good idea, Ann?" her father-for the time being-wondered. "look, Dad, there comes a time when I have to learn to stand up for someone else."

"why?"

"if I want to live with myself, after Mum has died, that's why, Dad," Ann stated brutally.

"and Jules is the one that I intend to stand up for, now and always; Mum will understand. . ."

"I am more worried about the hospice: close relatives only."

"you are being evasive, Dad; if it comes to that, you and I know what to do."

"okay; but do you realize how much you are about to commit to someone not even yet in your desired image. . ."

"Dad!" a daughter's reaction, given how much this was a case of 'the pot calling the kettle black'.

⁂

No one said a word on the drive to the hospice; Ann and her dad knew where to go without having to ask or search and Julia followed them, Ann's hand in hers; no questions asked.

Ann's mother, while distressed, was nonetheless pleased to see them all, very much including Julia :

"You managed to get time off school as well, good one," she commented. "It's good to see all of you; I do ask you to keep up the good habit in future months; don't expect me outside ever again."

"isn't that a self-fulfilling prophecy, Clara?" her husband enquired.

"Doctor Samira says No; she has given me weeks at best; she will be with us later today"

"let's talk about something else," suggested Julia and told them what one of the boys had done in the lab:

"we were asked to measure magnetic force in the physics lab," she started, "and, to warm us up, the instructor plugged in the horseshoe and challenged us to move it. One boy tried, then the next; the third, Geoff who does astrophysics, managed to pull it off, so did Ainsley but Bill failed, predictably, as did our teacher. A few more boys tried and didn't manage but Heather got up and pulled it off with great ease. Eventually, someone noticed that Dennis was sitting close enough to the power

45

outlet to be able to whip a plug in and out at speed and started laughing, so everyone picked it up, including the teacher."

"did he laugh along with the rest?" asked Ann's by now almost provisional father.

"yes, he figured that's what he liked about physics; it was full of surprises."

"do you like him as a teacher?" Ann's mother asked.

"yes, we do," both girls answered. "He listens and manages to get into your thinking, then unpacks it by asking questions. He rarely explains anything but thinks of an example, then lets us work things out."

"the mark of a good teacher," Ann's mother agreed.

"You were right," Ann told her lover a few days later, hands firmly held." It turned out to be no issue at all. . ."

"me coming along to see your mum?"

"yes, of course; you also managed to bend me to your will, which is what I desire and deserve; now I want no longer to be able or allowed to resist you, ever; one day, you'll 'man' me. . ."

"do you want me to fuck you bitch today?" "let's," Ann complied.

"I know this place behind the poplars which I used last year to test the correlation between light and transpiration on deciduous trees. . ."

"courtesy of our botany teacher; bless him. . ."

"no, lover, it was the gardener we had working here last year who showed me". "does anyone ever go there?"

"no, Jules, most of us don't even know it exists, including our teachers."

"do you have half an hour spare this arvo, Ann? We are on different timetables today."

"yes, lover; I am looking forward to being expertly fucked."

"Just before you get there, Jules, watch out below," Ann had told her,

"I set up a kind of tripwire on either side of the copse' you'll have to crawl. . ." "did you mine our access?"

"no, nothing as ridiculous as that, Jules;" Ann giggled;

"I found sets of bush telephones we used to play with as children. . ."

"two tins with a wire in between them, you mean?"

"yes, as we were cleaning up after Mum had to go back to hospital. I put them far apart this morning so anyone, in the unlikely event. . ."

"we get to hear them and can hide. . ."

"in a bit of bush without anyone seeing us. . ."

"unless they search. . ."

"but why should they; if anything, it'd be someone else trying to hide."

The girls arrived there, separately, from either end, but at the same time.

"well-timed," said Julia.

"we don't have to whisper but do keep your voice down, no names; now strip me.!"

❧

Wordlessly, they relieved each other of their clothing, kissing all the time.

Julia forced Ann down onto the leaves lavishly spread underneath the trees,

grabbed her shoulders, forced Ann's arms close to her body, mounted her, encircled Ann's lower body with her thighs, in a pulsing movement, and kissed her hard.

Ann arched up to Jules several times then went limp in utter surrender, aiming to be held down, kissing Julia's hands, arm and fingers. Julia, in turn, nuzzled Ann's barely formed breasts, upper arms and shoulders. Several minutes later, she partly rolled off Ann, immobilizing her with her thigh, and proceeded to enter her with her fingers, teasing the unresisting girl into uncontrollable, twitching excitement, using her knee to arouse and subdue Ann further.

She then turned Ann over, using her hand inside the girl to control and stimulate her, reinforced by her knee, and covered Ann's legs and body almost completely with her own, using her free hand to explore the girl's utterly captive body; Ann kissed every portion of Julia's hands and arms, in explicit submission. Jules eased off Ann's body and withdrew her hand from inside the gently moaning girl, breathing heavy gusts of air.

"don't," wailed Ann.

"we need to get ready, clean ourselves and get dressed," Julia kissed her one more time, to which Ann responded eagerly:

"don't ever let anything or anyone get into your way, least of all myself," Ann surrendered herself.

"I can't wait for you to grow nuts and a bolt," she concluded.

"how about a beard?"

"highly optional, lover. . ."

❧

Meanwhile, Hector Landers was getting ready to face the specialist for his initial hormone treatment. Glen who was to have accompanied him, had rung off.

"I am the acting boss today; we are two people short and I have to supervise the preparation for a workshop next week . ."

"the one you invited me to, on new software in job searches?"

"Yes, normally, I would have wanted you to come in today, with your boss' permission. . ."

"no, we have been through this," with some exasperation,

"Glen. . . it is difficult enough to get to see that man; could you prepare some documentation that he'll need?. . ."

"I'll fax some through and upload a statement in support; I am not trying to have you face all this by yourself. . ."

Ann's 'father 'had hung up, only minutely mollified, and tried to get emotionally ready.

When he reached the specialist's office, the receptionist was all apologies.

"Mister Cartwright, (some consultants are not addressed as Doctor, remembered Hector), was called out ten minutes ago to attend to a person who was put on contra-indicated medication to deal with a knife injury and we were unable to call you, Mr Landers; I am so very sorry. . ."

"I was probably on the way and I turn my mobile off when driving," he suggested, "would you mind very much if I went to see my wife, instead, and get Mr Cartwright to ring me when he is free?"

"thank you, Mr Landers. If it is not too impertinent to ask, where is your wife?"

"the oncology ward," he answered curtly.

"my apologies; I really am sorry!"

"nothing that you or I can do about it now; you have my mobile number; alternatively, here is the number for the hospice that my wife is in; they are bound to accept Mr Cartwright's call. . ."

The receptionist had a brainwave:

"he is at the Royal right now; I'll ring him straightaway and he can catch up with you there. . ."

"is that where the patient is?" he asked.

"Yes, in police custody; they couldn't move him; bad anaphylactic shock, I suspect."

"Would it be an intrusion, Mr Landers, if you were to introduce me to your wife?" the consultant had offered, courteously, over the telephone.

"I need to be here for quite a while and you'll have to get back to work. . ."

"why would you like to see my wife, Sir?"

"It will make things easier with the Ethics Committee, especially as your future partner is not here."

"Fine, Sir, just let the ward know, would you?"

ॐ

"Did you have any trouble, Sir?"

Ann's father asked the specialist after he had entered the ward and introduced himself to the couple.

"No, the professor did have a bit of a moan. . ."

"he would have liked to be given more notice, I'd guess. . ."

"yeah, that's about it. I told him that I needed to interview Mrs Landers here, not that you, Madam, would be anywhere else, plus your husband would be here to see you, rather than go back to work straightaway; by the way, I am sorry Mr Landers. . . "Hector. . ."

"I am sorry, Hector, that you had to drive all the way to my rooms. . . well, Mrs Landers, could we move you into a conference room, please!"

"I can walk, Dr Cartwright. . ."

"Mr Cartwright, please, that's the convention."

"I am encouraged to walk short distances, to help my circulation. . ."

"quite so, Mrs Landers,"

ॐ

Once they were seated and had a steaming pot of tea in front of them, courtesy of the nurse,

"your husband must have told you of the nature of his future partnership. . ."

"not only that, I met the bloke. . . his future husband, so to say, and a son; we invited them home. . ."

"So do you object to your husband starting hormone treatment within the next few weeks?"

"will it be irreversible, Sir?"

"eventually, yes" ("but you won't get to witness that", the consultant added, mentally).

"Does the Ethics Committee need to hear from me as well?", Ann's mother asked.

"it would help, yes; as you cannot go out and they may not want to meet here; if you could write or dictate a statement. . ."

"that I have no objection to my husband's gender alignment so as to meet his future partner's physical and emotional needs, as well as his own, for a fully-fledged relationship; is that it?"

"very well put, Mrs Landers," the consultant admitted.

"It is a bit of an ask but would you make sure that you are not on any medication. . ." "not even an aspirin, Sir?"

"ideally, yes," the specialist assured her solemnly,

"Would you come back with your laptop, Sir?" she offered;

"and let the ward know to let me miss out on my noontime medicals and be back, say, mid-afternoon, I can dictate it directly onto your laptop; the ward sister can witness it, if you like; they must be used to that kind of thing. . ."

"regretfully, yes, I am sure," the consultant conceded." I shall need to check on my patient, the one with the stab wound gone septic and in allergic shock; so I can come back here.

Meanwhile, I'll instruct my receptionist to make another appointment for your husband.

May I, "he concluded" compliment you on your approach to all this, at a time like this"

"thank you, Sir" Ann's mother said, simply.

The statement she dictated it later that day was simplicity itself;

"I Clara Ann Margaret Landers nee Wilson, of sound mind, hereby state that I have no objection to my husband's, Hector Alfred Landers, considering gender alignment and taking steps so as to be able to effect a future sex change, undertaken in the interest of a relationship that he may wish to pursue subsequent to my own forthcoming and, as I am reliably informed, un-preventable demise. signed. . . witnessed dated"

This turned out to be the very last afternoon to see Clara Landers in anything resembling good health, able to interact, not in too much pain and not too distressed. While nobody would have called her a believer in any sense denoting orthodoxy, she was a very aware person, both of herself and of others; nobody needed to tell her what went on in people's mind. Being as straight as a die, she did not take kindly to those trying to instill false hope or belittle her condition.

Ann and her-so far-father did not dare attempt to, and she had soon disabused nurses and other staff; she deserved to be treated with a healthy dose of realism and doctors, nurses and others respected her for it; not that some of the other patients did.

She was comforting a younger woman who dreaded the thought of having to leave two very young children behind:

"you are lucky, 'she told the startled girl," that your partner does not intend to leave it all behind."

("let alone change sex to try a different kind of relationship ", Clara added in her own mind). . .

"you are right, Clara,", she said, "but he is so helpless. . ."

"he won't be if he loves the kids, and as they grow up, they'll learn to look after themselves and him; girls usually do; they'll end up marrying him off, once again"

"how do you know that, Clara?"

"girls demand intimacy and they worry about relationships as much as we, their mothers do?"

"does your Ann?"

"oh yes, except that she's going about it in an unusual way."

"huh," the girl asked, starting to cease about her own worries, at last.

"I have said too much, Brenda, already," Ann's mother smiled, with some difficulty.

"Clara, that girl who is always standing behind her is not her sister?"

". . .but her future boyfriend," Ann's mother stated, matter-of-factly.

"may I ask?" "No, Brenda."

The mother of two, soon-to be orphaned little girls, laughed. . .

"I needed that; thank you;. . . I shouldn't have laughed at you; I am sorry, Clara." "don't be, Brenda;"

("you were worried about someone else, for a change," but Ann's mother kept that thought to herself)

❦

Doctor Samira, an Iranian-born palliative oncologist, had heard Brenda's fully- throated laughter and smiled as she entered.

"May I introduce myself, ladies?" she offered;" Samira Tafreshi, born in Shiraz,

"Ann's mother, astonished:" the world is a small place, to be sure?"

"What do you mean, Mrs Landers?"

"Clara, doctor, and this is Brenda"

"my pleasure," the young doctor replied.

"I used to live in Shiraz with my family when I was my daughter's present age, adored it; may I call you Samira"

"yes, of course, unless the Professor or Matron happen to be around," the resident answered sagely. "and may I add, Samira," Ann's mother requested: "try not to call the girls 'girls', when they are both here, I do it all the time but it is not a good idea, really!"

"whatever for, Clara?"

"you may find out if the girls are prepared to tell you. It's to do with what they went to see Professor Enderby for. . ."

"My ex-lecturer who was on the Ethics Commission?" "yes, Samira."

"did you let them?"

"Yes, we let them, but Julia's parents proved somewhat more difficult."

"are the girls in a relationship already?"

"yes, but it's going to be even more complicated than it is now. . ."

"and I wasn't even 'known' till was nineteen," the doctor admitted ruefully.

"In a scriptural sense, Samira?"

"yes," she replied; this time, both ladies burst out laughing.

It had unexpectedly started raining all over Adelaide when things came to a head in the Childers household. . . Julia's father was on his rostered day off and her mum had been unable to go to work; even her brother was home, trying to catch up on a project on the history of microbiology.

A fellow student had accosted him the day before:

"I saw your sister and another girl. . . Guess where?"

"when, rather?" wondered Stephen Childers; "you haven't been around much in the last few weeks, have you?"

"no, I am doing an internship at Victor Harbour Primary Health Care Laboratories. . ."

"not due till next year for your course in forensic microbiology. . ."

"normally, you'd be right, but I am doing an exchange year at Nanyang in Singapore, if you remember, and they won't let me do an internship there."

"okay, so where did you see my sister and the other girl; that would be Ann. . ." "who's she?"

"probably the one you saw my sister with, I'd say; they've been hanging out together ever since they started tutoring the Hazaras. . ."

"who are the Hazaras, Stephen; girls?"

"yes, Afghani girls from a persecuted minority; they need girl tutors; again where did you see Julia and Ann. . .?"

"Every now and then I have to go and see Professor Enderby; he is the only one who covers my future specialty at academic level in Adelaide; I had written part of a paper on detection of illicit blood products. . ."

"you mean, in doping?"

"yes, Enderby is on the panel for the Tour Down Under; anyway, I usually drop these at his publishers'; all of us do, from various campuses and labs, and I saw the girls leave the building with him; he must have wanted to drop them somewhere mid-morning. . ."

"they were meant to be at school. . ."

"maybe, at a bus stop. . ."

"did they see you?"

"probably not; I was just about to park and then go up to them; for I needed to speak to Enderby, anyway, but then a car drove out and I had to overtake it, then back into the spot that it had left.

By the time I was parked, they had gone, all three; the girls and Enderby were talking as if they had all known each other for ages."

"well, Jules wants to become a scientist," her brother said,

"seems to run in the family. Still, and all," he frowned. . .

He had ample reason to be shocked when he confronted Jules as she got home from school.

"Norm saw you and Ann at Professor Enderby's publisher's office. . ."

"how come he knows us?"

"from his cousin at your school,"

"where everyone knows everyone else's business", Jules agreed.

"Did Norm tell you what Ann and I had gone there for?" "No," 'her' brother admitted.

Trevor Childers had listened to his off-springs' altercation with half an ear but, suddenly, he interjected.

"Stephen, what is this Professor known for; I seem to remember having read something in the Examiner a fair while ago. . ."

"forensic microbiology, much of that sports-related, such as cycling. . ." "nah, try again"

"soil microbes in your garden; he did a radio talk on local FM. . ."

"yes, I remember, wasn't that one. . ."

"he does give talks on medical and legal ethics"

"that's it; remember the mass murder in Nuriootpa; four people found in forty-four gallon drums. . ."

"vaguely; I was on that student exchange in Germany at the time, I think. . ."

"could be right; I took a particular interest because a workmate used to live there, same block. . ."

"but where did Professor Enderby enter; remember I wasn't here. . ."

"they suspected someone tried to blow himself up, along with the arresting officer and an otherwise totally uninvolved neighbour. . ."

"now I remember," contributed their mother;

"they all needed blood transfusion and the neighbour refused for religious reasons. . ." "like Jehovah's Witness?"

"something like that, Stephen; the Ethics Commission got involved; it appears that the paper quoted your Professor Enderby."

"who may have been on the Commission at the time,"

"is that why you girls went to see him, Jules?" 'her' brother asked.

"Anything to do with that brain-dead idea of you changing sex so you could learn to bonk Ann for the rest of your lives together?"

A long shot, admittedly: "what did he say to you 'girls'?". . .

"if I am to be even more blunt," 'her' brother continued; "the idea of growing a rod to make Ann your long-term root sucks, to put it kindly. . ."

"you ought to be talking, Stephen,. . ." Julia reminded him; "you are one big hormone. . ."

"granted," the boy admitted cheerfully,

"my approach to girls is highly predatory; not that they have minded, so far; but even I wouldn't warp myself. . ."

"you don't have to, Stephen," Julia laughed.

"As to what we were discussing with Professor Enderby, that is confidential, dear brother, but you won't be able to stop me, nor will Mum and Dad."

"would you, please, explain, Julia, in your own, carefully chosen words, how?" enunciated her sibling.

"Do you remember Edward Tanner?" she asked, instead.

"Is he still around?" surprised.

"he used to come to our school and do blocks on development education; I enjoyed those; what's he got to do with you wanting to become a boy?"

"himself, nothing, I agree," she explained to their parents:

"Edward Tanner used to work as an overseas development consultant and gets to do development blocks; I think he's moved back to Brisbane. . . Did he give you the talk on Mahatma Gandhi?"

"satyagraha; non-violent resistance. . ."

"backed up by?" Jules challenged 'her' brother:

"You must be even more brain-dead than you look," he reacted.

"No, I am not, any more than Gandhi himself was. . ."

"it is quite an aggressive technique, isn't it?" her brother commented thoughtfully. ("he is taking me seriously, for a change", Julia figured)

"yes, it was, but more than that, and it threatened nobody. . ."

"except the ones it was used against; the Ethics Commission mightn't like you forcing us into agreeing to something we shouldn't have to."

"they might appreciate my determination, though. . ."

"we, your parents, would appreciate some concern for us," their father interposed.

"you may not have noticed that you lost us somewhere; what has the Mahatma Gandhi have to do with Julia wanting to change her sex.?"

"for one thing, Dad," his son informed him,

"Gandhi had a very troubled approach to sex and to young girls, especially in later years; I'll let Julia here explain in words of not much more than one syllable if that can be done. . ."

"thanks, Stephen," Jules helped herself to another cup of tea and took a deep breath.

"Jules holding forth;" her brother recognized the symptoms:

"shut up, Stephen. Mum and Dad; not an easy one but if you wish to prevent me from changing my sex, now or even in some future, there'll be a fast unto death. . ."

"whatever's that, Julia?" her mother wondered.

"a technical term, Mum" her son assured her. "It's more than that, Stephen, "Julia corrected him:" it is, literally, deadly serious; call it a hunger strike for a purpose. . ."

"a very selfish one," her brother commented.

"look, you broke up with a girlfriend for reasons that a two-year old would laugh at. . ." that seemed to be not too far off the truth; for her brother went very quiet.

"Julia, you need to apologize for that comment," her father urged; "that wasn't called for." Julia considered that:

"you are right, Dad; sorry, Stephen." She paused, took another load of deep breaths: "unless Mum and you can find it in yourselves not to object to my going ahead, I shall not touch food and only a limited amount of water if any."

"how about school, sports, tutoring, Julia?"

"work has to go on as long as possible, that's part of the discipline of an extended fast."

"we might stop you from going to school. . ."

"no, you cannot, legally; I am required to attend school and it is your responsibility. . ."

"as it is to prevent you from hurting let alone killing yourself."

"that is between you and myself, so far; school involves a third element, a force majeure. . ."

"whatever that is?" wondered her mother.

"your lover Ann wants to be a lawyer," Stephen remembered. "some of that must have rubbed off on you. . ." "guess how?" his sister teased him. "Biophysics!"

⚘

Hector fronted Glen at a coffee shop off King William's:

"I want you and me to see Clara this afternoon, Glen, I was given word late this morning. . ."

"ah, ah, that's a bit awkward, work, you know. . ."

"no, I don't, Hector; but if we are to be in a relationship, this supersedes work."

"using heavy bore, aren't you, Hector. . . what shall we call you in future?"

"a different name, obviously, but that future hasn't arrived yet. If you don't mind, I shan't resume hormones until after. . ."

"I understand; I am sorry, Hector, at a time like this. When would you like us to go, and how?"

"we'll walk, Glen; it's less than twenty minutes from where we are now, off North Terrace; where do you want us to have lunch; here or at the hospice cafeteria?"

"is their food edible?"

"by and large, it is, speaking from experience. . ."

"then let's eat there; before or after we get to see Clara?"

"depends on how she is, I suppose. Let's finish our coffees and move. . ."

"Thanks for coming," Clara intoned as both men,-so far-entered the ward,

"it's good to see you here, Glen," she added graciously. "Tea?" she asked;

"no, I am a Coffee Pot, Clara. . ."

"could you start the jug, Hector?"

Her 'husband 'went to the wall, selected cups, teabags, coffee mixes, milk and sugar for the two men(?) and found some herbal tea for his wife as well. 'He' balanced the cups and some biscuits, kelp-based ones for his wife, on a tray and returned to their table.

Clara was able to sit, with a drip overhead. "I am on chemo," she explained.

"to limit the spread of metastases; a losing battle," she added, matter-of-fact like.

"what did the Prof tell you, love?" asked her husband anxiously.

"four weeks at the most, could be a lot sooner?"

"why the chemo, then, or shouldn't I ask?" queried Glen, concerned.

"no, it's all right; the Prof wants to control its spread until it overwhelms me which it will, of course, like you would drive a car that's beyond repair while you can get some mileage out of it, for essential transport. . ."

"are you feeling comfortable?"

"limited in what I can do, but yes, thanks."

"Ann," her 'father' had managed to get through to her school and she had been called to the office, with Julia standing behind her:

"you need to come to the ward right now; I asked your office administrator to organize transport for you. . ." ". . .and Jules, Dad, I am not going without her. . ." Her father sighed, not wanting to argue.

"fine,", thinking of the even greater difficulty of prying Glen loose from his work: "it's your Mum. . ."

"'course, Dad. . ."

"the lady told me she'd get your career counsellor to drive you; I suggest that she drop the two of you close to Parliament and I pick you up where we had the Apology screened in 2008, as close as I can to the twin bus stop. . ."

"right hand side from Town, you mean, Dad?"

"yes, Ann; I can park there for a few minutes; if you two get there earlier than I, wait at the bus stops; I'll drive us to the ward and we'll have a sandwich and a cup of tea at the hospital cafeteria. . ."

"you mean cardboard and dishwater, Dad"

"Ann, say Sorry; this is not the time to make such comments. . ."

"of course, Dad, Sorry; will we be tied up all afternoon?"

"if not longer, my daughter," her dad assured her quietly.

Ann suddenly realized how much her life would change, as of now, the suddenness and severity of it all.

"thanks for organizing it all, Dad. We'll get there as soon as we can. . ."

Meanwhile, the school administrator was speaking on an internal line:

"Celia, I think the girls are ready for you," she addressed the guidance counsellor;

"yes, both of them; Julia is in her protective mode and Ann won't go without her. . ." yes, I understand Ann's dad will pick up the girls somewhere halfway; Ann will tell you where, so you can get back here sooner and they don't have to wait;. . . five minutes? Is there someone with you, Celia? do you want someone else drive the girls?. . . no. . . okay; I'll make them a cup of tea. . ."

The administrator turned to Ann and Jules.

"shall I ring your parents, Julia, or will you ring them while on your way?"

"would you ring Mum, please, and ask her to ring me, hopefully before we get to the oncology ward. . ."

"where they won't let you use your mobile, you figure?"

"yes." Jules replied. "Could you also let our next teachers know, we are in different classes till well after lunch break. . ."

"I know, Julia; do you girls expect to be back today, Ann?" "Probably not."

"we understand," the administrator said: "I wish that there was something I could do; not that I am the only one here."

❧

The counsellor arrived just as the administrator was handing out cups of tea: "would you like one yourself Celia?"

"yes, Marg;" she was offered a cup, "no sugar?", took a sip and dropped her cup on a table:

"girls, take your cups along and drink your tea in my car as we drive. . ."

"don't forget to return these cups, Celia," the administrator smiled.

They would only let two people at a time when they reached the ward:

"you girls go first," Ann's father instructed them: "Julia you leave when you are ready and let me in; will you do that?" "of course; I shan't stay long, Mr Landers"

("in another few years, 'he' won't even be Mrs Landers," Julia thought, somewhat disrespectfully, only to reproach 'her' self at a time like this").

Ann and Julia headed straight for Ann's mother's bed. The nurses had been able to make Clara Landers sit up for one last time, having connected her to all kind of drips and monitors.

"it's so good of you girls to come and see me one more time. Julia, I hope you don't mind me calling you that; you do have a strong sense of duty for someone that young. Ann will need you, whatever form your relationship will take; will you promise me to look after Ann for as long as it takes; that's all I can ask from you at any stage in your life. . ."

"certainly, mother of Ann," a formula she had heard the Hazara people use, time and time again.

"could I ask you now to let Ann's father be allowed in? And thank you very much for being here with Ann, once again."

Julia took the dying woman's hand and kissed it gently, then left, tears running down her cheek.

"Ann's mum wants to see you," she told Ann's father, quite unnecessarily.

"thanks", he replied, whether he was grateful for the message being conveyed or for Jules having kept her time inside the ward short, was not clear; not that it mattered. "do you want to wait for us, Jules?" he asked.

"yes, Mr Landers; let me go down the corridor first where I can ring my parents; then I'll be back outside the ward."

"I'll ask one of the nurses if she can make you a cup of tea and, maybe, a sandwich; the ones downstairs weren't too great."

("barely edible", Jules concurred but not out loud).

Hector Landers entered, in that identity, to say Farewell to his wife of many years.

"It is all right to grieve", he told himself, "Clara and Ann will both understand, yet I cannot bring myself to do so openly."

He strode towards his wife's bed, took her hand in his and kissed her cheek.

Then he sat, as closely as he could without interfering with all that machinery. "Ann, sit with us," he commanded his daughter who obediently found a spot on the other side of the bed, equally out of the way of sundry pieces of equipment.

"is Glen coming?" his wife asked.

"he promised to be here any time after three," Hector answered.

"if it is important to him to be here, he will," his wife asserted.

"give Ann his number; let her go outside, ring and remind him, then come back, Ann.

Your father and I want to talk, the two of us only. . ."

"okay, Mum; I'll be back; Dad, give me his number. . ."

"no, Ann, use my mobile, it's on the display panel, under his name. Go outside where you are allowed to ring and also don't forget Julia; she's here because of you; then come back."

❦

"This is Ann Landers speaking, in case you don't remember my voice," she told her father's future 'husband 'once she got through to him:

"are we expecting you? You are in a meeting; I see, so are we, it is going to be the last time for Mum and us. . .; look, if you are serious about being in a relationship which will require my Dad to become my Mum. . . yes, that is how I am putting it, you'd better be here; I don't care whether you'll tell my father on me or not; it is he who is prepared to undergo a fundamental change to make you happy. . . let me tell you something and don't interrupt:"

Ann proceeded to tell Glen how Jules had made Ann, her father and the hospital agree to her visiting when it had become obvious that Ann's mother would never leave it alive.

"So, if my girl friend is happy to become a boy to please me and can get herself excused from school, so can you if you are the boss of a job service provider. . . Okay, your colleague is leaving later this afternoon and you need to talk to him; well, let someone else drive you both and drop him at the airport or wherever he or she needs to be. . . forty minutes max? Thank you; I'll tell them; see you then."

Jules had listened to Ann's side of the conversation without any difficulty:

"YOU DIDN'T REALLY NEED A TELEPHONE!".
"was I loud enough, you think? Hold me, please. . ."
Ann pleaded, kissing her lover's hands before she stepped away.
"I'll always love you," Julia was crying gently.
"now go back to your mum and dad; I'll be here when you get back."
"did Nurse get you a cup of tea?"
"and an excellent piece of birthday cake to go with it". "thank God for celebrations."

Two hours later, Julia was still waiting and Ann, ready to return inside where she would have to turn off her phone, had another look.

"Sh. . ." she started, "shivers,,"

"what is it, Ann?" Julia moved closer.

"ahha," Ann moaned. "have a look, it's a text message from Dad's future partner:

lft wk, drpd cnst arpt, strk nt 1 bt 4 plc trfc rdblks, 1st 2 wd nt pmt me phne, nw

@ rdbkl #4; pls fgvm!"

"do you understand that message, Ann?"

"yes, I do; could you let Dad know; meanwhile, I see if I can ring him."

Eventually, the girl got through and came straight to the point:

"Ann Landers here; I got your message. . ."

"did you understand it? I am so very sorry; I ought to have driven by a different way; is your mum still alive?"

"she was, a few minutes ago, but barely able to talk. . . one moment, please... look, I need to hang up. . .", the distraught girl told him.

Jules had come running out, her hands waving wildly: "your mum is going fast",

Ann ran inside so fast she stumbled but recovered her balance. She had dropped her phone in Julia's hand who then found Glen's number and rang back.

"Mr Hiddings, I am Ann's friend. . ."

"and future life partner, I understand;"

"correct; I am sorry that Ann had to cut you off; her mum is going fast and there are no more than two people allowed inside at any time. What happened to you?"

"Ann had caught me in a meeting with a consultant who needed to leave this afternoon; at her suggestion, I took him to the airport myself to continue to discuss work with him yet save time as well; except I did not,. . ."

"we know all about the detour near the tunnel at Mile End, it affects us when we go tutoring. . ."

"that, too," Glen agreed, "I got stopped four times. . ."

"police every time?"

"yes, licence, registration, roadworthiness; I am very sorry. . ."

"you'll need to share your sorrow with Mr Landers, not me."

"I realize that."

"how much longer will you be, Sir?"

"ten minutes, maybe, it is getting into rush hour. . ."

"I'll need to wait till someone goes inside to let them know. . ."

Meanwhile, Clara Landers' systems had broken down in the most painful way possible; her daughter and her husband were holding each of her hands, to not much avail; for she was struggling with an unexpected strength and force, threatening to tear the equipment apart that she was hooked on.

By the time a nurse had arrived, her mother was dead.

Glen Higgins made it a bit later, almost inconsolable at the delays enforced on him by the police and barely coherent with grief at having let his friend down.

"I failed you," he all but wailed.

Eventually, the girls took him aside.

"don't you think we aren't in a state already; we don't need your help," said Julia.

"my Dad won't ever bring it up, I promise you," added Ann. "I'll make sure that he won't. You'll have to come to terms with in yourself, but don't beat yourself up, not too much, anyway."

"don't cry, Sir!" commented Jules, not unkindly.

"did she suffer?" Glen enquired.

"the staff managed to keep it to a minimum," Ann replied, diplomatically.

("may be just as well he did not get to see Mum's final moment," she thought to herself, Hector joined them, eventually, accompanied by a nurse.

"Mr Hiddings was held up four times on his way here, Dad," 'his' daughter forestalled 'his' future partner.

"I am so very sorry; I shall have to explain and ask your forgiveness. . ."

"are you part of the family, Sir?" the nurse asked.

"you could say that," Glen replied.

"could I ask all of you wait for the Professor? He is very sorry he could not attend to Mrs Landers' last minutes; he needed to attend to an emergency but he paged me. . ."

They looked at each other.

"Of course, we can; it is very kind of you; anywhere that we can sit down in some sort of privacy?"

"yes, of course; I am sorry I should have thought about it; Matron will let you could use her office till Professor gets here. . ."

❧

Samira wondered whether she had misread the signals. Both men seemed to genuinely grieve for Clara whom she had come to admire, given that she had to administer palliative care to so many people at all ages.

"What I was doing back in Iran?" she answered Glen one afternoon.

"I trained as an oncologist and had a job with Iran's largest charity for children."

"how did you get yourself to Adelaide, may I call you Samira?"

"yes, Glen, as long as I am not at work, of course you may. . ."

She had been on her way to Flinders Medical when her car broke down. Glen had happened to pass, recognised her, stopped and got off his motorcycle.

"would you like me to help you? remember me, I meant to be with Hector when his wife died; I was running late that day because of roadblocks; never mind. . ."

he had lifted her Hyundai's bonnet,

"start her, please" which Samira did.

The engine emitted a gargling sound and then died.

"has that happened before, Dr Tafreshi?" he enquired.

"never before," she replied, in unaccented English;

"just now, a few times; it stalled and would not start again. I have to lecture and. . ."

"are you running late, Dr Tafreshi?"

"Soon I shall be; you are Mr Hiddings, aren't you?"

"excellent memory, considering how many people you meet.

Yes; I manage a work service provider, different from Hector's. Yours seems to be starter trouble; are you in the AA?"

"no, more's the pity."

"not really; I am and, moreover, I supervise apprentices at that garage across the road; let me get some of them to help get your car across. . ."

He raced across Cross Road and returned with a few young men. . .

"meet Trevor, Kevin and Greg, Dr Tafreshi; they'll give the AA a ring, on my account, unless they can fix it themselves; meanwhile; why don't I give you a lift to Flinders Medical. . ."

"on your motorcycle? Do you have a spare helmet. . ."

"no, Miss," one of the boys replied;

"but I'll lend him mine for the duration. We trust Mr Hiddings. . ."

Samira was whisked off on Glen's motorcycle before she knew it, noticing, over her shoulder, that the boys had begun to push her car away, giving a clear berth to cars on Cross Road.

Glen had agreed to wait till after her lecture; she had agreed to a coffee at a popular spot within the university.

"My cousin Atefeh lives here, Glen" she explained; "she had to leave Iran in a hurry, got her photographer boyfriend to marry her in Turkey and was eventually accepted here; he followed later; he works with an Iranian film maker in this city."

"of whom they are several here" "true"

"how did you get here, all the same?"

"I was able to enrol in a postdoctoral programme for palliative oncology. . ."

"did you have to pass a few extra exams?"

"I had passed IELTS in Shiraz, trained by an Australian, by the way; once on the programme, I had to do an internship. . ." "where?"

"where I met you and your, er. . ."

"future partner, Hector, you mean. . ."

"yes; once that was behind me and I passed an AMA alignment allowing me to practice in South Australia; I stayed on. . ." "enjoy it?"

"under the circumstances; these are dying patients, as you realize; but it can be very fulfilling. . ."

"do you still work with children?"

"yes, Glen; two weeks a month on paediatric oncology at the Royal Adelaide. . ."

They sat, companionably admiring some birds picking up crumbs off the well-kept lawn.

"It's so rare to be doing this. . ."

"doing nothing for a minute?"

"reflecting; letting go; taking things in. . ."

"enjoying the moment. . ."

"enjoying the company if I may say so. . ."

She sighed:

"you are not wrong; would you get me another coffee before we leave", she asked Glen.

"don't you have to go back to work today, Glen?" she wondered.

"I rang my office, telling them that I checked on some apprentices today. . ."

"which you did, thanks to me," the oncologist smiled.

"do you have to go back to the office later on, anyway. . .?"

"I'll start very early tomorrow; we are on flextime, Samira; all I have to do for work today is visit some of our interns and their supervisor. . ."

"won't they have gone home, Glen, by the time you have dropped me and gotten there. . ."

"there are on shift which won't have started till after four o'clock."

He got up for next round of coffee when he was hailed:

"Glen; oh, that is you, Dr Tafreshi!"

Ann's father came rushing closer to their table. "do you want to join us for a cuppa, Hector?" his unpleasantly surprised future partner remembered that his 'betrothed' very much preferred tea to coffee "tea, please, Glen. . . May I join you and Glen, Dr Tafreshi?" he asked, courteously.

"Ccll me Samira; Glen here does," the graceful young woman told him, following the retreating figure with her eyes, a smile lighting up her face.

"do you work downhill, at Flinders Medical, Samira?" Hector enquired.

"I held a lecture until a few minutes ago; I used to train there for my palliative oncology, Hector."

"did you do oncology in Iran, Samira?"

"not originally; I started life as a paediatrician and then worked for Iran's leading charity for cancer in children"

"so you had to qualify?"

"yes, and subsequently, I had to, again, for the palliative version here in Adelaide. . ."

"same as a general nurse has to qualify for geriatric work, I suppose," he mused.

"something like that. . ." the doctor agreed.

Hector, not having taken an interest in another woman since Ann's mother's death, was perplexed about Glen. As if the girl had read his mind, she explained:

"your future partner Glen. . ."

"is that how he introduced himself to you?" Hector asked before he could stop himself.

"yes," Samira said, suddenly somewhat reluctantly:

"anyway, I was on my way here when my car stalled and wouldn't start; he was nearby to check on some apprentices. . ."

"oh, at that garage near the South-eastern Outlet; so what happened?"

"he got his apprentices to shove the car off the road, got the manager to ring the AA and gave me a lift here. waiting till I finished. . ."

"lecturing, on what if my may ask without sounding an impertinent know-all, Samira. . ."

"I am sure, Hector, that you are not; let me assure you that I am so very sorry. . ."

"thank you; it takes some wrestling with, it affects Ann likewise,"

"as I can imagine," the doctor replied:

"I was lecturing on the prospects of controlling certain cancer cells by changing their energy metabolism. . ."

"they manage by fermentation, don't they, instead of oxygen-induced combustion, or am I wrong?"

"not necessarily; how do you know, Hector?"

"high-school biology; but you should listen to Ann's friend Julia. . ."

"I remember her from your visits ; a scientist in the making?"

Hector was about to answer when Glen emerged balancing a tray with one hand while trying to open the door; a girl student helped him, eventually.

"thank you, love," Glen assured her.

"how are you getting home, Hector?" he asked, innocently worrying about his future partner.

"aren't you a bit blatant, Glen?" Hector replied.

The young doctor who had enjoyed herself, so far, was beginning to feel uncomfortable.

"would you like me to get a taxi instead of giving me a ride back to that garage?" she ventured.

"I shan't forget the helmet that you borrowed, Glen?" she promised.

"let me ring the garage first," he offered.

"look, Samira;" suggested Hector, somewhat surprisingly:

"I came here to return some textbooks to Flinders Library; I am an external reader in sociology here and borrowed a work vehicle; so I can give you a lift back to your vehicle. . ."

"it is very hard to get taxis to come to Flinders as you probably know, Samira,"

Glen agreed while waiting for someone to pick up the telephone. Eventually, someone did.

"Glen Hiddings here; thanks for helping out with Dr Tafreshi's Hyundai; did the AA attend to it?"

"oh, the boys found a faulty connection."

"car electrics can be tricky, Malcolm" after a while: "they did very well,

I would like to pass on some money, plus I have to return that extra helmet; Hector Landers is a colleague of mine and he will drop Dr Tafreshi, complete with a bit of money for the boys and with Kevin's helmet so that he... oh, he keeps it at work; thank them, please:

I need to catch up with another lot of mine this arvo but I'll drop in and say Thanks in person. . . "Hector is about to take off now with Dr Tafreshi. . . I agree, rush hour; thanks again, Malcolm."

He clipped his phone shut, smiling first at the doctor, then looking at Hector.

"make sure you don't leave until Samira has started her car and it won't stall again, if you would, Hector," Glen was speaking from experience.

"thank you, both of you, and thank you for the coffee, Glen."

Samira could not resist displaying her most radiant smile ever, overcoming her natural reticence, a smile that reached into her eyes and her voice. She rose, picked up her lecture notes and followed Hector on the labyrinthine footpath to the car park, leaving Glen strangely disturbed.

Sitting next to Hector, Samira smiled:

"it is sort of rare to meet men like you both, even here in Adelaide, who feel neither challenged nor titillated by someone like myself. . ."

". . .an educated professional Iranian young woman, you mean? Aren't there many such like in Iran itself?"

Hector wondered.

"Oh yes, more and more so. . ."

"with some difficulty, with rulers like yours in Iran?"

Samira visibly hesitated:

"as often as not, women are at the forefront of demands for change and that puts them at risk as much as any misogynist ruling ideology. . ."

"anything like in Saudi Arabia, Samira?"

"oh no, not at all; women are not permitted in certain few jobs but are active in large numbers in any other way, huge numbers at university, in the professions and business, journalism. . ."

"highly separated from men, maybe?"

"not really; look, it varies according to region, age group and individual religious convictions, but not necessarily on principle, like in much of Afghanistan or throughout Saudi Arabia where women used to be enormously invisible in public," Samira explained.

"do you go home very often?"

"home is Australia, not Iran any more; even though, legally, Iran will always consider me an Iranian, not an Australian citizen," she elaborated to him;

"yes, I do get to see my family in Shiraz and, whenever I can, I carry Shiraz wine from the Riverland. . ."

"like coal into Newcastle, as they used to say", Hector commented.

"yes, it is funny that the first place where wine was grown and made may have been Shiraz; yet you cannot get any legally there, even grapes are not as common as they once were."

"won't they check for any alcohol when you enter Iran?"

"there are ways around it," she assured him, clearly enjoying their conversation.

She could see the garage from the distance:

"I hope you don't mind and I am not even sure that it is my business," Samira began: "while Clara was alive I had to be very protective of her; now, would you mind if I asked. . ." she hesitated.

"how Glen and I relate to each other," surmised Hector.

"no, I shall answer as willingly as Glen would, if you were to ask him. . ."

"would you encourage me to, Hector," she smiled uncertainly

"no reason not to, Samira," he affirmed.

"Glen and I are committed to each other; yet neither of us is gay. . ."

"how did Clara feel about it; she knew, didn't she?"

"oh yes, and she, I would not say, approved but certainly accepted it. . ." his words petered out, his grief obvious.

"no, Samira; remember how upset Glen was when he was late on the last afternoon of her life, more than I was."

"I noticed; you had been with that situation a lot longer, Hector, for sure; he is divorced, is he not?"

"yes, been that for years. . ."

"would it not have been easier for either of you to find women to relate to, rather than each other, if you are both. . ."

"heterosexual, you mean?" he asked.

"we perceive something within each other that resonates, not detected with anyone else. . . now, I wonder."

"thanks for being so open; would you mind swapping phone numbers with me?" she wondered, handing him her phone.

"let me punch in Glen's number as well as mine," he offered, handing over his phone to her.

"we will both always treasure your friendship, Samira; do stay in touch;" he assured her:

"we are here; I'll wait till you get your car not just started but running for a while, as Glen said." Samira left his car:

"I am so glad I got to have spent this time with you both; do thank Glen. . ."

"why don't you ring him, Samira; he will be most pleased if you do"

Glen had been very restless all evening when he got home. His son rang him asking about the trip to Swan Reach:

"Is it all right to bring Bridget along?"

"yes, but we may have to organize an extra tent for the two of you, then"

"why, Dad?" asked his son.

"you know Hector's daughter, Ann? She insists on bringing Julia along with her. . ."

"her future boyfriend? Makes some sense, though; same as you and Hector want time with each other, is it not?"

"I suppose so. . ."

"in your case, it is work that puts a spanner into closeness; in their case it is school and their clique."

"do you mind?" Glen asked his son, worried.

"no, nor will Bridget worry too much; we, too, need a bit of time for ourselves, what with study, work and other people crowding into our lives. . ."

That last comment did touch a raw nerve; Glen barely heard what his son was saying next:

"This Julia, or Jules, will have a bit of a battle on her hands getting her family to agree. . ."

"quite," his father concurred: "it does not seem to stop her; I can see what Ann sees in her but to have this sheer force in your life for the rest of your days. . ."

"look, Dad, I haven't even asked how you have been. . ."

"work-wise, you mean?" "that, too, but just like not everything in life is work. . ."

Glen decided to take a slight yet calculated risk:

"You remember when Hector's wife was still alive in that Hospice, with that Iranian doctor of hers. . ."

"I never knew about the doctor," his son commented; "how come you mention him. . ."

"a 'her', Samira Tafreshi. . ."

"impressive, Dad?" his son teased him; "won't Hector be jealous!"

The fact that his father said nothing told his son more than he really wanted to know.

"You turn away for a few minutes and my Dad gets himself into endless strife; it is a waste of time to try and raise one's parents. . ." his son would not let go.

"lay off, don't you start," his father mock-threatened him.

"well, you are old enough and she is likely attractive enough. . . well, okay; I see where we can get a tent or maybe a small caravan from, and I shall try to persuade Bridget to join us motley mob this holiday"

They had spent a rewarding and rather relaxing time on Glen's friend's farm near Swan Reach, fishing, motorcycling, helping out on the farm and in the kitchen, generally staying away from telephones and computers; for much of the farm was out of signal range. The agreement was to watch nothing but the evening news on telly and not even listen to Regional Radio except during breakfast for sheep and wheat prices.

Glen's friend also grew oranges, olives and table grapes. Hector and Glen spent a lot of time on tractors and quads, welding things in the shed and generally following each other around, as did Jules and Ann who hung out with the young blokes, fencing and having a dip in the dams;

"even the girls are boys here!"

It did rain, on occasion; not that it stopped people from working or relaxing.

Once or twice, they all spent time on the houseboat owned by Glen's friend's family; Hector and Glen ended up in one room, tactfully given space by everyone else.

"we don't do 'intimate' much, do we?" Hector asked Glen on the bunk beds, having spoken little all afternoon.

"unlike the young ones," his future partner agreed.

"your son and my daughter, for one, but not with each other. . ."

"good grief, no," Glen laughed at the thought." It is the two of us who have to learn. . ." "to reach out into each other. . ." "it won't work unless. . ."

"let's get physical. . ." Hector intoned, smiling gently, rolling against his putative future lover.

"enjoyable?"

"yeah; time slows down and has no more meaning." More silence.

"You know," Glen started,

"I once read an account of the Brendan Voyage; someone would make a comment and someone else would answer half an hour later if at all."

"what a good idea; we ought to introduce it at meetings. . ."

"yeah, but don't talk about them, not here, not now. . ."

"yeah," came the reply many minutes later.

Meditative silence descended upon their cabin.

("closeness may not be a mere matter of hormones,")

"only people comfortable with their own company can truly relate to others."

"never thought of it that way," Glen agreed, "yet do we really need each other?"

"yes, we do," many minutes later, following a thoughtful silence.

"we both are very highly self-reliant, through work and also privately; yet we match each other."

"what we might do, later tonight, do something very old-fashioned?"

"dinner by candlelight?"

"this is a solar-powered boat with a wind turbine thrown in; light is not a problem. Let us do something 'prehistoric'; we 'll fill a piece of paper with what we need to tell the Ethics Commission. . ."

Many moments later:

"let's see whether we can put it in words without having to write it down, instead, and work through it every day while we are here. . ."

"set aside a time each day, you mean?"

"no, talk about it at times where we are together."

"our joint project, so to say. . ." "of course!" More meditative silence.

Bridget was, meanwhile, busying herself on top of Roger, making his body move as one with hers, guiding him with her knees and rump, as a good rider does, grabbing his balls for better balance. She straightened up without letting go of her boyfriend and dutifully emitted a heartfelt moan, followed by several more as her body got her boyfriend's full feel inside and underneath her.

Bridget was merciless and would not stop, eventually cuffing his hands on his shoulders and making him kiss her fingers and lower arms. She moved further up, forced his mouth open with her thumb and forefinger and thrust her hardened breasts inside it, one at a time, pushing her thighs and knees against his torso, dominating him. Finally, she let go, rolled off him and possessively covered his crotch with her knee:

"Why does Ann want Julia to turn into a boy?" she wondered drowsily; "it's so much more fun doing it, or being done like this, as a girl," Bridget opined, "whether by a boy or another girl".

"maybe she likes her partner to dominate her. . ."

"as do you," his girlfriend affirmed knowingly.

"but why does she not prefer it the old-fashioned way. . ." boy bonking girl lying on her back or belly, opening herself to all kinds of suggestions"

"Bridget's got a one-track mind, one-track mind, one track mind," he intoned; "I must have it too!"

"would you consider yourself a male lesbian, Roger?"

"if I have to, but never in public," he conceded.

"do you prefer 'old-fashioned bonk'?" she enquired, stiffening his tool with her knee.

"with you on top, I don't," he replied truthfully.

"you do know what's good for you," she mimicked a growl while mounting him again.

❧

Ann lay next to Julia whose knees were resting on Ann's thighs.

"you'll make a good boy, Jules, one day soon," she assured her underage lover.

"why's that, bitch?"

"if you promise to kiss me hard, I'll tell you."

Having been duly and lengthily rewarded, she did:

"you get on with the boys; you are a devil on the bike; tools fly into your hands; you can even talk while doing a repair, without having to look at what you are doing. How come, lover?"

"my brother and his mates taught me, as did Dad, once Mum left us for a trial period. . ."

"what did that have to do with your Mum, lover mine, she did come back that time, didn't she? So what does it have got to do with mechanics?"

"household goods, Ann, and small motors; Mum had learnt to repair them because she did not want to have to wait for Dad or Stephen to be home if she needed work done."

"did she learn how to, Jules?"

"oh yes, she got very good; so Dad decided that, while she was away, I needed to pick up some skills to help keep our household going; very useful, he said, for someone wanting to be a scientist. . ."

"not wrong," Ann agreed. "Anyway, you can do it with the best of them; how's your chain-sawing. . ."

"didn't you see me cut a strainer yesterday, Ann?"

"I heard the chainsaw; I was on a paddock where those sheep got loose and they wanted me to run the trail-bike to Trevor. . ."

"true; you went piggyback behind Kevin; what does it feel like sitting behind a boy, with your arms around him. . ."

"I want to sit behind you, with my hands arousing you, you'll stop the bike, lift me off it and drop on top of me. Do it to me now, without benefit of trail-bike, or chainsaw!"

"you are a greedy bitch, you know," Julia obliged her. "Open your legs; you know what to do. . ."

⁂

The day had come to face their first session in front of the Ethics Committee whose chairman opened proceedings in a nondescript meeting room inside the Royal Adelaide.

"First of all, I like to remind ourselves of the Elders who maintained this land from since Time Immemorial," he paused.

"I would then like to thank the hospital to allow us to meet here once again," he continued, "before I greet the petitioners and their respective friends and families; lastly but as importantly, I express my thanks to the members of this committee, all of us busy people in our own right, who nonetheless are prepared to have enmeshed ourselves into this case and are here now, to listen and to deliberate its merits."

He spoke without notes, glancing at the two girls, Julia's father ("Mum had to do a sudden shift for a colleague who went to attend a funeral," Julia had explained to the chairman) and Glen and Hector, accompanied by Glen's son Roger.

"These are not criminal let alone punitive proceedings, nor do they lend themselves to litigation," the chairman intoned.

"rather, they are mandated by the very nature of the request for gender alignment, coupled with its unusual motivation." He paused again.

"before I delve into it, let me reiterate the Committee's appreciation of the meticulous care with which both sets of applications were thought through, reasoned out and prepared; I especially appreciate the quality of the language in which they were drafted. . ."

(Julia smiled at Ann who had, in fact, researched, drafted and edited all the

documents, having spared no effort);

"I now ask our Convenor to summarise the two sets of pleas before us, if you would, Professor."

Julia looked the most relaxed among those present whereas Ann kept crossing and uncrossing her legs and both her father and his future spouse were visibly not at ease. The convenor began:

"I awarded each of these two briefs to a group of my colleagues, the two sets then to form a panel.

Allow me to start with the petition preferred jointly by Mr Landers and Mr Hiddings, requiring Mr Landers to have his gender aligned, the rationale being to become a spouse to Mr Hiddings fitting to the latter's legal, physical and emotional needs, whereby he hopes and intends to meet his own.

I admit to being impressed by the very mature way in which they express their mutual need and attraction for each other and their reasoned view of life together. Their plea is based, and also focuses, on both being highly heterosexual people; yet they chose each other rather than – forgive me-ordinary heterosexual partners each, an approach which I am to take very seriously.

Let me now introduce both Mr Landers and Mr Hiddings to their interlocutors and ask their party to move aside; dealings will be on a first-name basis; tea coffee and mineral water will be served, along with biscuits; any one of you may interrupt or even terminate proceedings at any one time. I trust that all telephones have been turned off; otherwise, I have to ask all of us here to rely on visual signals and messages only. We will meet here again before we end transactions for the day."

He then watched the committee members chosen to talk to the two adults in the room before addressing his colleagues, the girls and Julia's father:

"Mr Chairman, my colleagues, Mr Childers, Julia and Ann; let's get started.

Meet my colleagues, Dr Mrs Withers, medical ethologist, University of Adelaide, Mrs Raedel, Youth Worker and Guidance Counsellor at St Mary's College for Girls, Dr Sathianathan, situational ethicist at Flinders University, Bart Reichelt, Assessor on behalf of the Teachers' Union, Helen Wohlfahrt, medico-legal specialist on call to Elizabeth Hospital, late of Deakin University in Melbourne, our chairman, Professor Edward Baumer, Interfaith Council of South Australia; myself last, Henry Diamantopoulos, alternative dispute adjudicator in the Arbitration Centre of South Australia." He paused to allow everyone take breath. "you girls realize that my three colleagues working with the adults will be interacting with you next week. . ." "why that, Sir?" asked Ann.

"partly because their session involves your father but, mainly, that all of us need to listen and talk to the four persons seeking a ruling. Our chairman and I will then run the matching 'adults' session; we'll all get together briefly later. I have spoken enough." They were all quiet for a while till Julia raised her hand. "Well, Julia?"

"a practical point first; are the two of us to be, er, interrogated separately or together? also, I'd like to make a statement which you may ask Ann here to confirm it, not that we have agreed on it before. Is that all right, Sir?"

Mrs Withers, the medical ethologist, answered: "We'll talk to both of you together as well as separately; I also hoped that you meant 'interrogate' in a ironical sense, did you?"

"yes, Madame."

"now, I am sure I speak for all of us if I invite you to tell us what you want to say; do you mind, Ann?" she turned to the girl.

"no, I want to hear it myself; I am curious." "Go ahead, Julia,"

"I got into trouble at our school, St Brendan the Voyager's, when I first sent Ann a message offering lifelong love on our school's intranet system. . ."

"trouble? I reckon," Bart Reichelt mumbled.

"do you girls not code important intimate messages?"

"we do, Sir; unfortunately, the entire system crashed and they got the company specialist to get it working again; since mine was just about the last message, and a coded one, as you said, the contractor decided to enter Ann's inbox in the process of reassembling the works. . ."

"did he think that your coding contributed to crashing it?"

"possibly, Sir. Ann then told me something". . . "via email?"

"no, in person, the next day."

"what about, Julia?"

"I can't tell you the factual information; for to do so would get someone else in trouble who is not here to defend himself. . ."

"what do you like to tell us, Julia?"

"let me share an inference, based on a 'he'."

"and what, say, is that inference?" Helen Wohlfahrt asked, her medico-legal antennae up and waving:

"that her devotion to me needed to be directed to a boy, for her to feel the same long-term commitment about me,. . ." "meaning, Julia?"

"loving and being loved by someone who is me and none other, yet this love and need coming from, and being directed to, a boy, not a girl."

"and you are trying to tell us that, if you are to be both source and object of her love and lifelong devotion, which Ann would want to share with a boy, that you would want to be that boy?" queried

Dr Sathianathan, the situational ethologist, shaking his head" Well, I never. . ."

"I could not have put it better myself, Sir," Julia replied.

"May I ask you, Ann?" asked Edna Raedel, the guidance counsellor.

"yes, Madame, what would you like me to say?"

"first of all, whether that is how it had happened; then; if you can tell us anything about that 'he' to have encountered prior to Julia proposing to you; thirdly, if you feel that people your age ought to propose or be proposed to in such a fashion and, finally, whether that is how you feel and is that what you want to happen to the two of you."

"Before you do, Ann, though;" Helen Wohlfahrt interjected,

"can anyone tell me who drew up the petitions?"

"Yes, Ann here," Jules replied.

"including the one for Mr Hiddings and your dad?" "yes, Madame."

"did you have any help or ask anyone, Ann?" "no, Madame."

"we'll need to ask you, Mr Childers, about the statement you and your wife are prepared to made concerning Julia," the chairman intervened. "I'll let the other team do that later, to complete the picture. Would you comment on the documents, though?".

"yes, I am impressed, in spite of myself," Jules' father conceded:

"Ann is a girl of many talents, hidden and otherwise."

About an hour later, they all met in the original meeting room.

"I would like to think that we had two very productive sessions," the Convenor summarized.

"we'll swap groups next week and then finalise these interactive sessions because we are all very busy people. This coming week will give all of us time to reflect on what has happened today. I'd like to make two comments before we tie today's musings together.

Firstly, thank you, Mr Childers, for stating what you did, in writing, no less; the fact that your statement did not feature much today does not mean that we do not appreciate the sheer soul-searching that must have gone into it."

"thank you, Sir," father and daughter said, in rare unison.

"that, and the sheer depth of your preparation, girls, as evidenced by the quality of these petitions and of your answers and comments today, was what made the Ethics Committee, want to listen to you, rather than reject you out of hand. . ."

"is that what you would have tended to do?" Julia's father wondered.

"without a doubt," the Chairman answered

"now, let us briefly devote ourselves to what Hector and Glen. . . I hope you don't mind first names, gentlemen. . . (they nodded agreement) have had to contribute; would one of you two point it out to us, please?"

They looked each other, then Ann's father spoke:

"ours did not start with the intense physical attraction that my daughter and her future partner evidently feel; we met in Mildura, under work-related circumstances, and were attracted to each other, inevitably-what a word-being able to satisfy each other's purposes and needs in life; I do not want to elaborate on it any more; except to share with you that our impulses as to partnership between Glen and myself." ("well put, dad" his daughter had thoughts of praise for her usually unassuming parent) "if acted out differently, are of comparable intensity with, those that the girls must have trusted you with."

"thank you, Mr Chalmers," the chairman concluded.

"I realize that you and Mr. Hiddings have unburdened yourselves to my colleagues, something we shall go through one more time next week, same place, same starting time. Thank all of you for your patient and intelligent contributions which has made our work delightfully easy so far, if that is the phrase to choose," he ended on a smile.

"Looking forward to see all of you again here next week; now, let us go back to our own working lives," he recommended. Handshakes all around.

"How are you girls getting back to school?" the guidance counsellor enquired."

"we were given time off but if we are on your way, Mrs Raedel,"

Julia took the initiative, as always, "so that our dads can go back to work."

"will you be allowed to talk to us on the way?" Ann wondered as they got into the car:

"on the margins, girls," the youth worker replied." Like what do your classmates have to say?"

"most of them know us as an item but we haven't told any of them why we are here. . ."

"does anyone at your school know in any detail?"

"our biology teacher; he covered for us this morning, Mrs Raedel." The guidance counsellor turned around:

"don't you agree that our Committee was gentle on you girls?"

"we do," replied Ann, "but would you, please, explain?"

"once I am past that nut holding up our lane," the youth worker shot back, grinding her teeth at someone who had managed to stall his car while attempting a right- hand turn on King William Road, causing a serious holdup. The lady spotted a minuscule gap, stepped on her horn and whizzed through, cutting off a delivery van. "oof!" she mouthed. "Where were we? Underage sex, that's where we were," she challenged the girls.

"don't you think that we let you off lightly, what with that ephemeral boy of Ann's, and by not querying your present intense relationship in graphic physical detail. . ." "no need to," asserted Julia.

"you certain? Well, we did not; let's take it 'as read '; ("'implausible deniability'", she thought to herself)" but what was it that you girls really wanted to know? I may be able to guide you in the right direction. . . oof, this is becoming an obstacle course of imbeciles on the road. . . did their mums teach them to drive pre-World War Two or did they find their licences inside a wheelie bin?"

"not impressed, are you, Mrs Raedel?" Julia commented drily

"no, girls," answered their driver while passing a car that refused to stick to its lane.

"Mid-eastern driving, I call that. . ."

"How do you know?"

"I used to work in Egypt; you encounter to all kinds of road maniacs over there."

"is it safe to ask you now, Mrs Raedel? If so, may Ann ask you. . .?" "yes, Ann?"

"what is the Committee's thinking on us, or Jules here, rather, being able to 'convert' when she turns sixteen?"

"presupposing a lot, aren't you girls? Short answer: I may not tell you even if I knew which, very short answer, I don't, not just yet. . ."

"would it be all right to run my thinking by you and would you be able to comment?" "try, Ann."

"given that we'll be free to engage in consensual physical sex once we turn sixteen. . ."

"given,"

"and that that implies, at least arguably, our freedom to choose the nature and orientation of our sexuality, again if consensual. . ." "arguable, so far. . ."

"even though legislation in Australia does not yet reflect that uniformly; correct?"

"yes, Ann ("my future lawyer," Jules thought, rather proudly); South Australian law tends to agree with you; I can see where you are heading. . ."

"yes, of course; I aim to find out whether the Committee was comfortable with extending freedom of sexual orientation, if we accept that as a given for the moment, to include gender alignment. . ."

"at age sixteen, without requiring parental consent?"

"not necessarily, Mrs Raedel; with or without?"

The youth worker hit the brakes very hard so that the girls had trouble staying in their seats.

"Seatbelts on?" "Yes. . ." the girls breathed.

"maniac number sixty-five," the counsellor counted.

"now, this is the ten million five hundred and sixty-five thousand dollar and seven cent-question, is it not, girls? Having said that, your legal logic, Ann, is as close to impeccable as to make a fiery argument; and you, Julia, are you working on your parents? Your father, I must say, was very supportive today; will your mum be with us next week?"

"as far as is known, yes, either both of them or just herself, if Dad cannot make it next time."

"To sum up for the prosecution:" their driver stated:" you have hung in so far; go for it, girls!

And get ready to be dropped off; your school is around the corner but I have to be off immediately; have your bags ready. . ."

"thanks, Mrs Raedel."

⚘

The following week, the Convenor opened proceedings once more, this time with a parable:

"Early on in the Mahabharata, with Bhima, Arjuna and his brothers having already been banished the first time, the brothers joined a Mela whose highlight was an archery competition. The prize was Draupadi, the daughter of a local ruler and as beautiful as the stars at midnight. The challenge was to face a row of axes of uneven length and weight turning in different directions, at varying speed; moreover, the openings on each top were of different size and shape; an arrow had to be sent through these apertures such that it would stop all axes at once. None but Bhima managed to even tighten the bowstring and only Arjuna managed to send the arrow through these opening; the rest, you could say, is history. I feel stronger than Arjuna and his magic arrow, in that I managed to get all my colleagues to agree on a venue and a time, not once but twice, and arrive in one body, on time. This will be the last session before the Committee is to deliberate and arrive at a ruling; this time around, those dealing with the girls last week will work with Mr Chalmers and Mr Hiddings, excepting myself who will join my colleagues who have yet to interact with Julia and Ann. Our Chairman will lead the deliberations concerning Messieurs Chalmers and Hiddings, starting just about now. Later, we will constitute the full panel one more time and then adjourn. I may be able to predict the timing of our ruling before we end proceedings today. Off we go; same arrangements; tea coffee biscuits and sandwiches, no mobiles, please!"

The committee members sat in a circle, with Hector and Glen among them but seated apart.

"First names all right, gentlemen?" the chairman enquired courteously. "Certainly, Sir"

"let me start, then, Hector and Glen," the youth worker began, "seeing that I ended last session by driving the girls to their school; no, I did not pass on anything confidential but I learnt a lot."

"please, explain!" Ann's father demanded.

"with pleasure; your daughter already manages to argue like a lawyer. . ."

"her mum used to call her 'my favourite bush lawyer'."

"whatever; she outlined a very problematic but quite convincing case for gender conversion at age sixteen. . ."

"the combination of intellect and determination is hard to beat," added the medical ethologist, "with good looks thrown in, if I may be forgiven for sounding sexist. . ."

"we'll forgive you, this once, Dad" "us!"

Glen countered, mock-seriously.

"For the record, to get us started, I acknowledge Hector as my future partner and I feel that I can speak for him by saying that he is making our relationship contingent upon his change of gender; do you agree, Hector?"

"Yes, otherwise a long-term relationship of any degree of ongoing closeness would not make any sense; moreover, it was I who offered, totally unprompted."

"you already documented that, Hector," the situational ethologist confirmed.

"have you started hormonal treatment," the medico-legal specialist wondered.

"not yet; for one thing, I wanted to await a ruling; for another, my long-service leave is coming up soon and I intend to extend it by several months of unpaid leave. . ."

"do you want to change occupations, Hector?" asked the chairman, concerned.

"It may be quite difficult to front your workmates after a sex change."

"may I say something?" offered Glen. "While I may not formally offer Hector a job in my agency; for that would constitute an inducement, I had already done so when we first met and when I was promoted and transferred to Adelaide; as it is, I'll help Hector find work in our field, quite possibly as an independent consultant or contractor; his IT skills are second to none in our industry. . ."

"forgive us if we sound a bit like the family law court," the counsellor cut in,

"but do the two of you intend to live together, when and where?"

"with Hector; for my own son is about to leave home, as instructed by his girl friend, whereas Hector will have Ann and Julia to live with us, in her new incarnation, if it comes to that."

"what will you do with your own home, Glen. . ."

"rent it out long-term, possibly sell it, given a very good offer. . ."

"will you use that income to help establish Hector in employment or business. . ."

"I cannot admit to that here; for that would constitute an inducement, would it not?" he asked the medico-legal specialist.

"arguably so, Glen; for our purposes, it is enough if both of you are prepared to help one another materially as can be expected in a functional relationship; unless our chairman rules otherwise, we'll accept your word for it; we are not trying to trap Hector or yourself."

Meanwhile, proceedings went apace with the girls and with Julia's both parents present, this time.

The convenor opened by asking them to make a statement:

"We have had some documentation from you, as is proper; would you like to elaborate or alter your stand, before we interact with the girls?"

"yes, we would," answered Julia's mother. "First of all, I'd like to apologize for having missed last week's session. . ."

"we understand, Mrs Childers, the demands of work spare nobody; least of all us members of this Committee,"

"Julia's father and I had a talk with our son and his most recent girl-friend who made this very perceptive comment. . ."

"which was?"

"first, she asked: would we be very upset if Julia turned out to be gay, Lesbian, that is. . ." "answer?"

"yes, but it would not stop us accepting her. Then she wondered if we objected, if Julia were, indeed, Lesbian, to her possible choice of a girl friend or future spouse?. . ."

"your comment. . ."

"no, we would make every effort to include such a girl in our family. Then she asked if that included Ann whom we had come to know." "your reply?"

"Ann is a lovely young person; we feel that they are both a bit too young; but neither of us would hesitate to consider her one of our family. Then she challenged us; likewise, would we thwart Julia if she had decided that she was unhappy as a girl and wanted to change her sex."

"we are all ear:"

"naturally, we would be upset, but we would, in fact, support Julia. Then she concluded that our only ground for any objection was not the sex change but the motive. . ."

"you have our full and undivided attention now!"

"thank you; we have come to the very reluctant conclusion not to try to prevent, or interfere with, Julia's intention to change her sex for the purpose of living with Ann; we even accept that it may be advantageous to doing it as early as can be physically arranged and legally secured so that both she and Ann and, in fact, all of us, get used to it which, we hope we will, in time. End of speech." "Mr Childers, please!"

"nothing to add, except to thank your Committee for your tact and understanding."

"will you depose on that, o parents of Julia?" "write and sign a deposition, you mean?"

"yes; today, here and now if need be, duly witnessed by this Committee; we will accept it with grave reservations, as you can, no doubt, understand and so record it."

The idea had been for the Ethics Commission to notify them, once it had come close to a decision.

A few weeks after their hearings, Julia and her parents were invited to yet another one such and Ann had persisted; she had, eventually, been permitted on the understanding that she not contribute anything unless expressly invited.

The Chairman greeted them in his usual courteous manner.

"I am glad that you could come; did you have any difficulties getting time off school. . ."

"none in particular," Jules said, "Mum rang the office and told them that a distant relative was leaving for the United States today whom we were not likely to see for several years. Thanks for wanting to see us again, I suppose," she hesitated.

The Committee members were seated, looking at a sheet of paper placed in front of each of them.

"we had our note-taker draft this, almost word for word what we now know that your friend and agreed-upon future partner Ann told Mrs Raedel. . ."

"how could you?" Julia fumed at the youth worker.

"calm down, try to, Julia; I did not tell my colleagues until after they had agreed on the position and formulated it, more or less as we are about to read it to you. I was not involved in the wording at all and did not comment until we had it in front of us, in one piece. If anything, Julia, we owe the consideration we are about to share with you not so much to Ann, remarkable, though, how closely she argued it, but to your brother's 'most recent' girlfriend, the way your parents put it. But do make yourself comfortable, girls; you also. Mr and Mrs Childers."

They all waited for the Convenor to lift his sheet of paper, adjust his spectacles, tried different angles and distance for best focus and then read the prepared text:

"The freedom to act independently and responsibly in sexual matters once a person has reached the age of sixteen, if otherwise a minor, is embedded in law and has been recognized in both South Australia and elsewhere in the Commonwealth. While ordinary biological heterosexuality continues to be considered the norm, non-heterosexual activities and consensual relationships are now viewed, by and large, as covered by that same consideration; such, at least, is the situation in South Australia that the minimum age of sixteen applies there as well. The lawgiver no longer disallows consensual non-threatening physical relationships as of that age, however much society might disapprove of these, some very practical difficulties notwithstanding; nor do we, the Ethics Committee of South Australia, try to prevent them, once the two people concerned have reached that age and the required consensus. What the Committee has had to come to terms with is your attempt, Julia's and Ann's, to create an evidently physical, yet 'non-biological ', not to say artificial, heterosexual relationship, achieved by Julia's undergoing gender alignment from female to male. While this Committee has had to determine on occasion the ethical validity of changes to establish non-heterosexual 'couplings, 'both among teenagers and adults, this is the first time that ongoing explicit heterosexuality was what all of our petitioners wanted. As you know, we decided to deal with both these petitions at once, not only because Ann is Mr Chalmers' daughter but, more importantly, because both aim at allowing sex changes for the sole and openly-stated purpose of creating opposite sexes to enable, and function within, these highly- sought and determinedly argued-for lifestyle choices."

The Convenor paused, looked at his colleagues, at the Chairman, at Julia's parents, then continued:

"We decided to deal with this sequentially; first, we would determine if we could agree to, or at least permit ourselves not to disapprove of, the intervention necessary to effect such a change in biophysics, to put it neutrally. This ruling would apply to both the two of you girls and to Messieurs Chalmers, Ann's father, and Hiddings.

Secondly, we needed to arrive at a position on the minimum legal age for such an operation, including the treatment that needs to precede it; for if we held that sexual freedom as of age sixteen did imply the right to undergo a sex change, then we'd struggle to argue for a delay beyond sexual legal maturity, provided we had already decided not to obstruct gender alignment per se for the purpose that it had been sought."

"Would you allow Ann to ask the Committee a searching question?" Julia asked, unexpectedly, all eyes on her.

"what about, and why Ann?" her mum demanded.

"because we are a couple, in case you didn't know, Mum," her daughter shot back,

"and it is her role to ask, even though I thinks it concerns me. . ."

"what makes you say that?" wondered her dad.

"very soon, I may no longer call it Feminine Intuition, may I?" Julia countered artlessly and got everyone to laugh helplessly.

"wonderful," gasped the Convenor. "we need more quick wit in our morbidly serious deliberations. Do I detect a consensus among my colleagues?" he made up his mind:

"Ann, ask us whatever you have in mind."

A lengthy silence descended upon the assembly while Ann took a few deep breaths, confronted as she was by all these adults, none of them unfriendly, yet the only real support came, she felt, from Julia having placed her hand on her shoulder.

"We determined, did we not, that gender alignment may be a valid way of demarking the nature and purpose of a relationship. First, let me make a comment, though: This committee's ruling do not always coincide with existing legislation; true or not?"

"arguably so; we may hold a situation morally reprehensible yet not necessarily contrary to law, yet it may offend our sense of right and wrong," the Chairman began.

"likewise, we may rule something to be morally acceptable or arguable which is prohibited or restricted by law; the ban of consensual homosexual acts till recently between very young people in Tasmania would fall in that category, as is the treatment of couples whose one partner turns into the same sex as the other."

"Is the Committee ready, therefore, to accept or at least not to try and prevent, my father's intended sex change or, for that matter, Julia's, regardless of any future legal problems my dad and my lover may have in getting their new identity established and accepted. Again, true or not?"

"again, arguably so, at least, Ann. What is next on your agenda?"

"would the Committee try to block doctors or suchlike professionals from helping my father or my lover change gender in order to achieve 'relational heterosexuality'? If not. . ."

"let's stop your train of thought, Ann," the youth worker said.

"bring it to a screeching halt, girls; if I may be allowed to say so on all our behalf, that this Committee will not thwart anyone sufficiently professionally qualified and skilled in South Australia to initiate the treatment and conduct the operation/s needed to eventually let you young people, as well as your father and his partner, emerge to function as the kind of couples that all four of you want to be."

❧

Julia's parents took a while to follow the argument that was going on around them: "So the Committee does not object to, or disapprove of, my daughter becoming a boy?"

"no, if she does it with the intention of being Ann's future, hopefully long-term, opposite-sex partner."

"does that apply to the foundation of the intended partnership between Ann's 'father' and Mr Hiddings as well?" Julia challenged.

"again, your logic is unarguable, girls," commented the medico-legal specialist.

"I, for one, admire your very keen minds. . ."

"which is why this Committee was prepared to entertain your petition in the first place," concurred the Chairman.

"would you allow me to restart my train of thought?" Ann smiled at the gathering.

"well, why not?" invited the Convenor.

"now that you, the Committee, have seen fit not to disallow either my father's or, in principle, my lover's intentions, is it true that you are prepared to view the age of general sexual consent our sixteenth birthdays-as the acceptable minimum age to commence gender alignment, especially since Jules' parents have already agreed to not disagree?"

The committee was silent, as were Julia's parents, as were Ann and Julia. It felt for a while as if the two were alone with each other, even to Julia's parents and to the committee. Julia's steady breathing could be heard as she placed both her hands on Ann's shoulders, in a gesture both protective and possessive. Julia's mother broke the spell:

"I know we made that statement but would it matter very much if you waited another two years?" Ann looked up and asked: "may I answer that question, instead?" The chairman looked around and answered:

"you girls surprise me; I won't let you, Ann, with all due and, believe me, genuine respect for both of you. Let Julia answer her parents' question, ours also; we'd like to know!" Julia did her usual strong and even breathing before she spoke: "Mum and Dad told you that they could see an advantage in my being transformed sooner rather than later, so I can grow physically into being a mid-teenage boy before becoming an adult male. But that, dear Committee, is not the main reason why I wonder.

It has a lot more to do with what Ann, I am sure, had meant to ask you.

Do you really view the moment of consent to sexual acts-a sixteenth birthday-as a legitimate trigger for a decision on sexuality and sexual orientation, heterosexual or otherwise, and if so, for the 'biophysical 'change I wish to undergo to combine our permanent sexual partnership with our unashamedly heterosexual orientation which latter we ought to be free to decide and act upon, once we are both sixteen?"

Once more, the committee members did not quite know where to look.

Eventually, the Convenor smiled:

"As we have come to expect, you girls have put the finger on the spot. Yes, our Committee is not fundamentally and implacably opposed to your proposed sex change at the earliest admissible age. To argue from the top of my head for a moment which, admittedly I should not, we would prefer if you delayed the process, as your mother suggested, regardless of what your parents were prepared to state previously, to their great credit and with an enormous amount of soul-searching for which, I hope, you will always be grateful," he added solemnly.

Julia nodded and encouraged him to continue, by looking at him expectantly: "To sum up our response to your query, in fact, to the second challenge facing us, the timing or, more precisely, whether sexual as against full maturity under the law, allows for a decision on sexual orientation and direction-we hold that it does, with some misgivings. This permits us not to oppose outright the process of your sex change, consequent to your choice of both a relationship and your orientation; there, we admit that we have yet to define-and refine-a ruling."

Another moment of silence, then:

"does that time factor apply to Ann's father and his future partner, if I am permitted to ask that?" enquired Julia's father who had not spoken, so far.

"You ought not to have asked that," decided the chairman; "my apologies, then," "no, but in all honesty, since these are fully functional and responsible adults in every sense of the word, our intended ruling applies as soon as we make it; may I rely on your discretion, by the way?" Julia's parents nodded, as did the girls.

"In your case, girls, while we are prepared not to disagree with your intention – Julia's, that is – we have yet to decide on its timing; that is, we have to work out if her sixteenth birthday, the earliest age for sexual consent, is a suitable time for a course of action normally to be decided on, and answered for, by a legally responsible adult." He paused:

"we will commit, here and now, to a day when we shall have made and conveyed to you a ruling on that matter also. . ."

"a fortnight from today?" Julia bargained.

"a month," the situational ethicist argued.

"let's split the difference," suggested Julia's mother: "Three weeks; here?"

"why not," they all agreed.

Glen and Hector were invited to attend to the Committee the following week; as a sign how familiar the group had become with one another and with the intended couple, they all sat in no particular order, with Hector and Glen, in fact, facing each other.

The Chairman greeted the Committee and its clients in his customary courteous and good-natured manner:

"Glad to see you again, Mr Chalmers and Mr Hiddings; we would like to hear from you one last time and to share how we, the Ethics Committee of South Australia, intend to rule."

"may I ask a question, Hector?" asked the Convenor. "Did your daughter tell you anything about last week?"

"not in great detail, she didn't; nor did Julia; you had stressed confidentiality which the girls respected. . ."

"very good," commented the youth worker.

"before we expound our ruling," the situational ethologist took up the thread,

"would one of you state your position. . ."

"as a last-ditch argument?" queried Hector.

"no, as a kind of template, if anything," replied the medico-legal specialist.

No one said a word but, equally, nobody seemed unduly perturbed or nervous; a companionable silence reigned.

"here goes," began Glen. "As you know by now, we met – Hector and I, that is- in Wentworth where we conducted an IT upgrade training session arranged by Hector's employer to comply with changes in support service delivery; we both found the missing link in each other almost immediately. . ."

"Mrs Chalmers was still alive, wasn't she?"

"we knew, as did she, of her almost imminent demise, Sir."

"I am not trying to put you on the spot; I am sorry if it came out that way. . ."

"you'll be forgiven once again, this once," commented Hector: "let Glen continue."

"it took almost no time at all for us to uncover our need for each other; I cannot quite say when we started to discuss explicit gender change. . ." continued Glen;

"but once we did, it was so very obviously the best fit, really the only one in the situation," added Hector.

"how did your wife feel about it; sorry if that question disturbs you."

"thanks for being concerned; I do grieve but any pain associated with her death has become bearable; I have a daughter to look after, a relationship to look forward to, as well as responsibilities associated with work. To answer you: surprised but very accepting, both of Glen and of our unusual intention."

"how about the girls?"

"likewise; she really adopted Julia into our family in the last few months of her life." Hector was silent and nobody dared interrupt for a while.

"How it emerged that it would be I who needed to change my gender," Hector spoke at length, "we do not know but we never argued or doubted the need."

"can you imagine yourselves in ordinary heterosexual relationships, with all the intensity and passion both of you might have experienced in your previous marriages?" the guidance counsellor wondered.

"not as much as we might have at ages eighteen or twenty-eight, even thirty-eight, "Glen smiled,

"but we already do feel a sense of belonging and of not having to explain ourselves to each other overly much; we are beginning to be comfortable with each other and, once Hector starts the programme during his long-service leave, we expect to get used to being physical also."

The Committee members looked at one another, wondering who among them should start.

It was the medico-legal specialist who eventually did:

"you must both wonder why we asked you to cover the same ground once again. . ."

"did you ask us about our thinking so as to align it with yours?" Hector ventured.

"more or less. We, too, had to engage in a leap of faith, much as the two of you ended up doing. . ."

"where did that leap take you and where did you land?"

"we, the Committee, found ourselves agreeing with you, in the sense that we will not disapprove of Hector undergoing a sex change at your convenience or try to prevent a competent and qualified professional in South Australia from being involved."

"what would happen if we decided to go elsewhere, for any number of reasons?"

"you'd be able to quote our ruling and we, the Committee, would be willing to be contacted on that matter," the Convenor explained. "you might, however, have to seek the pleasure of another ethics committee if such were required elsewhere."

"naturally; we appreciate that. Does the ruling extend to hormonal or any such treatment needed before the operation.?"

"yes, to the extent that it appears necessary to facilitate future gender alignment," the medico-legal expert told them.

"our ruling does not require anyone to offer you such treatment and undertake the physical interventions that you will need. All it does is protect relevant professionals, provided they exercise the utmost skill and care."

"clearly; we live in hope," concluded Hector.

"yes, we do; we shall make the ruling incontestably official in due course; you may use that document at any time you like and we, in turn, shall uphold our decision whenever challenged. Thank you, all of you. . ."

"thank you," in unison.

"this Committee is, for your purposes, adjourned."

The Chairman looked at Hector:

"Your daughter did not tell you, good on her, but we did decide in favour of young Julia being able to go ahead; what we have yet to determine is when. . ."

"in a few months or after two more years and a few months, you mean?" asked Ann' father.

"yes, but we committed ourselves to have a ruling ready in about another two weeks."

The committee did even better than its word. Julia's parents received a note that they wanted to see them, and Julia, at their earliest convenience. Julia caught up with Ann the next day:

"Would you like me to share a secret with you?" she asked.

"let me share one with you, instead, Jules," Ann whispered, so as the other girls would not hear.

"I have this mad fantasy, without having to close my eyes, of the two of us in a room, with images of myself naked, in positions of sacrificial sexual surrender, at least a few of them on your phone showing me being aroused or entered. . ."

"and on everyone else's as well?" Julia asked.

"psst! How did you know?"

"I nearly said' feminine intuition '; soon, I shan't be allowed to state that any more; basically, knowing you. . ." "in a Scriptural sense?"

"that, too," Julia agreed.

"how about your secret, lover?"

Ann was seated on a bench, with Julia standing behind her, her hands resting on the girl's shoulders as if glued.

"we, my parents and I, are to front the Committee one more time. . ."

"to hear whether they'll give you the go-ahead as to when you turn sixteen or not?"

"yes, as they promised the last time."

"I am coming, too."

"I would not have it any other way; my parents. . ."

"Jules," her lover admonished her:" you bent me to your will when we went to see my mother these last few times; never mind what my parents or the Hospice had to say; now let me be stubborn; it was you who said that we were a couple, and so we are. . ."

"yeah, I suppose,"

Julia was uncharacteristically doubtful; Ann remained adamant:

"I shall always be subject to you, Jules," she stated, "but that does not make me a totally submissive doormat; you don't normally give in to your parents that easily: I won't let you."

"keep your voice down," her astonished lover admonished the girl.

"okay; I'll ring you when we are about to leave and you may have to find your own way. . ."

"rather than fight your parents, Jules?"

"it's called Economy of Effort," Julia replied blithely.

Ann was silent, busily working out what to do next.

She had a brainwave and rang the Royal Adelaide administration.

"we are doing a project on medical ethology and would like to book the facility for a simulation session. How about. . ."

After a few tries, over several days, she managed to get this reply:

"no, you'll have to tell Professor Enderby that the meeting room and the smaller group settings are booked on next Thursday, starting two o'clock. Would any earlier do?"

"probably not, Madame," Ann answered politely;" let me check with him; he might have to shuffle us around a bit."

"ring us as soon as you know. Your Professor Enderby is a remarkable man, letting you girls organize everything," the office lady commented, "best way to learn, I suppose."

⚜

If Julia was surprised at Ann not asking her any further about the final hearing, she did not show but confined herself to spending time with her, using every opportunity to hold the girl tightly.

Ann rang the refugee association and Mrs Weatherby answered.

"Julia and I may not be able to tutor the girls next Thursday," Ann told her.

"any way you can tell me, Ann?"

"It's to do with a biology project, it's still in a bit of flux and we may be able to leave in time to tutor a bit later. . ."

"good if you can; it's hard to replace you girls. . ."

"I know, Mrs Weatherby, and thank you for understanding; can you spare staff?"

"not really, Ann; I may have to do a session myself; the sooner you girls can make it, get here, please, so you can take over and let me catch up on some work; I'll need any help I can get, as per usual."

"we'll make every effort," Ann assured her, genuinely grateful to that motherly woman.

Ann was not really surprised at how the news had stirred her; intelligent as she was, she realized that her reaction was as much 'bio-physical' as mental; ninety-plus percent of all sex happens in your mind, she told herself. Nor was she put out when Julia failed to ring her in time for that final committee session; she did not put it past her lover's parents to confiscate her phone. Wondering since they had made no attempt to prevent Ann from attending all earlier sessions; why now? The look of surprised delight on Julia's face was reward enough.

"I knew you'd find a way," this usually very confident young person embraced her, giving Ann a sense of power.

"do you think. . .?" Julia's father began.

"we are a couple, Dad, and I doubt whether the Committee will mind."

"maybe not," her mother shrugged her shoulders.

"how did you find out, Ann? Not that you aren't welcome. . ."

"Jules is doing all this for me; it's the very least I can manage. . . well, I asked the right person the right question. . ." "which was?"

"were these facilities available. . ." "and the answer?"

"no, they were booked for this time", the girl replied artlessly, watching her future partner's parents break out in helpless laughter.

"let's go inside."

The Committee members were more than merely accommodating; they had become friends with Ann, Julia and her parents, much as they had become comfortable with Hector and Glen.

"Julia and Ann," the youth worker asked anxiously, "would you mind if we talked to your parents first?"

"Yes, I would," retorted Julia's mother, annoyed. "These girls are very mature young people and soon. . ."

"Mr Chairman, what say you?"

"let us proceed to our ruling here and now; it will be final by the time that we write it down but we'll let you briefly discuss it with us; some of us need to be somewhere else at about three. . ."

"so do Jules and I," interrupted Ann; "forgive us, Mr Chairman, we are expected to tutor as soon as we can make it this afternoon."

"well, that helps; I can see that tea is being served; one last time; and let me assure all of you, and ourselves, that these have been rewarding occasions, challenging all of us and stretching us beyond limits we were not aware of. . ." commented the Convenor. "would you do the honours?" he turned to the situational ethicist who began by clearing his throat:

"This Committee, duly convened on the Ethics of Medical Operations and Practices, has determined that Julia will be free to initiate treatment that will ultimately lead to her changing her present gender, i.e, a sex change; on the understanding that her parents, you-Mr and Mrs Childers-continue to support her and abide by your agreement with us, however reluctantly given, which we sympathise with.

Secondly, this Committee requires that whoever is to be professionally involved with both the treatments as well as any final sex-changing operation here in South Australia first seek to establish and verify our thinking if such operation was to be carried out before Julia's eighteenth birthday as she so clearly wishes, her parents' rather conditional agreement notwithstanding.

If treatment and the concluding operations were to be carried out outside of South Australia, in whole or in part, we likewise recommend that any such professionals contact us first, without mandating it, given that our reach ends at our state borders."

The ethicist took a deep breath and fell silent, as did everyone else.

Ann whispered to her lover:

"don't complain; I have done some research and shall do some more. . ." "tell me?" "only as a reward for an exceptionally good fuck. . ." Ann countered in style, ensuring that they could not be overheard.

Aloud, she rose: "Jules and I thank this committee for your ruling and I think that I can speak for her. . ."

"why, Ann?" Julia's father butted in. "Naturally, we thank this committee for its patience and understanding and for this ruling which does open avenues. . ."

"exactly what Ann was trying to say," Julia agreed with her parent.

❦

Ann's father was beginning to uncover an organisational flair akin to his daughter's.

One day, at work, he fronted his boss over a cup of tea:

"Ryan, could you spare me a few minutes later during the day?"

"funnily enough," his boss commented,

"I had wanted to talk to you within the next few days. We might as well do it now; anything you can get off your desk within the next hour, Hector?"

"I was meant to see a software writer right now. . ." "will he. . ." "she, actually. . ."

"keep you very long, Hector?"

"half an hour; she's working on one of our youth training packages. . ."

"the very thing that I wanted to talk about with you; an hour from now?" "yes."

That hour had come and gone and the young woman machine code writer had left.

The two men entered a conference room, nursing cups of tea. "You first, Hector."

"what I need to talk to you about, Ryan, is best kept confidential for the next few months; I can live with it if it comes out but I'd rather not. . ." "anything unlawful?" "no; you know Glen Hiddings, don't you, Ryan?"

"yeah, they tell me that you were very close at that workshop in Mildura that I got you to conduct over a year ago and you have been seeing him since quite often. Can I rely on your sense of confidentiality, by the way?"

"yes; but any such issues have not come up very often; he did offer for me to work with his setup but for the very reason that I want to discuss with you. . ." "which is?" "I intend to undergo a sex change and be Glen's spouse, in a long-term partnership."

His boss appreciated sitting on a chair, under the circumstances.

"No wonder you want to keep this quiet for a while; for how long, by the way?"

"we were given clearance by the Ethics Commission of South Australia; my long- service leave is coming up and I had wanted to start treatment at about that time." "makes sense," commented his boss, "but that will take longer than three months, more like a year, won't it, even before any actual operation."

"quite right, Ryan," concurred his employee. "What I am worried about is whether I'd be able to work here any longer afterwards; that is why Glen had offered for his company to employ me. . ."

"which they would, unhesitatingly." Hector paused:

"I don't want to, while we are to be a couple, it pays not to work for the same person" "I can see that. What would you like me to do?"

"employ me on a consultant basis or as a contractor a few months after I finish my long-service leave."

His employer said nothing for a while, finished his cup of tea and poured Hector and himself another round.

"I can do one better, Hector, which is why I had wanted to speak to you: I had really wanted to wait a few more days. . ." "for what?"

"we are considering a tender for a youth employment and education programme in the Micronesian Federation. . ."

"is that not part of the US?"

"yes, but not to the extent that others in the Pacific region may not tender. . ."

"our dollar is weaker these days than theirs, so it makes some sense. . ."

"besides of which, AUSAID is funding our bid as a Youth Education Training and Employment Programme to cover the entire Pacific. . ."

"where youth unemployment has been endemic for years," Hector agreed.

"the girl whom I just saw is originally Micronesian and she was commenting on it."

"get her to formalize her input, likewise yourself, with the kind of package you would normally deliver; do some research, of course, and have it ready next week. . ."

"and then, Ryan?"

"I am sending you to Saipan. . ." "close to Guam, is it not?"

"yes, there to set up, run it and train some of their local people for three months; afterwards, if you like, you may stay there for your long-service leave while I set you up as our Pacific contractor. The Kiwis have got the market cornered but that may change," Ryan informed him, with some relish.

"That is very strange, you offering this opportunity. . ." "why that, Hector?"

"I'll explain in a few minutes; but may I ask you if we are guaranteed that tender."

"more or less; the department approached me a few days ago; for very few agencies have had our experience and success, due, in fact, to you, with that particular IT application, combining superior software with ease of use for staff to employ it and young people to get skills and jobs."

Ryan paused to finish yet another cup of tea, then added:

"I would have nominated you anyway, I should think, but your forthcoming change makes it even easier to consider. . ."

"yes, it does, Ryan; for Ann did some research on alternative locations for preparing for, and undergoing, gender alignment, and she came up with Saipan, or, rather, a particular doctor."

"how come that?"

"she is involved with a girl who is to undergo a sex change. . ."

"so Ann's girl friend is to become a boy, instead?"

"yes, and Ann found this clinic that will start treatment on underage young people with parental permission, because the law there does not appear to forbid it."

"amazing; and what did the Ethics Committee here have to say about it."

"they won't block it; they very strongly recommend that the clinic, or anyone else outside of South Australia, got in touch with them, but won't mandate it, unlike with any South Australian practitioner."

"if it works out for you like this as well, I'd be the first one to congratulate you, Hector,"

Ryan smiled. "Meanwhile, back to work; can you draft a package for tender within a week?"

"I have the templates ready; all I need is the official tender document. . ."

"which is, with a preferred-tenderer statement, in three days, or else we would not offer."

"why that?"

"to test their willingness and whether they have any alternative but us to go to; also, you'd be the first to know that we will be busy for at least another year, even without them."

"nice feeling."

"I agree; one last question; that young Micronesian software writer, does she have anything to contribute, other than her cultural background?"

"Oh, definitely; a wonderfully simplified and very well-edited version of the yardsticks-or benchmarks-and some very sound ideas on how to incorporate these into training."

"well, integrate these as if you were to include her and her contribution into our team effort. . ."

"meaning to offer her to join us on Saipan?"

"yes, if it comes to that. What is her name?"

"Aline; raised in Auckland and Brisbane; she followed a boyfriend to Adelaide. . ."

❧

Hector rang Glen from work and they met in the park on South Terrace, not far from St Oswald's.

"How about the Mongolian restaurant for some really bad food which even their dogs won't touch?"

"why not if washed down with some arak?"

It was a lovely autumn evening and the walked the length of the park, closely in step with each other, saying very little.

"I think Kumyss it is, not arak?" "what is that, Glen?"

"fermented mare's milk." "we try everything once."

Once inside the restaurant, they ordered reindeer kidney embedded in larch needles, with a traditional salad of Altai herbs and chilled mugs of kumyss. They started, hesitantly, but realising how hungry they were, they made short work of their food and ordered another round of kumyss, saying little while eating. Eventually, Hector told his partner what had transpired at work.

"I can see how that may work," admitted Glen. "I'd spend as much time out there as often as possible and we can decide on having the operation there or here later on."

"what we'll have to work out at some stage is which house to keep and which one to rent out;" commented Hector; "failing that, sell or lease out both, on long-term rental, and buy one which would suit us both, as well as our sons, daughters and assorted boy-or girlfriends, such as Julia, in due course,".

"for the time being, which of our homes do you prefer?" Glen wondered.

"mine, mainly because Roger is about to move out of yours and I have to think in terms of both Julia and Ann living with us this or next year. . ."

Meanwhile, Julia demanded to find out what Ann had been researching that had made her so confident:

"that you can get me to become a boy in spite of what the Ethics Committee has ruled.?"

"did you notice," Ann countered with a question of her own,

"that the Committee were urging us to find someone outside of South Australia to do you, or at least start you on hormonal treatment. . ."

"well, you are the lawyer," surmised Julia, "you should know; but do explain. . ."

"I shan't unless you fuck me first and take some meaningful photos of me, naked, before and while you do it. . ."

"with my phone and Mum and Dad checking it?"

"no, Jules; let me show you my special. . ."

The girls were on their way to their next tutoring session and their bus was stuck in a traffic jam, "as usual", Julia had complained.

"I got this dedicated prepaid phone for you which you'll have to hide somewhere, unless I am to hide it for you. . ."

"why not; but give me an idea what we are talking about."

"do you remember Brendan McGroom from your science project; you told me. . ."

"yeah, he of the creative scientific invention. . ."

"did he not make up an entire series of year-long experiments out of thin air?"

"yes," Julia assured her friend; "he had done some genuinely pioneering work on menopause and nutrition; he decided to publish on heavy metals and hormones but ended up making up most of his data including the controls and not verifying the genuine ones; plus, he used tests resulting in significant differences when they were not, in fact. . ."

"which is what people noticed, was it not. . ."

"eventually, he lost his approbation which is quite tragic because such links have since been documented; what has he got to do with the price of eggs in the supermarket."

"that is Stephen talking!" "yes. . ."

"I sometimes read the paper and there was a section Insight a few weeks back; it said that he was due to be readmitted and had relocated to the Federation of Micronesia as a consultant until such time that he was fully permitted to practice. . ."

"he would have specialised in sexual medicine, no doubt. . ."

"well, we'll have to work out a time and a venue for you to film and fuck me," stated Ann, "then I'll show you what I found, not just on the Net. . ."

The bus had moved ahead several blocks, then stopped again.

"We might as well get off here and walk the next few blocks," suggested Julia, "are we late?"

"No; let's take a small detour; there is a park here, with a tool shed hidden behind a hedge," Julia remembered, "how about if I did you in there; the blokes finish at three thirty and I have a gadget to open the lock; have you got a torch, Ann?"

"no, but there's an El Cheapo half a block from the Refugee Association; batteries extra, no doubt. . ."

Their session, enjoyable as it was, and much appreciated by their Hazara girls, as usual, who were rapidly getting used to the easy-going ways of Australia, could not end fast enough.

"You go first," suggested Ann, "straight then left, so you can open the shed: I'll head off in the opposite direction and turn right, head for the shed and, if nobody is looking, step inside; if there are people, I'll lean against it and knock against the wall, indicating the minutes I'll wait."

"that might work; have you got money for the torch?" "Oh, nearly forgot, but yes. . ."

Julia took Ann's hand, lifted it against her cheek, let go of it and left.

Ann arrived at the shed about ten minutes later, having had to buy the torch and avoid a lady with a particularly nosy but friendly dog. She stepped inside the shed and Julia barricaded its door with two wheelbarrows stacked end to end. Ann handed her the torch which Julia tested, shielding it with her hands; she then took the phone out, set it up for pictures and began to strip Ann with her free hand, taking pictures of the girl with her arms raised, then another one with Ann arousing herself, her mouth open. No word was said.

Jules laid Ann on a stack of fertiliser bags in the corner, wedging the torch into the framework above and cast her legs around Ann's body, continuing to take pictures. Eventually, Ann stretched herself, raised her arms above her shoulders, against the shed's wall, and pushed her feet against each other, wedging her thighs apart. Julia, having put a pair of lab gloves on, entered her with one hand while opening Ann's mouth with the thumb and forefinger of her free hand, readying her to be entered with her breasts, one at time, in quick and fierce succession.

Ann raised her arms even further and pushed against her feet, thus extending her thighs and knees, inviting Julia to explore her fully, to be teased, aroused, probed and skilfully controlled.

Julia sat astride her and filmed Ann's utter surrender; she then flattened herself over the full length of her lover's body, with one hand remaining inside Ann and the other cuffing the girl's wrists, kissing, licking and biting her and not omitting to take photos by placing the phone on a rafter, pre-setting the timer, to obtain a sideways shot of Julia fully covering, entering, stretching and cuffing an utterly suppliant Ann.

A sudden low bark from outside the shed startled the two girls, interrupting their lovemaking.

Julia, letting go of Ann's wrists, placed her hand on the supine girl's mouth:

"Don't moan, don't scream and don't laugh out loud whatever you do; don't make a noise. . ."

meanwhile, the dog kept barking its head off. The girls could hear an elderly couple argue outside:

"who do you think is inside the shed, for Bruno to carry on like he does?" wondered the lady.

"must be some teenagers either bonking or smoking pot inside; Bruno must be able to smell it; I can't."

"your sense of smell has long since gone, Eric," his wife agreed: "no matter what I cook for you."

"look, blame me for the accident at work; it has put us on the pension."

"several litres of ammonia, a miracle you are alive," his wife agreed, for a change.

"Bruno, stop it! I can't hear myself think. . ."

"try harder!" suggested her husband.

"we should ring the police, Eric," she urged.

"over my dead body," "Eh?"

"remember the places where we went 'courting, 'as we told your parents. . ."

"yeah, I suppose. . ."

"and some of the stuff that I and my mates got up to, inside sheds such as these!

No, leave them alone. . ."

"but if they had vandalised or stolen anything, Eric?"

"think logically, Emily; I know that's one activity a long way from home!"

Meanwhile, Julia had urged Ann to get dressed, shielding her torch with her hands so Ann could see.

It was not enough; Ann lost her balance and crashed into the wheelbarrow left to bar the door.

"Shit," murmured Julia, with Bruno the mutt's bark getting even louder. Drastic measures were called for; Julia, only half-dressed, opened a window and called out: "Bruno, does your mum love you?"

The dog, astonished, ceased barking, enough for Ann to get dressed and move the wheelbarrows.

The elderly gentleman started laughing:

"Is that your boyfriend inside?"

"No, she is to be my boyfriend next year!"

Ann called out, emboldened by the sheer absurdity of the situation.

"We don't do drugs," Julia called out;" we merely decided on a rehearsal. . ."

"rehearsing for what, dear?" the lady asked, unsure whether to smile or be annoyed.

"were you about to steal or break anything?" she wondered.

"no, Emily," her husband had meanwhile looked inside,

"they would have done their damage and gone; and the gear you need for drugs doesn't look to be in there, either. . ."

"how do you know, Eric?" asked his wife, suspiciously. "Bruno, be quiet!" which did not stop the dog; Julia, however, did.

"Bruno, talk to me!" she commanded the animal which responded by walking to the window and licking her hand.

"amazing," commented the elderly gentleman; "he doesn't normally do that. what were you doing inside? Bonking?"

"what else?" Julia agreed. "Aren't you a bit young?"

"I didn't know that girls did it to girls. . ." the lady commented helplessly, "in public, too."

"not quite," her husband interposed; they entered a shed and closed the door behind them; "very civilised, girls; now, tell me is it merely a case of raging hormones or did all this serve a purpose?"

"yes, Ann here promised to give me some information about sex change for which I had to bonk her first. . . Pardon, Madame!" Jules added, seeing the lady's reaction. "Sex change? why would a sexy, smart girl like you, forgive me. want to do that?"

"to please my girlfriend and future partner here," Julia said simply, clearly speaking the truth.

The elderly couple shook their collective heads, called the dog and waited for the girls to emerge.

"you two are a bit young. . ." the husband commented, "but we shan't hold that against you, provisionally and for the time being. . ."

"how about the police?" wondered his wife. Ann and Julia had the sense to say nothing; for Eric had a look at the lock, having spied the inside of the shed and seen nothing missing.

"tell me, girls, did you break the lock? not that it looks like it. . ."

"no, it is fully functional, Sir?" Julia offered to show him.

"how do you know, girl?" The wife wondered, only slightly mollified; Bruno the Mutt, however, did not want to leave the girls but kept licking their hands.

"because," Julia answered patiently, "one day when Ann here was not around and it was raining cats, dogs and the rest of the fauna, Adelaide's famous horizontal showers, you know, I raced here and found that one of my keys opened it without too much difficulty; I can show you if you like. . ."

Having fully dressed herself, meanwhile, she snapped the lock shut and proceeded to open it again, so as to secure the door from the outside, with Bruno eagerly sniffing her fingers.

"anything you left inside, Ann?" she asked. . .

"a bit late; no, I don't think so, Jules," the girl said, unfazed.

"What are you girls doing around here, other than bonk. . ."

"we are homework tutors at the refugee centre. . ."

"on the main road; after school; seeing that you are in your school uniforms. . ."

"yes, St Brendan the Voyager, at your service. . ."

"well, don't voyage inside this shed again, if you get my meaning, girls; do each other somewhere else, if you would?"

"even if it were to rain, Sir?" wondered Ann.

"cheeky, aren't you? I like that in a girl. . ."

Julia the diplomat knew how far she could go:

"Let me apologize for my girl friend; thank you very much, Sir, and you, Madam. for your understanding; before we go, could we say Good Bye to Bruno?"

At the sound of his name, the big dog trotted over to her, sniffed Julia up and down and proceeded to jump onto Ann, licking her face and leaving imprints on her uniform.

"I am so very sorry, girls." intoned his owner.

"don't give it any thought, Sir."

"how are you girls getting home?" the elderly gentleman asked. "By bus?" "Yes, Sir?"

"in another twenty minutes, you can catch the express bus around the block;" he assured them;

"isn't that a set-down stop only, Sir?" wondered Ann, matter-of-fact-like;

"no, not during rush hour."

The bus had dropped a few passengers and the girls got on, showing the driver their school passes.

"it's not a pick-up stop, girls, not till next week, anyway," the driver commented,

"but insert your tickets at the next stop and find somewhere to stand; there's no more seats. . ."

"thank you," the girls intoned, smiling.

They forced their way into the aisle to gain some space for themselves and their school bags.

"now that I have done what you wanted me to do," began Julia," would you be kind enough to tell me what you found out. . ."

"not here in the bus," countered Ann, "but let me tell you what I tried to do. Remember Dr Mac Groom from our biology class?"

"yes, you reminded me before. . ."

"you are the scientist, Jules; what did they get him for, do tell us?"

"making up not only results but entire fictitious experiments."

"how did people find out?"

"someone read the published articles, then got someone to replicate the experiments; the rest is history. . ."

"so what happened to him?"

"well, all I know is that he was struck off the medical register as a result. . ."

"how long ago?" "twenty years, I'd say?"

"Jules, let me tell you that he is about to be reinstated very soon. . ."

"how do you know,"

Julia stopped herself from saying 'bitch', afraid that it would not go down well inside a crowded bus.

"I got in touch with him, initially to help Dad;" "why that?"

"Dad's company suggested that he bid for a youth training and employment software programme for Micronesia. . ."

"that's fine, let's hope he gets it. . ."

"you don't get it, lover?" Ann chided her.

"Dr Mc Groom has been based there for years; he runs a clinic for a local investor as a medical director and Dad could be there for the next six months, with luck, if you include his long-service leave which he can spend anywhere he likes and still be paid."

"I can see it work for him," phrased Julia.

"I see that I'll have to pass on the entire message over the phone, what do you think?"

"Mum and Dad will get to read it. . ."

"why don't I direct it to them, instead?" wondered Ann; "they'll have to find out, or so Dr Mc Groom said, anyway."

"how do you know, Ann?"

"I got in touch with him, that's why, lover." Ann answered proudly.

❧

"Dear Ann Landers, let me first state how much I admired you tactful allusion to my having been struck off the register in South Australia which is, of course, common knowledge; I am about to be reinstated and, once that is to happen, I have been offered my final approbation for the Federation of Micronesia.

As you have discovered, Ann, through your diligent study of the Net, I am the director of a specialised sex clinic, acting as a medical adviser, consultant and administrator, for its proprietor; my staff is fully equipped and qualified to supervise the kind of treatment and carry out the operation you have in mind for both your father and your lover, even if I were not yet in a position or simply too busy to do so myself.

I continue to be in touch with the Ethics Committee of South Australia; I shall need to have decisions and all relevant documentation covering both your father and your lover forwarded, rather than myself approach the Committee, even though I shall, nonetheless, also do so at some stage.

Your father's case appears more straightforward than that of your lover, in the light of what you have communicated to me, mainly due to her very young age. (let me stress that I am inclined to use personal pronouns and gender-related titles rather guardedly, in this context!), I am also pleased, on his behalf and because it will ease his treatment, that he may be able not only to spend his long-service leave with us but also to work here which will render it more affordable to him and his future partner whom I also need to hear from in due course.

As to your lover, I shall also need to get to know her parents' thinking, having been informed-by you-that they have already agreed, in principle; if they saw fit to allow your father to act in loco parentum, then I could have her treated and, eventually, operated on at more or less the same time.

Schooling is available, or else I can arrange home schooling or a combination of both, same as we already do so for the families of Australian staff. That may help remove her-and you, in her company-from your original school while she is undergoing hormonal treatment and thus avoid an awkward situation for you both.

As to fees, if we can arrange to treat both your father and your lover simultaneously, I have permission to either reduce them throughout or waive those for your lover and cap them for your father, in return for both of them being willing to subject themselves to learned papers, with their names withheld and confidentiality guaranteed, all this in view of the, so far, never-before documented background.

This, too, would require your future partner's parents' approval, or at least, their readiness not to prevent publication as long as my team ensures our habitual utmost discretion; likewise, your father 's partner's participation, if not outright consent, would be highly desirable throughout, even though he may not be physically present for much of the time, what with unavoidable work and family commitments of his own.

To sum up and repeat, dear Ann: I shall need written statements from your father and his partner, from your lover, her parents, and yourself, more or less such as you would have prepared for the Ethics Committee. All available documentation issued, or viewed, by them will have to be forwarded, since I wish to consult them, as they themselves appear to have recommended.

In due course, my clinic will work out a programme for accommodation and schooling, including costs, medical schedules and outlines of the publication/s that we intend to prepare, with the consent of all involved, subject to our utter discretion.

Let me admit to a sense of great personal and professional curiosity, on behalf of my staff and myself; we genuinely look forward to getting to know, and work with, all of you in person and in due course.

High regards Brendan Mc Groom Medical Advisor, Consultant and Executive Administrator, Obstetric Gynaecological and Sexual Specialist Clinic Saipan, The Federation of Micronesia"

The girls' workplace was abuzz with 'new talent '; for Jean-Claude Duvalier had arrived to help teach teenage Hazara refugees. The girls, in particular, could not keep their eyes off him; for he spoke fluent Pashtu and passable Dari. While he made every effort not to intrude in Ann's and Julia's classes, he managed to explain or at least smooth over awkward situations, arising not so much because of misunderstandings but of what the young Afghanis had missed out on for not being able to go to school for several years prior to their arrival in Australia; He knew what it was like where they and their families had come from.

The boys were impressed, too, in spite of themselves; for they could see that he took them seriously even when he clearly disagreed with their view of the world.

The refugee association staff, at first unsure of this confident newcomer and his assured manner, was easily won over; not only did he know what he was talking about but he was very patient without being patronising. Halfway through one such session, they called a tea break; Julia and Ann managed to sit on either side of the boy.

"why aren't you black, Jean Claude?" asked Ann, cheekily, with a ready smile. The boy's face went dark for a while; then he laughed.

"Very funny, Ann. . . haven't heard that one for years; no, I am not Haitien (pronounced in the French manner); my father did work there before the earthquake. We are French Canadians, but he still had to learn Creole. . ."

"is that the French equivalent of Creo that used to be spoken in Central Australia and further up North?" asked Mrs Weatherby, interested.

"I was not aware, Madame," Claude answered with his customary courtesy,

"of Creo being spoken in Australia but, then, my family has only been here for a few weeks. Carribean Creole is a kind of basic French written as it is spoken and organised as if it were a l local language,"

"very little grammar?"

"yes, that also."

"you are French Canadian, Quebec or Montreal?" another tutor, Clem, asked him. "Quebec; my father has tenure with Laval University and is here on a sabbatical; my maternal grand-bon-pere-great-grandfather, was Rene Vallieres. . ."

"the White Slaves of North America?" intoned Mrs Weatherby.

"you know!" Jean-Claude smiled;" I didn'think that anyone in Australia did."

"I did Marginal Literature at uni and it was on an optional reading list; such an unusual title."

The tutors drank their tea silently, not quite knowing what to say next. Ann broke the ice, as usual:

"how come, Jean-Claude, that you speak these Afghan languages like a local?"

"I wouldn't say 'like a local', "countered the boy:" I did not realise how much I had forgotten till today; to answer you, Ann, though; our family lived in Pakistan for several years. . ."

"did you ever get to visit Afghanistan, Jean-Claude?" wondered Julia.

"yes, Dad took us along a few times. . ." "us?" "my sister, Helene, and myself. . ."

"could you bring her along next time, Jean-Claude?" asked Clem.

"I had meant to do so today," was the reply, "but she was 'crok'. . ."

"you mean 'crook'?"

"yes, not well; and she's off on a school trip next week but I shall bring her along soon."

"is she as good with languages as you?" wondered Julia.

"no, she never got to hang out with the girls as I did with the boys, like playing football and cricket and racing motorcycles; girls in that culture can't really do that, and she was never into it all that much, unlike myself. . ."

"will she come, nonetheless; our girls would love her. . ."

"no doubt," her brother agreed, "and I am beginning to feel that she misses that experience. . ."

"probably because she cannot talk to anyone else about it, other than you and your mum and dad," Ann surmised.

"I never thought about that," he smiled at the girl.

"I am sure you are right because that must be why I made it here in the first place."

"Jean Claude introduced himself to the Multicultural Centre on King William Street one day after school and they couldn't send him here fast enough," explained Mrs Weatherby.

"did your dad worked with Afghan refugees in Pakistan; Jean-Claude?"

"yes, millions of them, including Hazara; you appear to have more of them here than we do in Canada," explained the boy.

"Dad is a planner and worked with universities in Quetta and Peshawar where there are a lot of Afghani students whom he trained in work with NGOs to benefit their fellow Afghanis stranded there. . ."

"ever since the Soviet invasion, in some cases," said Mrs Weatherby.

"quite, Madame. I went to school with boys and hung out with their friends, almost all of them former Afghan kids."

"so you learnt Pashtu and Dari from the Horse's Mouth. . ." do you have a saying like that in French?"

"no, but I know what you mean and you are right," agreed the boy:

"I think that is where my sister sort of missed out. . ."

"did she never learn these languages?"

"Dari almost not at all and she understands Pashtu better than she can speak it. . ."

"would the girls understand her, though?" asked Julia, disappointed.

"she'd get by and she's sufficiently familiar with the background to enjoy it when she gets here. . ."

"but she hasn't got your confidence, is that the case?"

"maybe; I'll bring her, and she'll like it, as will your girls. . ." and boys, maybe? "he pondered."

"meanwhile, we are very happy for you to be here; how long is our dad's sabbatical to last?" wondered Mrs Weatherby.

"till September, which is when our academic year starts in Canada," he replied.

"Let's get back to work," the lady told them; "would you partner Clem, Jean-Claude; you girls, shift your groups into the next room and leave the doors open; see what happens. . ."

It worked very well: Jean-Claude picked up quite quickly how he was expected to tutor, with Clem's help, and the Hazara girls would shout Dari or Pashtu words whose meanings they did not know in English into the corridor and repeat their translations after Jean-Claude, among much giggling; even the boys smiled.

"That was fun," beamed Ann, sitting inside the bus, in front of Julia, on their way home.

"Bitch!" gnarled Julia and removed her hand off Ann's shoulder.

"'bitch 'yourself," Ann turned around: "look at you; your eyes are shining; your face could light up Hindmarsh Stadium; you've got the 'hots 'on him, don't you?" "speaking for yourself," grumbled her lover, by now very jealous. Ann was quiet for a while, then:

"listen, my mum once told me this: 'look, there's a number of men I met over the years I could have been happily lived with or been married to, and I know for a fact that the same applies to your dad, the other way around; but I for one had made up my mind, and so had he. . .'"

"meaning that we need to stick with each other, Ann?" "yes."

"I am sorry. . ." "don't cry!" her lover comforted her:

"we just never get to meet boys like him, so we both have the hots for him, quite natural. . ."

"the boys we know are losers compared to him; the sheer confidence and courtesy. . . nothing like lovely manners to melt a girl," mused Ann.

"true," commented Julia, "he takes you seriously, doesn't patronise you, knows who he is and what he knows and doesn't; he'll have no problem finding a girl for himself. . . was your Brian like this?" she added.

"a bit younger, of course, and he hadn't been around quite like that, even though his father would have. . ."

"he was an international consultant?"

"yes, based in Brisbane," explained Ann: "you are right, though; Brian's got that same quiet confidence and can-do attitude without being pushy and he, too, listens as much as talks. . ."

"no wonder," concluded Julia: "you expect me to live up to all that?"

"you are doing very well, lover dear," Ann assured her.

❧

Glen met Hector at work, for a change, a few days after he had been told about Ryan wanting to send his partner to Saipan to develop, set up and run a youth training IT software programme, along with Aline. They shared a huge pot of tea, as usual, and were sampling some new software in Glen's office, following up on the workshop where they had first met each other.

"Is this particular one similar to what Ryan's asked you to develop and apply in Micronesia?"

"in principle, yes, Glen, like two model cars may be similar. . ."

"could you develop one from the other. . .?"

"a bit like creating a molecular compound from atomic elements; it can be done but it would not be the most straightforward approach, same as it rarely is in chemistry. . ."

"where did you get to argue like a scientist from, Hector?" Glen wondered, amused.

"blame my future son-in-law, Jules, as Ann calls her" They both laughed.

"remember she wants to be a scientist. . ."

"good on her," agreed Glen. "I am asking for a reason; as you know, our agency is expected to develop and put in place programmes throughout Central Australia. . ."

"the point, Glen?"

"being that there is a small group of Tongan people living and working in around Barrow Creek. . ."

"that's north of Alice Springs, is it not. . ."

"yes, about two hours by car; vineyards and orchards which the Tongans who live there have been working for generations; the government wants us to conduct a block with some of their young people to help them set up small businesses. . ."

". . .rather than train them for work that does not exist locally, I suppose."

"'hole in one', Hector. From what you have just told me, your software may fit that particular purpose better than what we have here. . ."

"you want me to join you up there, develop and trial my software?"

"more or less; we need to use this one here as a control. . ."

"will your company pay ours a licensing fee?"

"I would pay for your availability and, quite possibly, that young software writer's of yours as well. . ."

"Aline; why? Oh, I see, she is from Saipan, though, not Tonga!"

"not quite the same, eh?"

"well, similar enough, I suppose."

Hector helped himself to another cup of green tea, without sugar, and contemplated what to say.

"If you are prepared to sign a disclaimer on whatever software I develop and match with yours so that your company undertakes not to use or further develop it without our permission and upon payment of a royalty, and if you mean to hire myself and also Aline, for the three of us to go there; why not?"

"would Ryan be agreeable, do you think?"

"It would give the system a trial run among people who are not as substantially different from Micronesians as they might be from ordinary urban Australians. . . will the government allow you to budget for software other that what we have here?"

"No, Hector, but they'll allow consultants; Ryan will have to settle for the disclaimer which I am happy to issue. . ."

"and abide by? I have to ask, Glen,"

"I know; yes!"

A week later, having flown from Adelaide to 'the Alice', they were travelling in a vehicle belonging to Glen's partner agency, Glen, Hector, Aline and Lisa, a young programmer working with them. They were talking animatedly but also spent time in companionable silence, each lost in their own thoughts, looking at the starkly beautiful lateritic plateau they were crossing, hidden in the sheer expanse of Australia.

Hector realised for the first time, apart from his brief encounter with Samira, how much he had missed the company of articulate, intelligent and, he was more than ready to admit it, attractive young women, ever since Clara had died, much as he continued to grieve and feel incomplete without her. He noticed Glen unbend and felt a pang of jealousy at the ease with which his future partner interacted with Aline, in particular, as if it had been he, and not Hector, who had known and worked with her for quite some time now.

Andy Prescott, the caretaker at Barrow Creek Golden Bed Motel, was about to finish a very long day' work. Among many other things, the gearbox on his rather ancient ride-on mower had gone phut and he had to ring a mate in the nearby garage to help him fix it; likewise, his brush-cutter had seized up and needed to be coaxed into life.

Jobs that would have taken a few hours were only now nearing completion, late in the afternoon, with sunsets in Central Australia a sudden and drastic affair. He was about to give the finishing touch to a stubborn edge where some opportunistic asparagus had found its way into a grassed corner and had just lowered the blades to cut the next swathe when. . ."

"Oh shit, bugger!" he had remembered too late the pipe partly hidden under some tufts that had grown rapidly during the recent unexpected rains; light was fading fast and gallons of bore-water were pouring through a brick-lined retaining wall into the motel's basement at alarming speed and with the appropriate gargling noise, carrying topsoil, mulch and leaves as well as bits of mown grass with them, a veritable brown if not yet altogether smelly mess.

To make things worse, Greg, his mate had already knocked off work and lived too far away to come to his aid again in a hurry. His Tongan off-sider had been given a day off in order to be able to attend the IT workshop to start the next day; the owners of the motel had yet to return from a funeral in Tennant Creek and Doris, the housekeeper, had gone home for a short breather before night duty.

Still cursing, Andy found a torch and tried to remember the joint where the line joined the bore, as well as look for something, anything, that he might wedge in there to stop or slow down the water. Having rained so much, the ground was too saturated to absorb much water which would normally have happened.

He grabbed the stilton so as to partly unscrew the joint and insert a piece of long-suffering hardwood into the gap to reduce the flow which he did manage, to some extent and very much for the time being. The priorities were: sandbag the verandah and ring several people, starting with the proprietors, hopefully on their way back from their relative's interment, the housekeeper to prepare her for a load of unwanted and unexpected extra work, and Greg, for some more advice.

He never even bothered to ring a plumber; for not only was there none around for hundreds of miles but, barring a miracle, none would have turned up without charging an emperor's ransom as his call-out fee, just for getting there.

He, finally, managed to ring Mrs Bristow who, with her husband, was the chief vintner and orchardist in Barrow Creek and who had pickers' huts available, as well as a meeting hall used by the Country Women's Association as well as the weekly prayer circle.

Andy had another brainwave: while the plug lasted, he would fill jute bags with dry leaf-mould compost which, he had been told in Tennant Creek, held three times its weight-or was it volume?-in water;

these he quickly laid into the somewhat slowed-down flow of water from the bore.

That done; he filled half a dozen bags with building sand from a recent extension which he placed at the base of the rather useless retaining wall; he then went to retrieve his phone and started ringing, to not much avail; for he could get no signal for his employers ("out of range, as usual") and then found that he had very little credit left.

Fortunately, Doris picked up the phone. "Andy, what's up?"

"Can you ring me back straightaway; minor disaster here and I have no credit left. . ."

"nor with mine, Andy!" Doris intoned sweetly.

"next door's got a landline, don't they; could you ask them very nicely to let you ring our landline in the office. . ."

"do you have a key, because I locked it. . ."

"sh. . . it; could you ring the Bristows, please. . ."

"gone, cut off. . ." Andy's language petered off into the utterly unprintable.

The Bristow family, alerted by Doris, came to the party, seeing that the motel was not fit to accommodate anyone; they were also expecting a Council road crew to arrive and start work within the next few days. Brad Bristow arrived with a pump and a length of lay-flat tubing to drain off the bore until he and Andy could insert a high-pressure valve which Andy's friend had yet to machine on his turning lathe, using a defective one that he had available.

Gwen Bristow and her daughter Fiona prepared a meal and started worrying where to put up the 'A-Team' which was how the motel proprietors had described them, once they had gotten into range on their return from the funeral which Brendan, their son, had also attended.

"The girls can have my room for a night or two;" Fiona offered.

"How long will it take Dad and the motel people to get rid of the water and dry out and clean up the damage, Mum?"

"a day at least, that's what it took us after that last bit of storm we had a few days ago; you were at College at the time."

"is Brendan coming back tonight?" the girl wondered.

"no, he'll stay in Tennant Creek till the weekend."

"the blokes 'll have to share his room then for a night or two," the girl decided; "we'll have to keep the sleeping and cooking area clean for the Council crew, don't we?"

The meal was a success; the Bristows had served their own wine; mother and daughter had done themselves proud; "at such short notice", Glen said in appreciation of their effort.

"Thank you very much, Mr and Mrs Bristow. . ."

"Brad and Gwen, for you. . .," Brad Bristow countered; "Consider it outback hospitality; we were doing it for Tom and Eileen as much as for you, their guests; you'll be with us for at least two days; we'll help you set up your gear at the community centre tomorrow," he added.

"would you introduce your team called the A Team, that's according to Eileen, when she rang us on her way home. . ."

"after Doris got through, finally," Fiona added.

Glen thought how best to phrase it:

"Hector sets up templates and develops the type of software that's needed; Aline then writes it and Lisa takes it through its paces to make it work. . ."

"and yourself, Glen? Aren't you being too modest with yourself?"

"rarely so," Glen smiled. "I who am the least computer-adapted person alive gets, nonetheless, to design and then put in place programmes which are in need of Hector's software and the girls' skills."

Eileen and Tom had been invited, too, while Doris had taken Andy home to have tea with her family, with the motel kitchen firmly out of bounds for the time being. Everyone around the table did justice to the fine meal in front of them, involving asparagus, wild capres, vine leaves, fish caught in the dam and all kinds of greenery, not to mention the clear home-grown Rosé which Barrow Creek is famous for.

"But why here, and why our Tongans?" asked Tom, the motel keeper.

"not that we aren't pleased that you are here and doing this, not least because our own worker stands to benefit."

"is he with you right now?"

"Colin was not well enough to work these last few days; he's with his parents but should be ready tomorrow; but again, why here and why our Tongans?"

Hector answered: "Glen's company's reach extents all over Central Australia but Aline and myself want to use this as a dry-run for a project that I am to set up in Micronesia on a much larger scale. . ."

"Micronesia?" repeated Fiona. "My boyfriend and I went to Guam last year for a diving trip; the cyclone damage was colossal; would you like me to show all of you some pic's after tea. . .?"

"yes, please; but do not let us even think of finishing this lovely meal. . ."

"may it last forever," Glen agreed.

"These were fantastic pictures, weren't they?" Lisa asked Aline when they had finally settled down for the night in Fiona's room

("are you sleeping in your parents' room tonight?" they had asked the girl. "Yes, for the first time since before primary school," she had agreed, laughing, "a bit of a culture shock for mum and dad, no doubt!")

"phenomenal food as well. How do you feel being with us, Lisa?" Aline wondered.

"yes, it is more than work, it is not?" the girl agreed.

"Did you notice that the gentlemen in charge of us have been trying their level best to keep their hands off us. . ."

"or display any form of the Hots;" Aline stated.

"how about you? I'd certainly be able to want them for either, or even both, of us, and not hesitate to be very obvious about it;."

"not to say explicit. . ."

"except that it may not be a good idea to get that closely involved, any more than you inevitably do with people whom you work and get on and spend quality time with."

"no, regretfully not, Lisa. How about your boyfriend?" "how about him?"

"who and where is he?"

"Lionel is in the Middle East and I am in two minds to follow him," Lisa confessed.

"unless it's Saudi Arabia, I would not mind at all," confided Aline.

"It is Saudi Arabia; Lionel is already in Dhamman, working with a highway construction company; they'd be prepared to employ me to build their IT network."

"Is he ready to marry you?"

"what a question, Aline!"

"the one he needs to pop before you even go to Saudi Arabia; for you are just about immobile as a woman there unless accompanied by a husband brother or father, an uncle, in a pinch.," Aline explained.

"How do you know?" aghast.

"my own loser boyfriend's cousin was offered a job by a doctor in Tais; she managed to get her brother employed as security, otherwise she would not have gone; she's still there, earning lots of money; so's her brother."

"What do you suggest?"

"do you want to be with your boyfriend?"

". . .and get to see the world; of course. . ."

"or find a brother, yours preferably, and arrange for him to come along, paid or otherwise. . ."

"Brent is between jobs right now and may be sisterly persuaded. . ."

"all you need to do is put the thumbscrews on your boyfriend to establish him to live with you in Dhammam. . ."

"food for thought," the other girl scratched her head.

"Now about boyfriends, seeing that we are both in heat. . ."

"speaking for yourself?" Aline smiled: "Kieran is better on the keyboard than in bed if you want my honestly biased opinion. . ."

"did you meet him at work. . ." "more or less,"

"what do you want to do, Aline?"

"dump him before I follow Hector to Micronesia."

"would you take up with Hector, instead? I would, given a fifth of a chance; he's a widower, is he not. . ."

"yes, but he's supposed to be in a relationship with Glen," Aline informed her calmly.

"whaat!"

"Lisa, their room is next door!"

"but they are neither of them gay, the opposite!"

"true; what I know is what I picked up on the tracks; they both keep very quiet about it but that's also why they aren't getting involved with us girls as they'd probably like, apart from sex being a workplace hazard. . ."

"seeing that I am not getting a handle on any of them, as you say, and that Lionel is not here and that I am in heat, as you also agreed; would you bonk me, please?"

"any preference, Lisa?" "Just do me!. . ."

"psst, Lisa; this is how it's going to be: first I'll strip you, then stand you up, naked, and cuff your hands behind your back, then lay you on our bed (a draw-out couch normally in use by Fiona and her boyfriend), mount and sit astride you. . ." "like horsey. . ."

"then kiss you, pin your arms down and split your legs, finally, roll you on your side and spoon you; you'll end the night and wake up in the morning naked, spooned and imprisoned in my arms; agreeable as a menu?"

"my own personal, not to say intimate, sex-ecutioner; how sex-citing," crooned Lisa. "ravishing," concluded her new-found, forceful lover.

Glen and Hector realized that they had never shared a room let alone a bed, other than on that brief afternoon on the houseboat on the river Murray.

"What do you think the girls are up to?" asked Hector.

"why do you ask?"

"they got on as if they had known each other for years. . ."

"in a Biblical sense, you mean?"

"I don't know. I am very poor at sensing those things," Hector admitted.

"we are a good team, though, work-wise and as people. . ."

"which, in itself, can be quite challenging when you find it easy to relate to such smart intelligent and confident girls. . ."

"tempting, to say the least," agreed Hector.

"not that it would pay to get too intimate when you also got to work with them."

"we are tempted?"

"yes, of course; who would not be; yet. . ."

"it is good to be alive," sighed Hector, "even though it can be very difficult, at times."

"do you feel guilty?" asked Glen, perceptively.

"of course; then I remember that Clara wanted me, us, to be fully here, with half our lives ahead of us."

"come closer," urged Glen and started breathing rhythmically, with Hector following suit.

"soon as I know for certain. . ."

"certain of what?" even though Glen knew what Hector was talking about; "the tender. . ."

"why, any doubt. . ."

"not really, otherwise Ryan would not have offered to equip me; once the dots have been connected. . ."

"does this one have anything to do with it?"

"no, it's more by nature of an argument that there is scope to try my system on Pacific Islanders without having to leave Australia; Ryan has to persuade Micronesian authorities, not merely the department. . ."

"who both like to avoid risks and cover their fleshy parts," ventured Glen.

"you are trying to tell me that you'll start hormonal treatment as soon as you can see your way clear. . ."

"quite."

"my mum once said that relationships had very little to do with sex and a lot to do with both partners actually having work. . ."

"true, not only because we met at work but it also determines how far we can go and when. . ."

"have faith," urged Glen;

"and start treatment now?"

"not here in bed, this very minute, but in Adelaide, Hector!"

"this is not a request, Glen, is it?" "not really."

"let us sleep on it, then."

"ok, let's find out who snores the most."

"it's a contest!" Both won, in the end.

❧

A few weeks after Jean-Claude had been first introduced to teaching the Hazara kids, he brought his sister and a friend along, called Doug. The girls, while pleased and quite surprised to hear a Western girl speak Pashtu and even Dari, soon realized that Denise was not as forthcoming as her brother, nor particularly girlish. The boys, while wary, were nonetheless trying to impress her, and they were determined to stay on Jean-Claude's good side, being aware that a brother's acceptance was vital if you wanted to get friendly with a girl.

Julia and Ann felt that Denise was pulled in two directions, more than Jean- Claude had been.

Their patron, Mrs Weatherby, was inclined to agree with the girls.

"I think part of her likes being back among young people from the culture where she grew up, and the other half wants to be fully accepted by her peers, boys in particular, she meets at school." she observed, quite perceptively,

"whereas Jean-Claude is equally happy in both worlds and thrilled to be back in this one, even for no more than a day a week."

"How about Doug?"

"How about him? He is very quiet but awfully good at explaining things and very patient, easy to understand and speaks very clearly. . ."

"without patronizing anyone," Julia agreed.

They went back to work after their tea break, coffee for Denise and Jean-Claude, thank you.

"we are very French, really," the girl had admitted.

"Do you prefer French to English?" Mrs Enderby had asked.

"Why, yes," Denise started, "but then. both Jean-Claude and I grew up with totally different languages as well. . ."

"which puts things in perspective," added Ann.

The girls had gotten used to listening to Jean-Claude, explaining things and finding suitable expressions in either Dari or Pashtu, at times asking which term young Hazaras would use a in their own language.

Towards the end of their classes that afternoon, they realized that Jean-Claude was nowhere to be heard, nor Doug to be seen.

"How are you and your brother getting home, Denise?"

"We'll catch a bus to the uni and Dad drives us home. . ."

"but I've never seen your brother on our bus?"

"we use the 100; it takes longer but we don't have to change. . ."

Two weeks later, the girls fronted up to Mrs Weatherby.

"Let's hope that Jean-Claude, Denise and Doug get to continue," they said.

"why, girls; are you leaving us soon; we'd miss you?"

"it's great fun and we like it here," answered Ann, mindful how Brian had first rescued, then ravished her; some of the boys who had then threatened her were still in class. Brian had been right:

"Mullah Abdullah was deported, wasn't he, Mrs Enderby?"

"yes, thank God," the lady agreed. "but how come you girls are leaving us, and when?" Ann replied: "My Dad got his long-service leave coming up and also a consultancy in Micronesia, starting perhaps as soon as June. . ." "and you, Julia?"

"I am to go along," the girl informed her.

"I see; but how about your parents?"

"they are slowly coming around; in an ideal world, they'll take a holiday later this year."

"well, let's make the most of the time that you are still here," the lady concluded.

"I can see what you mean, though; it is good to have replacements ready. . ."

"not just replacements," protested Julia, attracting a strange look from Ann,

"they know more languages than we do and they are very good at what they do."

"true," admitted Mrs Weatherby.

That same afternoon, the girls left after class, along with a few Hazara girls, till they reached the bus stop.

"Let's walk a bit further," said Ann, once they had seen the girls onto the bus,

"and catch the tram, instead. . ." "and then get into a bus at Westend? why not?"

Julia consented and grasped Ann's elbow, walking her further down the footpath. Suddenly, Ann's free hand shot out and closed Julia's mouth.

"shht," she told her surprised lover.

"take me inside that doorway," Ann urged, keeping her voice down.

Julia looked up to see Jean-Claude and Doug embrace and kiss each other a few dozen yards away.

Once inside the doorway, the girls looked at each other. "Kiss me," urged Ann.

A few minutes later, the girls emerged, only to see the two boys walk towards them, hand in hand.

"you saw us," challenged Doug.

"look, Jean-Claude and Doug; we didn't mean to," Julia frowned,

"how come that you, Jean-Claude, and your sister didn't use number100, as you usually do?"

"Dad is not at uni today but helping set up an exhibition on North Terrace, in a gallery that belongs to Flinders Uni. Doug here can get on a bus close to Mile End so we decided to walk," the French-Canadian boy informed the girls,

"as did you; why?"

"we decided to catch the tram till Westend, then get a bus to Regency; we are doing a project with another girl today."

"don't tell anyone what you saw us do!" Doug informed the girls threateningly."

"Doug, your manners, please. . ." "you and your manners, Clodie. . ."

"having a domestic?" enquired Ann drily. Suddenly, they all laughed. "Just don't tell anyone, will you?" Doug affirmed.

"why don't we all take the tram?" suggested Julia; "it might take you a bit longer but we get to talk as we walk. . ." So they did.

"how long have you known that you were gay, Jean-Claude?"

"keep your voice down, Julia," warned Doug.

"sorry; but will you boys tell us?"

"I discovered it when I was in Quetta, playing with some wild kids. . ."

"did it get you in trouble there?" Ann asked.

"no, not while we were younger. . ."

"does your sister know?"

"she does but she is very uncomfortable with it. . ."

"but also loyal. . ." added Doug. "I sometimes think that Clodie's parents left Pakistan. . ." he began;

"it's outlawed in Afghanistan and considered haram in Pakistan, even though common," added Jean-Claude.

"Dad's time had come to an end, more or less, so my parents decided not to try and extend our time there, with that hanging over us, much as we wanted to; we all miss it so much"

"even Denise?" asked Doug thoughtfully.

"she least of us, but even she was at a loss at first."

"is she happy here?"

"yes," the boys replied; "more than in Quebec," her brother added.

"a surprise, I don't know. . ." he shrugged his shoulders in inimitable Gallic style and kept walking.

"how did you, Doug, get to be. . ." Julia probed.

"gay, you mean?" the boy countered. "At football, mainly. . ." he paused, lost in a memory."

"how did you find each other?" wondered Ann.

"that was hilarious, actually; we attend the same chemistry class and were both racing through the corridor, not looking, because we were late and in a hurry. . ."

"we banged into each other, instinctively held each other up and then. . ." Doug stopped:.

"kissed, very quickly," Jean-Claude explained; "we barely knew each other at the time because I had only just arrived; it went on from there, I guess."

"did you have a partner at school before Jean-Claude?" Ann again.

"no, nor did Clodie, he was new."

"how about you, back in Quebec?"

"no, girls, we weren't there long enough back from Pakistan; it was enough of a struggle without getting involved," Jean-Claude sighed.

"You girls are a couple, aren't you; yet neither of you are gay, are you?"

"no, but how do you know?"

"Clodie is very observant," his boyfriend commented.

"but even I noticed, not knowing you quite as well; so what's the secret?"

Doug being the more forthright of the two.

"Too complicated to explain, Doug,"

"Try us," challenged Jean-Claude.

"Where do we start?" wondered Ann, looking at her lover.

"By getting on the tram, for starters; it is coming towards us," concluded Julia. . .

A few months before her untimely death, Clara Landers had, while already at her hospice, idly flicked through a women's magazine and spotted a quiz inside; doctor Samira who happened to be around, nursing a cup of tea, had offered to help. "Alternative Shi'ite pilgrimage, Clara?" she lightly fisted her head:

"brainwave, please," she demanded.

Her face cleared, almost immediately; she took another sip and declared:

"why, the tomb in Mashad, of course; how stupid of me!"

"you are not stupid, Samira," protested her patient.

"you are smart beautiful confident accomplished. . ."

"do leave me blushed," countered the young woman.

"my parents took all of us on an Alternative Haj because we could not afford the real one. . ."

"Mashad is in Eastern Iran, is it not?" wondered Clara; "very cold winters, lots of snow. . ."

"how do you know, Clara?"

"I am, or was, on the board of the Orange Foundation which finds accommodation for new arrivals, including temporary visa, in those days; one such lot were Afghanis who had fled to Iran and, rather than being repatriated, decided to escape. Some of them had managed to make, and keep, photos of their time near Mashad. . ."

"yes, we had huge camps there; we still have quite a few Afghanis live all over Iran," the young doctor affirmed.

"Is that why your daughter gets to teach Afghan girls, Clara?"

"I'm sure it has a lot to do with it; never thought of it, though, in that sense. How about the clue, though, Samira?"

The girl finished her tea, then smiled:

"Mashad leads to another line; make it Mashed Potato,"

"when you connect it with: Tibetan sanctuary, Potala, and Central Spanish Cathedral city known for steel-making", added Clara.

"depending on how you spell that city of ours in English. . .", concluded Samira.

"let's complete the quiz, then, and find an envelope."

"do you want me to post it?" doctor Samira offered. "Yes, please."

"So much for the passage of time," wondered Hector, by that time back from Barrow Creek and sitting opposite Glen at their favourite café.

"what do you mean, Hec?"

"let me show you, Glen," his future 'wife'replied, showing him a letter. . .

"which I received in the post while we were in the Northern Territories. Want to read it?"

"no, give me a summary, please, in words of no more than a syllable or two and no more than seven letters. . ."

"how demanding! Well, it seems that Clara did one of the magazine quizzes and was the only one who got the key clue right. . . Remember Dr Samira?"

"don't we all?" sighed Glen, unashamedly. "What about her?"

"I was running late yesterday, dropped Ann at a bus stop, took the letter to work and opened it there, then rang Samira and asked her," Ann's father explained.

"what did you ask her, Hec?"

"well, I noticed the deadline for the competition and worked out that Clara would have had to be in the hospice at the time, so I asked whether Samira could remember Clara doing such a quiz."

"and why is that important?"

"yes, she had, and what's more; Clara won the contest. The letter says that, due to changes within the company. . ." "a merger, probably. . ."

"likely, Glen," agreed his partner. "Anyway, they now decided to award the prize. . ."

"which was. . ."

"a trip around the world. . ." "for two?" queried Glen. "Yeah, what else."

The two men looked at each other, not quite knowing how to react.

"Do you continue to be eligible as the partner to the exercise, now that Clara is dead?" asked Glen, eventually, finishing his coffee as he was talking.

"I asked doctor Samira to tell me which magazine the quiz had been in; she'll ring me back. . ."

"something to look forward to. . ."

"oh yes," Hector emitted a long sigh.

"I also asked our standby lawyer whom to consult; not only did I want to use her. . ."

"who is she?"

"curious, Glen? Natasha Bertram; you know her?"

"yes, a youth lawyer; she took on a firm on unfair dismissal of one of our young internship clients. . ."

"and won, didn't she? The kid was a South Sudanese who had been fired for devoting too much time to coaching his mates in soccer. . ."

"yes, she got stuck into the company for neglecting its duty to the community and to disenfranchised youth, seeing that they made and marketed sports gear to. . ."

"among other people, youth," Glen reminisced.

"what did Natasha have to say; it seems that our paths tend to be littered with attractive not to say sexy women. . ."

"sight unseen! She suggested herself; for she is now an entertainment lawyer. . ."

"did you get in touch with her?"

"Her law firm is holding an Open Day, in honour of a partner of theirs who won a medal from the Uni of Adelaide."

"when, Hec?"

"want to come along? Day after tomorrow, Hatfield and Partners. You know them?"

"yes, close to Keswick train station. What time?"

"any time in the afternoon. I'll take time off which I am entitled to, to follow up on anything to do with Clara's death. . ." "which, of course, it has," Glen smiled.

❦

Natasha turned out to be an extremely attractive and incredibly attentive young woman; she shook their hands, made them sit down and listened intently.

"Sorry about Clara's death. . ."

"how do you know about it?" Hector was surprised.

"my aunt was in the same hospice as Clara; I have the advantage over you, and I know doctor Samira because of that. . ."

"How is your aunt if I may ask?" Glen asked.

"she is out of treatment and out of the hospice, for sure," the young woman informed them.

"healed?"

"It takes five tumour-free years to determine that; but yes."

"did Doctor Samira tell you?"

"about the quiz? Yes but not that Clara would have won it; that would have happened too recently, plus there is an issue of doctor-patient confidentiality involved; did she tell you what magazine the quiz had been in, Hector?"

"she faxed it to me at work today. . ."

"did you bring the fax?" "yes".

"could you find a back copy on the net or by asking the publisher for an archive search?"

"yes; is it all right to call you Natasha. . ."

"certainly; go ahead."

"I have a group of interns whom we train as researchers; field agents, to be precise; I'll get one of them to do that for me. . ."

"good practice," stated Glen.

"So it is," the lawyer agreed. "If I may suggest so, do show your appreciation to that young person afterwards without singling him or her out from your other trainees. I, in turn, shall get in touch with the publisher, once you find a copy of the magazine."

"isn't their decision final and not litigable?" noted Glen.

"Yes, but I can get a leg in; I take it that you, Hector, want to take Glen along?"

"either that or my daughter Ann, aged fifteen."

"if it is the magazine that I seem to remember Samira telling me about. . . have you got the letter on you, Hector?" He nodded. "May I have a look?"

Ann's father passed it to her; she read it and smiled.

"it's signed by my ex-boyfriend's sister. Adelaide is a village, I have known this for years. Words will be had, no doubt; do find that magazine, please."

Hector, even though his organizing ability had grown by leaps and bounds ever since his wife had died, knew, nonetheless, that it went nowhere near matching his daughter's; thus he decided to involve her and Julia in the search.

"We are on library duty on Wednesdays," she told her father.

"how many more days till they need to hear from you, Dad?" "Ten."

"what is Natasha the lawyer doing?"

"come and meet her next week, you and Julia; I think she knows the editor. . ."

"magazine editors do not like lawyers challenging them on the results of competitions," his future-lawyer daughter told him.

"Yet, what a lovely idea, to do a trip around the world together in honour of Mum. . ."

"and to celebrate being father and daughter one last time," her father added.

"do you want us to travel via Micronesia, Dad. . ."

"I am in two minds but probably, yes. . ."

Ann and Julia explained to the library teacher what they needed to find.

"We do have several online subscriptions, girls; I also have a few back copies at home. get to work, girls, and I shall ring my daughter. . ."

"is Nelly not at school?" Julia asked, surprised.

"no, she's got the bug, and she's got the test coming up, so I decided to keep her home, to build up her strength. I'll ring her and see if she can find the magazine. . ."

The girls got to work, found the title and scrolled through to back copies. . .

"Mum died in March, the competition could have been in February," Ann surmised.

"Jules, get on another screen and. . ."

"I'll look at early February while you do March and back till mid-February."

The next day, Natasha was a keynote speaker at a young professional women's gathering which she knew Nina, the magazine editor, would also attend. The two young women sipped wine before Natasha was to give her talk.

"Haven't seen you for ages," the editor beamed, the girls having kissed one another.

"Nervous?"

"a bit; I don't get to talk in public very often. . ."

". . .and you have to be careful, as a partner. . ."

"yes, you keep looking over your shoulder. . ."

("and what an attractive shoulder this is. . ." Nina thought)

"no wonder my brother was crazy about you," she found herself saying aloud, not meaning to; ". . .sorry; Tash. . ."

"change feet, Nina," her friend commented drily.

"would you wait for me until after the talk, or are you in a tearing hurry?"

"yes, Tash, I am; it is something to do with work?"

"yes, it does; I am trying to help a father and daughter whose mother has died to claim a trip around the world. . ."

"the quiz competition; you can't be serious, Tash; you know that the magazine's decision is final; how do you know that their mum did die?"

"I know the oncologist who treated her rather well; in fact, I was expecting her here; probably too busy. . ."

"oh, that Iranian girl," the editor replied. "She might be, it is working hours for many of us;" she smiled: "look, I shall wait; for I really want to listen to you also; we'll have another glass afterwards and you'll tell me about it."

The talk went well; the young women's faces lit up with every word the slender, passionate young lawyer had to say. As the talk progressed, Natasha warmed up to her subject while fighting images of Glen and Hector sitting in her office.

("What a strange relationship between the two; they are evidently neither gay nor emotional, yet very supportive of each other, and so incredibly attractive. . .?")

Shaking her head at herself, she continued with her talk on women-specific successful career strategies, surprised how much thought she had given to her own professional development.

("Maybe that's why Bart felt left behind," she remembered her former boyfriend, Nina's brother, members of a German-Russian family who had arrived in Adelaide from China in the years after Mao's takeover. Their last name was Barthold, namesakes and relatives of the once-famous linguist, people had called him Bart.)

"Excellent," his sister marvelled, over a glass of wine." it is good to see you in one piece and doing so well. . . you really inspired the girls. . ." she paused:

"Do you miss Bart in your life? Do you mind me asking, Tash?"

"yes and no; but he is alive and I hope that he finds someone. . ."

"he already has, lovely girl, different from you, very smart, very quiet, very loyal; but you wanted to talk about, I think, the woman who won our quiz competition." "would you tell me the winning line, please Nina?"

"oh yes, Mashed Potatoes; very silly, very weird, to actually get there."

"now, I asked Samira. . ."

"that's the girl's name; pity she isn't here; what did you ask?"

"she had talked to Clara about cities in Iran; for Clara, that is the now-dead wife and mother, had actually travelled in Iran several times; apparently, as soon as Samira pronounced Mashad in a particular manner, Clara had a brainwave, grabbed your magazine and completed your laugh-line: Mashed Potatoes, which Samira tells me is a way of spelling that city. Samira even posted her entry, duly signed by Clara. . ."

"who is now dead?"

". . . yes, incurable intestinal cancer, died in March."

"yes, we had a management takeover and I ended up being promoted," confirmed Nina;

"it took ages to get back to that competition; we had three winning entries and drew lots, none of the team being familiar with any of those particular entrants. That's why it took that long; the actual letter went out, say, five days ago; I signed it myself but I do many letters. . ."

"as I can imagine," the girl nodded.

"you've seen it, Tash?"

"I have it, Nina. The widower turned up with his new partner-strangely enough a man-"

"gay, Tash?" "no, but very close." "how come: you?"

"one of our senior partners won a medal from the University of Adelaide and asked that we held an Open Day in lieu of a celebration; we work with Hector's firm, a job provider. . ."

"and you, girl, are the in-house entertainment lawyer; I see the connection. Ok, what is up?"

"Hector wants to be able to claim the win, for two: I asked who he wanted to share it with, his partner. . ."

"did he?"

"no, his daughter."

"why, do you think?"

"so they can bond, away from work and school, have space to grieve and, at the same time, celebrate her mum's life by travelling around the world on her behalf."

The young women grabbed another glass of Riverland wine:

"Shiraz, in honour of Samira," Nina smiled, then grew thoughtful:

"you are a very naughty girl, Tash, for challenging the magazine on a quiz competition; still; we decide this as a Committee; if we can get the photo and story rights. . ." "hmm. . ."

"and if the girl's dad can organize a birth death and marriage certificate each. . ."

"in any particular order?" the young lawyer teased her editor friend.

"none, all in one piece, please; just to show that the young girl; her name, please?"

"Ann, she's applied for an internship with us; long-listed; she's still very young."

"to show that she is the actual daughter of Clara and, what's her father's name?"

"Hector Chalmers; he's a manager for Workfind;"

"a marriage certificate, please, and a death certificate to show that Clara did, indeed, die; you, as a lawyer, ought to understand the mindset of our own legal talent. . ."

"a bit painful but I am sure that I can persuade them on those documents; that's just typical bureaucracy; listen to me saying that. . ."

"coming from a lawyer," the other girl agreed.

"that bit about the picture and story rights; how would that work in practice, Nina?"

"either their own words and pictures, or else ours, and those from partner organizations around the world."

⁂

Ann and Julia were back in the library, this time to have a look at the actual magazine that the librarian had found for them.

"The feature on the quiz is on page seventy-five," she explained. "Do you girls know the correct answer?"

"Let's have a look," suggested Ann; "my mother was always very good with clues.... this is about Spiritual Journeys. . ." "like pilgrimages?" suggested Julia.

"probably. Let's go through the clues. . ."

"why, girls? Did your mum not solve it and would have won the prize had she lived?"

"yes, but I want to put myself into her mind once more," Ann replied, "plus, that lady doctor"

"the Iranian that your father keeps fantasizing about?" asked her lover.

"may have supplied the vital clue, such as, a Shi'ite pilgrimage, a valid alternative to Mecca. . ."

"what have we got so far?" the librarian asked.

"Potala. . . that's the spiritual centre of Tibetan Buddhism. Toledo; that's where the Camino Real ended. . ."

"not in Madrid?" wondered Julia.

"no, for one thing, Castilia and Aragon had not yet been joined. For another, it had to skirt the Muslim-held kingdoms still spread all over Spain at the time," the librarian, a history enthusiast, explained.

"we have yet to fit in the first clue," she continued. "now, Julia, you just said that the lady doctor who attended to Ann's mum was Iranian; have you girls met her?"

"yes, Julia met her twice and I a few more times; a very beautiful and elegant young woman; both my dad and his future partner are quite smitten with her. . ."

". . . explain, please, or perhaps, not; on second thoughts," concluded the librarian, "so she was Iranian, and your mum would have asked her for an answer, especially as it concerns a Shi'a pilgrimage. Let's ask Dr Google, then. List of Persian Spiritual Journeys. . . Qom. . . that sounds like a pun in bad French. . ."

"like Qoms frittes? 'ventured Julia.

"Yazd. . . such as in Jazzed-up, maybe on standby," the lady went on. "Isfahan. . . hits the fan; doesn't make much sense; Shiraz, wonderful wines, especially in our Riverland. . ."

"a spiritual journey going further than the Barossa; why not,." affirmed Ann.

"Mashad; also Mashed or Meshed-alternative spellings in English."
"Let's add it up,."

Julia, ever the analytical mind, spoke up:
"Mashed Pota-to: nutritious, simple, easy to prepare. Would you let us take photocopies. . ."

". . .that page and the front page, the one with the name of the editor and the publication details on it? Certainly; go for it, girls; haven't had that much fun. . ."

"would you say Hello and Thank You to Nellie, hope that she gets better?"

"yes, of course, girls!"

A few days later, Ann rang the magazine and was, eventually, put through to the editor, Nina, explaining why she was ringing.

"Ann. I am pleased you called," answered the young woman. "I was talking to Natasha. . ."

"the lawyer whom my dad and Mr Higgings contacted?"

"yes, I happen to know her. . ."

"I applied for an internship as a paralegal support worker in her office, but was it the right thing to see a lawyer about the result of a magazine quiz?." "No, Ann."

"would you like me to apologize on my Dad's behalf?"

"not really; us two girls worked out what to do, and I expect that Natasha would have reminded your dad to ring or see her"

"oh, he would like that; she must be very very beautiful. . ."

"aren't we all, Ann?" the editor laughed. "Yes, she is; let me give you a short answer; the magazine is happy to send your dad and yourself on a trip around the world, the one that your mum would have won and, presumably, taken your dad along."

"they were close and dad still misses her tremendously."

"how about you, Ann?" asked the young editor. "Consider me the older sister you never had. . ."

"not much older, I guess. . ."

"you are not wrong; but there are conditions, one to do with documents which your dad probably has or can get hold of."

"such as birth death and marriage cert's, you mean?"

"of course, you will be a lawyer one day; yes, the other is a condition that I'll let Natasha-called Tash-explain to your dad and. . ." "Mr Hiddings "yes."

"I know what to do," Ann decided," thank you very much. . ."

"call me Nina; if things go well; we'll see a lot of each other in the not too distant future," the editor added warmly.

Ann rang the partnership next:

"I'd like to find out about the paralegal internship I had applied for," she began;

"what about it?"

"I may have to delay it by a few months and do not want to disappear from your list because of that."

"I see; who do you want to talk about it, Ann?" asked the office manager.

"your partner who specializes on entertainment law. . ."

"would that be Natasha Bertram?"

"I think so, Madam; would you put me through, please."

"let me see if she's free; I know she's in," the administrator told her.

"Natasha Bertram speaking; what can I do for you?"

"Ann Landers here, Miss Bertram. . ."

"that's quick; call me Natasha. . ."

"your friend calls you Tash. . ."

"Nina does; yes, you must have been talking to her. . ."

"just now, Miss Bertram; I am ringing about two things; one is my intended internship as a paralegal's assistant; I would like to have it postponed; the other concerns the quiz competition that my mum won, except. . ."

"now she is dead, you wonder if your dad and yourself may 'inherit 'it?. . ."

"is that why you were expecting my father or myself to call you?"

"yes, Ann. Let me tell you that Nina Barthold, the editor, my friend, as you said, agreed in principle; she may have said as much, subject to some conditions. . ."

"which she indicated but not spelt out, fully, Miss Bertram."

"well, even though the two of us discussed, and agreed on them at a reception, not in my office or hers. . ."

"not involving a formal consultation, you mean?"

"yes, even then, there is confidentiality involved, not least because lawyers do not normally get involved with awarding the results of such quizzes. Do you know, by the way, what the winning entry was, Ann?"

"yes, Mashed Potatoes, and the clues were end points of spiritual journeys."

"did it say so in the letter that was sent to your family?"

"no, my future partner and I worked it out, with the help of our school librarian," Ann explained.

"could I ask you to be available, however briefly, to Jules and myself, as I do not want to take up any more of your time, nor enlarge on it over the phone. . ."

"in what context, if I may ask you, Ann?"

"it is related to the journey around the world, or at least one of the stops my father and I want to take. . ." "where?"

"Micronesia, actually Saipan, via Guam; and that is where it will impact on my future partner as well."

"you are making me curious; anything else that you would like to tell me now?"

"Do you know Professor Enderby?"

"Oh yes, we all do, but how. . . Brainwave; you aren't the two girls. . . and your father and. . ."

"Prof Enderby would have observed the strictest confidentiality, yet you must have. . .?"

"One of our senior partners was asked, on a hypothetical basis; so we did ask Prof Enderby; the very fact that he felt he could tell us almost nothing told us a lot. . ."

"I gather," agreed Ann. "When and where can we meet, yourself, Jules, myself?"

"early next week?"

"we tutor at the Refugee Association off Airport Road every Tuesday and Friday; Tuesday arvo after four-thirty?"

"take a bus to Light Square, girls; there's a glassware gallery with a café next door, wait for me; I'll ring the manager, we know them. . . do you want to meet my friend Nina, the mag editor, as well?"

"I was thinking of it."

"I see whether I can get her to join us there; seeing it involves both of us work-wise; leave it with me, Ann."

"thank you, Miss Bertram. Now, how do I go about postponing my internship?"

"leave that with me, also; I'll talk it over with the partner and our head of staff; you are on our list but you would have had to wait, anyway, for an opening."

The four arrived at almost the same time, Julia and Ann having raced off a 101 bus, whereas the young women had been struggling to find parking space in this central part of Adelaide at almost rush hour.

"What can we get you girls?" asked Nina, the editor.

"a pot of tea, please, green, if they have it," Julia ordered for the two of them.

"lime cordial for me, Nina," explained Natasha the lawyer;

"same for me," decided Nina and went inside the glassware gallery.

"rush hour is killing me," exclaimed Natasha; "how did you girls get here?"

"we used the Circle Bus and then nearly got stuck just off West Terrace, so we got off and ran to be in time."

"good on you, girls," said Nina, rejoining them at their table. "Your tea will be ready in a minute. . ."

"fifty-nine, fifty-eight, fifty-seven," Julia started counting backwards.

"don't take me that literally," laughed Nina.

"my lover Jules is a meticulous, literal-minded future scientist, much as I am the future lawyer."

"could we start with you, Ann?" asked Natasha. "Your mum would have won the trip around the world for two, herself and your father, I take it?"

"yes, had she lived. . ."

"look, I am sorry. Now, to listen to Nina here, her magazine can certainly accommodate you and your dad, provided he can organize some documents and allow them exclusive rights on what would be a moving story; you seem to want to extend that a lot further, it seems."

"yes," the girl answered. "First of all, one of our stops would be in Saipan, perhaps Guam. . ."

"that's in Micronesia, is it not?" asked the editor.

"Yes, we would like to visit Dr Mac Groom's specialist clinic for sex-related surgery. . ."

"whatever's next!" wondered Natasha.

"Can we rely on a degree of confidence?" Julia asked.

"You girls have our word, again in return for whatever exclusive may be involved."

"now, this would suit my dad; he expects to work there, in a few months' time, subsequent to his long-service leave. . ." "doing what?"

"run a youth training and employment programme for which his company is the preferred tenderer."

"what else has he got in mind which is to involve Dr Mac Groom?" the editor wondered.

"A sex change, that's what. . ."

All four were very quiet for a while, with the two young women obviously rendered at a loss for words.

"Whatever for, if we may ask?"

"Ann will explain it to you in a moment," Julia told them; "but let her tell you about our situation, first, because I shall also. . ." "become a boy?"

"Yes, Miss Bertram." More incredulous silence, punctuated by the pot of tea that chose to arrive at that very moment.

"Sugar, girls?" the waitress asked.

"nah, not for green tea, but thanks," courteously; "Ann," she continued: "tell Miss Barthold and Miss Bertram what we are on about; by the way, Miss Barthold, did your family live in Harbin or in Kashgar after they left Russia during the Revolution?" "We had relatives in both places, as far as I know; my mum and dad went back to China for the first time in decades. . . how did you know, Julia?"

"your family's illustrious relative, Vassily Barthold, who, it seems, was allowed to stay behind in St Petersburg, then Leningrad, and continue his work." Julia had six eyes set on her in amazement.

"My lover never ceases to amaze me," stated Ann, smiling.

"He would have been my great-great granduncle, to be sure," confirmed Nina.

"Many of us former Russians, or German-Russians, in our case, ended up in Adelaide once we had to leave China in the early Fifties; both mum and dad arrived as babies. But how come you know about Barthold the linguist; most people in Adelaide don't. . ."

"most people in Adelaide know very little," added the lawyer. "Do tell, Julia!"

"well, Stephen, my brother, he with the impossible girl friends, used to mentor a football team in his last year at school; one of the kids, Geoff, did you ever get to meet him, Ann? incredibly fast and aggressive, tiny bloke, was a history buff;"

"the one the other boys would tease, is that him?"

"yeah, they did, he was just different; he flattened them on the paddock; he's got drafted into the SANFL earlier this year. . ."

"what's that got to do with history, let alone my great-great-granduncle?" wondered Nina.

"my Dad is also a history buff; one day, Stephen brought him home and he spotted a volume of the man's essays on Ancient Iranian Inscriptions and asked Dad about it; we had to ask Geoff's dad to come pick him up well after nine pm, that evening; he turned up a few more times."

"what was the kid's background?"

"his mother is an Iranian Baha'i who had studied linguistics at the Uni of Adelaide. . ."

"Absolutely enlightening," commented Natasha; "now, Ann, put us in the picture, please; why does Julia need to be turned in to a boy, at Dr Mac Groom's clinic, no less?"

"because once she does, I shall be his one and only girl friend and, eventually, his loyal and obedient wife. . ."

"and you, Julia?" asked Nina.

"I offered to love Ann and spend my life with her; a boy is whom she wants in our relationship; I want her very much and wrote her an email on our school's intranet. . ."

"did that get you into trouble, lover!" agreed Ann: "I had this very special experience a short time before Jules declared. . ."

"do you want to talk about it?"

"no, except that it gave me an idea who and what my future partner ought to be."

"isn't it a bit unfair on Julia?"

"not really; we went to the Ethics Committee, as you seem to know, and got my own sex change approved, preferably on the basis that it did not happen in South Australia if I insisted on it being done before my sixteenth birthday;" Julia paused.

"Ann then contacted Dr Mac Groom who she found out, was about to be reinstated to the medical register. . ."

"that's how I remember the name," Natasha slapped her forehead; "wasn't he struck off for faux experiments?"

"yes," answered Julia, the budding scientist.

"now, my Dad wants to become my Mum, if you like," Ann took over the story; "in the sense that he, too, found a future partner, Glen Hiddings, a widower; to make it work, this, too, requires a sex change. . ."

"to be carried out by Dr Mac Groom as well?"

"or someone in his clinic, in case there was a delay in his reinstatement."

The two young women looked at each other: "You girls are not making this up, are you?"

"no, we are serious," replied Julia, somewhat annoyed; "as is Hector Landers, Ann's father, so to speak, and his partner; they, too, underwent stringent questioning by the Ethics Committee. If you doubt us, ask Prof Enderby," she concluded.

"he may be tied to confidentiality, Jules," Ann reminded her.

"not enough to be unable to tell you whether we are serious or not." retorted Julia sharply.

"if you girls allow me to sum up for the prosecution. . ." "or the defence. . ." Ann, cheekily.

"would you, Ann, want the magazine to award the trip to your father and yourself and also underwrite your dad's forthcoming sex change, as well as Julia's, so as to create the sets of relationships that both you and your dad are after?" The girls nodded.

"Nina, over to you. . ."

"girls, talk me through the difficulties you can see ahead."

"that's easy," explained Ann." Jules' parents have already agreed to the sex change, even to the extent of being prepared to see it happen in time for that sixteenth birthday, with reservations, to be sure. . ."

"why are we not surprised?" replied the young women, laughing.

Ann continued, unsmilingly: "My dad and Glen, his future partner, already have the Committee's permission to have Dad changed over by a professionally competent surgeon. . ."

"which Dr Mac Groom is, in all probability."

"so the two sets of people whom we would have to convince are. . ." Ann paused;.

"my parents and Dr Mac Groom. . ." commented Julia.

"why him, say?" asked the editor: "Oh, I see, he might not like the publicity, having only now been reinstated."

"nor might his employer," added Ann. "Have you, Miss Barthold, a very persuasive journalist on your staff, someone young but not too young, sexy but not overdone, very confident but not overbearing, a good emphatic listener,...."

"would you like a job, Ann?"

"I am already spoken for," replied the girl, "my internship at Miss Bertram's law practice."

"no flies on you girls," the lawyer approved. "Nina, have you got someone in mind such as Ann here described to us. . ."

"oh yes, Elanca; in her thirties, able to blend in, speaks several languages; she can make any company light up and gets on with women as well as with men. . ." she paused.

"Tash here and I will talk this over in the next few days; we do need to see your dad, Ann, and his future partner; this is such a weird proposition that it might work. . . Thank you, girls; where do you need to be dropped?"

Elanca Hartwig, the daughter of a wheat grower and vintner from the mid-North ("freezing in winter, I tell you") had been a key component of the journalistic husband-and-wife crack team of Grant and Elanca Hoogeveldt, inquisitive, persistent, chameleon-like in their respective ability to blend into almost any background, perceptive, observant, meticulous to a fault, pragmatic and very dependable.

In cultures and situations where women were expected to remain in the background, she did and contributed in that manner, while, at other times, she would go forth, smile and charm her way through every kind of obstacle, with her husband providing an invisible but distinct element of protection. Like many good things in life, their award-winning partnership did not last:

They had gone to Kirgistan to help one of Grant's colleagues, a former classmate from their Macquarie University days in Sydney, help unravel a massive water supply scam which had ruined several cotton-growing estates, when Tariq Kalmykov's house got blown up, with him and Grant in it, as would have Elanca, had she not been stopped at a roadblock.

A lady from the women's movement hid her for a few days, then smuggled her into the Australian Chancery garden, to the confused annoyance of several Australian diplomats who, nonetheless, managed her more or less orderly departure via Teheran, of all places, and Dubai.

Elanca then went back to her home state; having found work with the magazine, it did not look as if she would ever be adventurous again,

"Like a bird whose wings have been clipped", Nina had commented. "I am beginning to see signs that some feathers have started growing back, "she told Natasha two days later.

"bring her along," the lawyer suggested; "I have a spot free tomorrow afternoon; do you want me to pick both of you up somewhere?"

The days, while getting shorter, were still nice and pleasantly warm, the latest heat-wave having only just passed. The three women were walking through Enfield Cemetery, talking.

"I still find it difficult to wrap my brain around all this," admitted Elanca, her clear features showing the very first sign of attractive middle age.

"you are not the only one, Elanca," her employer told her.

"unpack, to start with, on why Ann wants Julia, or Jules, to become a boy;" offered the lawyer; "likewise, why her father is intend on becoming his partner's wife. . ."

"and thus Ann's mum, by default," continued the editor.

"if you can get us some pointers, good; for I am sure they exist, especially with the girls; otherwise, use it as an exercise in empathy, to get you into the mindsets of these four people," added the lawyer;

"something that you are very good at, better than anyone I know," confirmed the editor.

"am I the shuttlecock in your girls' verbal badminton?" the experienced journo queried, then laughed. "Did one of the girls have a light bulb experience, you think?"

"yes," the young women agreed.

"but how about her dad and, even more so, er, his partner."

"for you to find out and to determine whether you can use it or not; in any case, it will get you on track."

"next thing is, I'll have to get close to the other girl's. . ." "Julia's. . ." "parents. . ."

"which will take all your diplomatic skills, plus some;"

"even more so with Dr Mac Groom and his employer at the clinic; I am quite familiar with his case but I didn't realize where he had gone. . ."

"whether they'd like it rehashed. . ."

"I'll have to negotiate the conditions under which they agree to be in the picture. . .

"Dr Mac Groom has already been in touch with Ann and agreed to the operation, seeing that the Ethics Committee had cleared both. . ."

"yes, but nobody had thought of involving us, or any other media at that stage," objected the lawyer.

"the Ethics Committee will have to be consulted, too. . ."

"what with confidentiality?" the journalist wondered.

"ask Professor Enderby; he is not an actual member at present but he has ways of approaching them that won't breach the rules but support the story from their end. . ."

"or so we hope," admitted the journalist.

"you got your work cut out." stated her employer; "I don't know or have anyone who could do it better than you but, tell me, do you feel confident that you can do it by yourself; for you have always worked in tandem on such lengthy and complex stories. . ."

"with Grant, to be sure," Elanca concurred, "but I am ready; it won't bring him back but this is what I do for a living. . ."

"it's settled, then," the two young women looked at each other.

"draw us up a budget and a time-line and make some preliminary contacts by next week and finish or drop any other piece you are working on at the moment. . ."

"Carol is back," the journo reminded her boss; "she can take up some of my bits and pieces whatever I can't get done in the next few days."

"Right-oh, then."

The three women continued their walk and started talking about other things.

"Are you sure," Elanca asked the young women as they took their leave of one another at the cemetery gate,

"that one of them, Ann, most likely, had a life-changing experience sometime a year or so ago?"

"yes," her editor had replied unhesitatingly; "we put you in charge of finding out. . ."

"what if I do, Nina?"

"we rely on your journalistic skill to walk the girls through it without making it explicit, since it most probably involved underage sex. . ."

"or else I'd wreck the story before I even start; I can see that," agreed Elanca. "but how about the grownups?"

"it could involve loyalty and feeling out of sorts, being one half each in relationships that no longer exist," surmised the lawyer.

"not as powerful, maybe," asserted the editor;

"but every bit as real," concluded the journalist, speaking from experience.

※

Soon after her precipitate return from Central Asia, her editor had sent Elanca to Queensland; there she had been invited to cover a badminton tournament in Mackay and meet Australia's great next hope in badminton, Brian Chalmers.

"He coached and mentored some young players in your state almost two years ago," she had been told. "His mum was in Adelaide, on loan to your police academy for almost a year; he and his sister went, too."

"I'll ask the badminton association back home," Elanca had promised. "we were placed in Malaysia for a while and I followed the sport there," she told the organizers, "one of their coaches is now based in Adelaide."

"oh, that's Tariq Hasimuddin; we know him."

She then met and interviewed Brian Chalmers, watched him train and perform ("someone who is in control of himself, his tools, the court and his opponent, all at the same time" she marveled) and took photographs of him and his girlfriend, Heather ("I took a few days off work to see him, Elanca") and, eventually, got a few moments with the girl while Brian was working with his coach.

"I am proudly subservient to him," Heather admitted. "I made myself available to him on the evening of his sixteenth birthday, the first time we could do it legally; I willed him to take possession of my body and charge of my life. . ."

"did you have to order him?"

"not at all," asserted the girl. "But I am proudly owned-occupied by my present partner and future husband, much happier for it and not ashamed to show it."

"long-term, Heather?"

"as long as it suits Brian and as long as life itself permits it." "what made you do it?"

"his sister suggested it during a workplace party in his honour, Elanca."

"would you have made him bed you otherwise?" "eventually, yes."

did he have a slew of girls at his disposal before you, Heather? "A pitying smile:

"no self-respecting female would ever allow herself to resist someone like Brian!"

"he was in Adelaide for a while, was that before you. . ."

"became his? Yeah, his mum has come back to Brisbane only a few months ago; I am sure, before you ask, a few girls there would have found him as well."

"no doubt; so he had millions of them before you, none since?"

"none, other than myself. Ours is now an adult long-term relationship, however young he is. . ."

"you are rather older than he. . ."

"so what, Elanca?"

Elanca had often reflected on that conversation, even though she had never incorporated it into her feature at the time.

She had soon realized having experienced the same thing-'proud subservience '-but in reverse. Not only had Grant been fiercely submissive in bed, willing her to possess, immobilize and dominate him every night, but also determinedly subordinate to her at work, as often and as much as he could get away with it, much as a skilled accompanist brings out the best in a performer while steadfastly remaining in the background. The memory which Heather's comments had reinforced continued to cause her pleasurable pain, physically and otherwise.

Having gotten to know the girls, Elanca decided to test her hypothesis by telling them about that encounter, almost verbatim, as best as she could remember. "Now if you were to tell me that none of this relates to you, I'll accept it and do the best I can," she told the girls.

"if, say, you, Ann, were to tell me: No Comment, a wise decision, by the way, I'd apologize. One thing that I shall not do is try and develop this into a story in its own right."

"how do we know you won't and why are you telling us, anyway?" demanded Julia, sounding like the future lawyer that she would never become.

"because not only would you lose every bit of trust in me, I'd also wreck the feature which I was tasked to do by the magazine; not only would that lose me my job, I'd no longer be worth taking seriously."

"but why are you running this by us, Elanca? So Brian was in Adelaide sometime over a year ago and had scores of girls at his disposal, myself possibly among them, for argument's sake and to be denied if pressed," Ann stated, lawyerly: "but why go on about it if you do not want to elaborate on it in print?"

"succinctly put, Ann; because before I can even start on this feature of ours, I need to come to grips with whatever powerful motive is behind it."

"and what guarantee do we have, all four of us, that you will not put it in words somewhere in your story?"

"that's my task and my skill as a journalist not to have to," the journalist explained. "let me give you both an example: I myself experienced something of the kind but in reverse. . ."

"reverse," wondered Julia, the observant one;

"yes, in reverse but I would never, haven't ever, dwell on it; it is enough that you seem to know what I mean without my having to be incredibly explicit about it. . ." "in other words, you do not see yourself as a tabloid journo. . ."

"thank you, girls. Now, tell me, Ann, whatever is it that motivates your dad. . ."

"to undergo a sex change to fit his partner, same as Jules is prepared to do for me, so that he may be my future husband whom I promise to love and obey for as long as it takes. . ."

"there are certain kind of fish, and also worms who start life as being male then end up female," chipped in Julia, the future scientist," it could be that Ann's dad, long- term happily married to her mum, feels the need not only for another long-term partner to function the way he used to, as part of a tandem. . . sorry, Elanca, did we upset you; I forgot?" Julia was genuinely distressed.

"change feet, Jules!" Ann teased her friend. "Since Dad is not gay or bisexual, once he found his match, happens to be a man, he decided that a shift was in order," Ann took up the thread.

"to what extent that is emotional and in which sense you'd have to see it in biological terms as Jules does, is for you to work out and tell us but not in as many words, if you are the skilled journalist we believe that you are."

"you realize that I'll have to spend a lot of time with the two grownups, together and apart. . ."

"not easily done; they are always at work," commented Julia.

"moreover, I shall have to win over your parents, Jules."

"it may help them come to terms with my decision and my future," agreed the girl solemnly.

"Where would you like to start, and who with, Elanca?" asked her boss during their weekly editorial conference. "a timeline, to start with, Nina." "when and where?"

"I'd like everyone involved, that is the four of them, to be in Saipan, or at least Guam, in about six week, say, forty-five days from now, whether for work, as in Ann's father, home schooling and familiarization, or in a kind of countdown, as for Julia and, once again, Ann's father."

"as far as I know, Ann's dad is due for some leave, much of which he and Ann could spend on the bulk of their flight around the world. . ." "won by Ann's mother?"

"the one; we can control that, airline-wise, at least. Get one of our interns to work on that."

"how long can such flights around the world be undertaken?"

"a year from starting date, as a rule; I suggest you get Belinda to work on it. . ."

"I'll need to ask Ann's father to work out their itinerary with her and get him to clear both his long-service leave and his Micronesian consultancy with his boss, as well as arrange for extended leave for Ann, coupled with a very flexible home schooling system, within the next ten days. . ."

"Ann may have to join him somewhere; we can split their tickets if it means that she gets to leave just before the end of term, say, by mid-June. . ."

"I might have to visit St Brendan's, my sister is an alumna and I know people through her; I shall also need to contact Ann's father's boss, him first, then make myself known to Glen Hiddings'company. . ."

"he is very senior and perhaps a lot more flexible in what he can do and how long he can go away for. . .?"

"do I budget for him to stay with his future partner/wife for a length of time?"

"you may negotiate that with him."

"I need to bone up on Brendan Mac Groom," the journalist admitted;" I did not even realize that his reinstatement was anywhere near due, let alone that he had been gainfully employed in Saipan. . ."

"then you'll have to get in touch with him and his company, as tactfully but also as purposefully as only you can. . ."

"to assure them that some publicity will be unavoidable and that, in the long run, their enterprise will benefit."

"on the other hand, even with the degree of accommodation that the good doctor has promised Ann, the entire exercise would be unaffordable unless some media organization underwrote it. . ."

"the difference between Cleo and Geo. . ." they laughed.

"What's the most difficult thing that you have to do right now, Elanca?"

asked Gwendolyn, another reporter.

"Get Julia's parents onside, to agree to her extended absence, to home schooling. . ."

"which Dr Mac Groom has promised to help with and which we can part-fund, same as with Ann's," added their boss, "and not to revisit their decision to allow treatment and operation to go ahead within the next few months. The next difficult one is, definitely, reach an understanding with Mac Groom and his employer. . ."

"you may have to go see them. . ." advised yet another reporter.

"lucky Micronesia, the isles of permanent cyclones," intoned a young journalist.

"I have been there a few times on diving holidays," she said; "loved it but some of the inter-island shipping is barely past the copra stage, aircraft not much better, and the weather. . . we had some close ones, believe me!"

"It means," concluded Elanca, "that I shall make myself known to them soonest and get Gwendolyn find a suitable flight"

(The cheapest way of doing turned out to fly to Bali via Guam, then return via a low-cost airline connection to Adelaide via Kuala Lumpur.).

"Julia's family is next, within the very next few days," their boss ruled, then concluded the session.

Julia's parents were not inclined to want to see Elanca until their daughter got to work on them, receiving her brother's totally unexpected help.

"I know what it is like to make a girl happy," he told their astonished parents;

"you have done it often enough, to scores of girls; you should know," teased his sister.

"if Julia wants to be like me in that respect, why stop her; why should we, seeing that you have already agreed, in principle; plus, they agree to pay what we cannot afford, however much the clinic is about to bend over backwards. . ." realizing that his parents were still very doubtful about the situation, he suggested:

"Let me and Erin. . ."

"good grief," moaned his sister," how do you keep track of them all; she must be number. . ."

"be quiet, Sis, it is all for the good cause of equipping you for life. . ." "listen to him!"

Eventually, the three young people bearded Elanca at her office and were won over, as was Elanca.

"'course, I'll meet your parents in the Barossa Valley this weekend; my cousin owns a winery near Truro; we can all spend the nights there, Friday through to Sunday; they've asked me often enough and they have chalets on site."

"Ann is a very nice girl," Julia's mum admitted, "and we'd love her to continue to be Julia's friend; we cannot quite understand her determination, nor Julia's. . ."

"at first, we thought it was rather evil," her husband admitted. "We know that it is not; we have just never met with such willpower, both of them."

They were sitting on Elanca's cousin's winery's verandah, having been invited for tea on Friday evening, over bottles of homegrown pinot,

"our specialty and a good year, to be drunk only in very good company," their host had assured them.

"we had an excellent autumn and expect a good harvest," he shared, "not too much crush but outstanding quality,"

"it is always a bit of a trade-off, is it not?" suggested Jules' brother's latest girl friend, an obvious descendant of South Australian vintners and winemakers.

"Yes, and the price even for good wines is not crash-hot, either, good year or bad."

They all sat quietly, sated, taking in the beautiful country with its productive, busy atmosphere, at the end of a worthwhile day. Julia's parents, in particular, were so obviously more at ease than they had been in years, warmed by friendship, enchanted by this surprise invitation and amazed at the sense of unstated purpose they felt all around them.

"Cherish this moment," Julia's dad admonished; "it won't come back precisely like that, ever."

"life is for the living. . ."

"and death is for those who are alive," added Elanca. "Don't say that you are sorry for me; Grant did die quite senselessly but there is a purpose in what we do while we live; his death is a reminder. . ."

("single by default, facing three couples of different ages and configurations," she thought; "four if my cousin and her husband count")

"what I miss most is the purpose and sheer energy that goes into building a workable relationship," she continued, "young people faced with constant breakdowns, the generation of their parents' divorcing, their own first few attempts failing, often quite spectacularly and disastrously. . ."

"what are you trying to say about Julia and Ann?" Julia's mother had 'inherited 'her daughter's perceptive nature.

"constructive polarity," Elanca replied, without having reflected on that answer, as surprised as everyone else.

"meaning?" wondered Julia's brother.

"in a relationship, people grow into one another. . ."

"Julia, is that true?" asked her brother's newest girl friend.

"yes, except that I want to become what Ann sees in me which is also part of her own outlook; she's wanting to become the one I had sworn to devote my life to. . ." Jules replied.

"sounds. . . pulp novel. . ." confirmed her brother,

"perhaps," agreed his sister, "but it got me into trouble from day one. . ."

"how so?"

"I wrote it all down on intranet, then deleted all trace, or so I thought, except that the system chose that very moment to break down; they called the specialist who went and retrieved everything off every single hard disk, in case that's where the fault was. . ."

"was it?" asked Elanca.

"no, but they recovered a very explicit statement which our IT supervisor took exception to."

"is a relationship worthless unless you are prepared to get into genuine trouble for it?"

wondered Erin, looking at Julia's parents.

"yes," everyone around the table answered in unison, including Elanca's cousin and her husband.

The vintner refilled everyone's glass to a moment of thoughtful silence.

Nobody wanted to spoil the magic of the scene; dusk had turned into a starlit night, with the wine storage bins lit from a reflected distance and a low but busy hum permeating the atmosphere, as also the scent of slowly fermenting wine.

"what are your plans for Julia, Elanca?" her father asked, after what seemed hours.

"if you agree, I can organize a flexible online home-type schooling to start as of early July; at around that time, I imagine everyone to be in place,, in Saipan."

"is Julia to start treatment there and then?" asked Erin.

"that will depend on Dr Mac Groom and his staff, but yes, that's the idea."

"how about Ann's dad?"

"likewise if that can be managed."

They sat around a while longer, none wanting to get up and make the evening come to an end; eventually, Elanca's cousin's husband stretched and yawned.

"starts at quarter to five; I'm getting some enzyme in and need to get another tank ready; temperature control's already been set up. Good night all. . ."

"thank you, Kev and Doreen," Elanca assured the couple;

"good night and thank you for a lovely evening," they chimed in and watched, with a smile, Erin dragging her lover off. . . "busy night ahead. . ." commented his sister. "I miss Ann. . ."

Her parents smiled, for the first time in weeks, took each other's hands and walked off.

"we are at fault," Julia told the reporter; "we should have organised a 'controlled dirty weekend' a lot sooner; thank you, Elanca!"

"good night, Jules; unsafe dreams. . ."

Elanca had decided to head for Guam within a week after her time at her cousin's place in the Barossa which had proved so inspirational to Julia's family. She had sent and received several email from Brendan Mac Groom whose background she had researched; unsurprisingly, they had turned up mutual friends.

He was waiting for her in Guam, only weeks after a particular tenacious cyclone had hit the small island state.

"I saw scenes like that in East Timor," she explained.

"oh, right after the referendum," he agreed.

"you know, Brendan?" surprised.

"even though I was not licenced at the time, I was asked to lend my expertise to a visiting team. . . Dili hospital had that one American doctor, a few Timorese nurses, two Javanese orderlies married to Timorese girls, almost no equipment and half of it ransacked by the militia, on orders by the departing military to leave no infrastructure intact. We trained seminary students from Dare to survey their villages for drinking water, food storage and locally available medicinal herbs and herbalists; one such in Atauro ended up looking after Sydney-based Sister Shirley's abdominal cancer." "Yeah, I knew her, a Jesuit language teacher," Elanca remembered.

Dr Mac Groom had access to the university medical hospital guest-house with a view over the bay, close to the naval base,

"that is about sixty percent of the main island, Elanca," he explained.

They went into the kitchen and he cooked a meal which they carried out to the verandah.

He opened two bottles of San Miguel,

"cheers, Elanca, welcome to Micronesia. . ."

They ate the simple meal, Thai noodles, a pungent Vietnamese fish sauce, squid and a stew of steamed pineapple and finely-chopped rose-apple afterwards, using chopsticks throughout.

"you look happy and relaxed," commented the doctor, "you must be dead on your feet. . ."

"jetlag will hit me tomorrow," Elanca said, speaking from experience.

"I learnt to eat sleep and do everything at the same time as everyone else, as soon as you arrive."

"what I have in mind for tomorrow may help you adjust even quicker. . ."

"please, explain, Brendan?"

"we are heading for Saipan by boat, starting early in the afternoon. . ."

"and get there early the day after tomorrow. . . won't it be rough?"

"it may turn out to be," the doctor conceded, "the last cyclone-typhoon -was only six weeks away. . ."

"is the cyclone season over?"

"no, but we have had no wind warning and we expect no immediate weather change. . ."

"it'll be an experience," agreed the reporter; "I haven't been on a boat on the Pacific for years. . ."

"when was the last time, love?"

Elanca tried not to show her surprise at the term of affection:

"Grant and I were doing a story on the partial ceasefire in Western Mindanao, so we travelled by boat with some hundred illegal immigrants being sent back from North Borneo. . . we were shocked at seeing twelve dozen belts being flung on the ground just before the boat left Sandarkan. . .l"

"to restore what these people could have used to hang themselves with;" surmised the doctor.

"do you know that one of my trainees, a girl medical student from Biskek, knew Tariq. . ."

"our fixer in Kirgistan. . ." a look of momentary dismay crossed her face. "The world is a small place. How come, though?"

"seeing that I am yet to be reinstated. . . three days from tomorrow, by the way," the doctor answered her unspoken question.

"the université refugière uses me as a lecturer and consultant; we work to maintain academic levels among refugees and displaced people whose education was interrupted; Gulnar was useful in Kirgiztan whose ethnic Uzbeks were in conflict with the new government after a coup some five years ago; likewise we had her in Afghanistan to help with displaced members of Ahmed Shah Massood's. . ." "the Uzbek warlord. . ."

"yes, part of his clan; women have some standing in that community."

"When did you give up that work, and why, if I may ask, Brendan?"

("this is the first time in years that I have had an interest in a man, who he is, what he does, what he might be like in bed," she wondered; "am I finally getting over Grant, or do I merely miss the challenge of discovery, meeting someone for the first time?").

The doctor sat back, finished his beer and thought:

"how do I best put it, Elanca?" he wondered. "The Ethics Committee. . ."

"the same that my charges had to answer to, back in Adelaide?"

"it was their ex-liaison with the Medical Association. . ."

"Professor Enderby?" she guessed, surprised.

"yes, he intimated that I'd be reinstated provided I could get meaningful long- term clinical employment anywhere in the world whose medical standards were recognized. Here, it is quite difficult to attract and keep medical staff at almost all levels; for with the training available here, people can work anywhere, the US, the Middle East. . ."

"wherever pay is high; yes"

"what people do not realize that, while life is not exactly cheap, people can and do save here; for much is provided and a lot that you'd pay money for does not exist here; then you often get some very inclement weather, without much notice."

"are you trying to deter me from tomorrow's trip?"

"no, I would not dream of it; for if the weather holds, it will be a most special experience, believe me. . ." he assured her.

"anyway; so this entrepreneurial clinic of ours got in touch with the people who started universite refugiere, assured them that I would be available to them once every fifteen months and put me on contract as a director-cum-consultant. The university here offered me partial tenure as a nutritionist; for that was part of my original training, not affected by deregistration; now that I have not significantly blotted my copybook as far as the ethicists are concerned and have had these years of fulltime work under my belt, plus some uncontested peer-reviewed publications to my credit. . ."

"will you be formally reinstated. . ."

"no, but unless I, or my employer, are notified otherwise, I am to so consider myself by the end of this week. Now, tell me a bit more about how you spent these last few years. . ."

"after Grant and Tariq's murder?" she averred. "Well, I ended up in Teheran, of all places, immersed with the affairs of a group looking after women inmates of Evin Prison."

"whatever's next!" smiled the doctor.

"whatever was next was the Australian embassy there getting very nervous; for many of these girls were only a hair's breadth away from jail; so someone contacted my people in South Australia and Nina's predecessor at the magazine got to hear about it and agreed to do a feature on the girls if I were ready to leave them forthwith. . ." "did the women mind?"

"no, they wanted their story known, with some precautions; that was a full year after these massive demonstrations all over Iran. . ." "the Stolen Election?"

"yes; they urged me to leave them and make their experience known; the magazine did a series. . . then stopped it part-way; a few more girls got arrested and the group had to lie low for a while. . ."

"are they back in business?" "oh yes, Brendan."

She noticed that her hand was firmly held in his by now but made no move to withdraw it.

"Nina took over as their editor-in-chief and, young as she is, she noticed how shell- shocked I really was; so I have had some fairly bread-and-butter assignments till now. . ."

"so she must feel that you are up to some risk and challenge in your working life, love."

"definitely," the reporter agreed.

"you'll have your work cut out persuading my people, employer and staff alike, that publicity won't turn into notoriety. . ."

"given the nature of this unusual double sex change, can it be entirely avoided?"

"so, in other words, let a true professional do an exclusive job which we can control and which she is – you are-capable of writing up as delicately" "and intriguingly. . ." "as possible. . ."

"thus enhancing your reputation, if anything. Let's talk about it tomorrow, on the boat trip. . ."

"which is another reason why you chose it over a quick flight."

"yes, and the fact that we have an understanding with the service that I act as a standby medic so I shall share a cabin with the ship's doctor during the voyage. . ."

"talking about cabins, Brendan. . ."

"would you like me to show you. . ."

"no, would you like to share my bed tonight?"

"I'd be honoured; if you were a future patient or any close relative or such I would have to refuse, with great regret; if you feel that, as a journalist. . ."

"consider it borderline, Brendan; but do pass passport control and customs on that one. . ."

"so, if you are ready to re-join the world of. . ."

"energy, passion and purpose; forgive me if I am out of practice. . ."

"permanently granted; it goes without saying. . ." he concluded graciously and guided her away from the verandah.

He made her caress and then mount him:

"so you get a feel what it is supposed to be like. . ." he had explained.

Elaine started to ride him, hesitantly at first, but fiercely only moments later, her iron grip almost crushing his balls. Brendan placed his hands on her knees, in supplication, his eyes closed as he experienced her onslaught. She leant her arms on his chest, almost as if she were to revive him after an accident, then lowered herself down on top of his entire body, forcing his legs apart and pinning his arms down, kissing him almost angrily, her body remembering the way she used to make captivatingly aggressive love to her husband.

She made Brendan come several times and felt herself lose control, yet careful not to scream out.

She surprised herself with the sheer force whereby she had cuffed his wrists and bit his shoulders and upper arms, careful not to leave a tell-tale mark on his throat, much as she was tempted to.

Brendan tried to rear up but was held down firmly, possessively, and made to feel the weight and texture of her entire body. Eventually, she raised herself up, made him kiss her hands, wrists and upper arms, then urged him to roll over while she rested herself on his back, her hands continuing to explore him. Finally, they both fell asleep, back to back.

It was with some difficulty that Brendan was able to get up and make breakfast next morning but he did, toasting brown bread previously bought at a local bakery, with passion-fruit jelly, cooking porridge with goat's milk and arranging fruit salad consisting of papaya, rose-apples, slices of mango and bits of mangosteen, with Elanca asleep from her exertion. He covered the dishes on the balcony then entered their room, slowly lifted the sheet, finding her breasts while he kissed her awake.

"Come inside me," she demanded.

"no, your night of unbridled whatever that was is over; "he explained;" breakfast is ready and we need to get going."

"why?"

"hostel rules; unless we were to stay another night. . ." "can't we?" she demanded, still half asleep.

"wish nothing more than that; there's a boat leaving. . ."

"tomorrow?"

"no, every three days. . ." "we fly. . ."

"no, I am on call as an extra," he reminded her. "work is calling. . ." she was slowly waking up to where she was. "yes, for both of us, I am afraid," he confirmed. "a deluxe tropical breakfast is ready. . ." "describe it to me. . ." Elanca stretched her arms out towards him lazily, hungrily. "we'll have to repeat this under the shower". "that can be done," he obliged, "but it will have to be a quickie. . ."

And so it proved to be, with her sliding effortlessly on top of him inside the shower tub under a gentle setting of an umbrella of slightly more than lukewarm water, hoping for their delight to be drowned out, bathroom acoustics notwithstanding.

After their lavish breakfast, Brendan took Elaine for a tour of Guam University where he taught nutrition on a block basis, then stopped at a waterfront restaurant. . .

"for an early lunch and a drink before we board; we'll get a feed on board but it 'll be several hours away. . ."

"after such a breakfast?" she objected.

"nothing that a few squid and a glass of Californian wine cannot fix," he assured her, so he fed her garlic-roasted squid with fried sweet potato and taro chips which she ate with relish, amazed that she would be this hungry.

He cheered her as they drank their wine:
"under different circumstances, I'd drink to a lifelong relationship, love," he assured her.
"I know you are married; how and where is your wife?"
"Elaine is about to undergo an operation. . ." "oh, what am I to say?" she said, her mood spoiled.
"you did ask; you have nothing to blame yourself for; I wanted what you offered last night and I am grateful; we will not be able to repeat it, ever. . ."
"you may have news there, Brendan," she announced. "What is she being operated on, or for; it'll be one of your colleagues, won't it?"
"hysterectomy, love, and yes, Norman, a specialist surgeon of ours; she'll be in good hands with all of us. . ."
"I'll keep it in mind and I would definitely not want to be in her situation, but she's got you. . ."
"and I do not want to change that; for she stood by me when nobody else did, family and former friends and colleagues. . ."
"when you would have given mud a bad name," she realized, taking and kissing his hand.

"I was almost never out of work, even after I had been struck off the register. . ."
"for inventing an entire set of experiments,"
"you have done your homework on me, as I did on you, it goes with the job,"
he agreed, taking another sip of wine and helping himself to a taro chip, fried in coconut sauce.
"strange thing is, someone modelled his team's experiments on mine and got very similar results to the one I postulated; any explanation? To get back to Elaine: she stuck with me and I am to stick with her in what she is to go through. . ."
"even though you'll never again 'know 'her in a physical sense?"
"it is a small price to pay, don't you think?"
"I agree, and my purpose of coming here was not to tempt you but to enable my Gang of Four to. . ."
"have their lives changed; we need to talk about how to persuade my employer. . ."
"to allow me to feature them, and you, in their story. . ."

"with great delicacy, love; tempting me once again may not be wise strategy, even though I am grateful and wouldn't have wanted to miss the experience. . ."

They finished their food and wine, still holding hands; once inside the car, she massaged his tool while he was driving; he did not stop her, pointing out stunning tropical scenery, instead, much scarred that it was in the aftermath of the cyclone. At one stage, he stopped and let her continue to arouse him, kissing her and feeling her breasts. The sound of a distant siren stopped them both:

"that is the first embarkation call," he reminded her. "How much time left?"

"half an hour. . ." "is that enough?" "barring the unforeseen, yes."

The 'unforeseen' involved a police roadblock; yet the officers recognized him and let him through:

"I am on standby on the boat and Mrs Hartwig needs to be on it, for her work. . ."

"what work, doctor?"

"she's doing a feature on the clinic."

"okay, doctor Brendan; I'll radio the next squad and ask the harbour-master's office to hold the boat till the two of you get there," the platoon sergeant assured him.

Brendan had a designated parking lot with the port authority; he left the car keys with an attendant whom he knew. . .

"Gavin from the lab will pick it up; I rang him earlier, Troy."

"certainly, doctor; I think I know him, otherwise I'll ask for his licence. . ."

"get him to tell you the vehicle number without looking if you are in doubt," the doctor suggested.

"never thought of that," the attendant replied and spoke into his radio:

"Dr Mac Groom has just arrived with his visitor. . .;" he listened, then replied: "can be done. . ." opened the car door again and said, "Dr Mac Groom, they want me to drive the two of you right to the quai, drop youse at the gang-way and take the car back to the parking lot." "Thanks, Troy," they said simply.

The voyage was uneventful weather-wise; Brendan sought out the doctor and the two ship's nurses and they were invited to pre-dinner drinks by the captain who also found time to point out a few dolphin at play several hundred yards away, seemingly unperturbed by the craft and its many passengers watching and filming them, Elanca included. The sea and the atmosphere were calm. With Brendan being able to spend time with her, Elanca felt more at peace than she had in quite a while;

("I must have missed intelligent caring company more than I thought" she decided, realizing that she was being unfair to her colleagues:

"yet they have lives, and families, to go back to, whereas I. . .")

"but what you told me today puts things in perspective. . ." "meaning. . ."

"I may miss a man in my life, you or someone like you, but I don't anticipate being operated on; nor am I in the situation that many people I have reported on or that you have worked with. . ."

"true, love, and we need to remember this at all times" he confirmed, holding her hand against his cheek and leaning her against the railing.

"What is your managing team like?" she asked, in a more relaxed mood than she would have thought possible; the clear sky was dotted with a few high clouds and warmed by the late afternoon sun.

"I am part of it, you realize; my bosses know their stuff and expect everyone else to do likewise; they'll cut you some slack because they hate turnover and want to keep the entire team together for as long as possible. . ."

"how did they react when Ann first contacted you?"

"what do you expect? Surprise, of course; then a few leisurely enquiries in Adelaide. . ."

"with other media?" "Naturally."

"did they find out much?"

"enough to know it was kosher and had been approved by the Ethics Committee, with some gnashing of teeth. . ."

"did they ask you, Brendan, to follow up with any of your contacts?" she asked, pressing his hand.

"you know I cannot really answer that but I 'll reply Yes or No correctly if you ask me the right question and if I know. . ." "Professor Enderby?"

". . .was a classmate at some stage; I somehow picked up his idea of using the girls' stories for a series of learned papers. . ."

"to be peer-reviewed, Brendan?"

"yes; I'll show you once I have a rough draft. . ."

"which will be a few months away, at least, seeing that treatment is yet to start."

"was that Professor Enderby's idea, to begin with. . ."

"not only; the clinic decided to follow up a reference, people who were eager to have a systematic account of what our Gang of Four is about to undergo. . ."

"adaptive sociology?"

"yes, that's what the paper will be about."

"was that enough motivation for the centre to go ahead with the operation?"

"yes, even to remit the medical costs for Julia/Jules; for hers will be a far more complex sex change operation. . ." "likewise Ann's father!"

"agreed," concurred the doctor," except that 'he' has a job while here, apart from his long-service leave. . ." "due to start about now."

"So the centre is not averse to some well-focused recognition. . ." "well put!"

"and prepared to go easy on some of the quite immense costs. . ." "right!"

"but, you do realize, unless the costs for Julia's parents to be here at times, for support, for 'her' and Ann to live here, go to school, do their long-distance schooling and, finally, for Hector and Glen to remain here, were underwritten, they'd be hard put to go through with it, much as they battled the Ethics people in Adelaide to be allowed to.".

"even with Ann's father earning."

"some of the time. 'he'won't be able to. . ."

"I know, all of them need all the help they can get;"

"so do I need to stress to your management team that what I intend to do matches what the academics have already offered, by encouraging you to publish, except that we are ready to support Glen Hector Ann and Jules over and above what the centre is able to do. . ." summarized the reporter.

"You'll also have to demonstrate that your feature is as informative as it is non- intrusive; can you show us samples?"

"your team must have done some homework on me already. . ."

"I certainly have, love; I am glad that you are here!"

The clinic had sent a car which Brendan drove to deposit Elanca at a home- stay, "run by the parents of Rosetta, our office administrator; they'll treat you like family, it won't bite your budget to bits and it is walking distance to the clinic. You are expected at a meeting this afternoon; Rosetta's parents invited the both of us for lunch which is when I pick you up. Whatever the outcome, consider this your home while you are here, my love. . ."

"is Elaine at the clinic now and do you want me to see her, Brendan?"

"yes; I'll take you there after our board meeting and you can spend as much time with her as you wish. She'll like that; I can't devote as much time to you as I should; for I also have to get home and keep our household organized; Elaine won't be able or allowed to lift even a finger after that operation. . ."

Rosetta's parents had a cup of green tea and some plantain mesh, sweetened with raw cane sugar, ready for Elanca's breakfast:

"you are more than welcome, Elanca; I am Iris and this is Thomas, Rosetta's parents; Doctor Brendan is bringing her home for lunch which we will all have together, even though she normally eats at work. . . how does smoked shark with kangkung in coconut sauce and treacled green papaya stew sound, washed down with palm wine and mineral water. . ."

"for strictly medicinal purposes, I gather?" asked the reporter innocently.

"as a digestif, to be sure," her host assured her.

Elanca was amazed at the sheer appetite she had developed, in more senses than one. She walked around the house with its view, and smell, of the mangroves and its proximity to a jetty, then decided to lie down, massaging herself not only to revive memories of lovemaking but also to find some sleep; for it had been her misfortune to have shared a deck-side cabin with four matrons, all of whom snored like saw-mills. Sleep did not elude her, nor did pleasant memories, a not altogether unwelcome change from her state of semi-conscious attentiveness, burdened by grief and shock as she had been only a few days before.

She would have dearly loved to rest once again after the lavish lunch that Rosetta's parents had laid on, Rosetta having proved to be a tiny, rotund, cheerful but obviously very alert young woman who kissed her mum's hand and forehead and embraced her father, leaning against him, before they went to eat.

Elanca was seated between her and Brendan, with her mum and dad facing them across the table.

After a round of collective belching, everyone got up, finished their drinks- clear distilled palm extract diluted with soda water, going excellently with the smooth taste of smoked shark-and headed for the verandah where a pot of coffee was waiting.

"I'll need this to keep me awake," Elanca commented, wedged against Brendan; "I'll need all my senses about me and not offend your board by falling asleep."

"They'd forgive you, dear;" opined Rosetta's mum, "you must be jetlagged and you can't have had much sleep on that boat." "too right," agreed the reporter, yawning.

Somewhat later, she was sitting in the clinic's conference room, pots of tea and coffee and bottles of water placed in front of all. The clinic's director, a Micronesian of Filipino descent named Rodriguez, welcomed her with green tea and commented:

"We understand that your magazine is prepared to underwrite costs accruing to Mr Landers and Miss Childers in full or in part, those that Miss Landers might incur, as well as those of Miss Childers' parents, should they decide to stay with us for various lengths of time. . ."

"especially those, as Jules' parents could not otherwise have her here, your own offer notwithstanding, let alone themselves arrive to be with her/him," Elanca began.

"an act of kindness, no doubt," commented the director.

"we are also prepared to bear the full costs of Mr Landers treatment and residential stay here so that he can finance his daughter's time and schooling here with which we may also help. . ."

"have you a budget, Mrs Hartwig?" "Elanca, Sir."

"first-name basis it is, then; agreed, gentlemen; Doreen and Marguerita",

addressing two very attractive and competent-looking youngish ladies whom Elanca knew to be medical specialists, from her previous research.

"then I am Gordon; pleased to have you here, Elanca. Have you got some financial statements, such as a bank guarantee, on you.?"

The reporter opened a folder in front of her; she had come prepared.

"let me discuss that with your accountants, if you like. . ."

A bespectacled wizened man answered.

"I am Maxwell, not Maxwell Smart but Maxwell Carangoonan; the financial controller or, if you like my more imposing title, the Chief Financial Officer. Could I keep this copy, for me and my staff to study?"

Good manners forbade his stretching out his hand, even though he clearly wanted to.

Elanca, noticing, smiled:

"Let me keep a copy, Maxwell; you may have this one," sorting out her documents. "yes, as Gordon already commented, looking after young Miss Childers' parents while the girl is to undergo her gender alignment, would constitute an act of kindness; for we were worried, seeing that the clinic is only prepared to bear the girl's strictly medical and not any residential costs, let alone those of her parents; we were less concerned about Mr Landers and his daughter; for he will be here in an earning capacity, as I understand," said the accountant.

"to the best of my knowledge, acknowledged Elanca.

"that, once Maxwell is satisfied with the financial arrangements your magazine is prepared to make, leaves us with the task of deciding whether such publicity as a feature in your magazine is bound to generate amounts to unwanted notoriety or can be of some advantage both to us and to the pioneering sexual surgery that we are capable of," challenged the director.

"Elanca, would you address yourself primarily to our public relations and marketing officer, Diego Kinoskusan? Diego, over to you,"

he nodded to a slim, somewhat Mongolian-looking man, a pale image of a young ChouEnLai, perhaps, it seemed to Elanca.

"as you would have gathered, we did some research on your magazine and on your contributions, in particular, Elanca," the marketing manager began. "Let me say, on a purely personal level, that I liked your story about the Iranian girls working with female prisoners; pity, your magazine felt compelled to cut the series short. . ."

"for good reasons, Diego. . ."

"to be sure; let me say, on behalf of all of us, sorry for the loss of your husband in the course of his work, and yours; it shows how dangerous genuine journalism is, in this day and age. . ."

"thank you, all of you!" Elanca stood up and bowed.

"Now, some of us have read some more of your work, Brendan here, myself, Doreen and Marietta, from before you joined the magazine. Let me say that your magazine made a good choice."

He stopped and looked around.

"I want to state, on behalf of this board: I am authorized to offer you a choice: stay here for a few days, choose material for a mini-feature about us, not related to your magazine's clients, then write and illustrate it to the best of your ability- use our help if need be-and submit it to us, so that we can judge for ourselves; or else find material, your own or any that your magazine may have featured, with or without your input in the last seven years, to convince us that their approach-and yours-suits our need to be recognized for who we are and what we can do, without sensationalizing our work in general and the forthcoming operations in particular, however drastically unexpected these may appear."

The director concluded;

"be our guest, anyway, to get a feel for us, then tell Diego how to proceed; we'll give you a few days, say, a week, regardless of your choice. Are Rosetta's parents looking after you well?"

"yes, Gordon; thank you for your understanding ; you, Maxwell and Diego, also; I hope to get to know the rest of you also," the reporter addressed the board and sat down, sipping some tea.

The rest of the board meeting dealt with mundane things, day-to-day items necessary for the smooth running of the business. She noticed how well the team got on, with nobody pushing or trying to outshine others and everyone knowing each others' strengths and weaknesses, even making good-natured fun of them.

"Any other business?" asked Gordon, in his role as the convenor.

"yes, as your guest, if I may. . ."

"Elanca has the floor," he agreed.

"let me thank you for your friendly and very professional reception; let me also share with all of you the kind of feature I have in mind in the next few days which will help you, the team, get to benefit from an outsider's insight; I, in turn, get to understand the workings of this rather unique establishment from a somewhat unexpected perspective: I'd like to get to know, follow and interview some of your service personnel, your auxiliaries if that's what you call them.

They aren't likely to be your top earners attracting any attention but their contribution must be invaluable; would you not notice if they weren't working behind the scenes?

I'll run the details past Diego and also Rosetta, to be guided in the right direction, such as timetables, shifts, security and workplace safety, the nuts and bolts of your clinic and those who handle them every day. . ."

The team looked at one another with some surprise, then smiled and nodded. "A wonderful morale booster," said one who had been quiet throughout.

"a good recruitment device," commented another.

"a look at what we need to remember to appreciate. . ." stated Marietta.

"could you and Diego talk to us during lunch?" offered Doreen.

"that might be a good idea," admitted Gordon; "we'll catch up with those on different shifts. Could we have a show of hands, please? Those in favour of Elanca doing a feature on our support staff. . . Everybody? Motion passed; thank you, Elanca. . ." followed by clapping of hands:

"close of business, four-thirty pm; let's go back to work. Diego and Rosetta, take Elanca for a guided tour, please, and drop her at my office before you finish for the day."

Elanca, Rosetta and Diego started on their rounds, with the reporter taking some pictures of work areas she intended to cover by observing and interviewing the people responsible for their upkeep.

She also measured how many steps it took to move from one section to the next. . .

"where did you learn workplace assessment like that?" Rosetta asked.

"interviewing a workplace trainer and assessor in Adelaide last year for a feature on the mechanics of workplace safety for women. . ."

"have you an upload of that article?"

"yes, inside our electronic archive; will tomorrow morning do?"

"why don't you use my parents' setup tonight, how long will it take you?"

"is your net servicer slow?"

"web service can be; our intranet is not," commented the girl. "I'll ring mum and ask her to get her pc ready; she'll know how to upload it onto our workplace system once you have lifted it off your files. . ."

Eventually, they arrived at the director's office.

"Have a drink on the house, Elanca," he offered her a small glass of double-distilled mango extract;

"my in-law's special; you are invited there for tomorrow evening."

"will there be more of this special welcome at their place?" the reporter enquired, smiling at the rare liquid.

"My esteemed father-in-law may be able to arrange a limited supply for tomorrow night," he assured her solemnly.

"I think, and I am sure that I can speak for all of us that I agree with Diego: your magazine made a wise choice in sending you here; welcome once again to Saipan and to our clinic."

Elanca silently acknowledged the director's words and proceeded to show him some of the photos she had taken,

"by way of giving me some background on where and how some of your staff work," she explained.

"I'll ask Diego to get you to attend a few night shifts, Elanca. . ."

"that's where a lot of your action is?"

"naturally, like in any hospital or clinic or anywhere, for that matter, where you keep people overnight."

"how many such do you keep at any time, Gordon?"

"fifteen, plus or minus a few; right now, it is far fewer. . ."

"where do you park people for longer-term treatment. . ."

"such as your magazine's clients?" Gordon laughed:

"well, the gentlemen who wants to become his friend's wife. . ."
"Hector Chalmers"

"expects to have a job here, providing him and his daughter with accommodation. The young girl who's to be said daughter's future boyfriend and her parents, well, your magazine promises to foot their bill. . ."

"provided that you, Gordon, and your team let me do the feature," she reminded him.

"understood; Rosetta will help you find them a place to live and somewhere for the daughter,"

"Ann"

"to go to school; she does it for any new staff or associate of ours. . ."

"Rosetta's parents' place, for instance?"

"quite possibly, it's definitely large enough and they have adult children who have left home, so yes, or else, they might ask a neighbour or someone at their church. . ." "I'm not sure that her congregation would agree to sex-change patients?" wondered Elanca aloud.

"who knows?" acknowledged the director.

❧

Elanca had always been an excellent photographer but so, it turned out, were Diego and Rosetta; other staff members had photos to contribute; one cleaner even contributed a drawing her little daughter had made while seated on the verandah, showing a corner of the ocean, clouds in the sky and the expanse of the administrative wing.

The clinic had its own day-care centre, so a fair bit of footage went into watching their little ones at play and at the two young women who kept it going. Elanca interviewed about a dozen staff at length and was invited to a charity event that several of them had been involved in, to raise money for research into multiple sclerosis.

She was even asked to give a speech there in which she described the experience of a cousin who had been misdiagnosed, to begin with, and who had, subsequently, had had great difficulty in securing a pension, having just embarked on an artistic career:

"what she was able to, until very recently, direct a niece of ours to use special computer software, dictating sketches into it, which would then print it onto canvas, to be made into tablecloth, t-shirts, wall hangings and curtains. . ."

Elanca had brought a few samples along, like headscarves for her niece's Afghan classmates, and some small handkerchieves:

"Now, she is finding it increasingly difficult to speak clearly and she hasn't been able to sketch for years, even in outline; so she is teaching herself to guide a paintbrush with her mouth.

Our niece, Deborah, has learnt to straighten out the lines my cousin manages to draw, then scan and print them on whatever material is in demand, whether glass paper or cloth."

"is you cousin doing well on the proceeds, Elanca?" a charity organizer asked her.

"along with the pension, she gets by, because she manages to split proceeds with Deborah which keeps her income below the threshold at which she'd lose most of her pension, plus it earns our niece some money as well."

"what is her expectancy?"

"she could live for a few more years but lose about any degree of mobility; she is beginning to have difficulty swallowing. . ."

"do you have a photo of hers?"

Elanca obliged with a series of pictures taken over the years and ended up recording the event, including the displays.

Brendan Mac Groom did not get many moments with her; not only were they both busy with their respective tasks, he would make sure that he was never alone with her, much as he wanted to.

He did manage to introduce her to his wife who was being readied for her operation.

"Brendan is quite a fan of your writing style, Elanca," she told the reporter.

"how do you know?" the journalist smiled.

"he wanted to find out whether you'd do him and his background any justice," Elaine affirmed,

"not to mention the clinic; for they have done the right thing by him and his work depends on keeping them onside. . ."

"I seem to have been given glowing reports by whoever read features of mine. . . it is rare to have that kind of intense feedback, even when I was working with my husband on these knife-edge stories of ours."

"I am sorry that he is no more, if that is of any help to you," the patient sighed.

"at least, whatever is to happen to me, I have a husband living."

Brendan was seated by her bedside, looking very much at ease, not saying much.

"I'll catch up with you in a few moments, Elanca; for I want you to meet some of my technicians, two of them were away on family business, so you get to know and interview them also."

"I'll wait for you in the canteen, then," Elanca replied, casually.

"you love her, don't you?" his wife stated when they were alone.

"yes," he admitted, "and I may well be the first man she has wanted ever since her husband died; they must have been close."

"at least, you are being honest; thank you. What do you want to do; tell me!"

"nothing, Elaine; carry on as before. . ."

"I shan't be a wife to you any more, you of all people should know that."

"in an immediate physical sense, that's true, no doubt; but aren't we beyond that?" he countered.

"one never is," his wife felt: "I miss not being able to make love like we used to; yet it won't stop us from being a couple; I am in the best hands, under the circumstances, thanks to you working here and thanks to your employer."

She sighed and beckoned him closer:

"Look, do whatever she wants you to do to her, if you can both be discreet and know how far you can go; both you and her are very physical people, more than I ever was, even in my most sensuous moments; heaven knows, you gave me many. . ."

"we still have a life together, dear," he assured her, visibly moved, but also not trusting himself to promise what he might not be able to keep.

He re-joined Elanca, took her hand briefly and settled down to some green tea with her.

"Let me introduce my theatre aides; as I said, two were away. . ."

"are they related, Brendan?" she smiled.

"why; oh yes, same-family business, a wedding on another island, and we do not always have boats going there and back."

"it's all right, Brendan," she assured him. "I love and need you very much," she whispered,

"but you do not belong to me. I owe this experience a great deal; now,"

Aloud: "let us meet your staff and get my camera ready; where are we going, Brendan?"

He lifted her by her hand and pointed towards a store room.

"A lot of work gets done there, sorting reagents, equipment, dyes, even gowns, aprons, sterile stuff, the bowels, if you like, of our business. Let me know if that place is too dark; we can wheel in some neon lights if you need them."

He held her hand a bit longer, then gently moved her past him in the direction they needed to go, introducing her to his theatre workers as they entered the corridor.

Several days later, Diego asked her if she needed any particular help.

"Yes, I'll need some big screens, like they have for sports broadcasts. . ."

"we have them, for teaching displays. Do you want to splash your images across them, Elanca?"

"yes, some stills, others like a video. . ."

"how about text?"

"I'll upload captions and some interpretative texts on some smaller screens if you have those also; I have already bundled pictures and text into hardcopy but I'll need a few more hours to edit that; I never review it straight after I finish the original version but do something else first. . ."

"to view it with a fresh mind, from some distance?" "Yes, Diego"

"Will you have everything ready tomorrow if someone can help you with the screens?"

"anyone I have yet to meet?"

"for you to squeeze an interview or a pictorial observation in?"

"we live in hope, Diego. . ."

The public relations specialist merely smiled fondly at the reporter they all had come to like.

The presentation was a great success; it always amazes people to see themselves the way others see them and to have familiar settings thrust upon them from a different angle; this was no exception. There were tears but also lots of laughter. The director's in-laws had donated some double-distilled mango extract,

"strong as a donkey kick; the ultimate painkiller," as Diego described it, as well as other home-made liqueurs;

Elanca liked their passion fruit sherbet, slightly alcoholic, best; for it was very refreshing.

The kitchen had prepared snacks in honour of some very fine images and pungent characterizations having flowed from Elanca's pen, so to say; the one of an apprentice preparing a mash of noodles and onions for a quick roast was particularly enlightening; for you saw the rapt concentration on the boy's face, overlaid with the delight on seeing the recipe succeed.

The cleaners, too, had done well, image-wise, with shots almost as if they were lining up to prepare their floor waxers for an F1 start, all that was missing was crash helmets.

Their work had been commented on, perceptively but generously, as had been that of Brendan Mac Groom's theatre aides with their seamless team effort.

The gardeners' endeavour was rewarded with some close-up of orchids, mangosteen in blossom and swamp grass waving in a light sea breeze, a piece crafted by the garden lover that Elanca very clearly was.

"It gives me great pleasure to host Elanca's presentation,"

opened Gordon who had got everyone to attend it who was not inevitably delayed, such as Marietta and Doreeen, two nurses, a theatre worker, a cleaner and a housekeeper, needed to get a suite ready for an inter-island patient suffering from severe post-birth complications.

There would henceforth be no doubt about Elanca's ability to cover the tricky double-sex change in such a manner as to do the clinic and its entire workforce proud.

"What is our next move," Ann's father asked his boss after yet another meeting.

"have we heard back from the tendering agency?"

"only that we continue to be their preferred tenderer; we need the final okay from the government in Canberra to nail it which we have, in principle. . ."

"what are they waiting for?"

"partly bureaucratic inertia but also whether there's someone sufficiently interested and politically powerful enough to want to get our contract for themselves. . ."

"in other words, unless they have someone resist in the next few weeks. . ."

"yes, but I shan't let that happen," his boss assured him.

"what do you want me to do?"

"get back to the magazine editor, find out how close they are to get agreement with the clinic, then claim the bit of your trip around the world that will get you and Ann to Guam. . . we'll pay the gap to Saipan and notify our counterpart; it is then up to you and their team to put some pressure on the ministry in Canberra; meanwhile, I'll go there myself and try to get things moving. . ."

"a pincer movement, in fact."

"something like that." "How soon?"

"as far as work here is concerned, say a fortnight at most; if Ann is to accompany you, work it out with her school; if they need to hear from me if it is work-related or not, I'll help; have you done anything to line up home/online schooling?"

"yes, I have several very good programmes in mind. . ."

"part of which we'll pay; see if the magazine will pay the rest, as part of the deal for the feature. . ."

Hector got to meet Nina the following week, together with Natasha, while Ann and Julia were at school, having taken an afternoon off. Seeing Nina and Natasha together, he felt familiar urges, scarcely restrained by Clara's tragic death or his commitment to Glen; the young women seemed equally enchanted by his manners and comfortable with his presence:

"It's good to get to meet you, at last," Natasha told him:

"we have had the pleasure of your daughter and her friend, future partner. . ."

"Julia, to be known as Jules if not Julius?"

"the one; both remarkable and very committed young people" the lawyer agreed.

"you would doubtlessly like to know," said the editor, "how close we are to an agreement with the clinic in Saipan; the good news is, very close; our reporter is already in place and was asked to do an in-house feature which is complete and which their management seems to be very happy with. . ."

"you are telling me that the clinic is not likely to prevent you from doing that part of the feature that involves them and relies on the embedded presence of your reporter there," queried Hector.

"words to that effect; so we need to consider your role in the feature, not least the extent to which we shall support you presence and treatment. . ."

"as well as Ann's schooling."

"how much can your employer contribute, Hector?" asked the lawyer.

"not much to my treatment and subsequent operation, except my long-service leave. . ."

"before or after you have done your work there?"

"preferably afterwards, so as not to confuse or irritate my counterpart team there," the work provider replied.

"So you'll be on a wage throughout. . ."

"yes, provided that my company gets final clearance. . ."

"who or what is holding that one up, o father of Ann?" wondered the editor.

"no one in Melanesia, the ministry in Canberra is dragging its feet a bit. . ."

"but your company is their exclusive tenderer as well, is it not?" wondered the lawyer.

"yes; my boss figures that someone there is waiting for institutional or political resistance to emerge and does not wish to move unless certain there will be none. . ."

"very possible," agreed the two girls, in unison, speaking from obvious experience:

"what is your boss going to do about it?"

"a pincer movement; he will go to Canberra and be a bit of a pain there; meanwhile, I and Ann are to start our part of the global journey which will get us to Micronesia, there to actually meet the key people and get them to put diplomatic pressure on people in Canberra as well, to start the programme as promised."

"so you would want us to release that first tranche of your trip around the world, and then. . .? Because we shan't readily finance another journey there from Adelaide which may mean you and your daughter will have to stay there."

"well, if you are prepared to finance a proportion of my daughter's time there and of her on-line schooling and/or local enrolment, my boss is prepared to partly bear the rest, leaving me to pay about as much as I presently do for her education."

The two young women looked at each other:

"Look, as soon as we have word from Elanca, that's our reporter. . ."

"I haven't met her yet; more's the pity."

"you will, and you will like the experience, we assure you; but, anyway, as soon as we can, we'll let you travel and get there; we'll cover the distance between Guam and Saipan one way, at least, and make a contribution to your stay and that of Ann's, as well as her schooling.

You may have to take some of your long-service leave in advance until you get your final programme clearance; if your employer can reimburse you for whatever you may be out of pocket meanwhile, good and well, otherwise we shall try, from within our budget."

"thank you, ladies," stated Ann's father: "so I have your go-ahead for us to leave, set up long-distance schooling for my daughter, get there, familiarize myself with the clinic where I am to undergo treatment and, eventually, be 'gender-aligned,' to use that word. . ."

"hopefully, also get to know your counterpart organization and get them to put the hard word on the ministry in Canberra, as a flanking measure to what your boss can achieve there," the lawyer added.

"once Elanca gives us the word, we'll give you the final go-ahead; meanwhile, get yourself and Ann as ready as you can to leave at short notice. . ."

"how many days before Elanca knows for certain?"

"no more than three; for the clinic had given her a time limit also, as have we, at this point."

"Elanca," said the director one afternoon, during yet another meeting,

"you are always welcome during our meetings but, would you excuse yourself for a few minutes?" she knew what they wanted to discuss and decide: permission to let the magazine proceed with its feature on the twin sex change.

She grabbed a glass full of water, feeling quite dehydrated, what with the high temperatures and even higher moisture, being a truly 'dry-land 'girl from the mid- North of South Australia, then left them to their devices. Nor did she have long to wait:

"The good news is that we are unanimously decided to let you go ahead with your feature," Diego opened.

"what is the bad news, then?"

"oh; we want you to be in charge throughout."

"I see," agreed the reporter. "Could I ask you, the Committee, to let my magazine know, rather than let me do it; for it is my magazine which will do the work and be responsible for its quality, through myself, admittedly. . ."

"well, in that case," stated the director, "let me then rephrase the conditions: We agree to your magazine featuring our clinic and its efforts to prepare, and operate on, Hector Landers and Julia Childers for gender alignment within, hopefully, the next three to six months, provided it is you, Elanca Hartwig, who will document and write this feature, with help as we can give and as you choose. We shall abide by this agreement for the next three months and extend it for another three months unless required, against our will and by the most severe occurrence of circumstances, to cancel., alter or modify this understanding. If the magazine chose, or felt compelled, to rely on someone else, we would, in turn, feel obliged to review our understanding; likewise, if the period were to extend beyond six months, for whatever reasons, we would be likely to ask whoever were to take over from you to prove her suitability to our satisfaction and benefit. Likewise, if both the treatment and operation would have to be extended or postponed and, thus, affect your feature, we would also have to examine if and how both the clinic and the magazine were to continue, not least in consideration for the wishes and needs of our patients and their respective partners and families."

Gordon paused, looking first at Brendan, then at several members of his board, then smiled at Elanca: "Could I get someone to move this somewhat altered version of our decision?"

"Marietta; second, anyone? Doreen? All in favour. . . unanimously accepted." Clapping of hands.

"be assured, Elanca, that we want you to start on your feature forthwith and that we shall notify your editor accordingly. . ." Gordon smiled, looked at Rosetta and the other ladies:

"am I right in assuming that drinks and some refreshments have been prepared.?" The ladies nodded, grinning from ear to ear.

Yet another native of Saipan came to the somewhat unexpected rescue, Ramon Figueros, the grandson of a Filipino taro farmer who had settled in Micronesia, as had many before and after him.

Hector's boss had both a telephone call and an email, more or less to the same effect:

"Ramon Figueros, from your future counterpart office of the youth employment provider in Saipan; you might remember me from the tender process."

"Ryan Sanders here, Workfind Adelaide. I do remember you, Ramon; good to hear from you. . ."

"we were expecting to hear from you earlier, seeing that your specialist is our preferred tenderer," the workplace consultant explained. "we were wanting him to have arrived before now; for we need to get started before the end of the month, for budgetary reasons. I was under the impression that yours was the Australian government's preferred tender, also. . . or am I embarrassing you, Ryan?"

"yes, you are; I am heading for Canberra tomorrow to urge that all details are finalized."

"look, Ryan, let me do that, instead, and then fly over to your capital for the actual signing. I'll activate our team from Micronesia at the US embassy; I understand that they know the relevant people in your department who, I am sure, may want to avoid a diplomatic incident as much as we do. . ."

"thank you very much; I would have suggested that, unless you or I get to hear from our own department about a serious objection to my tender, and yours, and to their own approval process by the end of the week, that their documentation is to be made ready which it, probably, already is, waiting in someone's drawer. . ."

"in case, a high-and-mighty-one objects in the last minute or cannot make up his mind," agreed Ramon.

"my team will put the thumbscrews on your directorate; for one of them was to come home with the completed agreement so we can get started, and his leave is also due. . ."

"is that why you got in touch with me, Ramon?"

"more or less; they figured that they would work the Canberra angle and that I sort out with you when to get Hector here."

"can I send him off within the next few days, Ramon?"

"Yes; I'd like him to start next week, Ryan; may I suggest that, instead of tomorrow, fly to Canberra day after, unless you have work there which you probably do, I'll get my team to arrange a signing on Friday; you'd be more than welcome to join Hector in the next few weeks yourself."

"I may, Ramon. Last question: Can you slot Hector's daughter into a school or a home schooling system in the next few days? I have her academic details on file and can forward them to who-ever you nominate. . ."

"I'll get someone in my office to get going on that," Ramon obliged:

"we do have contacts to all the institutions and to some distance-learning people also, all over Micronesia. We may find a way to combine the two, but get her father to research distance learning compliant with Australian standards if he hasn't done so. . ."

"he probably has; I did ask him to be ready at short notice. In fact, I had wanted him to travel ahead, get in touch with you and your colleagues and. . ."

"get some movement from us, to loosen up your own people in Canberra; was that why you wanted to leave for Canberra tomorrow to be ready?"

"yes, call it the 'lobster's claws'".
"nice image, Ryan. Keep me up to date; I'll do likewise."

Hector had done even better; he had lined up home schooling packages for both Julia and Ann, Nina having promised that her magazine would reimburse him as soon as the clinic had agreed to the feature. Consequently, Ann's father had deposited down-payments on behalf of both girls and gotten in touch with the Childers, Julia's parents, who had, if not become friends, begun to accept Ann and her father as part of their extended family.

"It appears that we 'll have to get Julia ready as well, is it true that you and Ann are to leave before the weekend?"

"yes, decisions are being made all over," Hector affirmed.

"the Micronesians want me to start next week and the clinic will want to start treatment. . ."

"is the magazine paying for Julia's flight and accommodation," her mother wanted to be reassured.

"I am sure that Nina has been in touch with you. . ." "she has. . ."

"the feature is just about to be agreed on; she'll let you know; I'd say, get Jules ready right now; do you both want to accompany her?" he asked, courteously.

"her father can't get time off work but I might," Julia's mother replied.

"did the magazine not budget for us?" she wondered.

"Look, Eileen," Ann's father assured her: "Ann's and mine journey is covered; I'll talk Nina through it so that the magazine pay some, as shall I, if you and your husband can cough up the rest. . ."

"will you do that, Hector?"

"why not; we are family, thanks to the girls. . ."

"yeah, I suppose," the lady sighed. "see if the magazine agrees; it'd be the right thing, don't you think?"

Nina rang Natasha to let Hector know that all was set:
"The official approval came through a few hours ago, and the clinic management rang me, a bloke called Gordon, as did Brendan. . ."

"that is Dr Mac Groom?"

"yes, I am beginning to feel that Elanca and he have been seeing more of each other. . ."

"than is good for either of them; look Nina; Elanca is a professional, as is the good doctor, only just now reinstated. . ."

"you followed it up, too?"

"yes, goes with my job, Nina. I know that Elanca won't let anything or anyone detract from doing a good job; having said that, it may help, to a point, if they get on so well. . ."

"because they'll have to, I guess," agreed the editor. "Ann's father got in touch with me yesterday; his company wanted him and Ann to leave tomorrow. . ." "will he?" "no, day after, instead; for we had to rely on our travel agent work out a connection that will both get them to Saipan and which they can stitch into the next leg of their journey. . ."

"around the world, soon as Ann's father is no more, in a manner of speaking. . ."

"yeah, that is keeping our agent busy, seeing that it is us paying for the tickets," explained Nina to her friend:

"Hector offered to part-pay for Julia's mum to accompany her to Saipan and stay with her for a few days, then return, if we, the magazine, would contribute and the mother, Eileen, would fork out the rest. . ."

"and will you, Nina?"

"yes, we had budgeted for a certain amount, not for a full fare or accommodation, but towards it; now that our feature has been approved, we can allow her to go ahead; Julia was to leave next week; now they can both leave and Ann will be waiting. . ."

"how about their schooling, Nina?"

"Ann's father and his counterpart have been organizing it between them, and Hector's made a down payment for both girls. . ."

"which you will reimburse. . ."

"as it affects Jules? Yes, Tash."

Natasha rang a rather hectic Hector at work:

"Nina's asked me to let you know that the magazine's reporter's gained approval; so you and Ann will work with Elanca, as will Jules, of course, and her mother if she wants to come. . ."

"so Nina is prepared to part-pay for her mum?"

"what we'll do, Hector," the lawyer explained:" the magazine's travel agent who is organizing your ticket, and Ann's portion of your trip around the world, the one that will get the two of you to Saipan, will get Jules' ticket ready, obviously, paid for by the magazine, and her mum's. It will be prepaid by me, accounted for by the magazine and part-reimbursed by Jules' father and yourself, now, if you and he can, or else in the next few weeks, into my work account which the magazine and I set up through our law practice. You see, I owe you and your daughter, personally and professionally, a great deal of fun," the lawyer said happily.

"will you and your boss meet me and Nina tonight? Food's on Nina, drink's on me, taxis on you and your boss if needed. Sounds good? Nina thought of the Casino; for it is central."

"fine, except it'll have to be an early night, unless I can park Ann with Jules' parents." Julia's parents raised no objections:

"I can drop Ann at the airport so that Julia can see her off, Hector", her father said. "thanks for arranging Eileen's fare and accommodation. . ."

Ann's father had explained the arrangement to him.

"I'll reimburse the lawyer next week when I get paid; please, tell her that but I'll also ring her myself. Nina rang, "he continued," and her travel agent is working on Julia's, and her mum's, tickets; I'll need to confirm with the school; you would have done that, already, Hector?"

"yes, as soon as my boss told me to be ready at short notice. He'll be at the airport, incidentally, to fly to Canberra to sign us off."

"at long last," mused Julia's father." It must be a relief. . ."

"someone in the US embassy put the hard word on them; suddenly, you find decisions are being made. As for Eileen's fare, etc, I'll pay Natasha my share tonight, and thanks for having Ann. I'll ring the school straightaway. . ." which he did.

"It appears you are staying with us tonight, bitch," Julia informed her lover later that afternoon.

"same bed, lover?"

"I am sure that can be arranged, Ann."

"my dad and I shall then drop you off at the airport. . ."

"what we'll have to do this arvo, Jules, is go to my place first, pack and then get my gear to your home. . ."

"are you more or less packed?"

"yes, Jules; I just need to pick it up, get some personal gear, a few books and certificates. . . I know where they are. . ."

"your passport?"

"is part of dad's; I have a copy at home."

"will we have time to drop in at the refugee centre, Ann?"

"'course; we'll ask permission to leave early and get someone in the office to ring Mrs Weatherby. . ." mindful that they were not allowed the use of their own mobile phones during most of the day, Ann being the born organizer.

The scenes at the refugee association were quite emotional, even though there was a different class in attendance, Somali and Sudanese girls instead of the usual Hazaras. The girls were asked to help a few Ogadeni girls with their homework, as their regular tutors had not turned up; having talked the girls through a marine geography project concerning Yorke Peninsula they soon took their leave and ended up having their final cup of tea with Mrs Enderby and her staff.

"We'll miss you girls. . ."

"next time you see us, Mrs Weatherby, one of us won't be. . ."
"please, explain!"

"Jules is going to be my boyfriend when all this is over, paid for by. . ."

and they proceeded to tell the lady all about it. Mrs Weatherby's comment was priceless:

"remind me to take out a subscription; I wouldn't miss it for the world."

"They'll give you an exclusive; we'll mention it to the editor, our close friend Nina," Ann assured her.

Fortified with lots of tea, the girls went next to Ann's place, having been given a lift into the city centre, there to catch a more suitable bus which had turned up after only a few minutes, "a record for Adelaide", Julia commented.

Ann let them in: "are you going to make love to me here or fuck me at your place tonight?" she demanded.

"both, if it can be arranged," Julia explained. "But show me first what needs to be packed. . ."

"oh, bits from the bathroom, a stack of documents, mainly school certificates in the second drawer below the computer, the posters off the wall, half the clothing off the rack in my wardrobe, the drawers with the knickers and socks inside; that's drawers four and five in my bedside dresser. . . meanwhile, let me hit Dad's bathroom and get ready for some action, "Ann promised. . .

She proved to be unable to keep it, though. While Julia was lining up Ann's dresses to fit them into the bag her lover had thoughtfully left near the wardrobe, she happened to look out of the window;

"ah, give us an s–give us an h-. . . Ann, get dressed!" she yelled across the passage; "your dad's car is in the driveway."

Ann, having locked herself in the bathroom, could not hear, so Julia finished shifting her dresses inside the bag, closed it and ran downstairs, leaning against the bathroom door and repeated her message, just as the door opened.

"Julia, surprised to see you here; is Ann not staying with you tonight?" her father wondered.

"Yes, but she knew that she had not finished packing just yet. . ."

"no, she would have expected to do it tonight but she did have everything ready to be lifted and tucked away within minutes, that's what she said. . ."

"and that's what she did, Mr Landers; I just finished her clothing and was about to pick up stuff in her bathroom; but weren't you going to have an evening with your boss and the ladies tonight; that's what they told us at school, that's why we are here to get her ready. . ."

('anything to give Ann time to get dressed; let's hope she has the sense not to emerge just yet').

"you are right; I have to arrange for my share of your mum's airfare and accommodation to give to Miss Bertram tonight but realised that I had left my cheque book here, not at work; so I decided to nick in, pick it up, then take the bus to the casino so I am not tempted to drive home. . ."

"would you like me to make you a cup of tea?" Julia offered, to get him out of the corridor.

"no, thanks, Julia; I'll go and get the cheque book and some bits of paper while I am here; you finish Ann's packing. . . where is Ann, by the way?"

"she needed to use a bathroom and chose yours," the glib reply, "to give me space to clear out hers. . ."

"go ahead, then, Julia; do you want me to give you girls a lift?"

"yes, to East End, please; we can catch a bus to my place every fifteen minutes or less from there. . ."

"look, with all of Ann's luggage-I realised a long time ago that you can either shift a daughter or her luggage but not both-why don't I ring for a taxi for the two of you to arrive in. . ."

"twenty minutes, Mr Landers?"

"ok, and give you some money; meanwhile, finish Ann's packing and I shall have a quick cup of tea with her, whenever she emerges. . ." her father spoke from experience;

"then you join us; by that time, the taxi should be here and we'll all leave. Let me get to my office, get the cheque book and ring for a taxi. . ." he said and left Julia surreptitiously knocking at the bathroom door.

The taxi arrived just as Ann was about to pack her documents in her special bag, after Julia had amassed everything else that she thought Ann ought to have on her and what Ann had already placed in readiness.

Ann's father started grabbing several of these bags, dragging them downstairs, while Julia helped Ann get her papers into order and inside the briefcase which they had to carry between them so that its contents would not burst into a paper trail all over the staircase.

The taxi driver helped Ann's father stow Ann's bags, opened the door for Julia and Ann to slide on to the rear seats,

"I'll sit on it," offered Julia, looking at Ann's briefcase trying in vain to hold all the books and documents she could have possibly owned. That was, eventually, how they took off, Ann's father getting in next to the driver, then getting off at a bus stop and, having handed the driver a twenty-dollar note, was last seen running after a bus about to leave; he caught it, someone having alerted the driver who delayed his departure.

Hector arrived at Adelaide Central, walked into the Casino and sat down, looking around; Natasha spotted him, waved and called him over; the girls got up and he kissed them both; they took his hands, sat him down and showed him what they had ordered, trout braised in radish, resting in roasted mash, garnished with lightly steamed onions, garlic, broccoli and Brussels sprout, to be followed by caramel pudding in apricot jelly; they would drink a 2008 Riverland Pinot Blanc, very suitable for any kind of fish, the sommelier had assured the ladies:

"the way he looked at us," Nina told Hector, "he would have assured us of anything under the sun."

"so you ladies have ordered," Ann's father stated; "I'll happily join you; we'll ask for another plate and eventually tripartite the bill;" so it was done.

"here is my share in Julia's mother 's airfare and accommodation in Saipan, by way of estimate," he offered Natasha a cheque.

"we'll work out something," the editor assured him, "if we can recover it from our budget."

"not to worry, ladies. We are in your debt and I am in your most enjoyable company."

Julia and Ann arrived, not to a lavish meal but to dinner at the Childers' household, with Julia's brother and his girl friend also present. Conversation flowed freely:

"won't you miss tutoring the Hazara girls, Jules and Ann?" Erin asked.

"yes, it's so good to see them gaining confidence, not only because their English is getting better each time you work with them; they also learn not to feel guilty about getting an education and being made to work things out for themselves."

"what else do you miss?" wondered Julia's brother, taking the girls seriously for once. "not what, who," they answered in unison: "our biology teacher; a good person and someone from whom you learn how to learn. . ."

"he does not try to teach you all that there is to learn, even though he knows a lot, but he'll make you work out what questions to ask and where to look for an answer", explained Julia, the future scientist;

"he rarely explains but guides you by asking," added Ann, the future lawyer.

Julia's parents, while saying very little, were clearly enjoying the interaction of four very alert young minds in action; It was obvious that

that brief weekend in the Barossa Valley, on Elanca's cousin's vineyard, had changed their relationship to each other and to their offspring to within orders of magnitude. Nor did they object too strenuously when first Stephen and Erin asked to be excused, with obvious intent, followed suit by Jules and Ann, heading to the showers once they were free and safe to use. By then, Erin was doing to Stephen what she knew to do best, controlling and riding him with considerable force and an unshakeable sense of purpose, not laying off.

"rinse me down, Jules," Ann urged her,

the chilly water under their shower notwithstanding.

"my big blob brother and his super-hormonised bitch must have used all the hot water,"

Julia commented. "Mum and Dad will be absolutely furious".

"consider me hyper-pheromonal, in that case, but keep doing things to me. . ."

Ann demanded, leaning against Julia who upheld her with one hand and entered her with the other, playing her with both, biting her breasts, shoulders, upper arms and nibbling her earlobes.

Eventually, she turned off the water, grabbed the biggest towel she could find and began to rub Ann down vigorously, under her arms, spreading her thighs, working her upper and lower back, finally wrapping that towel around Ann's body: "do not take it off!" she warned the girl and pushed her towards the bedroom door which Ann managed to open in spite of her arms being covered by the towel. Julia then dried herself, brushed her teeth and followed Ann, closing doors behind her.

She made Ann stand up before her and drop the towel, then took her lover's hands and cuffed them behind Ann's back with one of hers, using her free hand to groom the girl, massaging her breasts, shoulders, hips and buttocks, making Ann rest her head on Julia's shoulder, kissing her lips, chin, cheeks, nose and hair in determined yet gentle moves, making Ann go limp and moan in submissive expectancy, giving herself over to the experience of her lover's dominance.

Eventually, Jules lifted Ann's thighs and made her buckle, then carried and pushed her onto the bed they were to share that night, with Ann's wrists remaining cuffed by Julia's fingers; Ann was mounted, kissed and explored, her legs wound around Julia's hips until she dropped them and allowed Julia to spread them as wide as she could, surrendering herself.

"Your fate is sealed, bitch," explained Julia, "but wait till I am a boy and do you in depth," putting her two fingers inside the girl, arousing and possessing her, kissing her, resting Ann's torso against her arm and utterly immobilizing her.

A few moments later, she let go of Ann's hands, only to force her arms above her shoulders, like a victorious wrestler might subdue an opponent; she then forced Ann's thighs together with her knees and rode her, still exploring her from inside, biting her in many places but making sure that her teeth left no marks on Ann's body, by covering them with her lips. Never had she controlled her willing lover so completely; nor would she again, for at least a few months in the future.

At one stage, she sat upright on top of Ann, manipulating her, nonetheless, with her fingers; she, finally, rolled partly off the girl, lifted her, fastened her arms around Ann's torso, pushed her back and allowed herself-and Ann-to fall asleep, ensuring that the girl would wake up a captive in her lover's arms early next morning, which is what duly happened.

Ann's father was at the airport, waiting for the girls to arrive, as was Glen who had been unable to make it to the Casino the previous night; he strode up to Hector, hugged and embraced him for the first time ever in their relationship, then greeted Julia's parents and the girls.

"I rang Natasha this morning," he explained, "then Nina; they'll ring you, Hector; let them talk to Julia and Ann also. . . pleased to meet you again," he turned to Julia's parents.

"won't you have to be back at work, Glen?" asked Eileen.

"yes, but I am here to see Hector and Ann off; I'll wait till they have checked in, in case of excess luggage."

The queue was enormous; they were to board the flight to Cairns, there to change into a United Pacific flight to Guam, for a connection to Saipan, a massive time difference but a total of eleven hours of flying time. Yes, and they were overweight.

"Not a worry," Glen assured them and, unleashing his credit card, arranged an upgrade.

Natasha rang just as they had finished, so Hector told her about it.

"We'll adjust that; let me talk to Glen and thank him," which the young lawyer did. She then talked to Julia's parents, finally to the girls, addressing Julia in particular: "one of us, either Nina or myself, will be here to see you and your mum off next week; have your passports ready and we'll have the tickets by that time; Nina is getting them today."

Julia's mum thanked Ann's dad once more, kissing him lightly, as they shook hands with Julia's father, with Glen walking them towards document control before leaving.

Ann's father had decided to let Ramon know what had attracted him to Saipan in the first place, even before his boss had entered the tendering process:

"As you know, Ramon, I am an independent entity for the purposes of working with your company, yet wholly 'owned' by Workfind, in Adelaide," he had written in an earlier email.

"I am also committed to Glen Hiddings, himself the director of a work provider, also in Adelaide, which will require me to undergo gender alignment, something I chose to, at Dr Mac Groom's entrepreneurial clinic, bound to be well known to you and your colleagues, all of whom I am looking forward to meeting and working with. I undertake not to let treatment interfere with our work and not to undergo the actual operation until its bulk has been dealt with, having the period of my long- service leave from my regular employer at my disposal. I may add that Workfind intends to continue to employ me after I have completed the tendered assignment which I am privileged to have been chosen for and after my, hopefully successful, sexual alignment."

As soon as Ramon had got in touch with Ryan, but before the tender had been finally approved in Canberra, long after the Micronesian Federation had signed it off, Ramon phoned Hector at home.

He introduced himself, made a few comments about the time difference and came to the point.

"You know, Hector, I could have stopped the process cold, once you had told me about wanting to come to Saipan for a sex change; actually, I sort of knew about it. . ."

"is there nothing secret on Saipan, Ramon?" wondered Ann's father.

"no, I am afraid not; not that Dr Mac Broom-Brendan-or any of his team had divulged anything. . ."

"anything to do with Elanca?"

"the reporter?" queried the executive. "Not directly; she, too, has a code of ethics plus an exclusive to be mindful of; her visit may have triggered some curiosity, and it is an island nation where everybody knows about everyone. . ." "a word here, a suggestion there. . ."

"correct, Hector. Anyway, my Committee decided that not only was that your own entirely private affair, we would not roll up the entire process; not only would it take too long, we are under a time constraint set us by the Administration. . ."

"plus," Hector added, "not too many people have worked with the kind of software that you and your department need, let alone created any such, even though I say so myself."

"no, it's been obvious from the beginning and, we assume, that changing your sex won't rob you of that ability and expertise, to put it rather inelegantly."

"my daughter and I are to be on my way to Saipan very soon; Ryan asked me to sit on our packed suitcases, more or less. . ."

"yes, so I suggested to him; I expect the two of you within a week, at the outside; it's taken long enough. . ."

"for which we must apologize to you and to Worklink for the needless delay caused by Canberra bureaucracy."

Ramon paused before answering: "Very annoying but don't beat yourself up too much; your boss and I are on top of it now, with the help of two very forceful Micronesian diplomats.

It all happened yesterday, sort of on the lines which your boss suggested. . ." "which were: unless we are given some profoundly significant reasons not to proceed within the next forty-eight hours, we shall turn up for the official signing, seeing that this tender has already been agreed on by both sides, and shall not be shifted until these tenders have been signed off; vintage Ryan, in other words. . ."

"to the effect; good advice, by the way, if you can find the right people to act on it; my Chamorro friends did. . ."

"well, thanks, Ramon;" Hector acknowledged. "so you are determined to see me and my daughter on the plane soonest." "yes."

Julia and her mum found that they had to stay overnight, courtesy of the airline, even though Saipan Airport was once again open for business; such had been the backlog. They got the girl at the counter to ring the clinic; someone on duty rang Rosetta who rang her parents:

"would you tell Elanca, Mr Hector and Ann, that their friends won't get here till tomorrow, due to a passenger backlog at Guam International; they are staying put in Guam at the Hotel Patria; I am looking for the number and shall ring them there," added the administrator.

Ann had just come back from school and Hector and Elanca had yet to return their session with Brendan.

"would you thank Rosetta," Ann said; "could she let my father know later today; and would you allow me to use your phone tonight to ring Jules and her mum once she gets the number?" she asked her hosts.

"certainly; we can find the number for you also, Ann. How was school today?"

"very different from back home, very enjoyable; I got on with my teachers and met some cool kids, boys and girls,"

("one, in particular." Angh Vuong, the daughter of the part-Vietnamese biology teacher, had impressed her very much with her graceful beauty and poise, as well as the ease whereby she spoke French:

"I had attended a convent school for two years at my grandmother's in Hanoi; French was the only European language which most of the nuns knew," she explained,

"except one who spoke Italian and another who taught English, in a fashion. . ."

"why did Mum not send you to an international school there, Angh?" exclaimed Ann.

"too expensive, booked solid and Mum wanted me to meet Vietnamese children, instead.")

Meanwhile, Elanca and Hector had gone to see Brendan to start Ann's father on his hormone treatment.

"Elanca, do you mind leaving us when I ask you?" the doctor had asked.

"no, I do understand confidentiality. . . just give me a few minutes' warning so I can conclude a video shot, leave you and continue when you want me to." Brendan nodded and turned to Hector.

"first up, I'll need to do a fairly thorough check-up of yours, today and tomorrow; we'll keep you here tonight because I want you not to have eaten or drunk anything for some of my tests, starting as of six o'clock tonight. I use a mixture of testosterone inhibitors and oestrogen, not that dissimilar from an anti-baby pill, to start you off, not that you'll notice any immediate effects."

"and you need to get the blend right, Brendan?" asked his patient.

"yes, apart from having to know your blood group, nutritional status, any deficiencies which might contraindicate the hormones, fitness levels, etc."

"Some of these things would do wonders for me," commented Elanca,

"without aiming for a sex change; others I need to know from you because it is I who is to budget for it all."

"point taken," replied Brendan, her onetime situational and, by implication, adulterous lover.

"we agreed to you doing the feature on the understanding that your magazine underwrite a substantial portion if not all of our expenses, at least as far as Hector was concerned; we trust you, you are here and we want you to be present; what we are dealing with at this stage is common sense and very basic get-to-know-your- patient, not confined to this clinic or our particular project," Brendan argued; "we'll let you film a fair bit and the rest we'll have to negotiate."

"I realize there'll be bits I can't film or report," admitted the reporter, "and I am not even too fussed about what I may or may not cover. Please, continue. . ."

"there isn't much more, Brendan, is there?" asked Hector. "You have all the medical details about myself that I can find and that I have been able to keep over the years; have you been in touch with my doctors?"

"yes, by and large; once we have done some preliminary tests, I have software that will match the results with what your medics in Adelaide have given me, already scanned into my programme," explained the doctor,

"and you'll always be able to sight it; are you ready to share those bits with Elanca which you and I agree on and which she may need for her feature?"

"how does it sound, Elanca?" asked Hector. "logical."

"agreed, then, Brendan. What do you want to test for and which ones may Elanca watch?"

Meanwhile, Ann had managed to get hold of Julia and her mother:

"I am putting you through," the concierge at Hotel Patria had offered, once Rosetta's mother had explained the situation to him. "Jules," Ann queried, "is that you?"

"yes, Ann; we made it to Micronesia. How's school; I got your last few email messages. . ."

"oh, you'll like it; the boys in particular," Ann teased.

"anyone I ought to be jealous of?" (Julia stopped herself from saying 'bitch', not knowing who might listen)

"no, the boys are just themselves, some quite bright, others a bit silly not to say immature, all of them likeable, so far; just people our age, from a sort of different background; I'll explain it a bit more when you are here."

(Julia understood that Ann, too, did not know to what extent their conversation was overheard).

"you'll have to get used to the climate; it is equatorial which means it rains a lot and gets very humid but rarely too hot or cold, day or night; every now and then there's a welcome breeze; everything is green and grows like mad. I miss you. . ."

"not much longer, Ann; Mum wants to talk to you. . ."

Julia's mother got on the phone:

"thank you, Ann, for getting in touch with us. . ."

"do thank our hosts, Rosetta's parents. . ."

"is she the young woman administrator at Dr Mc Groom's clinic."

"yes, Mrs Childers, Mrs Hartwig, the reporter, Dad and myself are staying here, so will you and Jules when you get here. . ."

"won't that get a bit crowded, Ann?"

"Dad's workplace accommodation is not yet ready; they also promised him a car. . ."

"I am sure we will cope; Rosetta's parents run a home-stay, don't they; do you like it?"

"yes; they are lovely people; you'll like them and also the house; all you ever imagined the Pacific to be like, orchids, frangipani, hibiscus, Japanese Lantern, all kinds of scented herbs and flowering shrubs; the ocean close by, corals right by the beach; you'll have to use thongs. . ."

"not like the beach at Glenelg?" asked Julia's mother, remembering a coastal suburb of Adelaide.

"nothing like it; the water's usually much warmer, for one thing."

It did get a bit tight for space when they arrived;

"Your dad can't very well sleep with Julia's mum, can he?" commented Rosetta's mum who had to worry about these domestic details.

"Rosetta is prepared to spend another few nights at the clinic, with some of the girls; if we put two fold-ups in her room, you two girls can share it with Julia's mum; where does that leave you, Mr Landers?"

"Hector, please; the hammock, for me. . ." "you can't be serious!"

"oh no, I am, I am quite looking forward to it, you'll get a lovely breeze on the verandah. . ."

"don't you have a tent-type mosquito net inside which a fold-up would fit," queried Ann, "which we can set up on the verandah, under the awning in case it rains. . ."

"but if we haven't got enough fold-ups. . ." wondered their host;

"in which case Ann and I shall share one in your daughter's room, next to Mum. . ."

Ann urged her lover to cover her bodily even before Julia's mother had fully fallen asleep, with Julia's thigh and knee weighing down on Ann's pelvis and thighs, the girls kissing and Julia raising Ann's arms and cuffing her wrists, as usual. Ann arched against Julia's thigh wedged against her body and let herself be kissed with intense abandon, ecstatically surrendering to her lover's iron grip on her arms.

Julia had been invited to sit in class the very next day, her official schooling not to start till the following Monday.

"we have a science lab session tomorrow on the raising of live mice, Julia", the Vietnamese-descended, gracefully attractive science teacher told the girls.

"I am dying to hear how you see your future as a scientist," she added, "you realise that you must not cease breathing between funding grants before you can even begin to think of doing any research. . ."

"people do not stop telling me, Miss," the confident budding scientist replied.

Everyone realized that the two Australian girls were taking things in their stride and enjoying themselves, with both boys and girls hanging on their every word and move.

Both Jules and Ann attended the lab session the next day, holding hands, or else Jules standing behind her, her hands on Ann's shoulders. Other boys and girls were doing likewise, so it attracted less attention that it had at St Brendan's. It was Ann who asked the most pertinent questions about how to feed and train mice for laboratory work:

"do you test their blood for electrolytes every now and then?"

she asked one of the lab assistants, having to repeat her query a few times; for the young woman had never heard Australian speech before, to much laughter. Jules limited herself to watching the animals go through their moves rather intently, having never before been allowed to do so:

"why are these four or five mice heading in a different direction from the mob?" she wondered eventually.

"Hmm, we put a few of the original control group in here to see whether they were beginning to match the trial group and how long it would take. . . you are not wrong, except that there were more of the original control exposed to the 'majority 'if you like," the biologist explained.

"will we do work on them at school?" enquired Ann, not least on her lover's behalf. "yes, those boys and girls who do advanced science?" "more boys or more girls?" she smiled.

"girls, of course," her part-Vietnamese friend replied, in tones of utter conviction.

Ann's father's first full day at work was also full of surprises; for Ramon had determined that not only his staff but two hard-to-help unemployed young Chamorro were to be involved in crafting the software, which Hector took in his stride, having worked with the Tongans at Barrow Creek.

"what would an employer look for in a worker?" he asked one of the boys. "where do you live?"

"Ok, but why?"

"because," replied the other boy, "he might be afraid that if a job came up closer by, the worker would take it."

Hector smiled. got very busy on his keyboard and crafted his first provisional template.

"what else do they want to know?"

"when was the last time you worked. . ." the boys replied, from bitter experience. "what do you say if you haven't had a day's work in your life. . ."

"if the boss does ask which he probably won't, he might wonder when we left school. . ." more entries on Hector's template:

"would he also ask for things you did at school, in a sports club or so, like a hobby. . ."

"that's what our guidance counsellors said at school but not many ask for that much info," again from multiple experience.

"would previous experience help?"

"depends on," one of the boys replied; "but you cannot get it without a job, nor can you get a job without having done something like that before; it's a mess. . ."

"what would help an employer make up his mind. . ."

"rescuing his niece as she was about to get run over, maybe."

"drastic measures might be called for," Hector agreed.

"But barring the unforeseeable, things you can do. . ."

"dress smartly but that costs money; get there on time and not out of breath but our dads do not always have enough money for fuel, let alone keeping their cars on the road; perhaps not even for bus fare. . ." they sighed.

"would a fare voucher help?" wondered Hector. "we can get those but we normally have to ask for them a day earlier; does not help much if someone rings our parents, or us, to come over at short notice."

"would a standby loan help, such as to buy smart clothes, work tools, monthly bus tickets or a moped. . ."

"these are available but only once you have been promised employment," commented a staff member.

"now let's examine what we need from your point of view, boys," continued Hector:

"what would you like in a job?"

"close to home," one of the boys countered.

"regular hours, rather than being phoned at odd hours or when my girlfriend has something planned. . ." they all laughed.

"a good work-place, clean, well-organised, with good workmates", the other boy.

"Dad once had a job with one of his workmates getting stuck into him; it was enough to make him give it up and he has not had a day's work since," he continued sadly.

"how would internships work?" enquired Hector, still busily typing in code to enlarge his template.

"we don't have too many. . ."

"not even at the hotels or resorts?" asked Hector, surprised.

"no, for insurance reasons; that's their excuse," commented the staff member.

"the ones that do exist go to some girl," added the boys knowingly.

"why is that?" demanded Hector.

They all gave him a pitying look: "Sex," decided the boys.

"girls are known, rightly or wrongly, to fit into a workplace better than boys, work harder and are said to be smarter," opined the staff member.

"could one design jobs that would suit boys?"

"no; for one thing, employers here would like them multi-skilled; besides, that kind of job requires prior experience, and we have very few apprenticeships here, mostly for clerical jobs, hairdressing, kitchen and counter service, retail and, regrettably, not too often for trades-men or–girls. . ."

"how about Guam or any of the other islands?"

"a bit more, maybe, but what Lorenzo here was saying; bosses tend to choose boys-or girls-whose families live close by."

"how about sales jobs?"

"too many," stated Felipe, the other boy:

"the latest is Field Agents where they are supposed to pay you for photos you take with your camera phone; they don't always pay even if they use your shot; then you get mystery shoppers and such crap; lottery tickets, post cards, souvenirs and trinkets. . ."

"pays little and the proprietors disappear. . ."

"fundraising is another one," added the Work Link staffer.

"door knocking?" "yes, and stall-holding. . ."

"does it pay? I used to see myself through as a student doing that. . ." remembered Hector.

"some young people are very good at that; but you need nice casual clothing, good presentation, confidence, the right approach to people; quite a few people object because not all the money goes to charity but pays the collectors and the companies that hire them."

"do you have call centres on Saipan?"

"why, yes, but, once again, they prefer girls, especially those who know languages. . ."

"such as Russian, Korean, Japanese, Chinese," figured Lorenzo.

"what I want to work on in the next few days," concluded Hector, "is design a template for surveys among employers; meanwhile, if I can get you boys to sort out companies, small businesses, corporations, public employers and so on, by size, locality, nature of business, number of employees. . ."

"won't we need maps?" queried Felipe.

"quite; let's have lunch first and then I'll show you boys how to set up blank mapping templates from existing software into which you'll then insert potential employers, by what?"

"type and size", ventured Lorenzo;

"nature, whether a hotel, a scuba club, a bar, a workshop, a club, a government setup, a paint shop, etc." explained Felipe.

"parking or public transport nearby," countered Lorenzo.

"number of workers for which we may have to ring people; can we do that from here?"

"in preparation for a survey, yes," informed them Agapito, a staff member.

"we will design a survey questionnaire which you'll use over the phone. . ."

"and there'll be times when we expect you to front up to places to complete them."

"will that get us a job?"

"nothing to stop you from trying but we may have to prepare you a bit; for it will be an official survey. . ."

"don't mess it up," intoned Lorenzo, to the tune of a popular Micronesian song, with Felipe taking up the next line:

"our beautiful love affair. . ."

Later that afternoon, Ann and Jules were wrestling with the first instalment of their online home schooling programme. Rosetta had set them up in an empty office, with enough computer space and capacity "to run a small army," as she explained when the girls had returned from school.

"It is yours for the duration. . ." she explained, "but you may have to time-share it with Elanca if she needs it by way of a workbench. I'm sure you'll come to an arrangement because she works different hours from yours," the administrator concluded:

"you may help each other, on occasion, even."

Elanca entered at that moment, wanting to scan and arrange some photos. "do you girls want to watch what I am doing?" she offered.

"it won't take long and you may be able to do it yourselves for school projects once you know my templates."

She had taken snaps of some of the rest areas, taking in huge swathes of ocean, coral and nearby mangroves, so much so that you could almost smell them. Hospital staff were relaxing during breaks; sails and outboards could be spotted in the middle distance on an unusually cloudless day,

"which is why I took these shots,"

"because we may not get such days too often this time of the year?" surmised Ann. "yeah; why don't I help you girls find and upload some weather graphs onto your project files; do they do meteorology on your programme?" Jules, the scientist, looked up the index:

"no, but general locational geography features under environmental studies. . ."

"soon as we have scanned some more pics. . . which ones would you girls choose for the feature, by the way? We'll find and upload those weather graphs onto your files. . ." just as Rosetta entered with a pot of green tea, sandwiches and soft drinks, courtesy of the canteen; Elanca and the girls were surprised how hungry they were. "won't happen every day," promised Rosetta, "leftovers of staff training. Ann, remind your dad there'll be a session with the exercise people tomorrow evening," she continued;

"did anyone tell Jules about her initial session?" "when, Rosetta?"

"at the crack of dawn before you get to school. . ." "if I am running late?"

"the clinic has a staff bus to drop kids at school whose parents work here on awkward shifts; we can fit you in, Julia, on mornings that we want to work with you, likewise on afternoons when we need you here quick smart. How does your mum like it here, by the way?"

"oh, for her, it's an unending holiday; I suspect she'll get bored soon, but at present, it's like a cat inside a lab full of mice. . ." Rosetta smiled and helped herself to a sandwich, hungry from seeing all this good food disappear. "I need to leave you to it," she nodded and left.

Several days later, Julia was told that she'd miss out on school that day:

"we'll have to do an ongoing series of tests and have already notified your school; we can't do them all during late-afternoon or early-morning shifts; we hope it will be the last time for a month," Dr Mc Groom informed the girls.

"Ann, would you take a note to her biology teacher to pass on Jules' project tasks to you? My apologies for running you late; we'll allow you onto our staff school bus, instead."

Going through her day at school, Ann decided to head for the science section mid-morning, there to be waylaid by Angh, the hauntingly beautiful daughter of the science teacher:

"Jules' s got those tests on, Ann? Will that happen more often? I don't know how to say this. . ." so she did not, but quite suddenly embraced and kissed the girl and gently held Ann's hands behind her back; Ann surprised herself by responding vigorously to Angh's ardent approach. It was only when Angh started to explore Ann while cuffing her that the girl freed herself:

"Angh, I am spoken for, much as I admire you. . ." "Jules, but why?"

"because she is undergoing treatment for us to function as a genuine couple. . ."

"is love between girls not authentic enough?" asked Angh, perturbed.

"of course, and I am sorry, but for us. . ."

"Jules and yourself, you mean, but she is a girl, is she. . . oh, I see" Angh, as astute and alluring as she was, took a while to work out the implications:

"I shan't say sorry; for I really love and want you, Ann; but I'll try not to make love to you again," kissing her once more then letting go: "you've come for Jules' project pack, haven't you?"

❧

"I was about to be seduced on my way to getting your stuff today, lover,"

Ann told Jules when she got home, having struggled with herself whether to keep it a secret or not ("it is better to be honest; also, Jules might find out from someone who saw us this morning").

"who by?" wondered Jules, somewhat idly.

"I didn't think any of the boys at school had it in them. . ." "not at all, a girl. . ."

"you bitch," interrupted Jules, by now not idly but enraged, "here I am undergoing tests so they can change me over into someone just to give you kicks, ever since fucking Brian bonked you silly last year, whereas you let anyone do you over who can grab you fast enough and hard enough, you. . ."

"slut," admitted Ann, so calmly that Jules was not only out of breath from her outburst but also at a loss for words, for a change.

"I am, but to be 'slutted'-if such a word exists-by you, only and ever-captive to you; that's why we are both here. . ."

"who was it, anyway?" Jules, still irate, wondered.

"no, Jules; for we have to attend school every day. . . one thing I shall tell you; for she was very perplexed and perturbed that I didn't want to be done by a girl. . ."

"why that, bitch?"

"because they can see you claim me in public. . ." "now you are blaming me, you cow. . ." "no, Jules," replied Ann, calmly, "I am telling you what they can see at school; I want you to claim me at all times. . ."

"they are all over each other. . ." admitted Jules;

"not that it seems to matter in Micronesian culture, almost like a massive extended family," confirmed Ann.

"so she challenged me, why did I not want a girl to fuck me-your words-if they could see you blatantly in possession; you are still a girl to them; for they don't know any better, so far. . ."

"did you tell anyone, you slut?"

"no, lover, but the girl who nearly did me is about to work it out by herself. . ."

"how come?"

"I had to admit to her that we were not really into same-gender sex, regardless what it looks like to them. . ."

"but who could spot that one, just based on a negative comment," wondered Jules, ever the scientist, then started mentally going through the possibilities.

"wait a second! That gorgeous Vietnamese girl, your friend; she might just be smart enough; her mother is the science teacher, isn't she?"

"yes, it was her waiting for me with your project pack when she tried. . ."

Jules had calmed down sufficiently to ask Ann:

"Look, Ann, I am not getting mad at you; I am not sorry that I did, but you need to tell me exactly what happened; I have to know, you can see that."

So, Ann told her lover a somewhat pruned version of the morning's event, carefully omitting her initial erotically stimulated reaction, but admitting:

"I was too surprised to react at first: I did wrench myself loose as gently as I could?"

"why gently?"

"well, in case anyone was around, for one; but also I don't mind admitting that I am fascinated by that girl." "at least, you are honest, bitch," acknowledged Jules.

"well, I can afford to because, as I told Angh, I am spoken for," elaborated Ann:

"I am yours physically and in every other way which nothing or no one can change, not you, not I myself, not even someone as sexy and attractive as Angh. . ."

"or another boy like Brian?" wondered Jules, seriously.

"possibly not even he," acknowledged the girl. "You own me and so I can say what I like, including the truth, because it cannot be changed," Ann explained. "I cannot see any alternative to being your physical captive, whether I am being immobilized by you or not; I don't know whether you realize the sheer sense of freedom when you are someone's captive."

"you begging to be bonked tonight?"

"what else? Because Dad and I may move out any day; I think that Work Link has finally found a place for us." Another thought entered her mind:

"you know, lover mine, once you are a boy, I expect you to want to bonk girls like her, smart, attractive, beautiful. . ." "would you like me to, bitch?"

"in a way, yes, lover; you are a scientist, and I would want these, what would you call them, predatorial instincts to kick in each time you get anything like close to girls who are as smart as you and physically more attractive than I," Ann explained: "call it Crude Darwinism: you a Predator and I your Prey." "what are you trying to tell me?"

"that I'd prefer you to keep these urges under control rather than lose them outright.," she stated.

"now, let's talk about something else, such as your project and my homework and what we'll have to do online in the next few days, seeing I may not be living this close much longer. . ."

So they went to work with a will.

Julia's mother was beginning to dislike the thought of having to leave Saipan and Rosetta's parents' household, much as she missed her husband, son and friends in Adelaide. Being a trained accountant, she soon found a series of small enterprises that were desperate for a bookkeeper and got onto skype one evening:

"Trevor, we have to talk. . ."

"is anything the matter with Julia?" the first thing that entered her husband's mind.

"no, Trevor, she is amazing," she explained: "I know she's always known what she wanted. . ."

"determinedly so. . ."

"quite, and nothing much upsets her; but to see her do so well, cope with a totally different environment and such a change, now that it is happening; I haven't got the words to describe let alone explain it." "what is it you need to tell me, Eileen?"

"I want to stay to live here, perhaps for part of the year?"

"work?" her perceptive husband suspected. "how do you know?"

"I've noticed that you weren't happy at work any longer; so what's happened?"

"I met a few ladies who put me in touch with their families who run businesses that find their compliance increasingly difficult. . ."

"so they want you to prepare audits, keep journals and manage stock-takes; haven't they got professionals of their own?"

"yes, they do; not enough of them, expensive and hard to get them in time, they tell me. . ."

"will they recognize your qualifications, dear?"

"I am articled, as you know; they figure they'll help me if I want to get chartered in Micronesia; I'll have to get used to different standards, anyway. . ." "software?"

"that, too; I had a look at what they use here, not impressed," his wife replied, then wondered:

"why are you neither surprised nor determined to make me come back to Adelaide; is there another woman?" suspiciously.

"strangely enough, no; if I need to apologize for not having had another female on standby, then I am profoundly sorry," Julia's father countered drily.

"so why are you so matter-of-fact about it, asking me all these bits, as if you had known. . ."

"because it doesn't come as a surprise," her husband explained sensibly.

"our son is beholden to Erin, not us, any more; our daughter will soon be a boy and she already functions as Ann's partner, or maybe sibling, rather than our child; your workplace sucks and you can always put yourself on leave without pay. . ."

"and yourself," queried his wife, "do you no longer see yourself as my fulltime husband?"

"I do: for I am not oriented towards anyone or anywhere else, apparently uniquely so in our particular nuclear family," he informed her, unperturbed:

"don't forget that I'll be in Saipan myself to see our child through this change," he explained: "if you like, I can arrange to use up all my annual leave and then some, as you'll probably have to. . ."

"when, Trevor?" his wife wondered, relieved.

"ask Elanca to what extent my travels are covered by her budget and see whether you can find us some accommodation through one of your business partners; make it contingent if you like. . ."

"of course. Right now, it is getting a bit crowded," she informed him: "the girls share a bed in my room. . ." "willingly, no doubt. . ."

"oh yes, but they are quite discreet about it; Ann's dad is about to move her and himself out. . ."

"has his company found him a place, then?" "it looks that way, yes."
"what is your home-stay like, Eileen?"

"Rosetta works for the clinic; I am using her room as she sleeps either at the clinic or with some of the girls most of the time, and her parents couldn't be more like family if they actually were; can't do enough for you; I think they are quite pleased to have another family stay with them and share, even from a totally different background." "will you be sad to leave them?"

"yes, mutual, I'd say; but if you want to come and stay with us for a length of time and if I am to work. . ." "try and find a point in time closer to the operation. . ."

"to give you more time to sort out the Adelaide end of things. . ."

"such as renting out the place, setting up Stephen and Erin; deciding whether to return to Adelaide, eventually, or remain in Micronesia once I get there. . ."

"look, don't get me wrong, darling; I am your full-time wife, separated by nothing but distance for the moment." Famous last words these; little did she know. . .

Elanca, almost as busy as Julia's mum was beginning to find herself, still found time to sit her down on their common verandah since Rosetta's parents gone off to a church retreat for a few days.

The two women had made themselves a salad based on amaranth, cassava and hibiscus leaves, as well as basil and some other herbs, sprinkled with tender neem shoots, all from the garden, laced with hard-boiled eggs, pineapples, coconuts found on the beach and skilfully split by one of the hospital workers, then shredded, and a dressing based on passion fruit, vinegar, grated onions, garlic salt and lemon juice. They ate it with rice crisps and drank homemade passion wine to which they had taken a liking.

"Finger-licking good, Eileen, is it not?" Elanca sighed.

"I haven't seen much of you; are you serious about finding work and staying?"

"yes; I skyped Trevor a few days back; he's not too fussed about me living and working here. . ."

"does he want to come and join you?"

"not permanently, for the time being; but definitely to be with us closer to when Julia is to be operated on; have you an idea when this will be, Elanca?"

"I don't get to see Brendan as much as I'd like. . . meaning, his wife's just had a hysterectomy. . ."

"but he hasn't. . ."

"don't I know it!" the reporter sighed. "I did get some footage with him and your daughter once again when she had to stay behind all day for these tests. . ."

"what did he say?"

"provided that Julia keeps up with the hormone cocktail that he's designed for her, he'll start exploratory surgery in six weeks. . ." Julia's mum was, understandably, very quiet for a while.

"we agreed for it to happen; with luck, if that's the right word, she'll be 'equipped 'close to her sixteenth birthday"

"are we learning suggestive language from our teenage children now?" the reporter wondered.

"afraid so," the mother sighed. "why was your husband not surprised, Eileen?"

"look, I haven't been happy at work for a long time now; our son has been all but hijacked by his girlfriend and Trevor's work arrangements are flexible enough to leave and return whenever he likes; he sounded quite happy for me to have a sea- change, quite literally. . ." looking out across the lagoon.

"Now you want to know whether the magazine's budget will cover that kind of arrangement?"

"yes, more or less. . ."

"well, your return ticket can be adjusted; if there's an expense associated with it, we'll split it if you like," the journalist concluded: "as to Trevor, we had provided for him to arrive in time for the operation, as a family presence needs to be covered by our feature; we'll just have to have an arrangement with our tame ticketing agent that allows him also to stay as long as you need him here. As to yourself, give me a dummy date for your return to Adelaide sometime next year, whether you go or not," she explained:

"be honest with me, would you want you to live here as a family, complete with husband, child and, who knows, future daughter-in-law?"

"to be very honest, I need to wait till he gets here to be able to decide that; I do miss him," the other woman said, "but I do prefer it here. . ."

"your daughter has settled in very well," the reporter commented.

"yes, I have no worries there, except that I still have to work through her ending up as a boy, eventually as another son, if your know what I mean. . ."

"well, tell you what I'll do," concluded Elanca, finishing her last bit of salad and speaking with her mouth almost full. "I'll get you to give me a dummy date on your return ticket and I'll arrange one for Trevor, with a use-by date set at about three months which will give him some six weeks, starting with Julia's first surgery. How does that sound, Eileen?"

"good; let's get to work," answered Julia's mum and finished her portion of the rather rich salad, lasciviously slurping her last bit of passionfruit wine. "Ah, the good life, Elanca. . ."

Ann's father, while making very good process at work and looking forward to training more young Chamorros, was getting worried about not hearing from Glen and not having his email returned at all for several days now. He was barely able to restrain himself when Glen did ring him at work:

"I know there's time difference but that ought to be the only thing separating us at this stage. . ."

"meaning what, Hector?"

"very soon, whatever changes I am committed to on your behalf will be irreversible. . ."

"even before the operation, Hec?"

"yes, so I am told; I am beginning to notice a distinct skin tone and I am sure you'd notice that my voice sounds. . ." "looking forward to the difference, Hector?"

"are you trying to be sarcastic, Glen?"

"oh, not at all," replied his contrite partner; "you would want me around at a time like this. . ."

"can't you, Glen? Julia's mother has arranged for their dad to be around in a few weeks when Jules' time has come. . ."

"You know, this posits a dilemma, none of your making, which is why I am ringing you now and from home, not work. . ." "what happened, Glen?"

"my company was offered the employment service provider contract currently held by yours; even though I am our managing director and did absent myself from the negotiations, we had included a provision in an earlier tender application so as to be considered if it were offered again which it has and which has resulted in your general contract being up for review. . ." long silence:

"your work in Saipan is not likely to be affected, Hector; for not only are you an independent entity for that particular purpose, your funding is from two distinct sources unconnected to ours."

"how does it affect you, though, Glen?"

"I may have to resign from my own company; for I cannot risk it losing out on those contracts, but also out of loyalty to you which I have had to declare, hence my not being involved with the negotiations. . ." "the consequences, Glen?"

"both you and I shall not have a job or a company to return to from Saipan, unless either of our employers find ways to use us outside of currently existing or, in my case, future, contracts; do you still want to go ahead, Hector?" "yes." "very well, I'll be in Saipan very soon; I'll let Nina know and get in touch with Elanca. . ." "they may be able to fit you in their budget; for you were to have arrived at some stage, anyway." "we live in hope," agreed Glen.

Glen's flight to Saipan was a sombre affair, in contrast to when his partner Hector and Ann had undertaken that same journey, full of expectations and treating it as a holiday. Not only was he very worried about giving up his very senior and well paid-job which he felt duty-bound to do but also that Hector would have no job to return to in Adelaide; "lucky he's got his leave loading to cover his long-service leave and that he's legally and financially on his own",

Glen kept telling himself: he also realized that they had yet to develop the kind of intimacy that had come naturally to the 'girls', "maybe because they are young."

Glen had decided to upgrade Nina's economy ticket to business class to better face the long flight, time difference and geographical changes he'd have to cope with within a short time span, without any stopovers. Nina had notified Elanca of his impending arrival; Glen had no idea what arrangements would be made. His flight from Guam having been delayed, he did not know whether anyone was waiting for him at Saipan International Airport.

Merv the Cobbler, the descendant of Filipino shoe-menders who had arrived from Negros Oriental five generations ago and of Chamorro fisherfolk, equally good with their hands, had made his fortune by developing the Reef Shoe, calculated to prevent corals from piercing the soles of your feet when crossing them barefoot or on thongs:

"Remember that corals are live organisms which can survive in your body, supported by nutrients in your bloodstream," a tame doctor had once told his parents, to stop their boy from running across coral beaches barefoot. A genius former classmate of his had come up with an advertising campaign featuring a superimposed image of the Great Barrier Reef inside a person's hearts and lungs, courtesy of wildly proliferating coral cells inside the bodies of those too stingy or careless to avail themselves of, guess what!

It was Merv's sister Antonia who had first approached Eileen, Julia's mother, successfully, as it turned out: "The boys need a book-keeper; Merv has gone through a few and his fellow Rotarians are struggling to find and keep any, "she had explained at a church dinner." our economy has simply grown too much but also too lopsided; so most of our kids can't get jobs. . ."

"which is what Ann's father is here for," agreed Jules' mother.

"but the few people with decades of work experience, like yourself in accounting, are few and far between and all spoken for."

"any worries with paperwork?" Eileen had been concerned.

"most of that can be dealt with via the Rotarians quite easily; bless Micronesia in that respect!"

Eileen had been impressed by Merv. his cheerful good manners and open, trusting nature, and by the way he had memorized every detail of his shoe franchise: "but it is getting too big for that; "he explained to her on her first day;

"not only do tourists, Russians especially, make our Reef Shoes walk off the shelves, you could say, we sell a wide range of shoes and leather-made goods; I just got hold of two Pakistani specialist tanners. . . the paperwork was frenetic, believe me, so I can expand my workshop; I also fund virtually all street cobblers here and on several other islands so they can continue to visit people at their homes and mend shoes and leather goods or work street-side. . ."

"how do you do that?"

"voucher system, Eileen. . ." pouring her another cup of coffee.

"I sell tokens through certain outlets which cobblers honour and get refunded; I also hand out vouchers which cobblers can get refunded if their customers pay cash, instead. . ."

"that helps those who haven't had too many calls on their services. . ."

"exactly; you would have to keep track of these vouchers; eventually, you may be able to train someone; it isn't that difficult and I have more demanding work for you; stock-takes, audit preparation, both internal and otherwise, payroll tax, internal revenue service returns. . ."

"how many days per week, Merv?"

"two, to start with," the businessman answered. "I want you to have time for yourself and your daughter, or else help some of my fellow Rotarians; work it out your own; do you need accommodation?"

Elanca had rung the airport, only to find out that Glen's arrival would be delayed; they'd let her know. Eventually, it was Rosetta who found out:

"Elanca, the flight has arrived but I have nobody to pick Glen up, nor can I go myself; can you?"

"he is my baby, or the magazine's, anyway; thanks, Rosetta; but can you ring Eileen if she can get him, instead of me, on her way back from work, and I shall ring Hector at work. . ."

"I forgot, Elanca, that you only have a scooter and that might not be enough to carry Glen and his luggage. . ." "if he were a Chamorro, it might; I have seen people do that here. . ."

"perhaps better not; I'll ring Eileen at work. . ." "where is she today?"

"at Wickedly Sweet, preparing a shop re-modeling. . ."

"talented woman; please, see whether she can get to the airport in time. . ."

She rang off and got onto WorkLinks instead:

"Elanca Hartwig here, the Australian journalist. I need to talk to Hector Landers and his mobile is turned off," she explained once she finally did get through to what turned out to be Lorenzo.

"I am outside for a smoke, Ms Hartwig," the boy told her,

"we are doing an audio inside a soundproof studio. . ." "for an intranet recording?"

"yes; would you like me to pass on a message?"

"yes, Lorenzo; tell Mr Landers that Glen Hiddings is about to arrive and that Jules' mother, Mrs Childers, that is, will pick him up and deliver him. . ." "here at work?" "yes, Lorenzo; I'll catch up with all of you myself; what time do you thing you'll be finished with the feature?" "another hour, tops, Ms Hartwig."

("these boys have come a long way in a short time," the reporter thought, having met them as part of her effort to cover Hector's work on the island.

"it shows what boys are capable of when you take them seriously, give them responsibility.")

Meanwhile, Eileen had found a space to park her car, lent to her by yet another Rotary wife:

"my daughter is in Hawaii studying at the East West Institute there; she carpools most of the time and it would have been too expensive to ship her car there, anyway; so it is here; feel free to use it; Merv will get insurance cover. . ." which turned out to be yet another service club member whose approach to paperwork was relaxed, to say the least, Merv having paid her first instalment.

Eileen remembered Glen so she was certain she'd recognize him. What she had not reckoned with was, as she later described it:

"we both knew when we looked at each other that something had changed; we looked again, rather than walk up to each other, as if pinned to the ground. Eventually, we walked halfway, then stopped again, as if having been hit; he then waited for me to walk towards him, opened his arms, hugged and kissed me and held my hand."

As if he had forgotten, he picked up his two suitcases and, with another bag slung over his shoulder, followed her to the car. Eileen opened the boot, all the time looking at him expectantly.

"you look different from when I last saw you," commented Glen, his worrisome flight momentarily forgotten.

"you look good, too, Glen, but very tired. I'll drive you to Hector's workplace; Elanca will be there, too." "do you actually work here, Eileen?" he asked once seated on her passenger seat, having dropped his cases and bag in her boot.

"yes, I book-keep part-time, Glen." "is Trevor here?" he remembered to ask.

"not yet; another three to four weeks, I'd say." "work?" "that, too," she evaded.

"do you want to stay in Micronesia instead of Adelaide?"

"yes, Glen; I feel freer and better than I have in years. . ."

"then I am very happy for you, Eileen." "thank you, Glen. You'll like it here, too. . ."

Glen sighed: "It is very beautiful and I like the warm tropical air all right. . ."

Their welcome at Hector's workplace was warm; Ramon spotted the car first: "Hector, it looks that Glen has arrived but I do not know the lady who is driving him,"

Ramon recognizing Glen from a video taken at a workplace safety conference in Hawaii way back.

"Oh. She must be Jules' mum," figured Felipe; "my sister saw her at school with the girls one day"

Glen and Hector embraced but not with as much warmth as one might have expected.

They stood next to each other:

"had a good flight, Glen?"

His partner shrugged:

"in itself, all right, I chose business, but I had too much on my mind. . . have you people finished for the day?" "no, Mr Hiddings. . ." "Glen, please"

"Glen, then," corrected Ramon, "but you are welcome to watch us or participate in our session on body language. . ."

"which I then try to code into software, a bit like we did at Barrow Creek, Glen"

"so Ramon here will then work out how to put into practice what you enact here and what you have keyed into software which anyone could tap into, an employer, for instance," concluded Glen "where may I leave my bags; but I also have to thank Eileen before she leaves. . ." which he did, with considerable warmth.

Eileen, having been duly thanked, drove off to the clinic to pick up Jules who, by then, would have finished her homework, to take her home to the place that the Rotary ladies had found and furnished for them:

"Sonya is on the Mainland, Oregon to be precise, to help her sister there cope with chemotherapy. . ."

"I am sorry to hear that."

"so are we; Regina is married to a lawyer there and there are children to be looked after; but you are welcome to her home," their den mother had offered whose husband's business was also to benefit from Eileen's vast bookkeeping skills;

"I rang Sonya yesterday and Merv will forward a monthly to her. . ."

"by way of rent?"

"yes, but mainly for her to have an income while she's in Eugene and cannot work so she doesn't have to live off her sister's family."

"well, I am sure Merv will deduct the relevant amount," said the accountant.

"Mum, what's happened to you?"

was the first thing out of Jules' mouth when she left the office where she and Ann had been working on their school projects.

"what's supposed to have happened?" her mum knew what her daughter had noticed. "I don't know what you are up to these days but would you like me to tell Dad when he gets here?"

"is there anything to tell, Jules?"

"I don't know but you look as if someone had told you that you had won the lottery but you weren't sure that he was right but half-hoping he was. . ."

Jules, the perceptive future plant ethicist, speaking.

"I picked up Ann's father 's future partner from the airport since the hospital had no vehicle or person to spare and Elanca wasn't sure that she could balance him and his luggage on her scooter. . ." "perhaps not, even though the Chamorros seem to manage."

"Glen is no Chamorro. . ." "Mum!"

Julia then scratched her head and put her arm on her mum's, shaking her head.

"parents; who'd have them"

(making a mental note not to tell Ann, much as she was as committed to ruthless honesty as her loved one). "where is he now, Mum?"

"at Work Link, taking part in an audio-visual to be put onto a net-based package."

"whatever turns them on," Julia commented. "Is her dad coming to pick up Ann later?"

"I'd say so; go and tell her, then come so we can drive home. Do you have any more work?"

"yes, some, which I can do on my laptop, Mum."

Ann's father sat Glen next to him as he drove to the clinic to pick up Ann after when he hoped she had finished both her homework and her on-line schooling for the day,

"a double burden, having to conform to two different standards, Glen. . ."

"but they seem to be coping cheerfully and well. . ."

Hector nearly stopped the car in the middle of rush hour so that horns began to blare, then started the car and drove off into a side street, stopping there.

To his credit, Glen said nothing but waited "We are both professionals and we both know what I about to say is true; like the girls, you have to set your own standards, whether you are rewarded or not. . ."

"of course, you are, in the long run," argued Glen;

"yes and we know so, including Jules and Ann, two very perceptive young people; but you must act in the short term and you are not likely to tell yourself if you do two sets of homework when everyone else does one that you end up with a Nobel Prize in sixty years' time."

"even if that were true. . ." mused Glen: "are you trying to develop a recipe against massive youth unemployment, Hec?"

"in a sense, yes; that's what we are here for. . . I'll put it a bit differently; nobody in Chamorro society goes without food, a roof over his or her head and at least one meal a day, that applies to most people in Australia, fortunately, still. . . but I think we have forgotten to teach young people to be ambitious for its own sake. . ."

"can you develop any software to remedy that, Hec?" "on a sense-of-play basis, perhaps. . ."

"you are telling me you never thought this through until I made this particular comment just now?"

"yes, Glen, at least in so many words," acknowledged his partner.

"but you seem not exactly depressed but preoccupied."

"this is understandable, Hec: You are about to have no job to go back home to once this assignment ends. . ."

"how about my long-service leave. . ."

"Ryan is fighting for that; It's likely to be absorbed by the period of notice that they have to give you. I wish I had better news, Hec. . ."

"and I wish, Glen, that this would not have caused the dilemma you are in; it is very decent of you to resign, rather than accept for yourself what was taken from our company. . ."

"well, in a sense, I had no choice but to recuse myself when your contract came up; my company did not seek it so much as got it by default. . ."

"because your mob is the only other one in South and Central Australia as qualified and able. . ."

"as yours; as it is, I do not have the grace period that's available to you with your project and your long-service leave. . ." "didn't they give you a payout?" wondered Hector, surprised.

"yes, because I withdrew because of a conflict of interests which the board recognized. . . it could have been worse."

⚹

Ann was waiting for them outside the clinic; she kissed Glen and leant against her dad, then entered the car carrying her satchel. "Jules was in the clinic all day for some tests and exploratory stuff."

"do you miss not sharing a space with her day and night?" asked Glen.

"yes, but she is doing it for me and I see her almost every day, all day; once we both study and work at different places, that may not be the case. . ."

"true", acknowledged her dad's future partner. "How do you like living here, going to school, making friends, absorbing another culture. . ."

"fine; I couldn't be happier, Glen."

Eventually, Hector and Glen were alone with each other.

"how do you feel, Hec?"

"strange, a bit like an insect might that morphs into a different life form. . ." "interesting comparison," said Glen, undressing.

"shower together?"

"yes; it pays to eat, go to bed, do things in the same sequence and at the same time as the locals to minimize jetlag. . ."

"wasn't what I asked, Glen, but it is true; nice to be thought of as a local; rinse me off, would you?"

"what did you mean by 'metamorphosis', Hec?"

"it sounds like Jules the scientist; but you are right," admitted Hector:

"not only am I about to lose my job, but also give up my gender, so it is a double new beginning, quite elating. You realize that some fish start as males, then end up female,"

"worms likewise," added Glen.

"let's go to bed," offered Hector; so they did, lying very close. Glen fell asleep almost instantly, Hector only then realizing that neither had eaten and that they had left Ann to her own devices.

"I'll get up early tomorrow and fix us some Micronesian breakfast," he vowed before he, too, nodded off.

That is what happened next morning.

"Did you get anything to eat, Ann?" he asked his bleary-eyed daughter, having himself got up with some difficulty, Glen having wedged himself halfway across their bed.

"yeah, I raided your drawer for some money and dialled a pizza, delivered by a boy- and-girl team in the most bombed-out vehicle I have seen since you took me to Central Australia two years ago. . ."

"with tyres even more deflated that theirs?" smiling, remembered that desert Aborigines tend to let air out for their cars to have a better grip on the terrain.

"almost as much; moreover, it was a manual and its gears shifted at random; amazing that it didn't wake you up," his daughter countered. "what is Glen like in bed, by the way, Dad?"

"sleepy," her father explained; Ann laughed.

Hector then set up breakfast: papaya, coconut milk, rice flakes, fried fish (the seller had just passed the house), amaranth salad and green tea. Glen woke up, showered and sat down:

"thanks, Hec; did I fall asleep on you?" "yes, you did" "did I snore, Ann?"

"both of you snore," she corrected; "I cannot say which one was noisier. . ."

"did you get any sleep?" "not much; I must admit I miss being in bed with Jules. . ."

"can't have everything in life," her father stated sagely, then reminded her:

"don't rush your food, the school bus will be here in twenty-five minutes; have you got everything ready?"

"yes, Dad; I did some more work last night and then packed everything. Do you have to go to the clinic today?" "yes, later; I can pick you up there, Ann. Glen, eat your breakfast; there's a good boy," he turned and faced his partner. "you sound like Mum used to, Dad. . ."

"soon, my daughter, your dad will be your mum," promised Glen

Eileen's conviction that her place to live and work was in Micronesia and no longer in South Australia was growing daily if not by the hour; her time in Adelaide as a wife, employee and mother was becoming more and more like a dream; the fact that Trevor was still there, running his company and Glen, Ann's father's putative partner, was nearby definitely helped; for she increasingly realized how smitten she was, based on that brief moment of instinctive rapport they had at the airport; she soon had a chance to reinforce that impression.

"Eileen, would you drive over to Work Find and interview some of their young ones,"

Merv asked her one day over coffee, pointing out a newspaper article.

"It's something to do with the youth employment programme that your Australian friends are involved with; the government decided to match their training effort. . ."

"Employment Readiness?" she queried.

"that's what they called it in the paper," he agreed, "by offering actual incentives. . ."

"makes sense; you cannot really prepare young people for employment if there is none, as we keep finding out in Australia; our apprenticeship system is in shreds, has been for decades, so that we don't have the tradesmen and skilled people we need. . ."

"that could happen here," admitted Merv, setting down his cup.

"drive over, anyway, Eileen, have a look, make contact with some young ones and choose one or two, maybe three, whom we can interview. . ."

"what kind of apprenticeships, Merv?"

"two as cobblers and general leatherworkers. . ." "hmm. . ."

"yes, I have these Pakistani master tanners, as you know; I had always wanted them to train someone locally; now with these incentives, I can."

"don't the Punjabis want to stay?"

"not really; Abed wants to move to the Mainland after a few years where he has relatives, Aziz wants to return to Pakistan to get married and take over his future wife's family's business; they both need to last another three or four years here, to qualify for the Green Card on the mainland or the business establishment bonus which is part of their contract."

"anyone else, Merv?" "a salesperson, perhaps two, to be trained by our staff, including yourself."

Eileen arrived in the middle of a coffee break shared by Ramon, Glen, Hector, Elanca, the two boys, and a few more boys and girls who had just ceased working away at their laptops, still casting looks at their screens even while drinking and nibbling on sunflower seeds and nuts imported from Vietnam. "You are morphing into Merv's business manager, aren't you, Eileen?"

Ramon greeted her, asking her to sit down and offering coffee.

"have you got tea, instead?"

"Vietnamese teabags, very strong; is that all right?"

"yes, Ramon; thank you," she accepted, having met him several times already.

"Elanca, good to see you; is that part of your feature?"

"that I don't know yet; I want to get as much footage and general material as I can; it is always easier to leave lots out than to have to make up for what you haven't got, "the reporter commented.

Eileen looked at Ann's father while stealing a glance at Glen.

"we met at the hearing, Hector," she reminded him

"true, but it is only now that we get to see you by yourself. . ." "very different?"

"yes," answered Glen, instead.

"very much so," agreed Hector. "You seem to fit into the place very well. . ."

"you like it here, Eileen, don't you?"

"yes," she addressed herself to Elanca: "It is as if I had never lived in Adelaide, and that is ridiculous; for I speak with an Australian accent; I grew up in South Australia and have never before lived overseas; now I do and enjoy every bit of it."

"it is good to see you here;" Ramon nodded; "did Merv ask you. . ."

"yes," she interrupted; "I don't know whether you read in the paper. . ."

"about the apprenticeship incentive scheme?" interrupted Felipe.

"Lorenzo showed me in the paper today but it seems that the team here knew about it already. . ."

"and we were wondering how soon a business would contact us while we were training. . ."

Glen explained. "are you part of the team now, Glen?"

She smiled to let him know that she was not trying to patronize him but genuinely wanted to know.

"Glen is at a loose end and wants to set up as employment consultant here, as soon as. . ."

"we quite like to have Glen's input, as a bonus to what Hector here is doing with us; for his background and perspective is a bit different from ours," stated Ramon; "nor does it cost us anything extra; we budgeted for ad hoc expertise."

"did you come to enquire about the apprenticeship incentive, Eileen?" asked Elanca. "no, Merv asked me to find among you a few potential recruits; if your team can help with the paperwork, I won't have to do it," she added practically.

"salesmanship?" asked Lorenzo;

"yes, and two cobblers and leather-craftsmen or – girls. . ."

"oh, to work with the Pakistanis," wondered the girls: "they are so sexy, like Bollywood film stars."

"they are also very skilled master craftsmen, I'll have you know," corrected Ramon;

"likewise, if Reef Shoes wants to train any of you as salespeople, you are in good hands with them"

"why don't we try the aptitude tests we are working on to see how you'd shape up," suggested Glen, looking searchingly at Eileen for the first time.

"we developed the original templates in Barrow Creek, with the local Tongans there," commented Hector,

"and now, we are in the process of refining them"

"you could stay if you like to see us in action," suggested Glen eagerly.

"I might, for a short while, to see how these work; but I'll have to get back to work; I have two more accounts to do, not just for Merv; send whoever wants to and scores on your system over this afternoon, say at three; maximum six, boys or girls; for we may need four."

"let's finish up here and get started, then," ordered Ramon. "Elanca, stay here and watch us also."

"happy to," Elanca agreed, "not just because of the feature. . ."

Glen and Hector drove to the clinic for yet another test and to pick up Ann who had stopped there, to do her homework and to be with Jules who, too, had to undergo a screening.

"You and Eileen. . ." began Ann's father.

"you haven't lost your roving eye, either," observed Glen.

"I realize that; doctor Samira, the girls at Barrow Creek, Natasha and Nina; yet," mused Hector:

"this one was different as if you were each aware what the other was doing without looking at each other; if anything, it seemed to me that both of you made every effort not to. . . and yet. . ."

"look, Hec; do you want to go ahead?"

"with my sex change? Of course; we have begun to involve too many people, but don't forget that the Ethics Committee made approval contingent on our ongoing relationship. . ."

"true, Hec."

"as turning myself into a woman is concerned, my main worry is how the good Saipan islanders will react if they encounter us as workplace provision consultants and me a female, to boot. . ."

"but that affects only those who used to know you in your present incarnation," stated Greg,

"if I understand rightly what you are offering me. . ."

"yes, a joint consultancy, seeing that we are both stranded, or I soon will be. . ." concurred Hector,

"as to our inclinations; I trust that we shall come to an agreement, might even be easier. . ."

"what makes you say that, Hec?"

"one thing I am certain, or would not be surprised, about Eileen not getting back to Trevor, or not taking him back if he were to turn up to share her life here; that's not necessarily anything to do with you, Glen, but it may help. . ."

"it's called a ménage a trois," smiled Glen:" "you are yet to turn into a female; Eileen has yet to disown her own husband, along with life in Adelaide. . ."

"of which she has taken the one step but not the other," added Ann's father;

"she may yet have to make an intentional choice between the two, much as she has already decided to live here."

"and Trevor has a business to look after, and staff and clients to mind, in Adelaide, not here," conceded Glen:

"I will admit to a sizably profound attraction and I also feel that it is mutual. . ."

"look, let it happen if it must," offered Ann's father, "all I ask and expect of you is not to back out. . ." "that I can promise, Hec; we are a team. . ."

Trevor rang Eileen a few days later:

"I hear you are gainfully occupied on Saipan, darling,"

"yes, Trev, four book-keeping clients and the running of the shoe franchise, my paperwork is about through for commercial residency in Micronesia; will you come?" his wife wondered.

"do you want me to?" Trevor enquired.

"do; I want you here. . ."

"but are you likely to come back with me once I leave," her husband enquired sensibly.

"no, but do come, anyway. . ." "is there someone else?"

"yes, your daughter is about to become a son soon. . ." "you know that is not what I mean. . ."

"but it is what I say, dear: our daughter will be operated on in less than four weeks, perhaps less than two." Forgetting his suspicions for a moment, Trevor said:

"does it not take years to get someone ready for gender change, Eil. . .?"

"yes, but these people discovered a kind of fast-track; hence Doctor Brendan's input. . ."

"is he a good doctor?" Jules' father asked.

"oh yes, he was reinstated two weeks ago and the locals respect him; a few women I talked to were treated, they or their daughters, sisters or close friends; they can't praise him enough for his bedside manners and his skills. . ."

"well, he is a gynaecologist; there are still people in Adelaide who speak highly of him," added Trevor." May I sum up for the defence?" he continued, "you want me to come for Jules' sake as much as ours but you are indifferent, to say, the least, whether I end up staying or not, whereas you will, for the foreseeable future, right?"

"yes, more or less," his wife agreed, "but do come soon!"

How soon, Eileen was to find out only a few days later when Brendan rang her at work.

"Dr Mc Groom here, Brendan. . . speaking," he began. "what is this call about, personal or professional?" asked Jules' mother. "the latter, really, but I am also ringing as a friend."

"has crunch time arrived?"

"for Jules; close enough, I'd say; could you pick Jules and Ann up at school, please, and get them here," he instructed her. "Your husband has yet to arrive?"

"yes, Trevor's been delayed with some business problems he hopes to get behind him within the next two weeks." "he may be in time then for the actual operation if it comes to that."

"are you seeing Glen and Hector at the same time, doctor?" "more or less, yes."

"Fair enough," Jules' mum agreed. "I'll let the school know and shall text the girls. . . can't call them that in plural much longer, can I?" "no," answered the doctor curtly.

Dr Mac Groom also rang Ramon at work:

"Is it all-right if I get Glen and Hector to come and see me tonight, Ramon?"

"yes, Brendan; thanks for ringing me first; for we have a specialist here from Guam. . ."

"what type of specialist, Ramon?" "a software linguist. . ."

"like somebody who develops translation software?"

"yes; only that she specializes in terminology. You have been with us long enough, Brendan, to know that medical nomenclature does not render very well in Chamorro but we do need to explain the implications. . ." "I have to, at the Medical Examiner's Court, except in reverse. . ."

"we only have Amelia here for a day; needless to say, both Glen and Hector are smitten with her. . ."

"close to being besotted?"

"you could say that," agreed their colleague; "she is quite fascinated with them as well; it also means they get on fantastically and we are getting a lot of work done. . ."

"so you would like to have them leave later in the evening. . ."

"can it wait till tomorrow, Brendan?"

"basically so, yes, except that I asked the young ones to come, along with Jules' mum; it would leave Ann without her dad."

"let me be a bit devious, Brendan; I'll let Ann's father know, closer to the time, and get him to ring you, to see whether he should make the effort; he and Glen can decide whether to attend to you tonight or wait. . ."

"if I get to see them tomorrow, would lunch hour be all right?"

"yes; you might share lunch with them, either in the canteen or at Rosetta's parents' home if they don't mind."

"and send them back afterwards; good idea? Does your Amelia want to leave on a late flight?"

"no, we've booked her on the dawn flight; she's staying at my sister's place who lives right by the airport, a few hundred yards of walking distance; she'll need to be ready at about the time that my brother-in-law comes back from nightshift. . ."

"does he work at the airport?"

"yes, he's the one who drove Ann and her dad to the clinic when they first got here. . ."

"I think I recognized him; say hello to him, please, and to your sister also."

Amelia was a short but well-configured young woman of obvious intelligence who evidently enjoyed her work and the company that she was doing it in, explaining her approach to two attractive men, good listeners both:

"see, Hector and Glen, we do not really have a unified term for unemployment, let alone youth unemployment in Chamorro," she explained, "and I noticed that whoever designed your software, used a circumlocution; why and how?"

"we had a young woman, herself of Micronesian descent, supervise another girl's writing it," smiled Ann's father,

"but I designed the template in consultation with Aline and Glen here made sure of a context that allowed us to be both specific and flexible. . ."

"which is, by the way, why you won the tender, Hector, against considerable resistance in your own capital city, I may add." interjected Ramon.

"In any event," the girl explained: "you gentlemen arrived at statements such as Not having any work, Needing paid work, Working for someone not your family, and I like your description of Unskilled Work as 'tasks anyone can do'", she smiled:

"It makes my work so much easier; besides, you trained Lorenzo and Felipe very well; would it be possible," she turned to Ramon, "to involve some girls?"

"yes, we have done so," he agreed, "but, as you know, it is usually easier for them to find work than for the boys. . ."

"plus, you didn't want the templates to turn out too gender-specific but you know what our society is like, Ramon."

"we have about four hours left, Amelia. We'll have a few girls here in half an hour; why don't you work with them?" "if I need help with the templates, I know what to do," she nodded.

"you seem to understand them quite well now" stated Hec.

Eileen had asked the school to put the girls on the clinic's school bus that afternoon, so, as soon as Jules and Ann arrived, in the computer room, they were surprised to see Jules' mother there.

"Is it all right, Mum, if we start on some of the online stuff from Australia. . ."

"before Doctor Mc Groom gets to see you? Yes, but why the online material first?"

"because it's close to overdue whereas our homework can wait till tomorrow afternoon, Mrs Childers" "we have a sports day tomorrow, Mum!"

"so you should get to bed early tonight, both of you," decided Jules mother.

The good doctor arrived about half an hour later.

"finish what you are doing, Jules and Ann," he advised, "then join me over a pot of tea in my surgery, please; you, too, Mother of Jules," he invited her: "your dad, Ann, is delayed at work, the two of them, actually, rang in about half an hour ago, Ann."

"will they be finished by that time we join you, Doctor Mc Groom?"

"we live in hope, Ann. I am heading back, please, join me as soon as you finish," he explained which they did.

"The rest can wait," suggested Ann, "I'll ring Dad when Doctor Mac Groom has finished with us, so he and Mr Hiddings can be attended to and he can drive me home afterwards. Could you wait that long, Mrs Childers?" she asked courteously "within reason, yes." They sat down in Brendan's anteroom, with him pouring green tea from his set, having first readied the cups with steaming hot water:

"the girls are preparing the theatre for a lady whose blood pressure has gone up suddenly before her operation tomorrow;" he explained: "we don't need it for what I want to find out from you, Jules, which is. . ." "let Ann have her say, first, Doctor Mac Groom. . ."

"go ahead, then, Ann." Jules had got up, her cup of tea in one hand and her other one resting on the girl's shoulder, as per habit. Ann took, kissed and held it, smiling: "I saw that photo of an incredibly sexy thirty-year old woman on the front page of the paper a few days back," she started, "I hope that I'll be as desirable as that and be as subservient and as sexually attractive to you, Jules, then, as I am now." She kissed her lover's hand once more and then let it rest on her shoulder.

"I want to experience you as a boy and, eventually, as a man, both inside my body and in my life. . ."

"so much is known, Ann," argued the doctor.

"yes, but what I am saying, Jules and Doctor Mc Groom, I'll accept whatever Jules decides for herself and for me, now and ever, whether she's ready for boyhood or not. . ."

"Julia?" wondered her mother.

"thank you, all of you," replied Ann's lover; "I'll go ahead as intended. . ."

"knowing that treatment will be irreversible from now on even if we were not to operate?" queried the doctor. "I am aware of that, from the changes that I have already undergone. . ."

"in that case," smiled the doctor, "I have some strange, possibly good news for you," Dr Mc Groom elaborated.

"it's actually bad news for a number of people; young Andy who has had an accident will not survive much longer. . ."

"how awful for his parents," agreed Eileen, "someone at work told me about the accident; his family and friends must be devastated, speaking as a mother myself," she emphasized.

"yes, Mrs Childers, they are, but they have had some time to get used to the idea that he would not survive having been impaled. . ." "how ghastly! "exclaimed Jules. "oh yes, but it is you who may benefit; do you remember the biopsy we did on you. . ."

"when I had to stay here all day, doctor?"

"yes, Jules," he replied: "Now while just about every single organ of his proved beyond repair, his tool, so to say, is not, and your blood and tissues are very highly compatible. . ."

"how unusual," commented the future scientist, "us being from such different backgrounds. . ."

"too right, but there you are, Jules, it looks as if we could fit you with a proper penis instead of a permanent implant."

Ann smiled a slow, lustful smile, kissed her lover's hand once again whose mother looked stunned.

"won't there have to be a period, doctor Mc Groom, to see whether the transplant will be rejected or not?" she asked.

"oh yes, but the odds are better than even, is all I can say right now," conceded the doctor:

"you are right, Jules, by the way; the original probability was very low; yet I have since found out that his maternal grandmother's actual father was a serviceman who died at the very end of World War Two. . ."

"so his grandmother was then married off to a willing suitor, I suppose. . ."

"yes, Mrs Childers, this is a matriarchal society but it was also a very conservative one in those days," mused the doctor,

"not that that thing wouldn't have happened quite often during the War. Anyway,": he continued, "I would like to schedule some very intensive preparatory treatment for you, Jules, and then operate, complete with new plumbing, soon as. . ."

"I know that my husband and I have already agreed to the Ethics Commission for Julia to have the operation before her sixteenth birthday," moaned Eileen, "but all this is happening very fast and your father is not even here."

"you and Jules' father did agree, so as to give Jules more time to grow into her new gender," Ann reminded her courteously but firmly; "forgive me if it was none of my business. . ."

"it is, Ann," offered Jules' mum, sadly "you are family now; you mean to say that, by coming here to be with my daughter, for the time being. . ."

"you found a new life for yourself, didn't you," completed her 'daughter'.

"still, I wish that your dad were here."

Julia did something she had not done for years; she left Ann, went up to her mum and put her arms on her shoulders:

"thank you, Mum; Dad should be here by the time I get worked upon, he'll miss the preparation which will keep me here much of the time, anyway; Dr Mc Groom?"

"yes, I'll want you here very early the day after tomorrow for another tissue test; so I'll arrange for you to stay at Rosetta's place tomorrow night when you come home from school; may I suggest that you catch up on as much homework and online project work as you can tonight and tomorrow night because you'll miss out on several days' worth, to start with."

"should I ring my dad now, Dr McGroom?" Ann enquired.

"good idea, Ann."

"can you wait, Mum, for, say, another half hour, an hour max, so Ann and I can get some work done?"

"yes, but don't overdo it; you girls've got sports on tomorrow; is it all right, Doctor?" she suddenly wondered.

"oh yes, if Julia's classmates can get used to her voice," he smiled: "I hope they won't test you for hormones, Jules. . ."

"am I beyond the limit, doctor, for competitive sports. . ."

"yes, these are also traceable as injected and ingested hormones, not home-grown ones; let's hope your school doesn't test. . ."

"only if Jules were to break the triple-jump record, of a sudden, Doctor Mac Groom," offered Ann. She turned to her lover's mum: "would it be a good idea to send Jules' dad a text message now, what with time difference, you wouldn't want to ring?"

"good idea, Mum," added Ann's lover; "if Dad is awake, he'll ring back, otherwise he'll get in touch with us tomorrow to arrange his flight; any day, doctor?" she asked. "Yes!"

The girls went back to work, sharing a gender for the last time.

"Are you looking for your dad to arrive?"

"yes and no; he is beginning to be surplus to mum's requirements. . ." answered Jules.

"why would that be?" "one last mother-daughter confidence, Ann. . ."

"I understand but, in future. . ." "for someone who keeps promising to be subservient to me at all times, you are a remarkably assertive, bitch." "don't you want me to, lover?" "of course. Let's not talk and do some work, instead."

The next half-hour saw them both busy behind their laptops and running the printers red-hot, the sound of which Ann's father heard when he arrived, with Glen in tow. He entered the girls' workroom, kissed both of them and asked:

"is your mum still here, Jules?"

"yes, she'll take me home in a few minutes."

"Ann, do you want to go home with Jules; Jules, could your mum take Ann home with you?"

"ask her, Mr Landers. . ."

"for not much longer, Dad; is that why you are here this late?"

"yes, Ann; the good doctor will want to pop the question and then finalise arrangements," her father agreed.

"same as with us. . ." "us?"

"well, Jules and I are a couple; it is Jules, of course, who'll be under the knife, possibly quite soon. . ."

"next few days, Jules?"

"yes, I was asked to be here day after tomorrow morning, so this. . ."

"could be the last night at your mum's for some time. . ."

"yes, Mr Landers. . ." with only the faintest discernible irony.

Ann's father and Glen then walked to the doctor's surgery labelled Medical Director, knocked and stepped in.

"welcome, both of you. . ." he got up and sat them all down behind a low tea table, with a Korean tea set ready; he steamed up the kettle, poured scalding water on all utensils and into the cups, then emptied the residue into a small drain, filling a strainer with pleasantly-scented tea leaves:

"Jasmine with a hint of pine and acacia, resin and lemongrass, a drop of mangrove honey," he intoned.

"I wish the wines in the Riverland were quite as tasteful," commented Glen.

"don't say that, Glen; you get some very good years, with a nice dry cool autumn, early fogs. . . I must be getting homesick. . ." Brendan paused, smiling:

"why don't you take Elanca home when this is all over," commented Ann's 'father':

"oh, please forgive me; I am so sorry; pretend I never said it. . ."

"I shall; food for thought, though. . . let's have some tea first and then confine ourselves to matters at hand. . ." the doctor argued.

The men sat and silently, slowly drank the hot, finely-scented tea as Brendan was pouring it out, cups being cleaned and refilled time and again. Glen, in particular, started breathing deeply, his worried frown disappearing, the doctor also relaxing while deep in thought. Ann's father seemed to be the most at ease among them.

Brendan awoke from a kind of reverie, induced by the tea ceremony.

"Let's keep it informal," he opened: "Glen, Hector, crunch time is here. . ."

"would you like to pop the question, Brendan?" "yes, Father of Ann. . ."

"not much longer; I am ready if you are," Hector replied.

"in that case, how many days can you take off work and how soon, Hector?"

Looking at Glen, Ann's father answered:

"we finished an interesting and quite enjoyable session, vital to our project, just before we got here; Glen here can run the show, along with Ramon and the team. . ." Glen nodded:

"it is Ramon, Hector, who does," he corrected, "but I can step in any time. Why don't we go back to work tomorrow; you take me through the template design one more time, along with the young ones, and then 'he' will be all yours, Brendan, for however long you need 'him' here. . ."

"where do you want me to stay for the duration; Rosetta's parents across the street. . ."

"most likely," the doctor agreed, "but I shall need you overnight a few times also. . . Glen,' he offered," could you stay here for a few minutes; I shall need to deal with Hector's centre of being in my surgery and have a few words with him. . ." "finality starts now?" surmised Glen.

"I need to put your penis out of action," Brendan revealed. "You are not erecting at the moment, Hector, are you?" "no, more's the pity," Ann's father laughed: "A wanker no more!"

"no more wanking," agreed Brendan gravely. "Lie down if you would and take your pants etc down, please. . ." "what's to happen next, Brendan?"

"a jab at the base of your tool to knock a gland out of action which otherwise draws in serum to engorge it. . ." "will it hurt?"

"not as much as if I were to put it straight into the top; that would also cause problems with urinating. . ." "so best not done, I agree. Do I need to be held down?" "no, if you can hold still for a minute or so and then lie down quietly without moving for about ten," explained the doctor. "when am I about to lose my dick altogether?"

"before the week is out, I'd say, but I need to engage in some craftsmanship before that can be done." "will I never be able to erect now?"

"if left to itself, eventually, you would; as I told you, it is up to you now as it has always been."

"go ahead," his patient instructed the doctor who proceeded to inject him to start the process that would eventually change his gender if not his life.

"I know that ninety-eight percent of all sex happens in your head," confirmed Jules.

"I can promise you that the remaining two percent shall reverberate through the entire length of your body once I am suitably equipped." They were on their way home, Julia's mum having agreed to take Ann off her dad for the next two or three nights, at least: "it will happen more often," Ann's father had told and thanked her, enabling her to take the girls home without having to wait for him. Glen did, however, while Hector lay stretched out, watching his tool shrivel even more. Eventually, Hector had to get up to pee and found that it was easier 'side-saddle 'than standing up ("a sign of times to come," he told himself); finally, Brendan let him go and so Glen drove the two of them home, too. "what does it feel like, Hec?"

"a bit neutral, Glen; it did not hurt; I noticed that there is a bit less hair around the spot and it feels different already. . ."

"what with all these hormones, no wonder," Glen commented. "Will you be able to drive tomorrow? It'd be awkward for you, not to; this place runs by car only. . ."

"very much like most of Australia, "stated Hector. "thanks for not backing out, Hec, at the last minute. . ." "thank you, too, for being here."

Hector, while unwilling to drive, felt up to cooking them a light meal involving coconut batter on calamari, fruit salad and sago roasted in Malaysian palm oil, along with bread rolls and honey heated up inside an electric frying pan, helped along with tea and washed down with San Miguel beer, "more common here than water," as Ramon had once commented.

"that may be the last time you can drink for a while," remarked Glen.

They went to bed and began to explore each other:

"we'll have to get used to each other's physicality," Glen mumbled; Hector started smiling and stretched himself luxuriously:

"you'll have to begin to imagine breasts and well-shaped buttocks where so far have been neither," 'he' commented:

"how do I sound, anyway, sufficiently submissive, gender-neutral or overly assertive?" 'he' challenged.

"as long as you do not pretend to headaches, mate," 'his' partner's touch on Hector surprisingly gentle. "who did you last practice on, Glen?"

"certain things you don't forget in a hurry. . ."

Jules dominated Ann in a far more convincing manner, given a lot more recent practice.

"Look, girls," her mother had said that evening, after a late dinner, "I won't keep you separate tonight, seeing that Jules may have to stay in hospital for some time now, but, please, stop what you like to do to each other by about midnight. You got sports day ahead of you and some very trying times, for Jules in particular. I ask you to know when to lay off as much as enjoy each other tonight. I suggest you have a shower-don't take too long, I need to shower, too-and then go to bed straightaway. . ." which is what the girls did, with Ann dramatically letting go of the bathroom towel that Jules had wrapped her in.

"I keep fantasizing about being claimed, taken and possessed with an almighty thud, like a jackhammer", she whispered breathlessly:

"imagine me lying naked on my back, utterly immobilized, my arms pinned down, being readied for the sheer voltage of your thrusts deep inside my body, each harder, more determined, ruthless and relentless than its preceding one," she continued, warming up to her theme:

"and fancy, as you sex-ecute me, dying of a slow agonisingly enjoyable and endless death, lying beneath you, unresisting, rendered totally helpless, at your mercy forever. . ." she sighed.

"dream on, bitch," commanded Jules.

"in future, never keep your hands off me," while Jules had already begun to move hers all over Ann's body; "but keep at least one on or in between my legs, my hips, buttocks, breasts, chin, and definitely around my arms or wrists, in short, all over me" which is what Jules proceeded to do, "to show me and everyone else who is in charge; let it never be me, ever. . ."

"sex-wise, I'll guarantee that. . ." agreed Jules, embracing Ann fiercely while weighing her down.

It was Elanca who discovered, or rather stumbled, into the penultimate episode of our drama; knowing that both Jules and Hector's operations were drawing near, she spent a lot of time interviewing and documenting the actors involved and the instruments and techniques they were likely to use.

Someone had left a set of foot-pedal scales on the floor of the corridor which Elanca attempted to cross without looking, having done so very often. She slid on the scale, pushing it away with her foot and herself with it for several yards, trying to regain a semblance of balance, when someone's hand stabilised her.: "You may have saved my life," Elanca smiled, "or at least my dignity;" looking up:

"but I know you," she realized: "aren't you the reconstructive surgeon who specializes on women; Medecins sans Frontieres comes to mind. . ." "and aren't you Elanca van Hoogveld," the young Chamorra doctor replied: "oh no, forgive me, that was your husband. . ."

"now dead; you are Gloria Paz; now I know," remembered Elanca. "Hold my hand a bit longer, please, till I step off this silly scale;" this having happened, Gloria squatted smartly and lifted the offending obstacle out of the way.

"let's sit down somewhere," she decided, still holding Elanca's hand, "how about a cup of tea?"

"green tea, a pot, in my workroom," ordered Elanca. "Now I know, I first met you in Yemen, working with Eritrean refugee women, six years ago."

Gloria had worked in a refugee camp set up at the beach northwest of Aden so as to deal with refugees who had swum, rowed or sailed from Eritrea, Djibuti or Somalia to escape multiple layers of violence and displacement. Not only had she helped multitudes of young women cope with the effects of infibulations but also made all Elders, men and women, abjure female genital mutilation, once called female circumcision.

She had trained young women on some simple interventions that would, nonetheless, enable girls and women to urinate without pain or the risk of constant infection.

Many girls had also presented with uterine prolapse, due to having given birth when too young and malnourished, to boot. There, too, she had developed interventions and non-surgical treatments that could help restore a measure of continence, often an associated problem.

She had later specialized on vaginal and fallopian injuries whether self-inflicted or due to domestic or public violence:

"Do you remember the girl in Delhi in India about eight years ago who was raped by about a hundred people inside a bus and finally impaled on a reo rod from a building site? She died in Singapore where a specialist colleague of mine tried to cope with her massive internal damage and save her life," Gloria reminisced over a steaming cup of tea in Elanca's studio.

"are you here because of Andy's impalement?" Elanca wondered;

"what is your considered opinion?" "he'll die, Elanca" said Gloria regretfully.

"could you have helped him had you arrived earlier?" asked Elanca. "when did you get here, in the first place. . ."

"early this morning; Brendan dropped me at Rosetta's parents' place for a few hours' sleep. . ."

"you won't get many, from now on," agreed the reporter.

"I meant to come here to help fashion Hector's vagina. . ." "much needed. . ."

"but Dina here discovered Andy's magnificent and miraculously intact tool, so I was asked not only to do some palliative work on him but help with transforming Jules' genitals. . ."

"to turn him into Julius." "sort of. And you are doing a feature, Elanca for whom?"

"a women's magazine in Adelaide who hired me after my husband's murder. . ."

"that's what it was, "Gloria slapped her head;" I had a memory loss of sorts, and I never heard the story. . ." "about three years ago?"

"I was kidnapped," explained Gloria, "while in Yemen at about that time for several months, until rescued by a special unit from Saudi Arabia. . ." "in the Hadramaut?"

Elanca well remembered the lawless corner in Yemen bordering Oman and Saudi Arabia:

"now this is something I vaguely remembered; but once Grant had been blown up, along with our Kirghiz fixer, I experienced everything through a haze."

"understandable, Elanca," Gloria concurred, reaching out for the other woman.

"thank you," said the reporter and poured some more tea. "Medecins sans Frontieres refused to use you in the field afterwards," stated the journalist "a bit like my magazine refused to send me into any frontline situations, until now. . ."

"so they are testing you now whether you can develop such a cutting-edge feature on your own, thousands of miles from any support system other than what you can create," elaborated Gloria, speaking from experience.

"Are you with a man at the moment, Gloria?"

"I have someone in the background, a former mentor of mine. . ." "who is married. . ."

"and a good Catholic, to boot, in Guam, which is almost as small a place as Saipan."

"so you can indulge only when both of you are away from home."

"Hole in one, Elanca," said Gloria; "and you?" "until a few weeks ago, nobody; now. . ."

"not Brendan, by any chance?" wondered Gloria. "what makes you say that?"

"he told me about you but used a different name. . ." "my birth name"

"yes, but the way he spoke of your role, I wondered. . ."

"yes, he, too, is married, his wife just had a hysterectomy and. . ."

"torn between love and loyalty," sighed Gloria, "same as Fernando, chair of nephrology, University of Hawaii. I am trying to get him to come here to consult on both Hector and Jules. . ."

"are kidneys a problem in such gender alignments. . ."

"they can be; not that Andy's could be saved; it would keep both of us sane, being able to spend a few nights together while we work during the day as close friends and colleagues; we are a good team." "did you team up with him after you disappeared from Medecins. . ."

"a few times, on working on women who had suffered multiple both internal and external injuries. . ."

"are you a consulting specialist these days, Gloria?"

"yes, loosely based on Guam where I live with my parents. . ." "also doctors?"

"yes, they run a Native Chamorro treatment centre specializing on addiction; how did you know?"

"the dimmest of memories. . ."

"will you show me some of your documentation, Elanca?"

"by way of background, Gloria? one more question; is this the first time that you and Brendan worked together?"

"not really; colleagues of mine, then on Hawaii, took up the very work that Brendan got struck out for. . ." "series of freely interpolated data on physiological changes in female menopause?"

"good one, Elanca," Gloria commented admiringly; "when we. . ." "we?"

"yes, they involved me at some stage on growing and transplanting mucous lining. . ."

"very handy on Hec's new vagina," commented the reporter.

"so, we found that our genuinely experimental and highly verifiable data matched Brendan's 'man-made' ones closely enough. . ." "to help get him vindicated. . ."

"yes, eventually, as happened a few weeks ago," Gloria agreed:

"more like we wanted to meet him, study the kind of genuine professional intuition that drives him and compare methods in case we, too, were accused. . ."

"but have you worked with him on patients. . ."

"not quite like this but he has been the medical director here for a while; until now, most of the hands-on work had to be done by others, under his guidance, twice in my case."

"could I interview you separately on those cases, Gloria, and may I cover your contribution now?"

"yes and yes, Elanca; I can certainly talk to you about these two previous cases, one a near-drowning with complications arising from the rescue, the other an attempt at impaling with a broken bottle. . ." "by a drunken husband?"

"no, a sober brother who disagreed with a choice of boyfriend. Names and actual dates will have to be changed. . ." "naturally. . ."

"and as to why you are here; the limits set you by the clinic if any are the only ones that apply. . ."

"just like with any other medical staff, with Hector and Jules. . ."

"quite; it will be Jules first, by the way; for Andy' penis can only be kept for at most ten hours after his death. With nerves, tubes, glands and vessels intact and, hopefully, able to function. . ."

"will you do some work on Julia before the implant?"

"yes, Brendan and I shall have a preliminary gander; you are welcome to cover that until we tell you not to. . ." "as per usual." "I guess so.," concluded the young specialist.

"How was your sports day, Jules?" enquired Doctor Mc Groom, Brendan to most, by now.

"I didn't break the record in triple-jump." "why, Jules?" enquired Elanca.

"bit of a gust of wind, of a sudden. I also did high-jump quite well but failed pole vault. . ."

"the wind, once again?" Gloria, this time. "yes, they had to abandon a few events, eventually?"

"how about Ann?" "she ran very fast and made second in her height-for age group. . ." (Jules had hit on an ingenious way of motivating the girl:" imagine Angh chasing you, for obvious reasons, and me chasing Angh to stop her from doing things to you; would you not run fast to get away from it all?" it seemed to have worked).

"she also did a decent long jump. . ." "but no podium finish?" asked Brendan.

"no, Doctor Mc Groom, but we had fun" (especially while fixing Angh with a basilisk-like stare which came close to upsetting that normally very poised girl, so much so that she was rude to a potential boyfriend, as a result; Angh's mother had given her an uncomprehending look).

"did you sleep well afterwards, Jules?"

"yes, I had the use of Rosetta's room; I saw you move in, Dr Paz, as I was leaving. . ."

"yes, I needed to catch up on some beauty sleep; for I shan't get too much of that in the next few days, now. . ." "you don't need it, do you. . ."

"'beauty' sleep; are you practicing paying us women compliments for when you are a boy?" laughed Gloria, delighted. "practice makes perfect, no doubt," intoned Brendan:" Jules, your muscle tone and tissue strength is excellent; we would normally subject you to very strenuous exercises prior to your sex change, along with more hormone treatment, but we are in a hurry to graft Andy's tool as soon as we can. . ."

"and you can't make me take too much hard stuff," surmised Jules, the future scientist, "because of the immune reaction you are trying to avoid afterwards."

"hole in one," commented Elanca, genuinely impressed.

"nor can we overdose you on hormones, for that same reason," explained Gloria,

"and there are certain interventions I have to do on you as soon as I have given you a general check-up, under Doctor Mc Groom's supervision. . ." "to do what, doctor Paz?"

"your urethra, for one thing, then begin to occlude your vagina enough to plug it with Andy's tool, eventually." "won't you have to shave her pubies first?" wondered Elanca.

"Brasilian style, you mean? Yes, of course," commented Gloria. "we'll probably get one of the girls to do the honours. . ." "will it hurt?" "a bit, and it may feel like sandpaper afterwards. . ."

"local anaesthetic?" enquired Julia. "yes, after you've been shorn. . ." replied Brendan.

"do you want me to film all this, Jules?" asked the reporter.

"do I get to see the finished product, eventually?" asked Julia, a girl for the very last time.

"before I edit it into a feature? yes, Jules, you'll have the right of first refusal and if doctores Brendan and Gloria don't want me to cover any of this, you will tell me, won't you?" the journalist asked, turning to them and holding out her cup in readiness for some more tea.

"I know that doctor Brendan has taken skin, mucous lining and soft tissue off me for tissue cultures," Jules commented; "they'll come handy, no doubt. . .do you need more than that, doctor Gloria?" "yes, Jules."

"how many days and nights do I need to stay this time?"

"three minimum after the operation, a week at the most, depending on your immune reaction," said Brendan: "your healing properties are very good. You ought to be able to get onto your computer within a day or so, to catch up on your work; make sure that Ann keeps dropping it in."

Meanwhile, Gloria had measured blood pressure, breathing, skin tone, knee reflexes, eyesight and hearing, even while they were talking with and around Jules, with Elanca recording everything:

"Do you mind me watching you getting shorn, Jules?" asked the reporter. "no, am I about to?"

"yes, the girl is here to do you," answered Gloria. "Anything else on today?"

"yes, some exploratory surgery along the labia. . ." "around my cunt?"

"if you choose to describe it like that." "will Mrs Elanca be allowed to record that as well. . ."

"yes, from some distance." "local anaesthetics, doctor Gloria?" "yes, Jules."

Later that day, Ann's father arrived after work for a final general check-up, with lots of green tea in Elanca's workroom,
"you'll be famous, as of now, Hector," she teased him." Is Glen still at work?"
"he dropped me and has gone back; I expect him in the evening."
"is Hector staying over tonight, Brendan?" the journalist turned to her onetime lover, briefly touching his arm.
"yes, we are putting you on dialysis so that we can modify your urethra later this afternoon?"
"I'll have to divide my time recording Gloria doing Jules and you, Brendan, working on Hector here," she commented wrily.
"you will manage," both doctors assured her.

For the first time in all the years after the death of his former ex-wife, Glen felt lonely; he missed Hector's presence both at home and at work, his enormous equanimity and decency, his empathy with strangers, family and colleagues and his sense of humour ("good company"); he did not mind in the least to have to carry on, on his partner's behalf, glad that Ramon's team had accepted him so very readily. He rang Eileen at work: "where are you now; at Merv's?"
"no, I am preparing a furniture shop for an internal audit which I shall train their regular bookkeeper to conduct. . ."
"could I come over with some of my young people to watch you do that?"
"yeah, if they don't mind giving us a hand shifting things," Eileen decided quickly: "I am sure I can persuade Oratio to shout lunch for all of us and dash them a bit of money afterwards; and they get to see how it's done; do you have anyone among them who's good with numbers?"
"yeah, two girls, Eileeen. . ."
"look, I am really looking forward to seeing you here, Glen."
Glen told Ramon what he had arranged with Eileen.
"I wish you had asked me earlier, Glen," Ramon commented.
"was it Eileen's idea?"
"yes, Ramon."
"you could have suggested to her to ring back while you ran this by me first. . ."
"I am sorry, Ramon."
"try not to let it happen again, Glen; I know you are taking on extra work while Hector's at the clinic," explained Ramon: "and, naturally, it is a very good idea to get some of them involved with actual work;

can you convert an audit into an algorithm that can be translated into software, Glen?"

"not yet, but I can ask Eileen to design a spreadsheet. . ."

"she's probably got one already," agreed Ramon;

"which you and I can either transform into a template or wait till Hector gets back; I wish I had the girls from Barrow Creek. . ."

"where is that?"

"Central Australia; one of them is Micronesian, by the way. . ."

"do I know her?"

"Aline Romario does templates while the other one, Lisa, writes excellent software at the drop of a hat. . ."

"Aline Romario?" mused his colleague; "look, I'll let you go with three boys and two girls but let me ring someone first; I think I know Aline's family. . ." which he did.

While Glen had a coffee. Ramon organized the young people to accompany Glen and a vehicle as well, then rang a contact, followed by someone else:

"Yes, marvel of marvels," he smiled at Glen; "her original family lives on a nearby island called Agrihan and Aline is due to arrive from Australia for a clan reunion. . ."

"she has done that before, even though, she was born in Australia," agreed Glen.

"so is there a chance to get her to join us for at least a few days? It would help greatly, while Hector is, literally, laid up. . ." he wondered.

"in principle, yes, she'll have to arrive via Guam and here; the only way to reach her people's island is from here, by boat...why don't you send her an email or reach her some other way. . ."

"through her workplace. . ."

"maybe; meanwhile, while you are at work with Eileen in Oratio's furniture shop I'll reach some of her family, as many as I know, and ask them nicely if we may keep her here on her way there or back if that helps our own young people. . ."

"what you call a busman's holiday, I am sure; it'll be good to see her again at work. . ."

"no doubt," agreed his colleague wisely, wondering to himself about his friend's lifeline to attractive and competently active girls providing him with him an opening into Micronesian culture, while genuinely missing Hector.

Glen smiled at himself, chatting with the young people driving to Oratio's workshop. The very thought of being about to kiss Eileen's hand if not her cheek cheered him considerably; he remembered how cheerful she had sounded at the thought of him joining her at work.

He suddenly had a brainwave: a professional if not personal 'ménage a quatre' involving a, by then, hopefully fully female Hec, an all-woman Eileen and himself, running a specialized team, involving Aline, with luck, as both another intimate partner and a highly-valued colleague.

"It will need all your persuasive skills, Glen" he reminded himself: "but there is bound to be a market, with all these unemployed young people, such as the ones we are driving; should 'we' concentrate on service or on some sort of manufacture?" he wondered.

Like people before him, he had rediscovered the principle of 'functional intimacy' in the workforce, often at the emotional if not physical expense of one's principal partner or spouse.

As soon as Glen arrived at Oratio's furniture workshop, ready to witness and help Eileen with her stock-take, the owner assembled the young people and gave them a combination of papaya extract and passion fruit prepared by his niece. Eileen then handed out work sheets listing items from a previous audit and set up three work groups, for them to shift and sift items, watching them go off to work with a will. Glen sat her down, with Oratio nearby:

"what are your plans for the next few months?" she asked, smiling.

"I had a brainwave on my way here," he explained.

"Hec and I want to remain here and start a labour development consultancy; now I mentioned a young woman who helped us train some Tongan in Central Australia. . ." "eh, Glen?"

"'grapes', Eileen. . . she also wrote into templates the software that Hec was testing for our work, another girl did the machine coding and I ended up designing the programme. . ."

"which brought you here which I, for one, am pleased with; now to your brainwave, Glen. . ." sounding already very possessive:

"would you be prepared to spend at least some time and effort to help us set up a company on Agrihan which is a pioneer resettlement?"

"Oratio, where is that island. . .?"

"oh, that is a fair bit up north, a boat every three days if you are lucky, a mail plane once a week, weather permitting," the manufacturer explained:

"it erupted several times some twenty years ago so everyone was moved. . ."

"are people going back, Oratio," she asked the proprietor who was slurping a cup of coffee.

"yes, the volcano people tell us it will be safe for a generation or so, but very few people have, so far. . ."

"no jobs?" guessed Glen.

"yes, no investment and almost no capacity, such as mine here; they do have shops and schools."

"activities, such as. . ."

"fishing, some cattle, a bit of hardwood forestry, orchardry, very good volcanic soil," added Horatio.

"I do know of plans to set up a renewable-energy based industry; it might bear some research, Glen; is that what you were thinking of?"

"yes, I'd like to involve Eileen in financial control, Aline whose clan lives there, Hec and myself as the conceptual planners and IT people, to set up the energy base for manufacture and infrastructure. . ."

Unbeknownst to Glen for a while longer, this vision of his came a step closer with a phone call to Ramon while Glen and his team were at Oratio's workshop to help, and learn from, Eileen.

"I do not know whether you remember me," said the elderly voice;

"Oh. Señor Nestor, what a pleasure," replied a truly delighted Ramon.

"am I ever so pleased to hear your voice."

"I realise, Ramon, that you were trying to get in touch with us; anything to do with my grand-niece Aline coming home?"

"yes, Señor Nestor; my colleague Glen. . ."

"the Australian consultant; there are two of them, are they not?"

"yes, Señor Nestor; you are well informed; they both worked with Aline and another girl in Central Australia. . ." "she told a cousin of hers about that; but why the sudden interest?"

"Glen and Hec (Ramon wisely refrained from using Glen's partner's gender-related first name) want to set up a company, together with another Australian, a lady accountant who works for your friend Horatio Calderon, and involve your grand- niece as well," explained Ramon.

"I remembered my wife having mentioned Aline in some context so I got her to ring someone who had to ring someone else to find out. . ."

"the women usually know how to find out things that way," agreed the Elder; "one of the girls rang a daughter-in-law of mine here on the island and then the penny dropped. What do you want me to do, young Ramon?"

"I want your permission to keep Aline here till the next boat and consult her."

"please, do; for that is what I was ringing you for; why, you ask?" elaborated the elder:

"we want to resettle our island, so do the various governments we are all of us dealing with, but we have nothing to attract, let alone hold, the young ones. . ."

"fisheries cattle tourism?" ventured Ramon.

"not in the way we are doing fish and cattle at the moment; it supports us all right but creates no extra wealth, let alone a business base for another generation. Tourism: you know, I have been to the US Mainland and others have been to Europe or Asia; places attract tourists with what they already had even before the first tourist set foot there: churches, temples, shrines, canals, buildings, old cities or villages, the sea, lakes, beaches, forests, hills and mountains, or else sports; it is very difficult to create a tourist attraction from nothing." He paused then continued:

"besides, it makes you dependent on other people and on events over which you have no control. Now, I had hoped that Aline would provide a vision which we do not yet have and which you might help her turn into something concrete; new situations require new thinking. . ."

"we may be able to do even better, Señor Nestor; because now we have the makings of a team with proven industrial skills already determined to do something which involves your grandniece and is set to happen right at your doorstep. . ."

"as of today, Ramon?"

"more or less, Señor Nestor, in the sense of a venture, at least."

"the government told us that if we could find someone to develop renewable energy for industrial purposes. . ." "like a miniature Sun City, you mean?"

"like they have in China, running every household, workshop, factory and transport on renewable energy and manufacturing everything in sight as well on that basis?" queried Nestor.

"yes, on a scale to fit you."

"Tell me about their background, then: you have an accountant and business manager, a woman?"

"yes, her child is here for some unusual treatment; she probably never thought she wanted to settle and work here but that's what happened.?" "the other two, gentlemen?"

"they, too, are here because of each other; one of them won a tender to help us develop software. . ."

"that is to do with computers, Ramon, is it? The young ones keep telling me about it; I leave them to it but it seems something you need to know about these days, perhaps even more than to harpoon whales or slaughter cattle. . ."

"both sets of skills are needed, Señor Nestor," the youth development worker replied; "anyway, Hec, too, is at Dr Brendan's clinic and Hec's partner who came to Saipan merely to spend time with Hec ended up working with us; he mentioned a particular skill of Aline's for which we also have a need at the moment. . ."

"where is that consultant of yours, young Ramon?"

"he is at your friend Oratio's workshop, to help Eileen, the accountant. . ."

"the lady with the child at Dr Brendan's clinic, you mean?"

"yes, Señor Nestor; he took our young ones to help with Oratio's stock-take and learn how to organize one themselves, again writing software. . ."

"can you reduce the world that we know to software, Ramon?"

"of course not totally, but some you can, and our young people need to learn. . ."

"how to do it?"

"no, Señor Nestor, not necessarily, but to deal with it, as well as organize work when there's nobody to teach or supervise them. . ."

"we used to teach them by doing it with them. . ."

"in a sense, that is what our colleagues are doing, except that these are different tasks and skills than what even I grew up with. . ."

"I suppose so," admitted the Elder: "you are welcome to keep Aline for a few days; it may help her get used to us again because it must be vastly different from Australia, a huge landmass where it gets very hot and can get quite cold and where everything is different; get her to help you with what you need from her but, while she is with you, try to work out with her what we need and can use on our island, because her life and her skills are so different from ours that we don't know where to start, but you and these three Australians definitely would. . ."

"yes, we can get the ball rolling here with her on Saipan; can you guarantee the various permits etc. . ."

"including permission for all three or four, counting Aline, to live and work here; oh yes, the authorities realize that those kind of people don't grow on corals; site permits, grants, if it helps us develop the industry and settle the kind and number of young people whom we need. I'll get in touch with a few people in the bureaucracy in the next few days; I might even get onto the boat, get to sort out some heads and then take Aline home, likewise as many of the three Australians as can be spared at the moment. Do you really think, Ramon, that the girl would want to live with us for some years, at least?"

"she'll always be caught between two worlds, Señor Nestor; we do not realize how much; but here she has the chance to start something on her own, with help, which she never would, in Australia, plus she can do it with, and among, her people. . . it won't be easy for her or for my Australian friends, very frustrating, in fact, but also challenging and, in the end, more beneficial and, perhaps, enjoyable than anything they could do, or be, back in their country."

The Elder was silent for a while: "you are a good, can't say Boy, you are a good man if still young, with a good head on you; you said there was a child?"

"actually two, Señor Nestor, teenagers, one belongs to Eileen the accountant, the other to Hec, our workplace training consultant; they are promised to each other. . ."

"I did not know they had that in the Western world," mused the clan leader, "you mean, like very young people used to, on our island?"

"yes, except that it used to be our parents who'd arrange it; these two very young people persuaded their parents to accept them as a future couple, nor will they look at anyone else their age. . ." "how old?" "fifteen and a bit, I'd say."

"very bright, Ramon?" "both are, in different ways, with different aims in life. . ."

"yes, us older people forget that the young ones, while they may love one another, have additional purposes in life to do with work and study, not necessarily stepping into our types of life and starting families like we have as part of our traditional lives. . ."

"why are you asking me, Señor Nestor?" "is our school adequate for such teenagers, I wonder?"

"well, they are at school here and do an extra online programme to meet Australian requirements, I understand, Mr Nestor. . ."

"it'll be an unusual experience for all of us, them as well as our own students," the leader mused:

"we might get some extra educational facilities; as you said, young Ramon, young people have to learn to cope with the modern world which is very different from the one I grew up in after the Pacific War, or even the one when you were a boy. . ."

"that is true. Señor Nestor; now if you know, would you tell me when your grand-niece is due?" "oh, she's supposed to be in Guam already. . . we have to get on our satellite phone or use radio to find out but I should know later today, Ramon."

"would you allow her to ring either Glen, Hec or myself as soon. . ."

"I'll tell her if I get to talk to her myself, otherwise I'll make sure she knows, let me have the numbers she needs to ring. . ."

Aline, having paid her telephonic obeisance to her clan elder as soon as she arrived in Guam where she had decided to stay for two nights with a cousin working there, to acclimatize herself from Central Australia, dialled Hector's number in some anticipation and came straight to the point:

"You probably realize, you and Glen, that both Lisa and I had substantial difficulties on keeping our fingers and lips off you men; did you two blokes feel likewise?"

"yes," admitted Hector, surprised "These days, I am being feminised. . ."

"you are what, Hector?"

"being gender-aligned, sexually repolarised, de-manned, choice is yours, Aline," he teased her:

"it is good to hear your voice again. . ."

"where are you, Hector?"

"at work but I am due again at the clinic for a day or two, prior to the final operation. . ."

"which is when and what about. . ."

"so you can't call me Hector anymore, for starters; nobody'll be able to," he added reflectively:

"the final prune and shape will be in about ten days, could be earlier; for Gloria's time is strictly rationed. . ."

"isn't she the wartime trauma reconstructive surgeon," asked Aline, "what a mouthful, from Medecins sans Frontieres? I read a feature on her a while ago."

"the one by Elanca Hartwig?"

"yes, Hector, how did you know?"

"because Elanca is here, with all of us, at Dr Brendan's clinic, writing a feature on my forthcoming sex change and that of my daughter's future partner. . ."

"into what; dare I ask?" asked the girl.

"a very macho boy, to satisfy Ann's heart's delight. . ."

"will it work? and who are you trying to oblige, Glen?" "yes, you guessed right. . ."

"so Lisa was right, after all. . ." "did she tell you before or after you made love to her?"

"before, but how do you know?" "don't forget, we were next door for those few nights. . ."

"yes, those were the nights," sighed the girl. "My grand-uncle is so pleased to have you both and Eileen-whoever she is. . ."

"Glen's subsidiary love interest, no less, and a very smart accountant and business manager, like for Merv the Cobbler and Oratio's Outstanding Furniture. . ."

"Uncle Nestor knows them well. . ." "which is important in your culture. . ." "in any culture, Hector."

"So is she smitten with Glen or he with her?" she asked, amused.

"he's impressed and she is smitten."

"isn't he meant to be yours, seeing that you are about to turn your manhood into sheer femininity for him, whatever that'll be like; aren't you going to be jealous?"

"no, consider the lot of us a work-related seraglio, to be wholly based, and partly resident, on your ancestral island. . ." "including yourself and myself?"

"our seraglio, and 'manned', if not necessarily headed, by Glen and his, soon to be, all-female dream team. . ." "I quite like being 'manned' by the right man. . ."

"but remember, Aline," Hector added a note of caution to the girl's unbridled eagerness, "that relationships have as much, and more, to do with people working than with sex per se; plus we want your clan to accept us. . ."

"as we are and where we each of us are best at," conceded the girl:

"we'll find ways to meet each other's needs as well; let me ask about Eileen. . ."

"the Other-Woman-syndrome, Aline?"

"yes, partly," she admitted; "mainly, see I know what brought you to Saipan, and now I also know why Glen is here but where and how did she originally fit in?"

"she is mother to Ann's future boyfriend, called Julia last year, Jules at the moment, to be morphed into full-fledged Julius, entire, do not laugh. . ."

"with a genuine tool on 'her'?" intoned Aline, incredulously yet also perceptively:

"doctor Gloria's doing?"

"yes, but really due to a well-equipped boy's tragic accident. . ."

"his family must be devastated," she commented, aware of close-knit Micronesian families.

"at least, he was able to gift his most precious organ to a worthy recipient."

"oh, you like Julius as your future son-in-law?"

"yes, imagine me as someone's future mum-in-law. . ."

"trying, Hector," the girl complied, then rang off.

Her next call was to assure Glen of her undying lust for him.

"This is well known to us," Glen confirmed when she got through to him, nursing another coffee at Horatio's workshop. "is she nearby?" Aline asked.

"oh yes," knowing that the girl was talking about Eileen. "I'll tell her. . ."

"do you have to, Glen?"

"remember, we all have to work together," unknowingly echoing Hector's earlier warning. "let me tell you that I am very pleased to hear your voice again. . ."

"will we end up working together, then?"

"it depends on your people on the island, naturally. . ." Glen surmised.

"in that case, rest assured; I have already talked to Uncle Nestor, our clan leader and my grand-uncle; Señor Ramon must have been in touch with him; it was Uncle Nestor's own granddaughter who gave me your numbers, Hec's and yours," she explained, "and he's all afire, prepared to set us all up with land, documents, permits, even funding. . ."

"for what?" "Uncle Nestor had been approached about a core unit run on primary energy. . ."

"yours is a volcanic island. . ." "yeah. . ."

"so there'll be geothermal and then tidal energy, solar, wind and gravitational; how about water?"

"not enough for a turbine, I think," she explained, "but we could distill a lot with all the energy that we produce, in addition to rain and underground water; we have a lens in one place but the rest is quite sodic. . ." "distillation or reverse-osmosis, if we produce enough energy. . ."

"I can hear your brain at work already. . ." the girl praised her future lover.

"we all have similar minds and backgrounds," Glen acknowledged.

"I think that is what my grand-uncle noticed and is hoping for; we have not been able to resettle the island in large numbers because there hasn't been anything special so far to attract people my age, with young families. Let's make sure that this is about to change. . ."

"and the people say Amen," agreed Glen.

He turned around to face Eileen.

"Another admirer, Glen," she smiled and briefly took his hand.

"she is related to the clan leader on the island where they'd like us to set up what's essentially to become a primal power provider; I would very much like you to be involved. . ."

"will we be based there all the time?"

"not necessarily and always but we'll be registered there, hopefully including permanent residence for all of us, site permits, funding; for the government wants some such unit established before there can be any trade or industry. . ." "including fishing and beef?"

"yes, clearly," argued Glen, briefly kissing her hand then letting go.

"think of cold storage, battery recharge, boning and processing unit, workshops."

He paused and looked at the young people he had brought.

"let's go back to work on your audit preparation, but also let me say this: it'll be a pleasure to have you in my life, as a colleague and as a very intimate friend if that sounds all right with you?"

"I'll happily settle for that, so, I hope, will this young woman who just rang you; how about Hec. . ."

"he is my principal partner," affirmed Glen, "and that will not change."

Eileen looked quite happy:

"I'll have to ring Trevor. . ." "Jules is being done today, isn't she?"

"or tomorrow, at the latest, but I expect that to be a series of operations not just one. I want Trevor here for that, of course," confirmed his supplementary love interest. "but, basically, I shall have to put him on notice, at least geography-wise. . ."

"look, I'll never not relate to you man to woman, Eileen, nor to this young woman who just rang me, but I do owe my main loyalty to someone who is, arguably, giving up his basic definition of himself for me; will that do?" he. looked at her expectantly, smiling.

"Yes, Glen, it will be enough for me to know what else to tell Trevor. . ."

A few hours after having made these fateful telephone calls, a very sleepy Aline was woken from a doze by a call by her friend and sometime sexual sparring partner Lisa:

"Oh sorry, love, did I wake you," noticing her friend's drowsy voice:
"I should have realized. . ."

"no, thank you, Lisa, I need to sleep at local bedtime to get over my jetlag quickly. . ." Aline assured her: "listen, did you ring me a few hours, about six hours ago while I was still on the plane?" "more like seven", the other girl answered; "why, Aline?"

"let me tell you about the experience. . . I had eased my mobile deep inside me, relying on its pulse to stimulate me sexually if someone rang. . ."

"did it; I am pleased to be of some use!" "yes, I had finally fallen asleep. . ."

"what a way to wake up another person!"

"agreed," agreed Aline: "but there was a stern warning over the intercom to turn off all devices. . ."

"for obvious reasons," confirmed Lisa, "did you manage," her curiosity piqued.

"yes, through some mighty internal contortions. . ." "painful ones?"

"not exactly, love. . ." "your innards must be well trained. . ." "I guess so."

"delighted to have given you some pleasure," breathed Lisa. "Now let me fantasize a bit about having my body writhe in sexual anticipation at the merest touch of your fingers, under your control not mine and from such a distance; would you dial my orgasm tonight, as my captor and remote-controller, please, please. . ."

"dial your hormones, all right, you are just one big hormone, bitch. . ."

"I am yours as much as of any man who can control me through my urges like you can. . ."

"does anyone at present?"

"no, more's the pity," the girl sighed: "please, I beg you, dial every one of my hormones tonight!"

"when, Lisa?" "I'll be at home in an hour; not any earlier, I might be stuck in a traffic jam. . ." she started laughing. "how often?" "as often as you like, within another hour or two. . ."

"how long each time?" "five to seven minutes," Lisa answered with clinical correctness, "then allow me as much time again to pee. . ."

"will you have to take the mobile out each time?" Aline was interested.

"I'll try not to; I'll send you a text message if I need to, for a length of time."

"an experiment all right; do you want to picture yourself while naked and being dialled up?"

"why not; and I shall upload it for you; for I want you to see me under your total control. . ."

"a bit like do-it-yourself porn. . ."

"on one level, I wouldn't mind that either; perhaps not, though."

Eileen rang Elanca:

"is Jules being done today?" she asked; "if so, I need to take time off work, don't I?"

"is it like that now, Eileen?" the other woman wondered, "a mere few days ago, you were here simply as a mother to a young person about to change her gender, in itself quite life-changing; now you are a working woman who has to find time. . ."

"almost like in Adelaide. . ."

"you don't say Home any more, even, Eileen," admonished the reporter.

"yes, poor Andy died about two hours ago," she continued.

"in much pain?" asked Jules mother. "How awful for his family."

"yes," agreed the journalist; "I made friends with them over these last few days, courtesy of a local journalist; come and meet them. . ."

"do they know their son's tool's last resting place?" Eileen wondered.

"yes, and they are secretly delighted, even though they are good Catholics as well,"

Elanca replied:

"I would not call it 'rest' given the workout that your Jules is about to give it in both the immediate and the distant future. Are you at work now?"

"yes, Elanca; I am doing an audit preparation and training Glen and his team at the same time; why?"

"Be here in two hours if you at all can do so, is all I can say; Andy's funeral is tomorrow, starting at St Mary's; be there, along with all of us. . ." "Is Jules in the theatre, already?"

"no, she actually went to school for the day but was recalled and went to work in her workroom; give her a ring. . ." "is Ann here?" "expected at lunch hour. . ." "how about yourself?"

"I'll be allowed inside the theatre and so should you and Ann; I'll remind them, to be certain;" the reporter replied; "I do not yet know how much I'll be able to cover. . . get here soonest, mother of Jules!"

Eileen's telephone rang:

"oh, I meant to ring you this very moment, Trevor; Jules is about to be done within the next three hours, I'd say. . ."

"day after tomorrow is the very earliest, Eileen, that I can make it," her husband replied: "that only because I hired another manager who can relieve Anna who'll run the place while I am away. . ."

"she's a good choice," admitted his wife, "but you did right in finding someone who can take over some of her workload." she paused.

"anything you want to tell me, beside Jules?" Trevor asked perceptively. "About us?" "yes, I am glad you asked; come here soonest; but also know that, whether you get to stay or not. . ."

"is that it, Eileen, after all these years?" Trevor asked, hurt and upset.

"it is because of these years, good years, productive years, and I have always loved you, Jules and Stephen and your work and mine; this period of my life is over and I am not going back to it, or to you. None of this is your fault, or any of your doing. . ."

"is Jules to stay with you, rather than come back with me?"

"likely with us, Trevor; it'll be her decision, and Ann's, but I'd say, yes to Micronesia. . ."

"am I to be cut out of your lives altogether?"

"no; we need to work out a Modus Vivendi, a way to make it work. . ."

"does all this involve another man, Eileen?" asked her husband reasonably.

"yes," countered Eileen, "but he's but one reason, perhaps not even the main one."

"so you would have decided to remain in Micronesia, anyway, with or without me, or him, for that matter?"

"very succinctly put, Trev. The bloke is Glen, by the way, whom you may remember from the hearings."

"but how about Hector who was to become his 'wife'?"

"that will still happen, Trev; Hec is about to be operated on, too; they have a specialist here, Gloria, who will put the finishing touches on both Jules and Hector; you'll meet and like her. . ."

"be grateful for small mercies," her husband mumbled.

"oh, she is more than that; she used to be a women's wartime trauma specialist in the Middle East and Northeast Africa till she was blacklisted for preventing female 'circumcision'"

"do you want me to make an offer for her, by way of compensation for losing you, Eileen?"

"men!" sighed his wife. "Get in touch with Elanca's magazine for when you are due to leave Adelaide"

"done that, already; I'll get my ticket tomorrow. . ."

"still within their budget, is it?"

"yes, I'll let Elanca know before I leave, or they will."

"keep ringing me; I may be out of reach sometimes. . ."

Andy's funeral was a sombre but in some ways also joyful affair; Father Ernesto Alvarez, a diminutive elderly Filipino, had allowed the family to play the boy's favourite songs; shots showing Andy's family, his girlfriends and the boy with his mates filled a big screen all over the wall.

The ordinary Catholic funeral rite was followed in every other way, except that traditional musical instruments which the priest was fond of were used throughout. Many families had turned up, those of his work mates, some belonging to a gaggle of very attractive girls sitting close to Andy's sisters, Andy's own family and their close friends were in attendance, as was a delegation of the archdiocese of Guam, on Saipan to help write liturgy in the local version of Chamorro, made possible by the Second Vatican Council, to be used in the responses of the people for the first time, hence their interest.

People went past the coffin, according to a local tradition, gazed at Andy-the fence post having been skilfully hidden-some kissing his face, several girls making a point of looking at where his favourite tool would have been, older women holding hands and keening in almost unison;

Halfway through the service, a Chamorro song bewailing the loss of fishermen at sea was sung, with the lyrics slightly altered. Flowers were in evidence everywhere, as were bands of coral strung in the most artistic fashion by the orphans of St Mary's who made a good living from selling such ornaments to tourists.

The clinic had donated-and decorated-the bier with Andy on it and had paid an embalmer who had done wonders, aided by Gloria and helped by the fact that most of Andy's injuries had been internal; several girls were in constant tears yet could not stop looking at his face, holding hands or having their arms wrapped around, and comforting, each other.

The usual 'suspects' were in attendance, Oratio and his tribe, Merv's, as were several boys and girls working with the Australian Youth Labour project, as it was getting known, as were several clinic staff, including Amelia and Rosetta, even Gordon, the proprietor and two of his younger daughters, former classmates of Andy.

Glen and Eileen were standing close to each other ("Jules' ll be allright", he kept whispering to her), as were others, not necessarily known to Andy's family or anyone else.

The Diocesan team had invited several dozen key people to a reception afterwards, to "repay the generosity of the congregation in trialling the new liturgy" was their face-saving phrase, at Father Ernesto's suggestion; yet it saved Andy's family a lot of money and effort; the funeral itself was paid for by the clinic, topped by a sizable donation in cash and kind, double-distilled mango extract among the latter, from Gordon and his clan.

Gloria's lover and onetime mentor, Professor Fernando Gutierrez, had arrived at the clinic during Andy's last hour and, while involved in Jules' operation, had persuaded Gloria to attend the funeral mass, then showed up at the reception with her for a short time, making their excuses and steering her out by her elbow when it came time to resume duties.

"People know you here, Fernando," Gloria remonstrated with him later for such proprietary behaviour towards her, much as she had secretly liked it.

"they might even know that I am married, dear; let them realize that you, too, are mine; I haven't thanked you for involving me in that almost bizarre set of operations," he confided on their way back to the clinic:

"I wouldn't have missed it for the world, even without you around," he continued to press her hand; "but having you with me if only for a few days is personal and professional bliss. . ."

"you unreconstructed chauvinist," she disbursed herself of terms of endearment,

"still I feel chuffed when you praise me and when I am with you. . ."

"you are putty in my hands," the ageing lecherous specialist admitted, "but your own hands are very good, not only on this old man's body but also very gentle yet adept at removing that poor boy's dick. . ."

"for a good cause. . ." "and inserting it smack inside. . ."

"what was left of Jules' vulva after I had reamed it."

"agreed, but look out for infections. . ." "why, Fernando?"

"traces of urine, I think," said her lover thoughtfully. "You may have to inject some antibiotics. . ."

"probiotics, you mean, Fernando," Gloria's speech, too, had become factual.

"I don't have your knowledge of pharmacology but do something preventative, Gloria; I am not certain that the two urethra fitted perfectly, however well you spliced them."

"will it flow properly?" she asked anxiously.

"keep Jules on dialysis for one more night, then observe renal function early this morning, or else Brendan or I can do it if you want to sleep after the operation and the funeral. ."

"let me see in a few hours, Fernando; don't you feel sorry for Andy's family?"

They had put Jules on local anaesthetics but waited with the actual operation till first Eileen and then Ann arrived, quite breathless from having hurried. They were seated on either side of Jules, holding a hand each, waiting for Elanca to take up position behind Ann's shoulder and Gloria's team to begin, closely watched by Brendan and Fernando. The nurses acted like clockwork, not having worked under Gloria before; the penis was brought in, Brendan checked Jules' original genital one final time with an enormous magnifier, then identified key points where Andy's penis was to be attached without involving mucous lining, stepping aside for Fernando to do likewise; the specialist nodded and only then did the girls commence, already having shorn Jules' pubic hair and eliminated certain follicles deemed to be in the way.

While Eileen could barely look, Ann could not keep her eyes away, opening her mouth and moistening her lips, looking sexy, Elanca decided who had not stopped filming as close as she was permitted to. Eventually, Gloria directed Jules' mum and lover to move away to give her and two of her nurses better access and made Elanca step aside, before deftly stitching in Andy's penis which the girls kept holding in place with steadfast hands, wondering secretly against their better knowledge whether it would erect or not, such had been the boy's reputation.

The operation had not taken that long, with both Brendan, as the presiding doctor, and Fernando, the visiting specialist, declaring themselves satisfied with what Gloria and her team had wrought. Eileen and Ann had been allowed to accompany Jules afterwards but had to wash their hands rigorously before being allowed to hold 'her' hand again.

"Your dad will have to go through all this soon, and repeatedly," explained Jules, trying not to show the pain that she was beginning to feel.

"do we need to hold your hands so you don't scratch yourself, lover?" Ann asked.

"do as you must!"

The doctors, having scrubbed and disrobed themselves, entered Jules' bedroom.

"who is next?" asked Jules, "why, your girlfriend's dad, as of tomorrow early morning. . ." Professor Fernando Gutierrez explained.

"Is he at work, Ann, today?" "yes, he left to conduct a training session. . ."

"we need to reach him," stated doctor Gloria, with Brendan nodding by her side.

"I would like to start him off in earnest tomorrow very early morning, before Andy's funeral."

"Ann, do you want to stay with me tonight or here?" asked Jules' mum.

"no, here, so I can be with both Jules and Dad, him for the last time before he is turned into Mum. . ." "we'll ask Rosetta's parents," promised Brendan.

Elanca entered, kissed Brendan and the professor, embraced Gloria and took both Ann's and Jules' hands in her own-"I did wash my hands very thoroughly"-then hugged Eileen before she set up her gear to take a group photo.

"I am so excited," she revealed, "and so very proud of all of you very remarkable people. I heard that Ann's dad is next; do you want me to ring him later this afternoon to let him know?"

"ring him now if you can get through," suggested Brendan who barely dared to admit his need.

Rosetta's mum introduced Ann to Gordon's in-laws who had come over for a card game and to share some of their produce: "We have heard about you and your friend through a grandson of ours, Cecilio," the matriarch told Ann while her husband dispensed liquid goodness from ancient glass bottles;

"it tastes better in glass than in plastic," Rosetta's father declared. Everyone had three glasses in front of them, including Ann, except that hers contained less alcohol and more tonic, in inverse ratio to what the adults allowed themselves to imbibe.

Ann, aptly describing the brews as nature's anaesthetics, liked the attention bestowed on her by these generous elderly Micronesians, nonetheless went to bed early, to self- satisfy herself for want of her lover but, simply, also to sleep; for the stresses and effort of the last few months was beginning to tell even on her youthful levels of energetic determination.

❦

Ann's father arrived at the clinic rather late, with them dropping in at Eileen's place first:

"to see if you are all right by yourself. . ."

"thanks, Glen and Hec," their future venture partner greeted them, offering them green tea and spicy noodles interspersed with bits of smoked tuna. "are you allowed to eat anything, Hec?" she wondered. "eight to ten hours before the operation," Hector reflected, "I shall eat a few chopsticks full, to do justice to your cooking and since I haven't eaten all day; green tea ad libitum, can you fill up some for me for later. I am allowed to drink till midnight. . ." he ate reluctantly, then pushed his plate aside.

"thank you, it hit the spot. . . what did you make the tea of, Eileen?" wondered Glen. "lemongrass, mint, green tea and dried jasmine leaves and buds. . ." she watched her favourite man eat to his heart's delight.

They sat on the verandah for more tea, overlooking a palm-studded slope lit by an almost full moon shining on translucently soft warm air, stirred by a slight breeze.

"Here's to plans and prospects," Eileen told her friends: "I have rarely been as fulfilled as I am now, even though considering that my teenage daughter is turning into a boy under my very eyes; even then. . ." she paused:

"may Jules, and Ann, find happiness under the sky. . ."

"so say us also," confirmed Glen, his hands on Hector's shoulders.

"would they want to live with us here?" he asked.

"no reason not to," Eileen assured him and Hector nodded in agreement.

"they like challenges at least as much as we do, and they have each other, as well as us, and whatever friends they will make here. . ."

"it will either strengthen or break their relationship," mused Glen, "but they are also very persistent." He took Eileen's hand and kissed it:

"thank you, it is a privilege to know you and have you on board with the two of us. . ."

"and Aline?" Hector nodded appreciatively.

"she, too, will pull her weight and she's our link with the community,"

"let me drive you to the clinic; it is getting late," offered Glen, reluctant to disturb the magic of the evening. . .They drove through the quiet neighbourhood, ending up along the bay.

"thank you, Hec, for being in my life and for doing what you have started. . ."

"change is the fundamental law of life," concluded Hector, studying his future partner in profile, conscious of the remarkable man beside him.

Hector was shown a bed and attended to by the three doctors. . .

"makes us sound like the Three Tenors, except that we don't sound as melodious. . ."

"I don't know; Brendan used to be in a medic's choir and orchestra in Adelaide and I have heard Gloria sing. . ."

"but not as a tenor," she protested; "I am, if anything, a contralto and Professor Gutierrez here. . ."

"Fernando", her lover corrected his mentee, "is a wonderful baritone;" she continued, unfazed, "I heard him rehearse liturgy for the funeral," she explained with some pride.

"I'll start on you at about six am tomorrow; definitely no more food, as of now, and nothing to drink after midnight; do drink a bit now; go to the toilet now but not during the night. Brendan, anything that I need to remember?"

"no, except to wish all of us good luck, likewise to Hec here; thank you for being such a good patient and for fitting in so well with life here. Will Glen be here for you tomorrow?"

Doctor Mac Groom remembered. "no, he'll ring, but one of us'll have to be at work," his future partner explained, "I expect him to arrive in the afternoon. . ."

They hauled Hector out at dawn, removed his penis which they kept as a transferable organ or for tissue culture, depending on anyone's future need, then began to implant lining and tissue to form as authentic a vulva as possible while keeping the flow of urine intact; Fernando suggested that Hec be put on dialysis for the rest of the day which they agreed to; since he was on an intensive yet local anaesthetic she was 'selectively' conscious when 'he' spotted 'his' daughter.

"May I touch. . . Mum?" the girl asked Gloria who nodded but also added:

"not quite yet; at present, Hec is neither dad nor mum yet; there'll have to be two more insertions. Professor Gutierrez and I are expected at Andy's funeral; Ann, do stay with your mum/dad"

"as in Mad, doctor Gloria?"

Brendan put his arms around the girl, to spare his colleague having to answer. "let's have a cup of tea, Ann. . ." "is my 'Mad' allowed to have one, doctor Brendan?" "not just yet."

Elanca had filmed the operation and gone to shower and shake off her sense of fatigue, then stood next to Brendan, their hands touching lightly:

"tea sounds good; I think Rosetta has some ready; shall I get some. . ."

"bring her in as well," the doctor offered:

"Ann, go and spend some time with Jules, soon to be Julius, then go to school; our bus will take you. . . but have some tea first. . ."

"you do love the journo, doctor;" commented Ann, "she can't stop looking at you, that's for sure. . ."

"it is good to have her here, Ann. . ." the doctor agreed, not wanting to commit himself any further.

Ann entered Jules room and took 'his 'hand:

"would you, instead of massaging your newfound dick?" she asked demurely,

"do me instead, from the inside, please?"

"how did you know that I was not to touch my newfound dick?" asked Jules whose voice had perceptively deepened with all that hormonal treatment.

"you got a one-track mind, bitch. . ." "vive la difference, lover," his girlfriend answered calmly.

"can you do me a quickie or are you too tired or in pain. . ."

"nothing's too good for you, 'sighed Jules and, allowing Ann to help 'his' torso onto several pillows for support, reached out to where Ann had unbuttoned her school uniform skirt in readiness for Jules' ministrations whose fingers had lost none of their skills, probing and teasing Ann gently but unmistakably. "strip me, lover. . ." breathlessly. "can't," answered Jules, matter-of-fact-like continuing to arouse her, with Ann leaning against Jules' hand and lower arm for better leverage, murmuring in satisfaction. Jules stopped suddenly, a look of pain crossing his face. Ann reacted quickly, moved Jules' hand from under her skirt, kissed it and cleaned it with some gel found on the bedside dresser.

"do you want me to get a nurse, lover?"

"it's something urinary," Jules diagnosed, ever the budding scientist;

"strange thing is, I am to be on dialysis, yet it feels itchy but also painful." "the operation?"

"probably but it feels more like an urinary infection I had years ago, from my first- ever boyfriend when I was a girl. . ." Ann could not help smiling; for Jules had only ceased being a fully-equipped female that very morning.

"which doctor is around?"

"doctor Gloria and Professor Fernando are off to the funeral service, doctor Brendan. . ."

"please, get him; then you must go to school for the both of us; promise?" which Ann did, heading off to find Brendan.

By the time that doctor arrived, Jules was very uncomfortable, not so much in pain but itchy and in discomfort. Doctor Brendan had a quick look and saw an angry red welt not so much along the seam but along the lower side of the newly-stitched penis. "urinary infection, doctor Brendan?" "either that or toxemia, Jules, does not look like tissue reaction," Brendan surmised and added:

"let us wait till Professor Fernando; for he is the renal specialist. . ."

"will you be able to use antibiotics?"

"I'll try them on some tissue of yours, first."

"is that because Andy was overloaded with them, to begin with?"

"you'll be a good medical scientist one day. . ."

"if I survive the ordeal. . ."

"we all live in hope," admitted the doctor. "look, I'll leave you with one of my nurses."

"the ones that operated on me are off shift now, aren't they?"

"yes, Jules, I'll get one of the girls who's just come on; if it gets worse, she'll know what to do. . ."

"are you sending Ann to school, doctor Brendan;. . ." "yes, our school bus is picking her up?"

"will you allow her to come back in the afternoon?" "why, she'll have to do her homework here. . ."

"where is she sleeping nights, with Mum?"

"I'd say so; I get Elanca to arrange that," he said and turned away to deal with patients and staff. Elanca came, leant against him briefly and saw the worry lines on his face:

"how are your two patients doing?"

"Hec is all right. . ." "what do we call 'her' from now on, Brendan?" kissing his hand;

"Hec will do, for the time being; it is Jules I am a bit worried about."
"how come?"

"'he 'may have picked up a urinary infection from Andy. . ."

"could you have anticipated it, Brendan?"

"the tissue tested clean, Elanca; we must have not flushed it properly somewhere along the line, quite literally. . ." "what will you do?" she held his arm for a while. "get Professor Fernando to have a very good look at it. . ."

"a good thing, in a way, that it happened so soon. . ."

"yes, you are right, my love," Brendan replied, somewhat distracted. "how about Ann?"

"oh, I forgot; could you ask Eileen if she can host her for the next few days at least while Ann's 'mum' is here?"

"I'll go and find her," Elanca promised and went to have a look at Hec who was awake and in good spirits. "what does your new identity feel like?"

"hard to say," commented Ann's 'mum'in a rather pleasant light tenor-type of voice.

"my voice's changed and my torso feels different but I am getting used to it so I am beginning to forget what my body was like. . . I like to get back to work. . ."

"that might shock your team if they have to get to know you as Ann's Mum. . ."

"yes, it'll be an experience. . ."

"perhaps best left till you start on Ariman Island where nobody knew your previous identity."

"you may not be wrong," Hec admitted, "yet I want to test my new identity in my old job... I hear that Jules is not coping well. . ."

"this place is like a village well, nothing's a secret," moaned Elanca.

"Is it all right if Ann stays with Jules' mum for the next few days?"

"yes, can you arrange it, please?" "I am going to see her; she should be at work by now. . ."

"say Hello; I hope to see her soon myself, here or at work. . ."

Elanca had a fair idea where Eileen might be but she did not expect who had turned up meanwhile.

Trevor had arrived at about the time of Andy's funeral, having been fortunate in his connections from Adelaide via Perth and Guam. The homeland officer, on arrival, at Saipan International, had been brusque to the point of being rude:

"Does anyone here know you, Mister?" To his credit, Trevor refused to rise to the bait, in spite of being tired after his uneventful flight:

"my wife might, Sir. . ." with an emphasis on the respectful appellation.

"what does she do for a living, Mr Childers. . ." looking at Trevor's passport and suddenly smiling: "isn't your wife the Bookkeeper?"

"yes, she is an articled accountant; she used to work for me before we married. . ."

"well, she does a lot of freelance bookkeeping here. . ." the Chamorro homeland officer had suddenly turned friendly:

"anyone else her who might know you, Sir. . ." emphasized.

"my daughter is at Dr Brendan's clinic which is really why I am here. . ."

"then I am sorry and apologize," offered the officer, stamped Trevor's passport and guided him to the airport curio shop:

"My sister works here, Mr Childers, and I understand that your wife has done their bookkeeping. . ."

"here at the airport?"

"not yet; they have several shops in town; your wife appears to have designed a stock- take template and they do expect her here any of these days. . ."

"likely when there are fewer flights and customers. . ."

"probably, Mr Childers; go and ask for Elyssya, my sister; someone there may be able to tell you how and where to reach your wife; I wish you a good time with your daughter as well," the officer concluded, by now respectfully.

Trevor entered the shop and was fronted by a young assistant whose nameplate he was trying to read. "Are you trying to find someone, Sir?" the girl noticed.

"yes, a colleague of yours, Elyssya, and then my own wife. . ."

"and who may she be, Sir? would we know her?" the girl wondered, not least at Trevor's Australian accent.

"the homeland officer, Elyssya's brother, told me that she was known as the Bookkeeper. . ." Meanwhile, Elyssya, hearing her name mentioned, approached them and was told who Trevor was looking for. "my brother directed you here, Sir? Are you Mrs Eileen's husband?"

"just arrived from Adelaide," Trevor admitted: "is she at work?" "yes; somewhere in town. . ."

"look, Elyssya," interjected the other girl, "Manon is about to drive into town; let her give Mr Childers here a lift and find out where Eileen is working today; do you have your wife's mobile number here, Sir?"

"oh yes, but I haven't had a chance to get a sim card or a new phone. . ."

"obviously; just give it to Manon and she can find out and then drop you. . ."

It happened to be their mother-shop near the boulevard where Eileen had just been to pick up their accounts to drop them at home, prior to going to the clinic.

"I'd best drop you at the clinic itself," offered Manon, "so you get to see your wife and daughter at the same time. Do you have any other contact?"

"yes, someone called Elanca, a feature journalist. . ."

"yes, she's been to our shop; you'll realize that Saipan is a small place. . ."

"as is Adelaide, be sure," answered Trevor. "Let me give you Elanca's number also."

❦

Elanca had gone to witness Glen and Ramon at work with yet another group of unemployed young people. "Trevor, good to hear your voice," Elanca sounded enthusiastic: "are you heading for the clinic? I'll be back; I only left it this morning; looking forward to seeing you again. . ." "How's Jules?" "operation successful, but some complications."

Meanwhile, Gloria and her part-time lover had returned from the funeral mass and the reception, to be whisked into Jules' room.

"I scrub up and have a look straight away," the professor decided while Gloria hurried to do likewise and organise a nurse to get frocks.

"I meant to put you on dialysis," the professor told Jules, "but let's see first."

Jules, obligingly rolled over for the specialist, by now scrubbed, robed and gloved, to investigate.

"hmm; does this hurt?" he probed.

"a sort of stinging pain right through my body," answered Jules.

"a bit of a welt here; Gloria, get hold of a magnifier. . ." he ordered, probing a few more spots. . .

"Gloria, have a look. . ." his former mentee and occasional lover, herself a specialist, did:

"what do you think?" "an infection, doesn't look like tissue rejection. . ."

"too early for that, Gloria. . ." "but a bit toxic, nonetheless. . ."

Brendan had, meanwhile, returned from his mid-morning round.

"Brendan, did you people ever take that fencepost out of that poor boy?"

"no, Professor. . ." "but do you have samples. . ."

"specific to the steel post? I'd have to look. . ."

"meanwhile," the specialist turned to Jules: "I meant to put you on dialysis but I want you to drink some green tea now and pee as soon as you can; Nurse will help you; can you walk by yourself?"

"it hurts and chafes a bit and I have to walk very slowly because of the extra equipment between my legs. . ." "which you are not used to," agreed the professor, laughing:

"walk as soon as you had your cup or two of green tea. . ." "a known diuretic," agreed Jules; "yours is a good scientific mind, son," the specialist smiled,

"and then, once you have urinated to my heart's delight and yours. . . it may hurt, mind you, and fill up one of the vials, we'll put you on dialysis. . ." "as a control, Professor?"

"hole in one," commented Gloria. "Agreeable, Brendan?"

"yes, I understand you wanting to find out whether there was any contaminant on the fence pole itself that somehow found its way into Andy's urethra and was somehow reactivated. . ."

"in the hope it has not spread; yes," conceded the professor.

Meanwhile, Ann was back at school and Angh's mother asked her about Jules whom she had come to regard as her star pupil.

"Urinary infection?" she mused. "You know, Ann, that I am part Vietnamese; have a cup of tea, anyway," she offered, "and some Vietnamese sunflower seed; Angh is already busily nibbling these. . ." pointing at her daughter a short distance away:

"sit with us, Angh," she offered; the girls kissed and held hands for a moment.

"we have a mixed traditional-Western official system of health care in Vietnam which I studied while we were there, Angh and myself. . ." "you went to school there?" Ann reminded her friend.

"yes, the Samaritan Convent in Hanoi, Ann, fancy you remember."

"what I mean to say," interrupted her mother: "I grew to respect systematic natural healing if properly incorporated, works so well with infections, allergies and toxic substances. . ."

"Mum, are you thinking of marine toxins?"

"such as cuttlefish, man-of-war in the Caribbean, even certain algae within corals," agreed her mother.

"now, I understand that your father, his partner and Jules' mum are to work on Ariman Island with Señor Nestor." "are you thinking of the naturalist who was here last year?"

"yes, Angh; his was the first family to resettle after the eruption because he wanted to use fresh lava ash and ground magma for some of his medication. . ."

"what else does he use, Miss?" asked Ann.

"marine alkaloids, leaf and flower extracts, aloe pollen and honey."

"will any of this help Jules?" wondered Ann.

"it may, but remember she is in good hands at the clinic," commented the science teacher.

"who is looking after Jules, other than Dr Brendan?"

"Dr Gloria Paz from Guam and her ex-mentor, Professor Gutierrez, based in Hawaii. . ."

"very reputable specialists, I know Gloria quite well and have certainly heard about Professor Gutierrez; run what I have said past them at the clinic. . ." suggested Angh's mother:

"do they listen to you young people?"

"oh, very much so, Miss; what's that practitioner's name, please?"

"Alcides Alvarez; would you like me to find out how to get in touch with him?"

"yes, please, Miss, thanks for the tea; see you at sports, Angh," replied Ann, kissed that girl's hand and strode off.

"Don't be too jealous of Jules, Angh," comforted her mother.

Elanca had waited outside the clinic; when she saw Trevor emerge from Manon's van, she walked over, introduced herself to the girl, took Trevor's hand, offered her cheek for his kiss, thanked Manon and led Trevor inside. "How is Jules?"

"as I said on the phone, she can and does move about; she's doing homework on their computer," explained the journalist, "the clinic has given the two a workroom where to do online study and homework. . ." "Ann?"

"at school; she drops in and stays as much as she can; I live with a Chamorro family across the street-you'll meet them-and Ann sometimes stays there, other times with your wife who, by the way, is on her way. . ." looking over Trevor's shoulder, she saw Eileen drive up, let go of Trevor's hand and waved:

"Eileen, guess who's here?" She then led Trevor to greet his wife, then asked:

"Eileen, can Trevor put his bags inside your boot?"

"of course, Elanca. . ." his wife embraced Trevor who kissed her tenderly; having dropped his suitcase and shoulder bag in the car boot, the two women guided Trevor inside the clinic and went straight to the work room. Jules got up and embraced 'his' father, walking awkwardly and being in obvious pain.

"does it hurt much?" Trevor asked solicitously.

"no more that did your sciatica some years ago, Dad, and you managed," Jules answered, "I remember you saying that you had not lost a days' work on account of it. . ."

"what do they think is wrong?"

"I seem to have inherited a urinary infection compounded by some toxic contaminant. . ."

"what is doctor Mac Groom doing about it?" Trevor was not exactly calm.

"Mum, close the door, please," commanded Jules. "There are three doctors, Dr Brendan-Mc Groom that is, doctor Gloria-Paz is her full name-a gynaecologist and reconstructive surgeon, and Professor Fernando-Gutierrez, a kidney and urine specialist, all attending to me much more than to Ann's, er, parent. . ." Jules explained.

"I'll be on dialysis later today and for a few days. . ." "why's that, Jules?" asked Elanca.

"why, that's to eliminate toxins, with luck, and as a control to ordinary pee, to spot any difference. . ."

"and then analyse it, if any?" asked Eileen. "yes, to determine the nature of any toxin."

"what's next?" "normally, you treat infections with antibiotics and toxins with chelates," answered Jules the budding scientist;

"as I need to be on immuno-suppressants, we need to go easy on antibiotics but chelates are all right, I guess. . ." "are you consulting doctor number four,?" exclaimed Elanca, amused in spite of the potential gravity of the situation.

"I'd be an even poorer patient," commented Jules, "but let me tell you if you don't want to ask; Andy's dick feels as if it had been part of me at all times. . ."

"even though it hurts?" wondered Trevor.

"it's not my dick that hurts, Dad, nor where it is joined up-a bit, maybe-but the full length of plumbing way back inside me," explained Jules patiently.

"it's good to see you, Dad, and thanks for coming here, Mum, and Elanca; could I ask you to go and see the doctors, perhaps also visit Ann's, er, parent, unless 'she's back at work, so I can catch up with online homework. . ." she looked at the three adults:

"I know you are worried," Jules intoned in a rather boyish voice, "so am I; but be assured, I am in good hands, so, please. . ." and sat down again to work but also because he could not stand for a length of time.

The three adults went to see Hec whose new name nobody had yet come up with; he, too, was walking around and about to sit on the verandah and read a file when she spotted them.

"come and follow me to the cafeteria," she offered and led the way. Trevor could barely keep his eyes off Hec; even Eileen and Elanca who had seen her more often were surprised at the change in personality, whether voice, gait or body shape; yet there was no mistaking the gentle insightful self-deprecating nature which they had all come to know and like.

Jules appeared to have dropped off midway through the conversation; 'he' struggled 'to concentrate on' his 'project work' and, at the same time, interact with the adults.

"so there is toxin inside me, toxemic or not?" Jules wondered.

"your body seems to be fighting it, hence the pain and the temperature, even though we did reduce your immune reaction. . .?"

"is there a reaction against my new dick that you can measure?"

"negligible; your tissue must have been incredibly compatible with Andy's. . ."

"is it that you dare not use antibiotics?"

"yes, because of the hormones that you are on but also because they do not interact well with the chelates we shall need to use against the toxin?"

"what type of chelates?" Jules asked the professor.

"we are testing the toxin in the lab against some standard ones which don't seem to work at all. . ."

"would you like a second opinion, so to say, Professor Fernando?"

Brendan and Gloria stared at the teenager but the professor nodded.

"Who were you thinking of, Jules?"

"my science teacher, Sir; would you like me to ring her; if nothing else so that she gets to hear from me. . ."

"it cannot hurt," suggested Brendan and Gloria also nodded.

"would you like to ring her now or wait for Ann, Jules?"

"I'll ring in about ten minutes when she is due for a break; she is part Vietnamese and studied under the mixed-medical system they have in that country to qualify as a medical scientist. . ."

"I have a great respect for their system, especially against burns and certain kinds of injuries. . . we had three colleagues in the field who had trained in Vietnam," explained Gloria.

To everyone's surprise, it was the science teacher, Angh's mother, who rang within minutes.

"Ann had given me your number, Jules," she explained. "are your doctors with you?" "all three of them, Miss," Jules confirmed.

"I'll get you to explain first, Jules, then I shall talk to your doctor Brendan; we met each other. . ."

So Jules explained, as best he could, the nature and effects of the toxin. . .

"which may have been triggered by a undiagnosed urinary infection. . ."

"change of pH, quite possibly," agreed her teacher; "now, let me talk to doctor Brendan first. . ."

Jules passed her on, then listened to 'his' side of the conversation:

"Brendan Mc Groom speaking; Mrs Van Thran; we met at the Mariana youth science workshop two years ago; how is your family, your daughter in particular; I remember her well. . ."

"Angh is fine and doing well in school; she's come to like Ann and is busily competing with Jules; we all miss 'him', as it is. . ."

"Jules figured that you might be able to tell us something. . ." "about the toxin?" "guide us in the right direction, please. . . none of us wants to see Jules suffer. . ."

"I was thinking of a person rather than a remedy as such. . ."

"a professional, Mother of Angh?"

"in a sense, he is a healer and lives on Ariman Island, Alcides Celeste is his name. . ."

"I seem to remember that Ann's by now mum and Glen, 'her 'partner, were expecting a young woman, born and raised in Australia, but originally from that island to join them within days. . ."

"I have heard of her; she's been to the Marianas before; I know Señor Nestor quite well, the clan leader there. . ."

"are you convinced that Señor Alcide knows his ways about toxins?" "yes, doctor Mc Groom."

"would it make sense if we contacted Señor Nestor, quite possibly through Señor Ramon. . ."

"isn't he a colleague of Ann's parent and 'her' partner?"

"yes, and they are planning a joint venture which, I understand, is to involve his young woman descendent as well. . ." "Aline Rosario. . ."

"would Señor Nestor be able to ask Señor Alcide if he'd be willing to come and see us, Jules in particular?"

"yes, that might be an idea if you rang him first and then I shall follow up through the parents of several of my students. . ."

"have you been talking to Ann, Mother of Angh?"

"yes, Angh is very fond of her, and I did mention Señor Alcide's approach but not his name if I remember properly," explained the teacher: "do expect Ann to approach and ask you to get in touch with me or else with Señor Nestor. . ."

"how would she know? Oh of course, through her parent. . ."

"yes, these are two intelligent young people;" explained the teacher:

"had Jules asked you also to ring me?"

"you are not wrong, mother of Angh, and we shall do as you suggest, today if we can. . ."

Ann arrived on the clinic's school bus, gravely listening to what Jules and the doctors had to tell her.

"Angh's mum told me about the traditional healer from Ariman Island;" she commented:

"Dad, sorry, Mum, is at work and I shall ring 'her'. . ."

"why that, Ann?" asked the professor.

"because she told me that a young woman who she and Mr Hiddings worked with in Central Australia has family on that island and is expected any day now; she is to work as part of their team, by the way." "go ahead, Ann," smiled Gloria.

Ann settled herself close to Jules who put his hand on her shoulder which she kissed and then dialed: "good to see you back at work, er Mum! How did the troupe react?"

"it did not make any difference, Ann. . ."

"this is the first time that I am hearing your new voice on the phone. . ." smiled 'her' daughter:

"look, aren't you getting that girl from Ariman on board?"

"Aline, that's right; Glen and I know her from Central Australia. . ."

"in a Biblical sense, Mum?"

"that did not quite happen, Ann. Why are you asking?"

"can one of you ask her to get in touch with her family on Ariman to ask their healer to help Jules get over a bit of poison that 'he 'picked up from the fence post that impaled Andy, the bloke whose funeral we just had? What a sentence, Mum. . ." she ended, allowing Jules to kiss her.

Aline did ring Glen that evening:

"I am so looking forward to being with you lot, working and whatever else there is for us to together. . ." "Hec is now no longer Hector, Aline, you realize that. . ."

"but still the person whom we all love and value," tendered the girl.

"look, I'll be on Saipan day after tomorrow if not earlier. . ."

"Aline, my love, have you rung your family back on Ariman since we last talked?"

"not since; I am about to now; why, lover?" "would you ask your clan Elder. . ."

"Señor Nestor, you mean, my grand-uncle?"

"yes, would you ask Señor Nestor to allow that traditional healer of his, to help Hec's daughter's lover Jules get over a bit of poisoning which the clinic finds difficult and which Jules who is now a boy needs to survive. . ."

"I shall have to break it down into what our traditional society can cope with but I shall do so," the girl promised, 'to make you and Hec happy and also to help these two young people. . ."

"does your grand-uncle listen to you at all, Aline?"

"yes, he often asks me about things, not least to get an altogether different view of things;" she asserted: "do you want me to ask him to contact the clinic? He does respect them very much."

⁂

Señor Nestor rang Merv the Cobbler that evening:

"Can you spare the Australian accountant part of the year, for Ariman?" he asked his old friend, after the usual courtesies had been dealt with.

"for you and the people on Ariman, always, my very esteemed friend; she is presently costing some of Señor Oratio's school furniture for you. . ."

"do you want me to send the boat over for that, Señor Mervin?"

"yes, if you can afford to have the boat wait here for two or three days. . ."

"that would help get my grand-niece across at the same time; she is in Guam, due in Saipan any day now. . ."

"that's Aline, is it not? She seems to know your two Australian consultants. . ."

"I agree, Señor Mervin," said the clan elder; "I think that it is for them she has come back to the Marianas for. . ." "happy to see her?"

"of course; moreover, I want her to spend a day or two with them on Saipan, to pick up some of their ideas and break them down for us here. . ."

"forgive me for pointing it out to you, Señor Nestor, but they do have some very unusual domestic arrangements which appear to also involve whom you call 'my accountant'," stated the shoemaker: "can you people live with that?"

There was a pause, then he heard his friend's thoughtful reply:

"Look, Merv, the girls tell me, not just Aline but her cousins who have been on the US mainland or at least on Guam. . ." "what do they say, Nestor?" the businessman asked gently.

"that people like our Australian friends make a clear distinction between their work ethic and their private life. . ." "which we islanders traditionally do not," agreed Merv.

"these people made decisions well before they were aware of our existence, let alone being in a position to help us. . ." "you do need them?"

"yes, they have the knowledge and are available; so we have to accept them and their personal decisions and get to like them as people and appreciate their commitment to us which I do not doubt. . ." "is you grand-niece to work with them, Nestor?"

"yes, now she has work, and a reason, to stay with us, rather than return to what is, after all, her home. . ." the Elder mused:

"she just rang and asked that we send Señor Alcide over to the clinic. . ."

"where that teenager who belongs to my accountant is being treated?"

"the one; Aline told me that she suffers from a toxin that she picked up through a transplant. . ."

"another aspect of what you will have to come to terms with, Nestor," his friend sympathized.

"yes, but not immediately so, except that parents are involved, the girl friend's 'mum', I suppose, and your accountant, a genuine mum, so to say. . ."

"will you send Señor Alcide, Nestor?" Merv asked; "if so, would you like me to ring Señor Gordon? Meanwhile, Señor Alcide can stay with us, or at the clinic. . . my wife is a distant relative, a cousin to a niece of his. . ."

"yes, ring Gordon; weather permitting, the boat should get to Saipan tomorrow mid-morning. . ."

"high tide?" "more or less; would you also let the harbour master know as well, Merv?"

❧

Rosetta had gone to the airport to pick up Aline, only to find Glen there as well, waiting.

"Flight AX 295 from Guam delayed and expected to arrive in forty minutes," came the tinny announcement in English, Korean, Russian and Chamorro.

"can you wait that long, Glen?" the girl asked: "I need to pick up some supplies for the clinic and will be back, hopefully in time for when she gets here. . ."

"yes, but, please, ring Ramon and Hec., to remind them that he is due at the clinic this evening. . . can you also let Eileen know that Ann will stay with her tonight and that I'll ring her later. . ."

"certainly," said the hospital administrator and drove off.

The plane arrived somewhat earlier than announced; Aline strode straight into Glen's arms and had her buttocks cupped by his hands. "alone, lover?" she smiled. "Rosetta from the clinic will be back soon; you can then choose who is to drop you and where?"

"are you here to claim me?" the girl wondered. "I am."

"am I here to be claimed?" Aline enquired. "Yes, you are. . ." "then, so be it," the girl accepted her fate: "I can see some practical, mainly physical, problems to being your concubine; you have a partner who has given up 'his' manhood, a lady who, I understand, who is about to shed her husband, and this girl-me-who has already 'fired' a boyfriend, all for the privilege of living and working with you; my clan's home island is a bonus. . ." the girl drew closer: "hold me tight, Glen, leave your hands where they are; I want your baby. . ."

"just like that, love?" "yes, but also for another reason. . ." "cultural, Aline?"

"yes, how did you know?" she asked, dropping her arms in submission:

"my clan would normally expect me to marry a local or at least a Micronesian boy. . ."

"are you not a bit too old to marry by Micronesian standards. . ."

"I am twenty-four, half your age," the girl reminded him:

"traditionally speaking, you are right, girls would marry as teenagers and boys wouldn't be much older; nowadays, mine is the upper allowable age to get married. . ."

"and you tell me that your clan would allow you to live and work with them, through us. . ."

"which they are quite delighted about, in fact," explained the girl, nestling against Glen's shoulders.

"without you having to marry an islander, provided you. . ." "impregnate me in time.

I have certain fantasies about the actual procedure, "she added," but it becomes feasible if you are prepared to be the father, as well as one of my bosses. . ."

"did you come to Micronesia to be 'claimed', if I may ask?"

"yes," the girl assured him, "by either Hector or yourself, or both. . ." "Hec is now about to be. . ."

"your main heterosexual partner, lover, so it is you alone who may claim me. . ."

"consider it already done, if you don't mind being in good company,"

"no, but I can see Rosetta coming through the door," the girl observed, with the benefit of being able to view across his shoulder. "It may pay to release me, strictly for the time being."

"Boobs are on your menu tonight, Hec," explained Gloria: "at least, I can start you on the process. . ." "how long does it take to 'boobify' me; do you like the expression?"

"unlike a booby trap. . ." the young woman mused.

"o sorry, you used to be a frontline doctor, I shouldn't have. . ."

"never mind," explained the girl; "I have to be in Guam in a few days but meanwhile tissue from your buttocks will settle and be ready when I am back. . ."

"when, doctor Gloria?" "a week, maybe."

"you've done a good job on my vulva, doctor Gloria," admitted Ann's newly-minted mum:

"how did you manage the mucous lining, complete with nerve ends?"

"easy," the young doctor told Hec, "I turned your testicular sac inside out and then merged it with part of your penis that I had inverted, so as also to keep your urethra intact. . ."

"the inverse to what you did to Jules?"

"in a sense, yes," she conceded. "Tonight I shall start with some bedding tissues which I cultured over the last few days", she continued: "Then I'll use slices off your buttocks. . ."

"a bit like calamari or onion rings?" Gloria laughed.

Hec had had a good day at work; the young people had taken 'her' altered nature- and voice-in their stride, gently joking at times but mainly content to work with, and learn from, her, realizing how much they benefited. She spent as much time at work as possible, not least to meet tender conditions and to live up to 'her 'obligations to Ramon's organization.

Gloria would see her before her departure, or Brendan did, in order to modify or monitor progress.

The lower bits more or less had begun to conform to some sort of female functionality so that Hec could, for instance, only pee standing up by spreading her legs and using her knees by way of suspension; it tended to be easier to sit or squat when emptying 'herself '.

"so boobs are next, both at once?"

"yes, Hec; you must have noticed that I have already made inroads into your buttocks over the last few days. . ."

"it made sitting down awkward, I admit. . ." a wry smile at Gloria.

"can I get back to work tomorrow?"

"if you don't mind being dropped by our school bus. . . only teasing, Hec. . ."

"not at all, if that's the bus that will take Ann to school. . ."

"I can ask Rosetta to arrange that; the driver can pick up Ann and you; I understand that they do that with staff whose children live in or around Saipan City itself. . ."

"thanks; now, I am ready for you, doctor Gloria"

Trevor had felt like a fifth or even sixth wheel ever since his arrival in Micronesia if not before.

Eileen was not only at work but also getting increasingly involved with her new colleagues, Glen, in particular. She had made love to her legally-betrothed husband but once, an almost loveless if physically challenging affair, with Trevor being mounted and rendered helpless for much of the night.

"Make the most of this night, Trev," his wife admonished him.

"you were thinking. . ."

". . .of someone else. . ." Eileen confirmed: "throughout; this happens." she lay down across him, grabbing his tool:

"if Jules weren't fighting toxaemia, I'd ask you to go back to your business; as it is, 'he' needs a parent's presence. . ."

"and you are too busy these days, Eileen?"

"yes, and I am not proud of it but neither am I willing to apologize," she stated:

"I admit I ought to have spent more time, 'he' and that's still difficult to express, has had more quality time spent by doctors, nurses, Ann, even classmates, than by 'his' parents; so, please, Trevor. . ." massaging his tool, she managed to get some more action, readying Trevor to be mounted one last time, her knees pinning down his hands, her hands gripping his buttocks and herself riding him fiercely.

Whenever Jules was not at work in the computer room, being unable to go to school while battling toxemia, 'his' dad would spend time with him, going for drives or walks as much as Jules could cope with, a drip stuck constantly in his vein.

Jules liked to spend much of his time along the reef, using a pair of Merv's Beach Boots, courtesy of his mum, to avoid further injuries; he and his dad would take test tubes, thermometers and acidity reagents along and record data, "as part of a project I am doing for online schooling, Dad" he explained in his, by now, sonorous voice, "but mainly because it's fun. . ."

"that's how I felt when I set up my business, Jules, knowing that it would take a long time before it really took off. . ."

"a bit like data; it takes ages to reach a conclusion, however exciting," the budding scientist confirmed.

"how is Ann taking it?" asked his dad. "the toxin, you mean?" "that and your future, Jules."

"she is hurting almost as much from the toxin as I am; but love-wise, there is this girl, Angh, the daughter of our science teacher here, she is keen on Ann and Ann likes her very much."

"would Ann be prepared to share you with her?" "in a physical sense, Dad?"

Jules, in his surprise, nearly dropped a test tube, neatly catching it in midair.

"Dad?" then he frowned, working his keen mind through the possibilities:

"two girls for the price of one. . ." shaking his head in wonder.

"her mum might have to say something about it," his father suggested.

"they are very close," admitted his 'son' "and I need to get better, quite possibly thanks to Angh's mother. . ." "why that, son?"

"it was she who suggested that naturopath from Ariman Island where Mum is to help set up that energy enterprise. . ." "any news on that one?"

"why don't you ask Señor Gordon; you are getting friendly with him, aren't you, Dad?"

It was true that Gordon, the clinic's proprietor, had sought out Trevor several times for business advice, over some powerful home-brewn liquids.

"we admire your wife's acumen as an accountant and business manager, Trevor," he had explained over an afternoon snack in the clinic's canteen:

"it'd be ideal if the two of you could stay on as a working couple"

Trevor sighed: "She won't let me, but nor will my own business in Adelaide. . ."

"I can see that," admitted the proprietor, "and I am sorry in a number of ways, not least as a friend; who runs the place in your absence?"

"two women managers, for the time being. . ."

"could they, or someone else, do it for a similar limited period of time, Trevor?"

"yes, I suppose so, Gordon. . ."

"do you want some more passion wine with some omelette, Trevor?"

"yes, certainly; where is this leading to, Gordon?"

The proprietor sat up:

"I would like you to return to Saipan, as my guest, from time to time; I want you, too, to consider us a home away from home, for me and others to pick your very considerable business brain. . ."

"don't you have US expertise to pick on?"

"or Korean, even Filipino, admittedly; but your perception is challengingly different." Gordon waited for Trevor to finish, then asked him to take his drink along while getting one of the girls to carry his homebrew to his office where they sat down in a corner:

"for starters," he began, "and that has nothing to do with the clinic but a lot with a telephone call I just had from Señor Nestor. . ."

"the clan leader from Ariman who Eileen, Ann's 'mum', that young girl from Mildura and Hec's partner Glen are to work with and for?" "and some good news, I hope. for Jules. . ."

"the naturopath, Gordon?" "how did you know?"

"Jules told me; it was his science teacher's suggestion. . ." a marvellous lady, brought up her daughter single-handedly; her husband is still inside a Vietnamese jail. . ."

"oh, I didn't know that. . ."

"yes; anyway, Señor Alcides will be on the next boat which is bringing in chilled fish, prawn and bamboo splits for some restaurants. . ." "places that Eileen did the books for. . ."

"two of them, yes, as far as I know", the proprietor concurred.

"In return for a load of school furniture and beach boots; day after tomorrow, depending on the tide. . ." "can't be too soon for Jules. . ." "undoubtedly"

"what else did Señor Nestor tell you or ask you about. . ."

"possibilities for additional industries, now that he has found a way to get primal energy generated in sufficient amounts to run them on. . ." "garments?"

"as a last resort, we have too many on some of the smaller islands already. . ."

Trevor sat down, nipped his drink and started thinking: "coral ornaments, printing, spare parts. . ."

"spare parts?" interrupted Gordon. "Let me make a phone call to someone at the Chamber of Commerce. . ." "would they still be at work?"

"oh yes, they are preparing a meeting for the Northern Marianas Business Association. . ."

"are you involved, Gordon?" "yes, and I am happy to invite you along. . . let me ring Agosto. . ."

In the next few days, Gordon, his friend Señor Agosto and Trevor would spend hours working out precursor materials, supply lines and cost factors on small-aircraft spare parts, usually whenever Jules was 'at work' or being treated;

("I can get the chelates to gather up the toxins but I can't get his organs to get rid of them so they accumulate," Brendan had admitted to Professor Fernando.

"They gather mainly in the spleen, very hurtful, but I can see it affecting Jules liver and kidneys," the scholar admitted: "at least, his bloodstream is largely free; I'll try different kind of chelates next, to mop up residues if nothing else. . .").

"Ever since that Chinese bloke started Sun City in this remote corner of Southwest China. . ."

began Agosto on the evening before the meet at the Saipan Chamber of Commerce and Industry;

". . .something which he first offered to Australia, to be set up in Central Australia. . ." "true?" queried Gordon: "what a wasted opportunity!"

"now we know how to industrialise small islands such as ours or remote communities such as yours, or theirs, in China," continued Agosto, the chamber's investment specialist:

"too expensive to cart raw materials and fuel in bulk, too remote to communicate to and from and too small to warrant a grid other than locally itself which, in the absence of energy. . ."

"other than any available renewable one," added Gordon, "would be futile to attempt without creating both materials and energy on site. . ." "the material being?" asked Trevor.

"China-clay, excellent for ceramics, paper and templates, to be converted to spare parts for light aircraft, boats and certain sports equipment," explained Agosto.

"the product is a bit like fiberglass, in different thicknesses, densities and strengths, incredibly formable yet very stable once finished, corrosion-proof, heatproof, good insulator. . ." added Gordon;

"except that it needs lots of energy to mine, purify and form it," concluded Trevor.

"I know the stuff, it's all over Northern Australia and much of Indonesia as well; a mate of mine in Adelaide uses it for sanitary gear."

"would you do us some sums before you leave, Trevor?" Agosto asked him.

"give us a bit of an outline at our meet tomorrow, please. . ."

"but still, spend as much time as you can with Jules," Gordon reminded him:

"that is more important than anything."

The three men finished their respective Gordon's elixirs and left the Chamber of Commerce.

Ann sat with Jules, having spent time with her 'mum 'before Hec was wheeled into the operating room.

"You have changed," she had told her parent, "but even though I was expecting the same of Jules. . ." "the other way around, though. . ."

"yes," her daughter admitted: "yet I struggle to cope with your new gender; do you?"

"no, daughter mine; I am content with myself, my work, my prospects and with life in general. . ."

"even though you are expected to compete with two actual women, one your age; Jules' mum, no less, and a very young one who could have been my older sister. . ."

"yes, consider us Micronesia's most unique harem," her parent smiled.

"I may yet make a good Matriarch in this society which is quite rich of them. . ."

"born to the role which you were not," her daughter reminded her.

"what are you trying to ask me, Ann?"

"You remember Jules' science teacher, don't you?"

"the one who thought of the naturopath on Ariman; let's hope that he'll make it soon and that he knows the remedy," her parent said: "what about her?"

"her daughter, rather, Angh. . ."

"oh that exceptional girl; if I were thirty years younger and still a boy. . ."

"that's exactly, except that she wants me rather than any of the boys we are with. . ."

"they may not amount to much to a very smart girl," Hec commented:

"do you want her in your life rather than Jules?" "no, but perhaps in addition to him. . ."

"why then don't you work out how you can share Jules with that girl and make her realize that that's the only way she can have you. . .?" unwittingly echoing the suggestion which Jules' dad had implanted into his son 's mind.

❧

Oratio, the furniture dealer, had a surprise caller whom he nonetheless recognized, in the middle of the actual audit which Eileen and Hec's trainees had worked so hard to prepare: "I haven't seen you for years, Miranda," he embraced Señor Alcide's grand-niece warmly, introducing her to Eileen whose services he had, once more, borrowed from Merv.

Several trainees also recognized and smiled at her. They stopped work and gathered around their workbench, wondering why the girl had come to call. Oratio's office girls were already busily preparing coffee and happy to see the girl as well.

She greeted a few of the young people whom she knew before Oratio explained her background

and asked: "a cup of coffee or juice, Miranda?"

She nodded in the direction of the pantry with its unmistakable whiff of strong coffee, then smiled:

"Señor Alcides, my grand-uncle, is not very comfortable with phones, especially mobile ones; he rang me from a public phone on our landline at the toyshop; I recognized Aunty Eileen from her book-keeping for us last week, then rang Uncle Merv who told me you might be here. . ."

turning to Jules' mum: "organizing the audit."

"I did see you at the toy shop, Miranda" the older woman acknowledged.

"did Señor Alcides want you to talk to me?"

"yes; my grand-uncle understands that your 'son 'suffers a kind of metallic poisoning due to an operation performed on him which the doctors cannot get rid of; true, Mrs Childers?"

Eileen, still reeling from having Jules described as her 'son', answered nonetheless: "yes, that is correct as far as it goes; Jules would be able to explain it better, as would his science teacher, Angh's mother. . ."

"as would the doctors," added Oratio reasonably. "what do you suggest, then?"

"when is Señor Alcides due?" asked Eileen.

"He is getting ready to sail on the boat that Señor Nestor is loading with prawns and limestone. . ."

"for me to return with school furniture and Señor Merv with Beach Boots. . ."

"for the coral cutters," agreed the girl, by now nursing a steaming cup of home- grown strong Robusta coffee sweetened with vanilla sugar.

"Does your grand-uncle want to talk to someone to enlighten him before he leaves, seeing that he does not trust a mobile. . ." Eileen wondered.

"not that he would get a signal on the way, anyway," stated the furniture dealer.

"because the clinic has several landlines," explained Eileen,

"and I could ask Rosetta to explain in Chamorro; doctor Gloria who can speak it is back in Hawaii and not expected for another two or three days. . ." she then proceeded to explain that young cosmetic surgeon's and her mentor's role in the scheme of things.

"Professor Fernando might, if he is in; he, too, was due to leave for a few days, to give forensic evidence in Guam," she added:

"Miranda, is there a landline on Ariman other than a public phone?"

"yes, at Señor Nestor's office, for he is the alcalde. . ."

"and he has already rung the clinic a few times, I know."

"look, use our phone," offered Oratio:

"the Mother of Jules will give you Rosetta's number; get her to ring Señor Nestor's office whose number she probably knows and arrange a conference call on my phone as well so you can talk as well; Rosetta will know how to do that. . ."

As did the girl, it turned out; she finished her coffee. got one of the girls to pour her another one, started nibbling a biscuit and got busy. Rosetta answered on the third ring and Miranda introduced herself to the girl:

"I am Señor Alcides' grand-niece, I am ringing from Señor Oratio's workshop, with Mrs Childers here as wellt. . ." she then explained what her kinsman wanted to know before he ventured on his voyage to Saipan.

Rosetta understood at once:" he may want to know which ingredient to choose, in case he may not find it here," she ventured.

Have you set up the conference call already, Miranda? "the clinic administrator asked the girl:" yes? will you ring Señor Nestor's office and give us a ringtone when Señor Alcides is on the line?"

Rosetta got hold of Brendan, explaining what was about to happen.

The doctor was between two patients but promised to go to Jules' computer room and get a connection, for the boy and himself to listen in. "how do I explain a chelate?"

Rosetta asked, to begin with, once connection had been established. Jules answered, instead:

"Chele is a word meaning a lobster's claw, a kind of scissors or pliers, to hold nutrients in the soil, keep them close to a tree's root, then open to release the mineral in one direction and have another ready when needed. . ." "nutrient meaning something that plants need for food?"

Rosetta, while querying, was already busily translating as well, in Chamorro, so that the ancient naturopath would understand.

"Yes, Rosetta," answered Jules: "The doctors injected some chelates to isolate the toxin which got into my bloodstream. . ." "coming from where?" asked the naturopath, via Miranda.

"an organ transplant," explained Jules, unsure whether he would offend the old gentleman by being more specific. Rosetta took over and described what had happened in more detail; Jules needed not have worried; for Alcides burst out laughing loudly enough for all to hear.

"The chelates have cleansed my blood, doctor Brendan will correct me if I am wrong, but my body seems to be unable to get rid of them and they collect in various organs of mine. . ."

"not a good idea," agreed the healer. "What is the nature of the poison?" he asked, using a Chamorran term.

Rosetta asked Brendan to describe it so as for her to translate:

"a bit of bitumen and dirt from roadworks – we have samples of each-primer paint from the fence post, minute buts of steel, urine, bits of muscle and serum; we found a minute tear in Andy's bladder, eventually, every other internal organ was pulped, as you know. . ."

"is doctor Brendan the doctor who performed the operation?" the healer asked.

Rosetta answered by outlining the various roles that each of the surgeons had played. "when is the young lady doctor from Guam expected back?"

"day after tomorrow, Señor Alcides," replied the girl, courteously:

"If you, Señor Alcides, were to get here tomorrow morning; she'd be here twenty- four hours later, in person; meanwhile, I would connect her to you on our telephone lines. Do you have any difficulty understanding or talking to us, Señor?" she wondered.

"no, other than that my hearing is on its way out."

"we can adjust our phone to suit you, so you will be able to talk to her and to Professor Fernando, her mentor, if you like, in Chamorro."

There was silence.

"Señor Alcides?" asked Rosetta anxiously; she then heard Miranda talk to her kinsman who seemed to relent:

"I may not have time to collect the ingredient I really need. . ." he stated.

"if you cannot, can someone else get it for you, on Ariman or from somewhere else?"

"here, no, there won't be time," the old gentleman replied.

"Is it available in Saipan, Uncle?" asked his niece, worried.

"no, but doctor Gloria may have to ring an old friend of mine on Guam. . ."

"if you cannot get hold of it before you leave, Uncle, could you get the skipper to radio Uncle Nestor's office and they will fax the name or a description of what you need to Rosetta or myself, at the shop; we girls will then get hold of doctor Gloria to see your friend in Guam so she can collect it from him and bring it; meanwhile, we'll make an effort to find it on Saipan. . ." "that sounds good, girl, is there anyone you can ask. . ."

"yes, my ex-boyfriend works for the Institute for Marine Science. . ."

"if you don't mind asking him; is Señor Oratio around, Miranda?"

"would you like to speak to him?" the girl was surprised, knowing her grand-uncle's habitual reluctance to talk on the phone.

"he is normally loud enough to be heard even without the phone," cackled the old gentleman.

Hec's boob base showed signs of settling down nicely, Glen thought when shown. "You look a sight, Hec." he said; "when are you getting the full complement?"

Glen had encountered Hec who had mistakenly entered the men's toilet at work, following a yet-to –be discarded habit; Glen had tactfully locked the door while Hec was showing off. "work of art, mate. . ." he commented, trying not to laugh.

"when is Gloria to finish sculpturing your torso? 'he asked, trying not to sound sarcastic.

"I am doing it for your immense physical needs," Hec commented, surprisingly placidly:

"soon to be met by Micronesia's first expatriate harem. . ."

"who knows?" agreed Glen. "Back to work; all eyes will be on you, not necessarily boob-wise but on your presentation of Mariana's first Jobsearch template, crafted by you. . ."

"with help from many, not least you, Glen," Hec stated graciously;

"now we have to start working on one for the Ariman primary power plant," she added as the partners went back to Ramon's boardroom.

They had already chosen the trainee who was to start the display of the Chamorro version, with a girl to activate the simultaneously-translated matching feature in Filipino-accented English.

The templates dealt with jobseekers matching their skills and preferences with the demands made by potential employers, taking care to emphasise traditional Chamorro kinship values; for everyone realized that enterprises tended to hire among their own families and those of friends which, however, involved most people in Saipan, at least.

Glen and Hec looked at each other with a great deal of satisfaction

("the lessons of Barrow Creek with those young Tongans have been well learnt") and Ramon's team appeared pleased, laughing at the right times; for the visuals provided for many light moments, some a bit unintentional. Glen and Hec had tried to overcome the imbalance that favoured girls for many jobs:

"we need to road-test these now," Ramon stated during a break.

"some we'll do by showing these to employers, others by sending our young people to sell the message," he said, over coffee: "we have an invite to present these at the Chamber of Commerce tonight, hence the hurry, you could say," he informed the team:

"guess who is also giving a presentation there later today?" Glen and Hec shook their heads.

"your friend Eileen's husband was asked by the clinic proprietor to develop an industrial scheme to make use of your primal energy plant on Ariman. . ." "for what?"

"aircraft spare parts, no less!"

Having settled on how many young people they would take along to the Chamber of Commerce and who to choose, they finished work for the day, celebrated the completion of the tendered-for templates with a drink each. Ramon Glen and Hec dropped off the remaining young team members and headed their minibus to Merv the Cobbler's premises, there to pick up Eileen on their way to the Chamber of Commerce. Glen helped her climb into the vehicle, holding her hand for a while. She kissed him, then noticed something: "anything I need to know?"

"yes, Mrs Childers; we are going to present the working version of Hec and Glen's work-search templates to potential employers. . ." "that I know, Señor Ramon," the bookkeeper acknowledged, "are we talking about our primal energy project om Ariman tonight as well?"

"the follow-up, o Mother of Jules, rather," explained Ramon courteously. "Er?"

"your husband appears to have teamed up with Señores Gordon. . ."

"the hospital proprietor and brewer of some powerful exlixirs. . ." "yes, him and Señor Agosto. . ."

"isn't he the current Secretary of your Chamber of Commerce? I think I met him."

"so he is," agreed Hec: "they picked your husband's brain on the next stage. . ."

"following our energy project, you mean?" "yes, love," stated Glen:

"they seem to want to propose a business plan for spare part templates, especially for light aircraft. . ."

"Trevor's job is a resource broker for, among others, armament people using extraordinary amounts of special clays, much of it confidential," she wondered.

"Señor Ramon, does Ariman have such a resource?"

"yes, very pure kaolin, to prepare which you need lots of energy and water. . ."

"that'd be distilled water, wouldn't it?"

"yes, in such large amounts, certainly; they used to do form-work during World War Two; the Japanese used an existing lens of fresh water," Ramon elaborated,

"which then took years to recharge and whose use has been restricted ever since. . ."

"one reason why resettlement has been that slow?"

"yes, Ariman relies mainly on rainwater, not scarce at all for domestic and farm use, even ice-making, but not any serious industrial uses. . ."

"Thanks for telling me to expect Trevor tonight," murmured Eileen:

"I am pleased that someone is using his expertise and his is as logical a follow-up as any; I hope they realize that he has his own business in Adelaide to go back to at some stage. . ."

"I am sure that Señores Gordon and Agosto understand that," corrected Ramon:

"they may have offered to host him from time to time whenever he can take time off; it'll allow him to remain in touch with Jules as well. . ." "very important," agreed Eileen.

Jules was in considerable pain that night, but rather than put him on painkillers, Brendan scheduled another round of dialysis which did help, while injecting more chelates, instead of antibiotics.

Eventually, Jules fell into an uneasy sleep during which his breathing and pulse calmed somewhat.

Brendan and a nurse dozed on and off, sitting on either side of him; as soon as dialysis was finished for the moment, Brendan injected Jules with a very mild barbiturate and sent the nurse to bed:

"be ready at five o'clock, for a very long day," he told the girl:

"once Señor Alcides arrives, we'll be very busy. . ."

"will you get some sleep, doctor Brendan?"

"yes, once a few more girls get on shift, I'll kip for a few hours by which time. . ."

"the resident doctor should have arrived," the girl agreed.

"who is that tomorrow?" "Doctor Ernesto, GP, seven o'clock rounds, doctor Brendan. . ."

"so, barring the unforeseen, five to eight, maybe half-eight. . . you go to bed; but would you ask the girls to get me another pot of green tea, please?" The nurse smiled and nodded.

⁂

Jules woke up not feeling particular well, uncharacteristically unwilling to go online, do homework or make love to Ann, had he been given that choice. She dropped in early that morning, having persuaded Eileen to drop her half an hour earlier, relying on the clinic's school bus to pick her up in time, held Jules hand, kissed him and fed him some green tea.

"Hungry, lover?" she worried. "not particularly; I might manage a weak nutri-milk shake later" (a mixture of soymilk, papaya and banana extract). "did I tell you what Dad suggested?"

"about Angh?" asked his lover; "if it is the same that 'Mum'also advised. . ."

"independently of each other, do you think, bitch?" "I think so;"

"Mum said to tell Angh to share you with me, not me with you. . ."

"Dad also, but not in as many words; am I to decide?" "of course, lover; always. . ."

"if her mum gets here. . ." "which she might, seeing that they expect the naturopath today. . ."

"that'd be good but how do you know?"

"I overheard Rosetta on the phone as I came in," remembered Ann:

"I'll certainly ring Angh's mum and ask her if she could get me permission to get back later during the day and herself to attend to you. . ." "and bring Angh as well if she can; good idea; good girl. . ."

"I love you very much," Ann replied, kissing Jules' hands: "I assume you know. . ."

"yes, and thank you; I do feel a bit better. . ."

Ann went to ask the nurse to prepare a nutri-drink for Jules, then went to wait for the school bus, meanwhile ringing Angh's number: "are you and your mum on your way to school already. . ."

"not yet, Ann; good to hear your voice" the beautiful girl answered.

"they are expecting the naturopath mid-morning. . ."

"Señor Alcides from Ariman as Mum suggested. . ."

"yes, Angh, but it seems that he may be short of a vital ingredient which Rosetta and someone else are supposed to find; they also asked doctor Gloria to organize a supply in Guam," the girl elaborated:

"we'll need your mum, both for the translation and for the science involved; it may be beyond not only Jules but even the doctors. . ." Ann paused: "is your mum nearby, Angh?" the girl, noticing Ann's inflection, smiled hopefully:

"no, darling; she is getting some papers and I am ready for school; why?"

"Jules and I agreed to let you share him with me, for the time being; we'll have to work out how. . ."

"and where, but thanks; I wonder what Mum will make of it. . ."

"how about a trial period; when is your birthday, Angh?"

"in ten days, love; Mum is getting ready; I'll ask her to come and bring me along as well; what time would you say?" "a bit before noon, Angh, but get her to ring Rosetta first. . ."

"good thinking, Ann." Angh approved.

⁂

Gloria rang Brendan from Guam:

"I managed to trace Señor Alcides' colleague here but he has yet to get the mixture, or rather, one of the ingredients that Señor Alcides was unable to organise at short notice."

"thanks for ringing, Gloria," Brendan acknowledged. "Can you help him find it, Gloria?"

"no, I am stuck with patients and some time-dependent research if I am to be on the flight tomorrow. . ." how about your Professor?"

"he had to travel to Hawaii to conduct some exams; the earliest will be three days."

"did you ask him for an alternative to the missing ingredient, Gloria?"

"yes, I did; Professor Gutierrez mentioned a different group of chelates he sometimes uses on external industrial injuries, and Señor Alcides' colleague mentioned an alkaloid which he feels that Señor Alcide already has; he'll pass on some but. . ."

"there usually is a 'but'", remarked Brendan: "what is it this time?"

"it is free-standing and does not fit into the compound that he feels his friend is trying to create."

"has it been used in this type of poisoning before, Gloria?"

"it is well-known against snakebite; people sometimes use it in food poisoning, especially if resulting from damaged cans. . ." "effects of corrosion, you mean, Gloria" "apparently, Brendan; look, I need to ring off; I'll have to drive across town to see a patient's family for some medical history."

"thanks for keeping me up to date, Gloria; say Hello to Professor Gutierrez when he rings again; we are waiting for him also. . ."

Ann's 'mum' was due in hospital later during the day, the need to be at work daily having receded now that the Work-search templates had been finished and were being tried; she had been pleased with their interaction at the Chamber of Commerce and did not mind Trevor's involvement in the least, more so since Jules' father had not sought it in the first place.S/he accompanied some of the youngsters on their visits to various small businesses, with Glen, Ramon and Agosto canvassing employers who had approached them the previous evenings.

Strange as it may have felt, they were all growing roots of a kind in this society. Elanca had promised to try and join them later during the day, in time for a pickup lunch.

First, she wanted to encourage Brendan and then document the naturopath's arrival and the beginning of his treatment of Jules' toxemia. She sat with her onetime lover over a pot of green tea as soon as Brendan had woken from a short sleep.

⁂

"Brendan, may I seduce you one last time," she wondered. "why last time, El?"

"Nina rang and also sent a message. . ." "by way of an ultimatum?"

"almost; I have most of my material and some totally different story has come up. . ."

"the HIV baby in the detention centre?" "yes; you must have heard about it also, anyway, I was given extra days, only because of the involvement of the naturopath from Ariman. . ." "which does make for readership," concurred Brendan" that's what Nina said but she also told me that there would be no extension, nor would she send anyone else. . ." "tough young woman!"

"she'll have to be, herding cats like she has to. Anyway, once Gloria and Fernando are back. . ."

"I shall find some time; I really want to, I assure you. . ."

She kissed him: "I know that you will not leave your wife or your job here." she led him to Jules bedroom where a nurse was conducting yet another blood test.

⁂

"I shan't do another liver puncture till after Señor Alcides' treatment," he promised Jules, "but I want to generate some serum to test his ingredients on. . ."

"did you keep samples of the actual toxin, doctor Brendan," asked the teenager.

"yes, to test the medium as well." "what in particular are we waiting for, doctor Brendan?"

"in a sense, I do not know. One thing that is almost bound to happen; did you have anything to eat or drink, Jules?"

"yes, Ann organized a kind of smoothy before she left for school, consisting of soy, papaya and banana extract. . ."

"perhaps not the best idea," argued Brendan, "even though you need to keep up your strength. You may have to vomit, Jules, before or after you get your first dose; there may also be a fever. . ."

"for my body to try and burn the toxin?"

"very possible; we'll have to dose the medicine very carefully, quite possibly over several days."

"when do I get back onto hormones," asked the boy.

"I shall take to ingest them for the rest of my life, not so, doctor Brendan?"

"I shall put you back on tomorrow unless they disagree with today's treatment," decided the doctor:

"you'll be on them as if you were on insulin, epilepsy repellent or an anti-retroviral. . ."

"or lithium," added Jules.

"exactly; do you want to work on the computer?"

"no but I'll try and edit some printouts to take my mind of things. . ."

"sorry Ann is not here; do you want your father?"

"did he not attend the event at the Chamber of Commerce?"

"yes, so I gather; I'll get Rosetta to ring him; someone from the investment bank wanted to see him, I was told last night. . ." "Investment on Ariman, you mean?"

"I'll go and get your dad for you, Jules," Elanca offered; they all looked up; for they had forgotten about her presence.

"can I get a vehicle of yours, Brendan?"

"yes, use my car," he threw the keys in her direction which a nurse caught, smiling, and passed on to the journalist. "do you have his number, Elanca?" "I'll get Rosetta to ring him."

Trevor had finished a very productive session at the Marianas Investment Bank:

"I can see the sequence," the banker, Orlando Ramirez, had concluded:

"your fellow Australians creating the basis for renewable industrial energy, base-load, indeed; and you being able to offer the basics on formworks, a welcome change to garment factories, let me assure you, Señor Trevor;"

"or ferro-cement boats, much as I like them. . ."

"sight unseen," agreed the banker: "yet, remember, these, too, are building blocks of our island economy; let me compliment you, actually all of you, on your ability to fit in so well; it is a pity that you alone won't stay. . ."

"I have a business to run, as well. . ." forgive me, Señor Orlando, my telephone." He listened, then turned it off and turned to the banker:

"Mrs Hartwig, the journalist from Adelaide, has come to pick me up for my parental duties. . ."

"Jules?"

"yes, we are expecting the naturopath from Ariman Island." "Señor Alcides. . ."

"she would like to take a photo of you, even ask you a few things. . ."

"I think I saw her yesterday at the presentation," the banker conceded.

"Yes, she too has learnt to blend in," commented Jules' father.

Elanca entered with a smile, took the coffee that was offered and asked Señor Orlando:

"you don't mind my easing Señor Trevor off you for a moment?"

"no, we Chamorro take family duties seriously. You want to ask me."

"yes, we were all surprised," the journalist began, "to see Mr Childers giving input on how to set up a formworks once the primal energy unit had been established on Ariman; can you, Señor Orlando, see it fit in with development needs?"

"oh yes, Ariman needs resettlement which its present economy does not guarantee. . ."

"the opposite," stated the journalist.

"sadly so," agreed the banker. "My friend Señor Gordon who I understand you also know quite well by now had the good sense to pick Señor Trevor's brain here. . ."

"how about firm business and production plans, Señor Orlando?"

"oh, we have enough talent, whether it be Señor Ramon's group, involving Señora Eileen and her future colleagues, her husband here, ourselves. . ."

"for a fee, no doubt,"

"yes, but also as our duty of care, as you will understand," he added courteously.

Elanca asked a few more questions of both him and Trevor, then eased him out of the office and into Brendan's car: "Excuse me if I rush you, Trevor; will you forgive me?"

"you'll need to explain, Elanca."

The reporter drove out of the parking lot, narrowly avoiding a delivery van failing to look while backing out." it would help if people looked. . ." Trevor commented;

"or better, still, if they backed in rather than out," Elanca agreed:

"Trevor, are you ready to leave with me in five days?" "why, the magazine budget?" "that, and Nina wants me on a different story and would have pulled me off had it not been for Señor Alcides and the chance to cover Micronesian natural treatment in action. . ."

He was used to making rapid decisions:

"It would give me great pleasure to travel back to Adelaide with you, Elanca," he told her:

"unless Jules' condition does not improve at all. . ."

"even then, Trevor, you would not be able to stay very much longer. . ."

"no, that's what my own team is telling me increasingly frequently," the businessman stated:

"Elanca, slow down and let that truck on the left change lanes," he warned her of a situation he had seen develop:

"Yes, I shall travel with you, if you need to get the tickets and hotels ready. . ." he concluded as soon as Elanca had let the speeding truck rush ahead.

"If Jules' condition worsens between now and when we are due to leave, I'll stay put as well." promised Elanca, surprising herself with that commitment and briefly reaching out for Trevor's hand, then continuing to drive.

❧

Oratio and Merv had barely arrived at the harbour, along with Eileen, when the boat from Ariman showed up on the horizon. Oratio brought out a thermos filled with coffee and offered his friend and his favourite bookkeeper a cup each as well.

"Let's hope it will work out. . ." "and the people say Amen," murmured Jules'

mother; the men, having heard her nonetheless, made the sign of the cross. Some of Ramon's team, boys as well as girls, were driven up in a minibus, to help unload the boat's cargo and load both furniture and beach boots destined for the island, thus putting some of their newly-learnt planning and organizing skills to the test and earning them much-needed money.

Soon as the frail but sprightly naturopath had stepped off the boat, years of practice belying his age, Merv arranged with the bus driver to take Eileen and Señor Alcides to the clinic:

"would you bring the minibus back as soon as you have dropped Señor Alcides and Señora Eileen, my son?" he asked courteously: "would you like a coffee first?" he offered. The driver nodded, at the same time making his obeisance to the elderly islander and the accountant, in that order. He then drove off with them, having helped to stow the naturopath's various parcels, bottles and bags.

Señor Alcides apologized for his limited English:

"Señora, I shall try to help your child, once your daughter now your son, not that I understand but I shall do what I can and know. . ."

"were you able to get everything that you need, Señor Alcides?" she asked; the driver explained and the healer replied:

"not the one bit that I really need but I can start with what I have;" he asked the driver to explain:

"that is with honey from a. . ." he showed them a cascading stand of coral flowers covering a rumbling wall, "that flower, one of the few on the island; then use powdered coral and bark extract; yet I need a root bark which has become rare and which I did not have the time to gather. . ."
"we know that my son is in the best hands," his mother assured the healer.

Elanca and Trevor had arrived at the clinic at the same time that the minibus did; Eileen could not help smiling to herself while waving to them as they pulled up: "Señor Alcides, Elanca es una jornalista del ciudad Adelaide en Australia junto con me casado, consultante de ciencia material australiano intendiente aplicarse per favor del isla Ariman," she tried in Spanish which, to her surprise, the elderly healer understood and appreciated.

Elanca showed the healer her camera and asked if she could take his picture among the team, including the reluctant driver, which Señor Alcides permitted.

Rosetta came, took the healer's hand and led him inside, with Eileen and Trevor following directly and Elanca a few steps behind. The nurses bade him enter the canteen and offered him green tea:

"do you want a pot with you when you start on the boy, Señor Alcides?" asked the girls.

"smart girls," commented the healer; "good idea. . ." he finished his tea and went to greet Gordon, his long-time friend, who then guided him and his entourage to Jules' room where Brendan and the nurse rose and greeted him with great courtesy.

Alcides lifted Jules eyelids, then made him stretch out his tongue, tested the elasticity of his skin and asked him to lie down, then massaged his pelvis gently. He brought out a jar of honey, emptied some into a teacup which he gave Jules to drink. It nearly caused him visibly to vomit; the healer shook his head:

"I would have preferred him to empty himself," the healer explained via Rosetta:"

I'll wait an hour then give the boy some more honey before I administer my medication. . . this afternoon, I want him to break out in a kind of fever which I shall also control. . ." Brendan nodded, understanding the rationale:

"doctor Gloria is expected any moment now, hopefully with the ingredient that you were asking for," he asked Rosetta to explain.

The healer drank some more tea and made Trevor and Eileen to sit by their 'son', gently singing a traditional song which Rosetta and the nurses hummed with him. Jules fell asleep, as-very nearly-did Brendan, not having had much sleep; he took the opportunity to look after other patients and monitor some trainee nurses.

"I am glad your friend made it," he admitted to his proprietor who was also making his rounds.

"Brendan, you are a very conscientious doctor," his boos took Brendan's arm and sat him down.

"here, have a minimal drop, a nano drop, if you like, for strictly medicinal purposes. . ."

"would you offer some to Señor Alcides, Gordon," his medical director offered while accepting a small glass filled with a treacle-like substance.

"I'll ask him whether it is safe to offer a special palm wine of mine to Jules. . ."

"to stimulate circulation," "or as a solvent; we never thought of that earlier. . ."

"well, ask your friend, Gordon, by all means; do excuse me, I'll be back in Jules room in another half-hour." "as shall I. . ."

Elanca had taken several frames of Alcides examining Jules and administering coral flower honey, then sat down close to Trevor and Eileen.

"Elanca has to leave Saipan and the project in five days and has asked me to leave with her," Trevor admitted to his, supposedly estranged, wife.

"what will you do, Trev, if Jules worsens by then. . ."

"I shall stay in that case, but not indefinitely," he assured her.

"Elanca, has the magazine run out of budget, "the book-keeper wondered.

"close, but Nina wants me to cover the story of an HIV baby born in a detention centre, quite possibly because of a sexual assault by a guard who turned out to be positive," the reporter explained. "had it not been for Señor Alcides here and the chance to see and record his approach, I would have had to leave." She paused and looked at the sleeping teenager.

"I was getting involved with Brendan when I arrived," she admitted, making sure that the nurses were out of earshot. "I did ask Trevor to accompany me to Adelaide, not only so that his travel is covered by our budget, as is mine, but also. . .”

"you are right; our days as a couple are numbered," stated Eileen, "through no fault of his, or yours, Elanca, or anyone's."

"then spend as much time together and with Jules, may I suggest. . ." began the reporter, "even though all of us are both caught up with our own very different involvement here. . ."

"true," Eileen concurred, taking Trevor's hand.

The healer had been persuaded to accept a mead-based elixir of Gordon's and asked if any of them were of any use in treating Jules.

"Yes, Gordon," the old man's eyes lit up: "I have some powdered bark here which is difficult to present; have you got an arrack based on swamp rice.?"

The proprietor nodded: "I shall send someone home because I do not keep it in the office," he offered: "I have some very little left, from Andy's funeral. . ."

Jules woke in time for another drop of coral flower honey, this time causing less of a violent reaction; instead, Jules declared that he was hungry, for the first time in days: "chew on this, then," offered the healer, giving him a bit of sugar cane, "just for a few minutes; concentrate on the fibre. . ." with Rosetta translating.

"now walk around the block with your parents several times, talk to them as if you were all going for a walk," which Jules did, taking his drip with him, as at previous times, his mum or dad taking turns holding it up.

"Mum and I are separating, as you probably know by now," began Trevor.

"you don't need to explain; are you travelling home with the reporter, Dad?" he asked:

"I saw you on the parking lot, out of the window. . ."

"did you overhear us as well?" asked his mother.

"I may have, I was dozing most of the time, other than being sick. . ."

"and you, Mum, will form part of Mr Hidding's entourage. . ."

"both personally and professionally; you are right, Jules. . ."

"how about us young ones; where are we to live?"

"choice is yours. . ."

"here, then, Mum and Dad, the three of us. . ."

"three?" his parents queried in rare unison:

"us and Angh, the science teacher's daughter, Ann's friend."

"Does her mum know?"

"she will," answered Jules confidently.

The healer looked under Jules eyelids again and mixed some pollen in with the tea, giving it to Jules to drink which made him break out in sweat; he had to sit down and started shaking; the healer nodded, as if anticipating that reaction. Gloria chose the moment to arrive:

"Señor Alcides, are you trying to shake the poison loose?" The healer nodded.

"I brought a very small amount of that root bark from Guam," she pointed at a minute amount wrapped in clear plastic foil:

"Señor Ilario told me that it was years old; he was not sure he'd get any more in Guam. . ." the healer understood:

"I'll send him some next time I go and collect a bit back on the island; I won't be able to do this climbing much longer. . ." he then directed the nurses to wrap Jules quite firmly.

After the shaking subsided;

"are you still hungry," he had Gloria ask the boy, half an hour later, who nodded and was given another very small piece of cane to chew. Gloria came closer and kissed the healer' hands.

"you are a good girl," the naturopath agreed, "and you will help cure this boy."

He looked outside at the level of the sun, as if for timekeeping, readied another powder, then asked one of the nurses if the proprietor's arrack had meanwhile arrived.

"I need to give this in very small amounts several times between now and sunset," he explained in English, for Brendan, Elanca and Jules' parents to understand as well, while carefully stirring his special bark powder into the liquid:

"drink and swallow it very slowly, a few sips at a time," he commanded Jules, also in English.

Gloria excused herself, having to prepare for her work on Hec's buttocks later that day, to further fashion his extended breasts, having given the healer his missing ingredient. Elanca filmed him ("first time that's ever happened", he commented) mixing it with some coral powder, more pollen and a small amount of pounded rock; ("volcanic; full of even worse stuff than what got into the poor boy here," he told Rosetta "to pick up that poison and the rest will force the body to get rid of it all."); he then gave a small amount to Brendan, asking him, again via Rosetta to test it on his sample; Brendan had a nurse wheel it in, in its liquid-nitrogen mantle, then put on special gloves and threaded in the mixture through a burette while being able to watch proceedings through a specially reinforced lens, with his onetime lover Elanca taking pictures throughout.

❦

"A bit too early to tell but I can see some sort of reaction," he commented and then offered to show the healer the kind of chelates he had used on Jules.

"they might do the job all right but I can't see how the body can get rid of them," were the naturopath's words via Rosetta, with Brendan nodding agreement.

Jules, too, was not surprised. "will these ingredients help?" he asked Rosetta, to convey that question to Señor Alcides who understood straightaway.

"tell him to expect some vomiting and raised temperature several times this afternoon; it should all be over by tonight and he will feel very very hungry for the next few days," he told the girl.

Gloria, having set up everything she needed to do the final cuts on Hec that evening, had a cup of tea, grabbed half an hour of shut-eye on a couch, then re- entered proceedings.

Jules had just been given the first instalment of Señor Alcides' special concoction and was, as pre-told, violently sick almost immediately, passing up some green-looking stuff.

"bile combined with copper," he figured, always the scientist; "amazing it didn't kill me, possibly some wire stuck to the fencepost."

While his parents managed to look disgusted, Señor Alcides burst out laughing when he had Jules' comment translated. "my granddaughter is a bit like that", he explained.

The teenager shivered wildly and was instantly wrapped in a moist blanket as his temperature had shot up, also as expected.

"do I need to remain on the drip?" he wondered.

"it does not seem to hurt to keep up your electrolytes," commented Gloria, asking the healer accordingly. He barely looked up from mixing some more honey with bark in a the last remaining bit of arrack and nodded once the girl had explained the contents of the drip.

"I might ask you to reduce the flow in an hour but, once all this vomiting has stopped, he'll need every bit of help that we can give him to recover. . ." then went on to stir his mixture.

"when will you give him that?" asked Gloria who had not seen Gordon's original brew brought in.

"after his second and third bit of vomit," the healer answered matter-of-factly, secretly pleased that neither Jules nor his parents could follow Chamorro.

Jules was slowly recovering from the sheer violence of his first bout but expressed an urgent desire to "visit the drop-in centre" meaning the toilet, which he did, helped by a nurse; he spent many minutes peeing and defecating, "more than I have in months," not that the girl wanted to know that, of necessity.

She quietly, and thoroughly, flushed and cleaned the toilet bowl, instead, then guided him back to his room where another load was being readied.

Señor Alcides stepped out on the verandah to look at the length of shadows, then returned:

"another fifteen minutes," he told Jules, in English, who smiled weakly.

Elanca silently touched Brendan's gloved hands then returned to her equipment; Brendan chose to look at his sample: "can you capture that digitally, love?" he asked her;

"the sample has just about disappeared." All Elanca was later able to show on her pictures was a grey smudge ("possibly zinc from the galvanizing," Jules had commented).

The science teacher chose this moment to arrive, with her daughter and Ann, hand in hand, in tow; Angh ran forward and kissed Jules' hands, then smiled at his parents.

"why don't you two take a few moments' rest," her mother suggested to them, not least to forestall any awkwardness resulting from her daughter's impulsive gesture of surrender to their 'son'.

"I am sorry I couldn't get off school any earlier or send the girls ahead of me; they both had to sit different tests, as will Jules here once he is able to; we can be here for the rest of the afternoon, and I'll take Ann home as well, as her 'mum' will need to be here tonight."

"why don't you follow me to my parents' house?" offered Rosetta as well, "for an hour or so."

"Good idea, Rosetta, take some time off yourself and be back in an hour if you could."

An hour later, time which the healer measured by the shadows settling over a verandah, accompanied by cups of green tea, Jules was treated to yet another few drops of mixture which, once again, made him vomit and increase his body temperature, to be cooled down by yet another moist blanket; he was made to chew yet more fibrous sugarcane and sip drops of honey dissolved in arrack, along with dried petals, this time.

"Headache?" asked Brendan, Gloria having gone out again to check on her preparations, having watched Jules close his eyes in pain. Jules nodded.

"is this normal?" Rosetta asked the healer.

"yes," said Señor Alcides, "make the boy lower his head, raise his feet and breathe slowly; meanwhile, I shall give you some lemongrass, my daughter, or have you any in the garden?"

"yes, Señor Alcides, we do; shall I get one of the staff to harvest some and cut it up?"

"yes, girl; and ask one of the nurses to boil water; if it persists, I'll get the boy to inhale lemongrass extract. . ." "we have lemongrass oil here as well. . ."

"use it at other times, for him to inhale, daughter;"

"will there be more headaches in the next few days?" she asked.

"very possible; the entire body will have to shed itself of the poison; all I am doing is to start flushing it out. . ."

"how many more times will you administer this treatment of yours today?" Brendan demanded.

"twice more, then a bit of coral flower honey late in the evening, pollen very early in the morning, then one more course; for I need to leave with the boat before high tide. . ."

"will you leave us some of your material?"

"yes, and instructions for the girl doctor from Guam. . ." "doctor Gloria?"

"yes, because I cannot write. . ."

"but I can write Chamorro, Uncle," insisted Rosetta, "and I can read it back to you if it is correct; doctor Gloria can read and act on them; for how many days?"

"I'll be able to say after the very next dose; for that will be a severe one; it depends on how the boy reacts to it. . . how is your headache?" he asked Jules, in English.

Jules was breathing regularly, as was his wont when in pain or perturbed.

"I'll manage," he told Brendan, "yet; I think Señor Alcides mentioned lemongrass. . ."

"he did, but how did you know?"

"he used a word in Chamorro which I have heard before; we had a unit on aromatics and one boy in science used the Chamorro name instead of the English one. . ."

"I remember," said Angh's mother, "I then held up a blade and asked you if you knew the English name which you did. . ."

"why do you want to know, lover?" asked Ann, oblivious to a certain amount of staring at her.

"because, if I could sit up, I could inhale it and my headache would disappear completely."

Several minutes later, a nurse brought a bowl filled with steaming hot water and bits of lemongrass floating in it and a towel which Jules put over his head, then started breathing even more regularly and inhaling, very slowly at first; for it was hot.

"Three minutes maximum, then wait and add a bit more hot water, then another three minutes," said the healer.

"I shall also use some of this in his next cup of tea, and mine," he added.

Gloria had come back in time for Jules' next dose.

"don't be shocked, daughter," the healer told her, "but keep an eye on your patient; this will be the strongest reaction yet. . ." "necessary?" the girl queried.

"yes, my daughter; ask the girls to give you some space and be prepared, you and his mother, to hold him; make sure he does not drop or damage the drip and have another damp blanket all ready; then turn the drip on full. . ." the healer waited till everything, and everybody, was ready.

"Drink it slowly and swallow it well," he admonished Jules who did and then very nearly jack-knifed his torso against his upper legs; Eileen and Gloria, having been warned, were able to hold him gently but with sufficient strength, while a nurse hung on to the drip, keeping it away from him.

He was running very hot and another wet blanket was put around him while he was still shaking. . .

"almost like a bad case of dengue fever,"

Brendan said more or less to himself but the nurses, Rosetta and Gloria all nodded agreement; for they all knew that bane from painful experience. Meanwhile, the healer had prepared a small amount of honey with pollen and some drops of arrack which he allowed to soak into some tissue paper which he gave Jules to chew and calm him down so he fell almost asleep.

"Don't let him sleep just yet," warned the healer; "he needs to have a very deep sleep tonight. I'll wait and then let him inhale some more; I'll use some mixture this time."

Brendan made the nurse boil up more water while the healer pounded some lemongrass, pollen, hibiscus and neem leaves and petals and some bark, all of which he spread on the surface of the hot water which the nurse passed him.

Jules who had watched him, sat up, held by Elanca and Eileen this time, to free Gloria to reset the flow of the drip, put the towel over his head one more time and inhaled deeply, sighing with satisfaction. "One more time, in about another hour. . ."

"will the reaction be as strong again, Señor Alcides?" asked Gloria on behalf of everyone else.

"I expect no more vomiting, a bit of temperature which must run its course, then I want the boy to walk for a few minutes, use the toilet which will take some time, then go to bed; leave one of the girls and myself here;" the healer ordered;

"you look after your other patient, so will doctor Brendan; the boy's parents can stay for a while and then come back tomorrow, as early as they can."

"do you want the nurse on night shift, give him tea with coral flower honey late in the evening and your pollen paste early in the morning and also wake you so you do not miss the boat, Señor Alcides. . ." "yes, please, but I shall sleep in my hammock, on the verandah, and will probably wake at the required time. . ." "it will be dark. . ."

"it never quite is when you are outside, girl; I'll know what time it is. . ."

"Angh and Ann, have a cup of tea and go to the canteen, eat a bit and do some homework in the computer room," the science teacher ordered them; "then come back for a few minutes to say good night to Jules. . ."

"Mum and Dad have your bedroom ready for you," added Rosetta; "they'll give you dinner. . ."

"and then to bed, no later than ten," said Eileen "come over early in the morning if you want to; we will. . ." meaning Trevor and herself, for perhaps the last time.

Elanca took a picture of the young people then watched them head for the canteen, hand in hand.

"girls girls girls. . ." she sang, smiling as Brendan whistled the well-known tune as well.

Gloria, meanwhile, had everything ready to operate on Hec for basically the last time, some future fine adjustments excepted; for she, too, needed to leave in another two days, hoping that she could spend one more night with Fernando when he came back from his coronial enquiry and exams.

Glen dropped Hec just as it was getting dark, his arm around his partner till they entered the clinic.

"Good luck, Hec. . ." "let's hope for completeness; will you stay?"

"yes, till Gloria shoos me out. . ." "which I shall do very soon," the young doctor said, having overheard them:" I shall allow you to watch Hec undress. . . have a cup of tea first, no sugar, both of you, then get ready, Hec, and as soon as I have Hec ready for the theatre, you'll have to leave, Glen. . ."

"go home then, Glen, and come back tomorrow; will I have to stay here, doctor Gloria?"

"yes, but not necessarily in bed." They had their cups of tea in companionable silence, then Gloria made Hec undress and shower which Glen was allowed to watch, then he was shooed out as expected.

He drove their work vehicle to the Chamber of Commerce slowly, thinking of their future lives and of all the work ahead; there was another evening session similar to the one the previous day which Trevor had surprisingly been invited to. Ramon, Gordon and Agosto were pleased to see him.

"How is Hec?"

"given the finishing touches by doctor Gloria; she asked me to come back early tomorrow before work. . ."

"pleased that you could come for our next session, then; sit down, Glen, a beer?"

"a very light one, I am driving. . ."

"no, Glen; a company car will pick all of us up later tonight, drop you and myself and pick you up tomorrow so you can collect the work car on your way to the clinic. . ."

"at five o'clock, Ramon?"

"in that case, my nephew who has to get up early will drop you at the clinic if you can get someone there to drive you here later in the morning. . ."

"have I met your nephew?"

"you may; he lives next door and is a cleaner; he does our office as well as some others. . ."

"all right to leave some dollars in his glove box?" "as you wish, Glen."

Meanwhile, Gloria went to work removing circular disks from Hec's buttocks, meanwhile asking her:

"have you any sensation in your new vulva?"

"do you mean if I tried?" "yes, Hec. . ."

"there is some; did you manage to insert some pressure points and leave some nerve ends intact, same as you are about to, with my nipples, no doubt?"

"similar principle," admitted the young doctor. "I cannot add any more but possibly reinforce a few. . ." "so I can feel the impact of a dick inside?" queried Hec.

"your comment, not mine; but I'll test for it tomorrow and day after; you'll be in Brendan's hands again. . ." "and Glen's,"

"don't be rude. . ." she smiled." I am leaving in two nights, three days max. . ." "miss me?"

"I shall, all of you, but you, Glen, Eileen will be here, or on Ariman, of course, so we may get to see each other in future. . ."

"something to look forward to, Gloria," her patient agreed and was then silent.

Being under local anaesthetic, he was conscious, but not of any pain; that would come later.

"I'll put you back on your hormones, Hec, before I leave; you'll have to be on them or on any that Brendan chooses to prescribe for the rest of your life, every day, like Jules, except that yours are obviously different," she explained: "It is a bit like being on hormone replacement therapy but stricter. . ."

Having harvested enough material to fashion two breasts, she got the theatre nurse to anaesthesise Hec's chest, then opened the initial base she had formed around the nipples and started attaching the disks she had cut out like concentric rings on top of each other, spraying an additional layer of skin on top of her creation, finally injecting a tissue bonding agent.

Hec had by then fallen asleep, as had-almost-the theatre nurse, Gloria had trouble keeping awake herself but was able to finish the operation without mishap, washed up and rang for another nurse to tidy up and find a bed for Hec.

"you go to bed for a few hours; are you on night duty?" she asked her assistant. "not quite; my shift ends at midnight, doctor Gloria. . ."

"find a bed or couch, anyway and, when you go home, arrange for someone to wake me at five; I'll put up a cot in Professor Fernando's room." she said, smiling to herself, in case her mentor and lover would find her there during the night.

"Dream on," she told herself sternly, drinking her final cup of tea for the night.

Jules fell asleep almost immediately after his last dose, so much so that the nurse did not want to wake him at eleven to make him drink the medicinal tea he was meant to have at the time; the healer himself, noticing the time, woke up, listening to Jules breath, nodded and went back to sleep himself, knowing that he only had a few more hours of sleep.

Brendan woke up shortly after midnight, tiptoed into Jules' bedroom and noticed the teenager tossing in a drugged kind of state. He went to the verandah and stood quietly next to the hammock.

Señor Alcides woke up and looked at the doctor questioningly who indicated Jules' room. He helped the old gentleman get up who went and had a look.

"no tea for the boy?" he asked Brendan in halting English. The nurse had to be found and asked.

"Jules was sound asleep and barely moving so I did not want to wake him. . ." which the girl repeated in Chamorro.

"make the tea the way you were meant to, girl," the healer ordered her,

"then use some tissue and let the boy swallow it off the way I made him do in the evening. . ."

Jules was groggily asleep when the girl opened his mouth and wedged the tissue inside.

He swallowed, then sat up properly, starting to breathe regularly again. The girl managed to pour some more tea onto a piece of tissue placed on his tongue which he chewed on then swallowed.

"tell him to continue to breathe the way he does when he is in pain," instructed the healer;

"he does that very well. . ." both Brendan and he waited till Jules had lain down, no longer tossing and again falling asleep.

"I had a reason to make the boy drink that tea just before midnight," the healer admonished the girl who apologized.

"Have you got the mixture ready for the morning which Señor Alcide is to give Jules before he leaves. . ." "I am not sure, doctor Brendan."

"then ask Señor Alcides to show you or make it up for you in readiness before he goes back to sleep. . ." "yes, doctor Brendan; I am so sorry. . ."

"just as well I noticed, don't worry too much; what time does your shift finish?"

"just about when Uncle here needs to leave; I can wake him then. . ."

"and I'll make sure there is a car and driver waiting," concluded Brendan and went to organize it all before going back to bed, asking the registrar to keep an eye on things.

Jules had to be woken from an even deeper sleep and given the medicine; this time, the healer indicated that the drip could be turned off. Jules' temperature went up one more time and another moist sheet had to be used but he did not vomit. He dropped off almost immediately.

He woke up when Ann and Angh entered the room and kissed his hands. "How do you feel?" the girls asked anxiously. "I think I have an erection," he told them sleepily.

"we are sure you do," confirmed Angh. "are we allowed to touch it, lover?" asked Ann, sensibly.

"better not, just yet. . . has Señor Alcides gone?" he wondered.

"Yes, he needed to catch the boat with cargo for Ariman Island,"

Angh, who had been able to understand most of his instructions the previous day, explained:

"we are both yours now and we can barely wait. . ." "were you bitches kind to each other last night?"

Jules enquired, by now more or less fully awake, still feeling a bit leaden but also very hungry, undoubtedly a good sign.

"yes, we shared Angh's bedroom. . ." "and my bed. . ." "and excited each other,," which the girls had done as soon as Angh's mum had fallen asleep. Ann had guided the Vietnamese girl's hand inside her own body, holding it, and done likewise inside Angh's, kissing her breasts, neck and chin, experiencing the other girl's free hand over her own body, between her legs, across her hips and erecting her breasts. She dropped on top of Angh, moving the hand that was not exploring Angh's body to force the girl's jaws open, then inserted her hardened breasts, rhythmically, one after the other, inside the other girl's mouth, opened wide in submission, making sure not to make too much of a noise, so as not to wake up Angh's mum. She then rolled Angh on top of her and allowed the girl to control and explore her in turn.

"Angh, love, we need to sleep now," she instructed her: "we want to be up very early. . ." they kissed one another and fell asleep, their arms and legs entwined, aware that Angh's mum had readied two cycles which would be safe to ride early before morning rush hour.

The girls enjoyed the early morning ride, with the scents of the night from the sea and the frangipani trees wafted along on an early breeze, untainted by the exhaust of ubiquitous two-wheelers. They stopped, arm in arm, looking at the expanse of the ocean at low tide, reflecting the light of a pale moon and of a few buoy lamps left on to guide boats into the channel leading to the harbour. They passed the quai where the boat to Ariman was being loaded, by way of a small detour

"Has Señor Alcides arrived yet?" Angh asked the boatmen in Chamorro.

"No, he has another hour, just about, before we have to leave on the low tide;" the captain told her:

"can you girls see that the tide is already turning; I hope he gets here in time, otherwise we use too much fuel to go against the undertow. . ." "will you wait for Señor Alcides, anyway?"

"within reason, naturally; Señor Nestor asked us to look after him. . ." he looked at the girls again in the dim light:

"are you girls friends to the boy whom he is treating in Señor Gordon's clinic. . ."

"we are his girl friends, Sir," answered Ann, in English, having understood the last question.

"lucky boy; I was getting married at his age," the captain confided, also in English,

"as was the way on our island then, and definitely not to two girls, and beautiful ones at that. . . please don't tell my wife; she'll divorce me from my grandchildren." he laughed and the girls solemnly promised, hoping that the other sailors had not followed the conversation.

"have an early coffee with me, girls; your bikes'll be safe, the boys will keep an eye on them," he invited them across the gangway.

"what time did Señor Ramon's team finish loading. . ." Ann asked: "my parent is one of their coaches. . ." "where is he now?" the captain wondered.

"she, Sir, it does get complicated, in the same clinic as our boyfriend, and for very similar reasons. . ."

"I am only a humble navigator," the captain admitted, rolling his eyes, over steaming cups of coffee which the steward had meanwhile served.

A mere ten minutes later, the girls had arrived at the clinic and made their way unerringly into Jules' room where they found the one who they considered as the rightful owner of their young bodies still asleep; they could also see the silhouette of the ancient healer curled up in his hammock on the verandah outside, ready to awake if the light, and the intensity of the breeze, was right.

'Manfully' resisting the impulse to feel for his newly-acquired tool, the girls gently grasped his hands instead and settled themselves on chairs either side of Jules, felt his forehead, listened to his regular breathing and slowly dozed off. The nurse who had arrived to administer Jules' potion and, subsequently, wake the healer, roused the girls, instead:

"I need some space, girls," she told Angh in Chamorro, yet she did not resist their help in getting a very drowsy Jules to sit upright. He drank his medicine, made a face, on account of the bitter taste of the bark and, slowly waking, gripped the girls' hands with surprising strength.

"I am very hungry," he told the nurse; "is Señor Alcides awake as yet?"

The nurse was spared an answer; for the healer had entered through the French window, agile as a goat at his age. He took one of Jules' hands out of Ann's grasp, used his free hand to lift the teenager's eyelid and held his ear close to Jules' face to listen to his breathing; he then tore a strand of hair off Jules' head, possibly looking for traces of toxin.

He nodded in satisfaction, asked the nurse to pass on his regards to doctores Brendan and Gloria, held the girls' hands for a while and then left, the nurse having rung for his vehicle to wait outside.

Eileen and Trevor arrived just as the hospital car was driving away; Señor Alcides made the driver stop and got out of the car. Jules' parents got out likewise out of the car that Eileen had commandeered from Merv's business premises and Jules' mum embraced the ancient healer.

"Thank you very much," she said; her husband-so far-added:

"soy muito obligado para Vd; muchas gracias para el Señor," and placed his hand above his heart, offering a bow. Señor Alcides acknowledged them:

"He is a good boy; I know that he not always boy but strong, very smart; two lovely girls with him," in his basic English. He re-entered the car to be driven off to the boat already waiting for him.

"this will be the last thing we do together, Trevor," Eileen commented:

"but we also need to see this through. . ."

"Jules seems to cope," Trevor added, "and I am beginning to be on countdown and Elanca even more so." "do you want to get involved with her, Trevor?"

"since I can't be such a big part of your life any more, I shall be glad if Elanca were a choice; I'll not be reticent with her, I promise. . ."

"she made love to Brendan when she first arrived, I am sure of that. . ."

"a doctor whose place is here and who has a wife and family. . ."

"exactly, and she knows it, too," his wife of not much longer agreed:

"good luck with her and also with your future; it will be good to see you here from time to time if that investment comes off. . ." "it will. . ."

They entered Jules' bedroom, finding the two girls seated next to Jules and Brendan and Gloria in attendance. "Jules is very hungry and doctor Brendan says he may have breakfast with us. . ."

"but he is not yet allowed to do homework or online studies just yet; tomorrow, possibly. . ."

"let him read a textbook, then?" "for limited amounts of time, today, yes," inserted Gloria.

"I could eat a horse, for the first time since the operation," confirmed Jules.

"You'll be put on hormones tonight, barring the unforeseen," added Gloria, "then you'll be even hungrier because of the extra muscle they tend to form. . ."

"exercise?" wondered Angh: "we got here by bike. . ."

"good idea," agreed Eileen; "that can be arranged; did you girls enjoy the cycle?"

"oh yes, we did," Ann confirmed. "doctor Gloria," she wondered, "am I allowed to see my, er, mum now." the young doctor contemplated her answer:

"go and see her now, then join us for breakfast. . ." "is 'Mum' not getting any?"

"oh yes, but I'll have to send it in; I do not want her to move any more than necessary today;"

"I'll share a pot of tea with my, er, mum, then join all of you for breakfast before Angh and I have to head off for school. . ."

"a pity that Jules cannot join us yet;" Angh indicated; "we all miss him."

Ann woke up her parent who was under instructions not to move further than the toilet, for "my boob tissue to settle down", as Hec explained to her without any sense of embarrassment.

"we live in hope," Ann commented sagely.

"may I ask you how you feel, not just like in well-being but as a. . ."

"newly-created and definitely not traditionally built lady, you mean?" Hec replied.

"in one way, not at all different, on another, running on an entirely different kind of passion and energy. . ."

"almost like a professional celibate?" Ann wondered.

"not in a personal or functional level; yet, mentally or spiritually, yes. . ."

"like being part of a intentional community, Mum?"

("takes some getting used to, still," her daughter thought, "unlike Jules, as a boy, no problems whatsoever. . .")

"yes, you'll see me live and work as part of a team. . ." "led by who?"

"Glen, most of the time, but essentially by whoever is best able and equipped for a particular task. . ."

"we studied project management as part of our economic studies," remembered Ann, "conducted by a parent who runs an engineering company. He told us that risk gets allotted according to tasks and to whichever participant is most responsible and best equipped to undertake a particular job. . ." "that's a good example," Hec agreed. "thank you for sharing early-morning tea, have your breakfast and get to school. . ."

"yes, Mum. . .".

Brendan had a few hours to share with his wife at their home:

"There is not much I can do physically," she said,

"I can barely lift a finger let alone else. . ." "but, darling?"

"I am beginning to feel like a woman again; we'll have to find ways to make use of that because the 'tunnel-of-desire' method no longer does much for me, not like it used to. . ."

"we'll work out something, no doubt. . ."

"agreed," she concurred, watching him eat sandwiches she had prepared for them;

"meanwhile, your needs are to be met, as do Elanca's. . ."

"she's travelling home to Adelaide with Trevor. . ."

"who has to go home and tend his own business. . ."

"yet, Gordon and the team on Ariman expect him to return within a few months, to guide the next load of investment. . ."

"Jules' mum will have to learn to be very flexible. . ."

"she's found her niche, anyway. . ."

"to return to Elanca. . ."

"yes, what about her?"

"find time with her, one last time," his wife advised him.

"that I may be able to," he assured her; "they are sending their regular onboard practitioner to attend a training course and he's asked for extra time because of some terminal illness in his family. . ." "have they been in touch with you, Brendan?" "yes, I had to ask them to be patient till I knew that Jules would get over that toxin and we could continue his normal treatment. . ."

"which does not really require you to be involved at all times?"

"yes; I have already agreed to be on board the Mercury day after tomorrow. . ."

"what happened to the Haparanda, Brendan?" "drydock, Elaine."

"ask Elanca to join you once again, for one last time. . ." "and Trevor will have to be fine-tuned."

"he could fly ahead and wait for her in Guam, or else wait here another day, with his son and join her when they are ready to leave for Adelaide together. . ."

"Elanca will be busy till the last minute, recording and editing her material. . ."

Gloria, too, needed to get ready to leave.

"Jules, as of tomorrow, you will be able to work on your projects as long as you like and, give us another day or two, you ought to be ready for school," she told the teenager.

"I am putting you back on hormones combined with vitamins and minerals to make up for your loss of weight and muscle tone; there are a few mechanical things need to be done, or observed, but the clinic can deal with that without me or doctor Gloria; I am travelling home to Guam by boat. . ." "with doctor Brendan and Mrs Hartwig, doctor Gloria?"

"more or less, we'll take turns doctoring the ship's crew and passengers while their regular doctor is onshore. . ." "whatever for, doctor Gloria?"

"leukemia in his family, and a training course in disaster preparedness which he is required to pass every few years. . ." "Mrs Hartwig's reportage is just about finished, is it not? "queried the teenager." Yes, and they expect her to deal with the recent story of a baby born with HIV in an Australian detention camp, fathered by a guard, it appears." "back in harness. . ."

"absolutely," agreed the young doctor; "as to you, don't overeat, not until you can start to exercise. . ." "cycling?" "sounds good, likewise swimming, Jules."

A short while later, she walked into Professor Fernando's open arms who had arrived unannounced and entered the clinic straight off the airport, spotting her in the corridor. She gave a deep sigh, as if she had never expected him to return, and dropped her head on his shoulder.

"I missed you so much, love," she murmured. "and I you; are you leaving us, girl?" "yes, lover, Brendan and I are taking turns on the boat leaving late tomorrow evening. . ."

"their doctor's not on board?"

Gloria explained to her mentor why the shipping company had asked Brendan to take their doctor's post for the round trip, and that she had agreed to join and take turns. . .

"to free him for some last bit of quality time with Elanca." "is her job finished, too?"

"yes, Fernando; you have not asked about your patients as yet. . ."

"they are in good hands, I know; you'll have to tell me about the naturopath. . ."

"Señor Alcides?"

"yes, I would have loved to have seen him at work, Gloria. . ."

"ask Elanca to show you; she recorded just about everything; Brendan and I have also kept samples for you to study; we'll need to administer a few more to Jules in the next few days. . ."

"the nurses can do that, no doubt. . ."

"they will, Fernando. Have a look at him, he'll be allowed to work in the computer room tomorrow; then go and see Hec who is still confined to bed. . ."

"you want to give the tissue some more time, girl?"

"yes, and could you check on some organ function, please, before I put her on full hormonal treatment. . ." "for comparison, you mean. . ."

He kissed her, then asked a passing nurse to have a strong coffee prepared for him and a pot of tea for Gloria. Jules was pleased to see him: "will you be here long, Professor Fernando. . ."

"no, I am afraid not; I am getting Rosetta to book me on the boat for tomorrow afternoon. . ."

"I heard about the epic voyage; my dad will be about the only one not on it. . ."

"it will give him more time with you. . ."

"yes, but you did not know that the Chamber of Commerce wants him back in a few months as well. . ."

"good grief; has Saipan suddenly become the centre of the commercial universe?" wondered the professor, with Jules having to explain what had happened in his absence.

"How was Señor Alcides?"

"very interesting, from a science point of view, very painful but quite effective as a treatment, Professor Fernando, He did tell us that he had a granddaughter a bit like myself."

"I have no doubt that you'll get to know her, too, Jules," Professor Fernando assured his patient ("quite possibly in the Biblical sense as well").

He then went to see Ann's parent who was in good spirits, studying women's magazines with a sense of absurd delight. "Elanca gave me some back copies. . ." "to break you in, sort of?"

The specialist could see the funny side of things as much as the next person. "Some were written by Elanca herself," Hec pointed out,

"like this one, a follow-up on several models who were HIV positive. . ."

"no longer the death sentence it used to be, in this part of the world also,"

the professor commented. "that's where Señor Alcides entered; he had remembered how we used to treat animal retroviruses and did so over the years on our early victims when we had almost no anti-retrovirals that worked, let alone today's multidrug treatment;"

Professor Fernando recollected:

"especially with TB thrown in. . . as normally happens. . ."

"yes, we owe him and his fellow healers a great deal. . ."

"how was your forensics, professor Fernando?"

"oh, I'll tell you, but let me give you a check-up which doctor Gloria asked me to do. . ." together with a team of nurses and technicians, he spent several hours doing that, then announced:" Gloria will put you on full-strength hormones and you will be able to return to work in two or three days; we'll all be gone by then as you may have heard." "by boat?"

"yes, in one way or the other; I am quite looking forward to it," he replied:

"you'll be on an normal diet, work and stay at home wherever that is, exercise but not extremely so, to develop tissue strength. Gloria will be back in a few weeks for some finishing touches. . ." "downstairs?" "among other bits. . ."

He then gave the same thorough check-up on Jules, apologizing to the teenager who had to cope with all the work that had piled up.

"consider this a break but I really need to do this; I won't be back for months and I need to be sure there'll be no after-effects; plus I want to see how the herbal treatment has worked all inside you. . ."

He gave Jules, too, a clean bill of health, as had his mentee before him. He saw some more patients inside the clinic, went to meet some doctor friends of his, then returned to get some sleep and to meet Gloria as she came off duty.

"I asked Rosetta to book me on the Mercury as well," he told her after she had kissed him hungrily. "she told me; yes; they gave you a double cabin. . ."

"for you to rest as well when you are not on duty. . ." "but on call," she reminded him;

"they would have given me a cabin but thanks. . . we'll find a use for it. . ." she started to work on her lover. Later, they lay drowsily entwined.

"what is it that attracts me to you, a happily married old man. . ."

"my intellect, no doubt," he teased her.

"yes, I learnt so much from you, yet you appreciate me more now I, too, am a specialist. . ."

"that's normal, love, a desire based on profound respect. . . look, get some sleep; I want to do the rounds with you early tomorrow morning. . ."

Elanca had started to edit her material, not expecting to have to add much more; even her text version was just about complete. Brendan had watched her for a while:

"up to another voyage, love?" "same journey?"

"different boat, but yes, back to Guam where it all started. . ."

"one last time, Brendan; why not?" "will you continue with Trevor, from then on?"

"yes, I offered to travel with him; if it leads to being his future partner, so be it. . ."

"so be it, my love, from Guam onwards."

"will you be on duty or on call on the boat, this time, Brendan?"

"both; Gloria is coming, too, so we take turns?"

"Professor Fernando is back; is he squiring Gloria?"

"yes, they have been at it since her student days."

"will she ever have a husband or partner of her own?"

"she's too busy, in many ways; I think the arrangement suits her. . ."

"and him; for he has a wife and family. . ." "who probably know and have come to accept it."

"likely. Anyway. . ." she got up and put her arms around Brendan.

"I'll have you on short-term loan only, courtesy of your wife," she sighed, "but I am content."

Sitting next to Trevor who was minding Jules, she had told him:

"Look, I have the chance to travel back to Guam by boat, the same way I came because planes could not land that day here on Saipan. . ."

"together with doctor Brendan, Elanca?"

"let's have some tea; Jules, would you like another cup as well?"

They moved onto the veranda, having promised Jules to return.

"will you wait for me on Guam, Elanca?"

"yes, I am in charge of our travel arrangements, Trev;" Elanca promised:

"whoever gets there first will have to wait for the other; we shall travel back to Adelaide together, via Singapore; would you like us to break our journey there for a few days?"

"two nights?" "thereabouts, Trev; I'll have to check our itinerary."

"and afterwards, once we get to Adelaide?" he looked at the attentive and committed reporter.

"entirely up to you; I am open to suggestions. . ."

"you lost your husband quite violently some years ago," Trevor commented,

"I am in the process of losing my wife now and still expected to return in a few month. . ."

"we won't dwell on it," she said and guided his hand to her forehead: "offer stands. . ."

"accepted with a grateful heart, Elanca; it will simply take time for me to live up to it."

Jules' father was genuinely grateful. He kissed her hand and held it for a while longer.

"meanwhile, enjoy your last time with Brendan; do you want to return one day for any specific purpose?"

"haven't thought of it, yet," she admitted honestly: "perhaps to accompany you come the time for you to come back here to monitor industrial investments, the way you do at home. . ."

"home will always be Adelaide, for me, at least," he replied tellingly.

"which does not apply to others in this story," the reporter concluded." I shall have to love you and leave you soon after we land in South Australia. . ." "your own work calling, El?"

"yes, you may have heard. . ."

Glen arrived during lunch hour to say Goodbye to Elanca and Gloria and to spend time with Hec who was struggling to eat while sitting up in bed.

"They do not want your boobs to fall off, makeshift as these are," commented her partner drily.

"anatomical casualty which they'd prefer to avoid." Hec agreed. "shall I feed you, Hec?"

"why not; let's"

"a spoonful for Ann, a spoonful for Jules, another for his mum, another for me. . ."

"how about your future part-time lovers?"

"guilty as charged, Hec. . . eat up; another spoonful for doctor Gloria. . ."

"there are times I wish I were still a man. . ." "bisex's not an option?"

"it appears to be my daughter's. . ."

"let me seal my lips, yet I love these young ones; you should see her with the Vietnamese girl and her and Angh all over Jules. . ."

"blessed be their hormones; talking about that, how about a spoonful for Aline?" "coming up, Hec. . ."

Ann's 'mum' managed to finish her lunch amid that much laughter that the nurse came to investigate, herself barely being able to stifle her giggles watching these two mature people engage in spoon-feeding. She had a brainwave:

"let me get Elanca to take pictures. . ."

"no, take them yourself and upload them onto her site later," advised Glen who had seen her and Trevor move out on the verandah:

"she is not to be disturbed at the moment. . ." the girl shrugged, took out her camera phone and urged them to continue:

"a spoonful for Señor Gordon, another for doctor Brendan, one for Rosetta, another for her parents. . ." The nurse smiled, closed her contraption and walked off to see to more serious cases on her rounds.

Señor Nestor rang Gordon later that day:

"would you like to come over to Ariman Island in a few days, along with Señor Agosto?"

"and with Ramon and the Australian team. . ."

Gordon had the feeling that the Elder had to stop himself from saying: "I suppose so" and asked:

"are you having trouble with their, er, domestic arrangements, Señor Nestor. . ."

"yes, but we are agreed on wanting them to plan and set up the primal energy project. . ."

"to be funded by the Marianas Development Fund"

"without which unit no one, the Development Bank or any private investor, will stake a follow-on unit which we need to attract and retain educated young people, our own, and their families," the alcalde sighed.

"you are right, Señor Gordon; I was thinking of the second step before the first. . ."

"all I can say, having worked with Westerners all my life, that these are people able to separate their private lives-and-loves-from their professional commitments; that even goes for some of their teenagers. . ."

"very difficult at that age, I remember," smiled the elder:

"are you thinking of the two young ones in your clinic. . ."

"three, by now, Señor Nestor."

"do not try to explain; I am only a humble island chief hundreds of years behind the times. . ."

"no, Señor Nestor; you are very switched-on, as my daughter would say;" contradicted Gordon:

"take Jules; while he was in pain, he still kept up with his homework, projects and all the stuff the Australian system made him do towards his matriculation; the doctors had to physically stop him, for Señor Alcides to work on him; thanks very much, by the way; what did he have to say on his return. . ."

"very much what you just did, Señor Gordon; he was most impressed with his patient. . ."

"also with the girls?"

"he appreciated that they came to see him very early in the morning so did not miss out on school but also that they were all over Jules. Generally, he liked them around because it helped his patient and Jules' parents having them nearby."

The Elder paused so that Gordon was about to ask when he eventually continued:

"Señor Gordon, ask Señor Ramon to send his Australian colleagues. . ."

"how about Aline?"

"we are expecting her; is she part of the team now? That'd be good."

"how about some of the young people?"

"the trainees? let Señor Ramon and his team make a choice among them. . ."

"how about the teenagers?"

"I suppose this extra girl belongs to the Vietnamese science teacher who recommended

Señor Alcides in the first place. . ." "did he tell you that?"

"not only he, believe me," explained Señor Nestor.

"If you can get her mum to come, I'll have all three of them as well. . ."

"could I send them to you a bit later, Señor Nestor?" "why; school?"

"yes, Jules needs to get back to studies; there is also his birthday to consider. . ."

"sixteenth, is it not? how about the two girls?"

"within days of each other and of him. . ."

"the law, I know, but then, girls were married at that age, even in our own generation . . teenagers." he paused:

"when would be a good time to have them and the Vietnamese teacher over here?"

"three weeks, in the lead-up to a mid-term exam," affecting, as it did, not only his grandchildren but the offspring of several of his staff as well.

"can they defer that exam till after they come back from Ariman?"

"yes, given notice, some of our kids here had to have it done earlier or later; we normally ring one of the girls in the department. . ."

"that's all it takes?" "yes, the department would not run without them. . ."

"nothing does, it seems," admitted the elder, "including my own office and family; well, that's it, then; if you'd be good enough to arrange for all of you, Señor Ramon and his people, yourself and some of your family, your friend Señor Agosto and whoever he wants to bring. . . any of your doctors available?"

"I'll ask around; for a spot of work in your health post, you mean. . ."

"mainly for a holiday, I'd say. . ." "they'd jump at that!"

"that's it, then, and we get the young ones to see us in a few weeks. Should I charter the boat, Señor Gordon?"

"that would be a good idea, Señor Nestor; regards to your. . ." "very large family, I know. . ."

On the very next boat to Ariman, Glen and Hec ended up sharing a cabin, as did Eileen and Aline.

Ramon had selected three girls and three boys to accompany them, as the nucleus of their new work force, and was accompanied by his sister whose husband was an original Ariman islander, as his wife could not get time off work. Two Chamorro doctors had joined them, to take turns in Ariman's health post, so that the other could do some fishing or generally laze around. Brendan was tempted to treat his wife for a holiday there but she wanted to get back to her work at the community college.

Eileen and Aline had brought out some deck chairs and enjoyed the sunset, a few bottles of beer between them. "have you put enough mosquito repellent on," enquired the girl.

"yes, Professor Fernando had left me with some neem screen from Hawaii where it is made and where you can buy it over the counter. . ."

"very hard to get in Australia; I do use neem soap which I stocked up on in Mildura. . ."

"the business at hand", Eileen reminded her: "are we agreed to want the same thing from the same bloke?" "hopefully not at the same time, though," wondered the girl. "do you want to do me tonight, instead, as for such times that Glen is unavailable. . ." "such as doing Hec, you figure? Interesting thought, on several levels. . . no, not the full length, even though I may let you try; you have some practice, I take it. . ." Aline smiled and explained: "I may be seductive; I am certainly very highly seducible if that is a promise; with Glen, we just have to act when opportunity arises. . ."

"as does, hopefully, something inherent to the man. . ."

"the centre of his being, to be worshipfully adored and blissfully enjoyed in all his glory. . ." sighed the girl.

The next few weeks saw some feverish activity at school and at their respective homes, with Jules living with his mum close to Señor Merv's, Ann with her 'mum' at the quarter Micronesian Work Search had organised, and Angh with hers on Saipan's subsidised school premises. With Ann's and Jules respective parents mostly on Ariman, however, Angh's mum had taken on the role not only of home tutor but also of den mother.

There were opportunities, through, such as changing after sports when Jules had let himself in through an open window in the girls' change room whose outlay he remembered from the days of his girlhood. Ann and Angh had shared a lengthy shower when he, noticing their feet from under the shower curtain, lifted it briefly and let himself inside the cubicle, closing the girls' mouths with his hands. "strip me and get ready, 'he ordered,

"we have about four minutes; teacher has gone for a coffee. . ."

He then explored each girl while they did their best to lift whatever clothing had to be got out of the way; he lifted their breasts, chins and elbows, then he made Angh massage his-originally Andy's tool-while exploring Ann from inside her, routinely cuffing her wrists behind her with his free hand.

"what's your name, bitch?" "Ann, lover," she managed.

"as soon as you legally can, you will call yourself Ann Childers," he ordered.

"eventually, you may think of yourself as Mrs Julius Childers, in a few more years. . ."

"may it be done to me according to your words," a very submissive Ann agreed, to be kissed in a most possessive manner before he turned his attention, and his hands, to Angh whom he made to relinquish his tool, for Ann to take over. "I cannot change your name. . ."

"which is Angh Vuong Minh," the girl offered: "nor will I marry you." "take me nonetheless," she agreed: "as long as I may share you with Ann at all times. . ."

"consider it to be done. . ." spoken, with his hands taking possession of her leaning against him.

Hec and Glen had a somewhat rare chance at intercourse on Ariman island, having discussed 'the young ones' at length. "up to not much good, no doubt. . ."

"depends on what you define as good," argued Ann's parent;

"they'll probably see it as Christmas and Easter falling on one day. . ." "doubtless. . ." agreed Glen.

"free yourself of any excess clothing, massage me and be prepared to open your legs. . ."

"at the slightest provocation?"

"yes, more or less." "I do not know whether my current hormone level will allow that. . ."

"try crossing my leg with yours and then come on top of me. . ." "'the things we do for love'"

Hec, laughing, grabbed the 'centre of Glen's universe,' as his somewhat more authentic, female companions had called it. Glen suddenly rolled Hec onto 'her' back, inserted himself inside his partner's carefully 'hand'-crafted vulva:

"brut", his partner managed to moan very convincingly. "I can be made to like the approach. . ."

Glen demonstrated what it involved, in physically drastic detail, not excluding a surprisingly expert examination of the breasts that Gloria's skills had created out of Hec's hind parts, the remnants of which Glen then gripped in utter ruthlessness while keeping his tool wedged inside Hec's body.

"brut," repeated Hec and let the experience of someone else's age-old biological instincts take over, much as she suspected had happened with Ann, her daughter, not to mention with Angh, that exquisitely alluring and sophisticated girl, boy Julius' most recent prey.

www.ingramcontent.com/pod-product-compliance
Lightning Source LLC
Chambersburg PA
CBHW050552190726
48283CB00007B/2115